Locked Away

BOOK ONE

Locked Away
Copyright © 2022 by Amanda Bryk

Second Edition

Hardback: 979-8-88590-813-9
Paperback: 979-8-88590-814-6
eBook: 979-8-88590-815-3

TikTok: @lockedawayseries
Instagram: locked_away_series
Facebook: LockedAwaySeries

LOCKED away

AMANDA BRYK

For My Husband

I measure my life in memories,
all of them beginning with you.

Until There Was You

TWENTY-EIGHT YEARS of questionable choices and regrettable relationships have brought me to this place, a jail in central Ohio. Never could I have pictured my life to look this broken. One more misstep and I could be on the other side of the desk. My whole life, I've tried to be a good person. I've tried to respect the rules, to bend but never break.

On my quest for love, I frequently stumbled along pathways masquerading as perfection. In hindsight, I don't think I was ever going to find happiness, not where I was looking. Too often, I assumed my thoughtfulness would yield appreciation, so I gave away the best parts of myself. Unfortunately, all I received for my troubles was a slap in the face and a kick in the teeth.

Now, if it's true what they say, that you have to love yourself first, I'm screwed. At this point, I don't even like myself. I barely recognize the person I've become.

Despite all of that, I wasn't quite ready to abandon hope. But, when your path crossed mine, my story abruptly ended.

One

I DESPISE the sound of an alarm clock. Repetitive tones make my skin crawl, and my neck muscles tighten, causing my head to pull to one side. Being assaulted by sound is a terrible way to start the day, but it's a necessary evil. I miss the cell phone I had in high school that allowed me to use downloaded songs as ringtones. Right now, I could be waking up to the sweet sound of 90s grunge punk instead of these fog horns. I can feel my brain exploding behind my eyes, jarring me awake. All I want is ten more minutes of sleep. Hell, I'd take five minutes trapped in my worst nightmare over another evening in this shithole apartment.

My current living situation is unfortunate but not entirely unexpected. I found this place online. It's the second story of a house that's been converted into a one-bedroom/one-bath living space, complete with a kitchen and living room. The best part is that it's a mere stone's throw from work and super cheap. I should have known there would be a catch. Lacking better judgment, I didn't see the apartment in person before signing the lease. A decision that can be filed away in the **BIGGEST MISTAKES OF MY LIFE** folder, along with most of my ex-boyfriends and my date to junior prom.

The stairwell leading to the second-floor apartment is so narrow and steep that it might as well be a ladder. Even with help, I couldn't get any of my furniture past the first-floor entry. On day one, I knew it was a bad omen when the couch I brought from three hours away using my stepdad's truck wouldn't fit in the staircase. I had to drive to work with it still loaded in the back. Then, as if to add insult to injury, it started to rain. My new co-workers were nice enough to notice and gave me a place to park away from the elements, but my fragile ego was already damaged.

Since I couldn't cruise around town with a couch strapped to the truck bed for the week, I had to call and ask my mother to pick it up. First day out on my own, and already my parents had to come to save me. It was embarrassing.

The living room here at the apartment is decent, with hardwood floors and three walls of old wooden windows. It's remained relatively empty except for the TV, cable box, and a vintage storage cabinet left by the previous tenant. Since I don't have a couch, the TV goes mostly unused. Unless it's a cleaning day, I hardly ever go in there, which is a shame because it's the nicest room in the house. Maybe I should get a couple of plants and make better use of all the sunshine and wasted visual space. Or maybe I should stop being stubborn and buy a chair. I could do that, but I won't.

The bedroom is pretty much the polar opposite of the living room, except that it's also old and half-empty. With dark brown 1970s wood paneling on the walls, it feels heavy and almost haunted. The gold shag carpet has become stiff and tacky with age, and the room feels coated in hundred-year-old grime. The whole place smells like stale cigarette smoke and bipolar depression, even though I was promised this was a non-smoking property.

There's a small window with an air conditioning unit in the bedroom, but little light comes in. Normally, when I'm sleeping, I keep the mini blinds shut and the heavy butterscotch curtains closed. Blocking out the day has been useful since I'm currently adhering to a vampire's sleep schedule.

A dresser would be nice, but I don't have one. There's a makeshift closet constructed out of plywood and a metal bar in one corner of the room, but the only thing I hang in there is my work uniforms. I can't bring myself to unpack anything else. The rest of my clothes are folded neatly in two large black duffel bags and pushed against one of the walls. These are the bags I inherited from my brother when he came home from the Army. Maybe giving them to me was his way of encouraging me to go off and find my own adventure. Or maybe he simply didn't need them anymore.

All I know is that I spent a boatload of money on college, and here I am, reduced to sleeping on a twin-size air mattress. Owning a bed would most certainly improve the quality of my sleep and my mood, but I can't commit. One of these days, maybe I'll bite the bullet and order something. After all, that would be the only way to get furniture into this place. Everything would have to come in one piece at a time, and then I'd have to build it. The only thing stopping me from considering that is the thought of having to take it all apart when I move out.

By far, the worst thing about this place is that it lacks a shower. The mint green, floor-to-ceiling tiled bathroom boasts a claw foot tub, pedestal sink, toilet, and one of those medicine cabinets hidden behind the mirror, but No shower. It's about as inviting as your average gas station bathroom.

I don't know about you, but I'm NOT a bath person. How can anyone feel clean when covered in soap scum and remnants of their filth? Allegedly, soaking in the tub is meant to be relaxing, but I don't buy it. The thought of bathing in that room sets my anxiety to eleven.

I'm not exaggerating when I say that a shower has always been the absolute favorite part of my daily routine. With the water hot enough to burn off my sins, when I'm lobster red and ready to pass out, I know I'm ready to face the day ahead.

Feeling depressed? Wash your hair and shave your legs. I promise you'll leave that shower feeling like a new person.

If I'm being honest with myself, I hate everything about this place, but I guess it's to be expected. Twenty-eight years old, and this is my first venture into living independently. Most people my age are married, have children, own homes, and invest in a 401k. They have a five-year plan. I don't even have a place to sit. Coming home to this sad excuse for an apartment makes me feel like a complete failure on a daily basis.

So, if you're wondering what brought me here, I'll give you the short and sour version. Like most disasters in my life, I put myself in this position because of a guy. Kevin and I met online, and I drove to visit him every other weekend for the first few months of our loosely defined relationship. Initially, I didn't think he was my type. He made a terrible first impression when he called me a liar and acted belligerent over the placement of my tattoos, but it was an unfortunate misunderstanding. Since I'd made the three-hour trek to see him and didn't feel like driving home after ten minutes, I opted to give him a second chance at a new impression. After a few drinks, the mood shifted, and we had fun together. His world was a nice escape from my usual routine, and I found the change of scenery refreshing. There were no bad memories attached to any of the streets or buildings here, unlike back home. Every place we went, everything we did, felt brand new.

When I was there, he always talked about how interesting his job was and introduced me to a few of his co-workers. Having never been arrested, I knew nothing about a jail's inner workings. So every narrative they told was fascinating. I found myself deeply yearning for more knowledge about the setting and a better understanding of the characters in their stories. I would watch their body language and focus on their tone as they spun tales over drinks at the bar.

Eventually, Kevin convinced me to apply for a position at the jail where he worked. I filled out the application to appease him, not expecting much to come from it. In theory, being a corrections officer fell within the scope of my Sociology degree, but I'd had zero experience with that sort of work. However, Kevin ensured my references were spot on, which was easy since he knew all the right people. Apparently, I came highly recommended, even though most of his friends had only met me once, at the bar.

The day I received the call to schedule an interview, I was nearly lost for words. The idea of working inside a jail terrified and excited me. Thankfully, Kevin would be there to show me the ropes and keep me safe. All I had to do was survive the pre-employment interrogation.

I remember posting on Facebook a quote I once heard, "I'm so nervous I can taste my heartbeat." That line stands out to me because one of my interviewers asked me if I was nervous, and when I said no, she repeated the quote back to me. I think it was supposed to be a "gotcha" moment, proving I was a liar and making me aware that they had stepped into my online footprint. But it was easy to laugh off since they were originally someone else's words. It was a clever line from a reality TV show I had watched and nothing more. Perhaps it was that moment when my level head guided me through their gauntlet, unshaken, that ultimately landed me the job.

To say I was overwhelmed would be an understatement. I was abruptly tossed onto a new career path in a town three hours from my home. And since I never considered I would get the job, I was completely unprepared for the next few steps. I had one week to quit my current job, find a place to live, and pack my car.

Staying at Kevin's house was never offered, so I hurried and took the first place I could find online. Then, I shared a quick goodbye with my co-workers back home and broke the news to my parents. Of course, they thought I was crazy, but that didn't stop them from accepting my decision and wishing me luck. My brand-new adventure was about to begin, and all I had to do was embrace the change.

Little did I know, as I was ripping my life apart to run off and be with some guy I met online, he packed his bags and left town. Turns out, Kevin was still a reservist in the Army. He was contracted to go overseas for a year, so it's not like he could say no. A little heads-up might have been nice. The last thing he said to me was, "I don't want you to put your life on hold. Don't wait for me." And I never heard from him again.

Banana peel, meet foot.

I would love to say that this situation was a horrible yet rare occurrence. Chasing after some guy, bending over backward, and contorting every aspect of my being to fit whatever version of a woman I thought he wanted, has become commonplace. Begging for someone to simply notice me is my new favorite hobby. The partner might change every six months, but the dance remains the same. I have a real knack for picking cheaters and liars. And if that all sounds pathetic, that's because it is.

The guy I came here for might be gone, but I'm still here. I accepted a job offer and signed a lease, so I'm locked in. Some of these streets and buildings now hold memories I wish I could erase, but at least I was never in love. I'm annoyed and pissed off, but I'm not heartbroken. Ultimately, I gave my word, which might not mean much to some people, but it is important to me. Thankfully, I never worked with Kevin, so the jail remains untarnished.

Despite all the bullshit that happened before I arrived, this quickly became my all-time favorite job. I work overnight, from 11 pm until 9 am. So, it's dinner when I awake and breakfast before bed. Most of the people Kevin introduced me to work on an earlier shift, which is probably for the best. As nice as it would be to know someone here, I don't need any part of me associated with him. As for the job, the stories I heard prior that sparked my initial interest did nothing to prepare me for the risky venture ahead.

The first day was trial by fire. Ten minutes into my training, a call came over the radio about a fight in C Block. I took off running with everyone else even though I had no idea where I was going, what I would find, or even what I was expected to do. Instincts I never realized I had kicked in, and somehow, I knew what to say and how to handle myself. That fight helped me to learn something important about myself, and on that day, I found my place. As it turns out, in highly stressful non-romantic situations, my emotions turn off, and I can act on pure instinct and logic. If only I could harness that superpower in my dating life.

I had no real expectations when I started working at the jail, but I did notice something strange. After everything was sorted out with the fight in C block, the officer I was training with could finally show me around. The warden requested that I wear long sleeves to cover my tattoos. I wasn't happy about it, but I obliged his request without complaint. However, someone asked me about my tattoos no more than two steps into A block for my first set of rounds. This happened over and over again in each block I walked through.

Within hours of beginning my new job, I learned three key pieces of information. One. Secrets can be passed through solid walls. Two. Wearing long sleeves was pointless since hiding my tattoos drew more attention than showing them. And Three. Someone had been talking about me.

I've been at the jail for about two months, and have learned a lot since that first day. In a weird way, being locked inside a building with 223 strangers feels more like home than this rental. Maybe it's because there's a shower in the employee locker room. Or it could be the giant kitchen with the industrial size ice maker. I don't know. Maybe it feels like home because, for the first time, I fit somewhere.

Throughout my life, I have often felt undervalued. Neglected. Easily forgotten. Temporary. As the old saying goes, "Out of Sight, Out of Mind."

But what is it about me that's causing this? Why am I not worth the thought or the effort? People constantly dump their shit on me, and I absorb all of it to the point where my head remains flooded with stories that aren't mine. I haven't so much as left a fingerprint on the people I've met, while they've left me with deep emotional scars. The only words of mine anyone seems to retain are the ones they plan to throw back at me during a fight later. The type of low blows that linger for an eternity.

I have not one lasting friendship to show for my twenty-eight years on this Earth. The group of girls I spent every day with in high school won't even acknowledge my presence at a reunion. I've attempted to reconnect with college friends who can't be bothered to respond to my messages. Kevin had to manufacture references for me out of his group of friends because I couldn't produce contact information for my co-workers or prior acquaintances.

Most of the time, I feel like a ghost who can't come to grips with the reality of being dead. Floating through the day-to-day, waiting for someone to see me.

Two

I'VE WASTED most of the day doing nothing, and now that the sun has moved west, it's time for me to get ready for work. Thankfully, getting dressed requires little effort since my attire has been pre-selected and government issued. My uniform top is a stiff, black button-down that holds my shape even after I've taken it off. Permanently creased, reinforced, and topped off with a badge, these shirts were not designed to flatter the female form. Under the thick polyester top, I wear a plain t-shirt, which keeps the scratchy top layer from touching my skin. The bottoms are black cargo pants and a utility belt that holds my handcuffs and walkie. Most of the guys wear combat boots, but I like to wear my black leather motorcycle boots. They add style to an outfit that was clearly made for a man. My shoulder-length hair, tattoos, and lack of makeup complement the utilitarian look. It's not like I have anyone there I desperately need to impress, so I keep it simple.

If I drive straight from my apartment without stopping for gas or food, my ride to the jail takes less than five minutes. I listen to a couple of songs and broker peace with my demons before I'm in the parking lot with time to spare. Sometimes, if I'm early enough, I hang out in my car and think about the choices that landed me here. I love this job, but I'm not sure it's a career. In the little part of my brain that craves stability and comfort, I could picture myself remaining here indefinitely. But I'm not sure lingering in this place will get me where I dream of being.

The Oak Falls Correctional Facility is a brown and beige block building located on top of a steep hill and surrounded by trees. It looks small from the parking lot, but the inside is surprisingly spacious. The terrain here is nothing like back home. It took me a couple of weeks to get used to driving slowly on the winding roads, with their sudden drops and blind driveways. Not to mention the box turtles. The other day I had to stop on a dime to remove one from the road and send him safely on his way.

I keep hearing about the national park not too far from here that is supposed to be amazing. Maybe I would go if I had some friends, but hiking alone in the woods seems depressing and dangerous. Mostly depressing. Nearly all of my time is spent alone or surrounded by criminals of varying degrees, so there's not much opportunity to meet people.

My mind is hyper-focused when I'm inside those cinder block walls and steel doors. Every possible worst-case scenario that can occur at any given moment passes through my thoughts in rapid succession. And while that might sound hectic, it's actually sort of peaceful. The constant if/then strategizing quiets my usual nagging inner monologue. Strange that the universe would lead me here. I found my purpose in the last place I would have thought to look.

Here at the jail, there are only a handful of positions a CO can be assigned to for the night. Intake, Booking, Tower, Minimum, and Blocks. Working 3rd shift has its perks and its pitfalls. For the most part, it's quiet. There is some overlap between the shifts, but the overnight staff is about half of what it is during the day, so that's not much backup coming if the shit hits the fan.

Intake is the most exciting position. Think of it as the welcoming committee. The fun begins once the police pull into the loading bay to drop someone off. Whoever's working intake has to pat down the prisoner, search for concealed drugs or weapons the other officer might have overlooked, gauge the inmate's level of compliance, collect their belongings, photograph them, fingerprint them, and put them comfortably into a holding cell. If the incoming inmate is male, my duties end there.

However, if the person is female, I have to walk them to the showers and request that they strip. I don't like watching random women shower. In fact, I think it's degrading. But we have to check for contraband. The part I do enjoy is the conversation. I guess most folks figure they have nowhere left to keep their secrets once they're naked, so the women tell me all kinds of interesting stories. Sometimes I smile and laugh with them. Other times I hold back tears. No matter what they confide, I listen without judgment.

As they dry off, I get them a uniform, which is little more than a pair of worn-out gray scrubs and some bright orange crocs. Then, our new resident gets a blue bed mat, a pillow, and a blanket. Our walk to the blocks is usually quiet. I'd imagine that's when the reality of the situation begins to sink in.

Men are housed in blocks A-D, the minimum-security area, and occasionally in solitary confinement. Inmates can also be sent to "The Hole" if they're being particularly nasty. Women are housed in blocks E & F, whose units have their own solitary cells if need be. For the most part, the women here are fairly well-behaved. Male and Female inmates are kept separated at all times. No talking. No touching. No looking. If you want to see someone of the opposite sex, you better hope you smuggled in a good imagination.

Booking is exactly what it sounds like. I don't have much to say about that position since I've never been allowed the opportunity to work there. The same two guys take turns every night. Mostly, they play solitaire on the computer and wait for someone to get brought in.

The tower is quiet and lonely, but it's also one of the most important positions. You sit in the dark for 10 hours watching the monitors, keeping an eye out for trouble, and unlocking doors for the officers making their rounds. From there, you control who goes in and who comes out. It's your job to keep everyone safe, so you have to stay alert.

Before starting on the floor, there's a half-day of training in the warden's office. He goes over levels of force, hostage procedures, and what to do in case of a blackout. It's all pretty straightforward.

As a CO, you are permitted to use one level of force higher than what's coming at you.

If someone yells, you can put your hands on them.
If someone hits you, you can use a weapon.
If someone uses a weapon, you can kill them.

During this discussion, I remember reflecting on my days as a Resident Assistant in the Kent State University dorms. If only those same rules of engagement had applied back then. In college, we were taught that when someone gets loud, you get quiet. By remaining calm, the belligerent underage drunk is encouraged to meet at the level you are on. Defusing a situation is always the best option, but inside the jail, you can't afford to look scared or weak.

Hostage procedures follow the old American standard. We'll do our best to get you out alive, but we do NOT negotiate. No one is safe if word gets out that doors will open once someone grabs a Corrections Officer. That makes perfect sense, but I didn't feel comforted knowing I was expendable.

As for the blackout procedure, the tower can't unlock the doors if the power goes out, so officers must use a key. Don't, under any circumstances, let an inmate get a key! As I said, pretty simple stuff.

The last two positions at this facility are checking the blocks and hanging out in minimum security. Those two jobs are similar in that the main objective is to count the inmates throughout the night and feed them breakfast when the sun rises. Going through each block usually requires two people working in tandem. One person counts the top floor bunks, and the other counts the bottom. Then you check your headcount against the log, and if it matches, you get to move on.

Between hourly counts, there's quite a bit of freedom to wander around and visit with co-workers confined to stationary positions. Officers assigned to the blocks also help with intake, relieve people for their breaks, and take off running if a call for assistance comes over the radio. Working the blocks is great if you need to get some steps in for the day. You also get to do a perimeter check around the outside of the building at the beginning of your shift, which is my favorite, depending on who I'm paired with.

Minimum security is the only section of the jail that sets my teeth on edge. It's a huge V-shaped room full of bunks, two bathroom areas with showers, and a large open area for meals. There are usually between 110 and 120 guys in there at a time against one little ol' me.

The majority of the people housed in that area are short-term holds or nonviolent offenders. For example, the guys serving a few days for unpaid tickets or a DUI and the old timers who only care about the coffee pot being hot and their mail getting passed out after breakfast. These guys want to do their time in peace and go home. But you also have your share of younger guys who long to prove their toughness. Those are the ones you have to keep an eye on. They like to play pranks and talk shit. I have zero interest in dealing with any of their bullshit, but it comes with the job. However, if they cross the line, I have no problem getting one of the big guys to come in and drag them out.

All in all, I'll happily accept any position I'm assigned to for the night. The job isn't physically demanding, but it can be mentally exhausting. You must always be guarded and remain fully aware of your surroundings. This sort of work isn't for everyone. In fact, I think I fare better because I don't stomp around like a tough guy. I treat people with respect until they start to run off at the mouth.

At work, there are a lot of guidelines and policies meant to keep everyone safe. But the most important rules are unwritten. Common sense can take you most of the way, so long as you always remember...

No matter how friendly an inmate seems, the ONLY people you can count on to have your back are the ones with a gold badge on their chest.

Three

TODAY I'M ASSIGNED to the blocks with Officer Kelly. He was hired around the same time I was, and we started on the same day. It's nice when we're scheduled to work together because we're on the same level. Like with any job, seniority and rank give you power. But Kelly and I are both nobodies, hanging out together on the bottom of the totem pole. Honestly, he's my favorite person to be paired with. When we're in different areas, our interaction might be limited to a quick "Hey, how's it going?" If he's working the blocks while I'm stuck in minimum or the tower, he usually offers to relieve me for my breaks or brings me things I can't retrieve for myself. More than once, I've chosen to stay and hang out with him instead of sitting in my car alone.

Whenever we work the blocks together, we have interesting conversations, and he's saved my ass a few times. Nothing life-threatening, but situations that would have escalated beyond my control had he not been close by.

Kelly was beside me that first day when the fight happened in C Block. I remember seeing him run straight toward the inmate who was all bloodied and beaten. The sight of blood made me nauseous, so I turned my back and assisted elsewhere, but Kelly didn't seem phased. From the beginning, I was impressed by him. Later he told me that he had considered becoming an EMT. He even went through all the schooling but applied here on a whim. And, like me, he fell in love with the job almost instantly.

His personality was enough to win me over, but he's not exactly lacking in the looks department. Kelly is in his mid-20s, properly fit, and drop-dead gorgeous. He's the type of guy who works out at the gym for fun, with the sort of physical proportions that might make a person social media famous for merely existing. He's the kind of guy women line the blocks to meet, willing to sacrifice their virtue for the pleasure of his time.

Kelly's about four inches taller than I am. So, if I had to guess, I would put him at 5' 11, 185 lbs. with dark brown hair and eyes that look almost black. He has one of those effortless beards. The kind that looks like it grew in perfectly two nights ago, and he hasn't bothered to notice. I don't know why, but I'm a sucker for well-groomed facial hair. Of course, Kelly seems perfect compared to everyone else in my current vicinity.

The pair of us talk nonstop during our perimeter check, cracking jokes and sharing secrets. I feel like I can trust him. The back and forth between us always feels natural, and I catch myself thinking of him after we part ways. Kelly is engaging, comical, intelligent, considerate, intense, clever, and occasionally flirtatious. These are all qualities I look for in a person but never seem to find.

I would have considered flirting back, but he's a couple of years younger than I am and so far out of my league that we aren't even playing the same game. Even on a bad day, Kelly looks photo-ready, whereas I'm happy to be invisible. If the jail were ever looking to recruit more female officers, they'd only need to print his image on the flyer.

Despite the disparity in our physical appearance, I might have considered the possibility of dating, except I have this weird thing about eye color. I've only date guys with blue eyes. I know it's an odd dealbreaker. And trust me, I know that it's dumb to limit my options so significantly, especially considering only 8% of the global population has blue eyes, and the majority of those people fall outside of my acceptable dating age range. Not to mention, I'm painfully single and getting older by the day. Maybe I should reconsider my priorities, but eye color remains on the list for today. Sometimes, my subtly changing eyes are the only thing I like about myself.

Being an overweight teenager made me an easy target for bullies. And while I might have frequently dreamt of waking up in a new body, that wasn't going to happen. So, if I had to come face to face with a mirror, I found comfort in looking myself in the eyes and avoiding the rest.

The blocks are their usual buzz of activity as we enter. It's only an assumption, but I get the feeling the inmates stay up late enough to see which officers are coming in at shift change. Then, after we pass through, most everyone goes to sleep for the night.

Walking along the top counting, I'm reminded of a video clip the warden showed us early on. Last year an inmate jumped from the second-floor railing. It didn't seem like a suicide attempt because he went feet first, but he also wasn't doing it for fun. Upon impact with the concrete floor below, the bone in his leg snapped and came poking out the side. Warden Lawson said some people would do anything to get out, even if it's only half a day in the emergency room.

Another thing to keep an eye out for, I guess.

I don't usually look directly at any one person as I trek the well-worn footpath through the concrete dungeon, but not because I'm afraid to make eye contact. It's important to be aware of everything simultaneously, so my focus is on the room instead of the individuals. If you fail to pay attention, threats can be easily disguised in the dark. When I reach the next door, I give Kelly my number, and he checks our total against the list. Each block only has about 16 people, so it doesn't take long to get through each one.

There's a door on either end of the balcony, connecting the units together. Picture adjoining rooms at a hotel; only these doors are reinforced with thick metal and bolted shut. All I have to do is stand by the exit I want to go through, and whoever is in the tower will unlock it for me.

As we walk through, it's not unusual to come across a mystery substance on the door handle. Most of the time, it's shampoo. The guys think seeing our reaction to their nighttime antics is funny, but I've become pretty good at spotting it before I get there. If I ask them to clean it off, they will, so I don't feel the need to make a bigger issue of it. Some officers live for write-ups, but that's not my style.

Kelly and I are though A and B with no issues. I love these quiet nights. The lock on the door ahead of me clicks, and I continue on my way. We're nearly finished with C when someone behind me says, "Officer Belk, hold up."

Inmates often stop us to request items such as toilet paper or envelopes, so I turn around expecting to hear something along those lines. However, when my eyes focus on the man approaching me, he already has an envelope in his hand with my name written on it.

"Here, this is for you. I wrote you a letter," says the heavily tattooed male inmate, taking one final step toward me. He's well over six feet tall and built like a brick shithouse. If it weren't for the smile, I might have been mildly intimidated by his sudden appearance.

For a moment, I'm caught off guard. This situation is a first for me, and I'm not entirely sure how to proceed. I know that accepting any form of personal communication sends the wrong message. But what if it's important? Not all information can be said aloud. He might be reporting a situation in the bunks or a threat we're unaware of. Or maybe he's shooting his shot with one of the only women he's allowed to lay eyes on from now until his release date. This letter is putting me in an awkward position, but I can't exactly stand here and ask questions.

"Don't hand me that," is all I can think to say. But he remains unmoved with my letter held out in front of him. So, I do what most women do when confronted with a man who doesn't listen. I repeat myself and add a warning. "Please, don't hand me that. It'll get you into trouble."

"I'm already in jail. There's not much else they can do to me. Take it. I wrote it earlier." His tone is friendly, and I have no reason to feel threatened by the interaction. He's smiling at me as though trouble is a welcome friend, but I'm the guest of honor.

"Fine."

Once I accept the envelope, he winks at me and returns to his bunk. Best to continue with what I was previously doing and sort this mess out after. I keep the letter in full view of the cameras as I walk through the last few blocks. What the hell could it possibly say? I remember this guy from the morning tray pass, but I can't recall us ever exchanging words. I show Kelly the sealed envelope as soon as we step into the hallway alone.

"Are you gonna read it?" he asks, as a look of curious excitement lights his face. Kelly looks like a kid on Christmas, and my impending doom is this season's shiny new toy.

"No! Absolutely not." Of this, I am certain. There's no way I want the rumor mill in this place churning out stories involving a guy from C block and me. Officers who engage in inappropriate contact with inmates belong behind bars. The only acceptable course of action is to take the unopened envelope to my supervisor and let him sort it out. Sergeant Hubble's office is across the hall, and I can hear him in there talking with someone.

I knock on the open door and wait in the hallway with my stomach in knots. There are three people already in the office. I seem to have interrupted some kind of male bonding moment between officers. They're looking at guns and ammo magazine and making plans to meet for target practice at a local range. Sergeant Hubble motions for me to come in. I assume the other guys will leave, but they remain seated, waiting to hear what I have to say. I hand Hubble the letter and explain what happened.

"Sir, I was walking through the blocks for headcount, and an inmate in C handed me this letter. I have no recollection of inter-acting with this person prior to this evening. And I thought it best to bring it to you straight away." My tone is matter-of-fact, and my statement is to the point. Whenever I have to talk to someone in a position of authority, I use my interview voice in hopes of being viewed as an adult.

After concluding my statement and handing over the enve-lope, a full second of stunned silence passes before all three men erupt in laughter. Clearly, I've overthought the possible severity of my current situation. Yeah, that feels pretty on-brand for me. I imagine my cheeks are painted red with embarrassment as he unfolds the notebook paper and begins reading.

"Do you want to see it?" He asks, holding the letter out to me.

"No, thank you," I say. But I'm not sure how accurate those words are.

"It's nothing bad, but you should probably read it."

He's still smiling when he hands me the folded notebook paper, so I guess it can't be anything too outrageous or offensive. I read it over once. Confusion mixes with my embarrassment. The problem I'm having is that I'm not exactly sure what some of these slang terms mean. I'm not from this area of the state, and my prison vocabulary is limited. I can't very well ask them to explain it either, so I do my best to play it off. You best believe I'll be on Google searching for translations the first chance I get.

"All right, if that's all, I guess you can head to minimum for the rest of the night, and Grant here can take Mr. Hillard to soli-tary. 30 days. We'll keep you off the blocks for a week or two and ensure there are no further issues. While you were reading, I pulled the file for Jason Hillard. 28, in for theft. Turns out he lives down the street from the house you're renting. He'll be out in a couple of months." Hubble's tone is nonchalant as if this is a normal conversation.

Okay. Well, this sucks. A guy was sent to solitary for a month, and I've been exiled to minimum security as a direct result of my overthinking. What was the point of his letter? From what I could grasp, he was talking about tattoos and life on the outside. If he's impressed by my ink, he could've said that shit to my face as I passed through and avoided this situation. I caught zero hints of flirtation or threat written on that page, and now I'm being punished for doing the right thing.

I walk out, questioning my decision and dreading the night ahead.

Four

THE MINIMUM-SECURITY AREA is at the end of the hallway across from the kitchen. Since I'll be alone with my thoughts for the rest of the night, I stop to get provisions. Currently, two male inmates are working overnight in the kitchen. As soon as they see me, they jump to their feet, in the classic "hurry up and look busy" move. The kitchen has its own break area, including a television, and they're watching a movie I don't recognize. The thinner of the two guys offers to fix me a plate, but I'm pretty sure I can handle it.

I grab a bucket of ice from the machine and a large Styrofoam cup. Then I take my diet coke from the fridge, slap some peanut butter on a couple of slices of bread, and throw some chips on a paper plate. There are leftovers from dinner that I'm allowed to eat, but I'm not in the mood for what looks like beef stroganoff and mixed vegetables.

"Don't worry about cleaning. I'll take care of it." A male voice calls over from the break area. I don't know which one extended the offer to clean up after me because they're some distance away, but I'll gladly accept.

I've noticed that the inmates working overnight steer clear of anyone in a uniform if they can help it. It's not that they're trying to hide something. In fact, it's probably the opposite. There are only so many jobs available for inmates, and there's a waiting list of names for all of them. So, as long as these guys stay out of trouble, they'll maintain their position. Each of the jobs comes with its own set of perks. For example, working in the kitchen gets you extra food. But even better than that, these guys get to change the channel on the break room television. Every place else in the jail, the officers control the TVs. It's meant to keep people from getting into physical altercations over the remote. However, I also feel like it's meant to reinforce power dynamics.

My train of thought continues on a new track as I carry my stack of rations from the kitchen into the hallway. As I approach the airlock, I hear the door click and pull it open with my elbow. I must have been a waitress in a previous life because I manage to get through both doors without dropping a single item. Sitting at the desk is one of the older guys on 3rd shift, and he's excited to hear that I've come to spring him.

"Any problems I should know about?" I have a pretty good feeling that I already know the answer to my question. There is more movement and conversation among the inmates than I typically see at this hour, and I sense that I've come in at the tail end of something.

"Oh, some idiot thought flooding the bathroom would be a fun idea. He's cleaning it now." Smith's voice is deep and gravelly, like a guy who's smoked unfiltered cigarettes since he was ten.

"Isn't that lovely?" I roll my eyes and let out an exasperated breath. This is the last thing I need right now. When one guy starts acting inappropriately, it's easy for the others to follow suit. It's important to be quick. You have to stop their antics before the escalation. Otherwise, it descends into chaos.

"I gave them a warning. One more incident tonight, and hot water and mail won't come out until noon tomorrow. So, don't take any shit from these guys. And call if you need backup."

"Will do!" I say, trying to sound confident. This night is going to go one of two ways. Everyone will settle down now that a new officer is here, or they'll steamroll me because I'm a girl.

"Want to do a quick head count together before I leave? That way, you're all set for the hour." He's nice to offer, and I don't hesitate to accept.

This is the V-shaped portion of the jail. My desk is at the edge of the dining area in front of the door at the base of the V. There are 60 bunk beds, 30 on each side, so that gets us to our 120 max. Currently, 113 people are being housed in this block. Once per hour, I'm required to do a head count.

Thankfully, it's almost midnight, so most of the guys are near their bunks. As I move along, I lose track of the count and have to start over, but eventually, I get through it. While walking along my half of the bunks, I ask the guys if they plan on making this a long night for me.

One guy attempts to reassure me but does little to alleviate my concern. "Nah, most of us hate Smith. The rest of the night should be quiet. We like you."

All I can do is smile to myself and move along. The last thing I need is another letter with my name on it, though it is nice to hear that people like me. I don't usually have any issues when I'm here. Unfortunately, as much as some of these guys might like or even respect me, I can't count on them to keep everything peaceful.

The numbers match the count, so Smith is off to greener pastures. As for me, I'll be here, in purgatory.

Don't get me wrong. I still love my job even when I'm stuck in minimum. This isn't a terrible area to be in. It's painfully boring but generally quiet. Mostly, the guys sleep until it's time for breakfast, which leaves me alone with my racing thoughts, crushing self-doubt, and a laundry list of regrets. I prefer order and silence when the alternative is chaos, but the quiet darkness doesn't offer much in the way of distractions. By 4:00 am, I'll be struggling to keep my eyes open, and the last thing I want to do is fall asleep. Trust me. I've run through that worst-case scenario playlist more than a few times, and it isn't pretty.

I stay behind the desk, close to the door, when I'm not counting the same inmates over and over again. Thankfully, I'm far enough away from the bunks that my constant crunching doesn't keep anyone awake. I'm not in the mood to deal with sleep-deprived criminals barking at me.

I'm not sure what it is, but lately, I've been eating ice like I can't get enough. And getting more becomes an all-consuming mission when I don't have it. I'm obsessed with frozen water like some kind of ice addict. The small cubes from the machine in the kitchen here at work are my second favorite and usually my go-to. However, If I feel like treating myself, I drive to the gas station in the next town over and get a cup of the good stuff.

It didn't take long for my co-workers to notice my odd craving. Sometimes, Kelly will bring me a fresh bucket of ice from the kitchen when I run out unless he's stuck in the tower. I wish we were still in the blocks together. I didn't realize how much I would miss having Kelly beside me until I was banished. Maybe we're better friends than I give him credit for.

I nibble on the food I brought while fiddling with the old desktop computer. It doesn't have access to the internet, only work-related stuff, but it's still better than nothing. Reading through the files helps keep me awake when I don't have a book.

Officers can search for people by name, or housing unit, so I pull up the list of names for minimum security and click on one at random. The photo of an older man appears on my screen, and I recognize him immediately. John Stetson. Sounds like he should've been a cowboy. Heck, I don't know. Maybe on the outside, he was. I don't usually look at the conviction or sentencing info, though we are encouraged to do so. What I find most useful is the names and faces.

During tray pass, guys occasionally hurry and eat or hide trays in their bunks to get in line for seconds. You have to pay attention because if you call the kitchen for more trays, look out! The cook is a heavyset lady in her 60s who is not one bit afraid to berate the officers. I hate when someone gets one over on me and steals a tray. In the blocks, it's easy because there are only a handful of people at each stop. But the line in minimum is too long to keep tabs on. Plus, you have to pass meals out as quickly as possible. It's a real cluster fuck. That's why studying the faces beforehand helps make it easier to spot the double. Bonus points if I can remember what their name is.

I hear the door behind me when it clicks to unlock, and I turn to see who it is. For a split second, I find myself hoping it's Kelly with a new bucket of ice, but a much larger figure greets me when I spin my chair around.

"Belk, I have another one for you." Grant seems amused by something, and I wonder if he's still laughing about the letter that landed me here.

Five

TOP of the hour and time for me to do another head count. I adjust the total on my sheet to account for our new arrival and head over to the bunks. Grant leads our newest inmate to an empty bed in the left section, so I start my count on the right. I'm nearly finished with the section when I hear, "Watch yourself, bitch!"

"Excuse me, what did you say?" My tone is sharp, and I can feel the tension solidify in my muscles as my eyes narrow.

The people here will test you because they have nothing better to do. Thankfully, it's never escalated past that, but the possibility remains on the table.

"I said you'd better watch yourself, bitch. You woke me up."

My jaw tightens when he doubles down and repeats his previous statement. I'm beginning to hate men and their insistence on speaking as if anyone wants to hear it.

"Get your ass out of that bunk and stand by the door." This is an order. I have no choice but to have him removed. I don't recognize this inmate from my photo scrolling. Otherwise, I would address him by name.

"I'm in here for beating my wife." He says, clearly in an attempt to shake me. He wants to see me scared, but guys like him are a dime a dozen in this place. He hasn't shaken me, and he isn't going to.

This guy isn't the first of his kind that I've had to deal with. The men in my past have often tried to make me feel small. Backing me into a corner. Silencing me with fear. And I allowed it to happen, time and time again, because I wholeheartedly bought into the idea of love. I thought I could change them if I did enough to prove myself. I believed all the bullshit lies I was fed in my youth, that relationships take work. I opened myself up to the punishment and accepted the pain because, after a while, I thought that was what love looked like. I don't like the idea of closing myself off, but at what point do I start caring enough about myself to stop the bleeding?

"You work at something until it's not worth working at anymore." A quote from my first boyfriend, who could best be described as a lying piece of shit, catfish. We met online and talked every day for about six months. Later, I would find out that he was living with his girlfriend of four years and playing me for a goddamn fool the entire time. There's a lot more to the story, but since it makes me look like a pathetic loser, we'll save that for another time. Needless to say, it wasn't a great first step into dating.

Sarcasm has always been my go-to weapon in a battle of words. So, I shoot back in my most ridiculous, rich old lady accent, "Your mother must be so proud."

Now it's a staring contest. But I have a secret weapon besides my wit. This fat, ill-mannered slop standing before me seems to have forgotten one crucial thing. I'm not the only officer in here right now.

Grant is a BIG guy. He's one of the officers on SRT (Special Response Team) and the sergeant's right-hand man. He loves getting called in to crack skulls. Metaphorically speaking. Though I'm certain, he could crack a skull if he tried. Grant is one of the guys who stomp around this place, itching for a fight to break out. While others, like myself, pray for quiet. So, when I see him, over the inmate's shoulder, with rage set into the muscles of his face, I know this situation is about to be taken off my hands.

Time not only unfreezes but seems to accelerate beyond the standard rate. The words come out of Grant's throat in a roar, "YOU DO NOT DISRESPECT MY OFFICERS!" He weaves one of his massive forearms through the arms of the inmate and locks them behind his back. With his other hand on the inmate's shoulder, he walks him straight to the door. The lock clicks, and they are out of the room without so much as a look back. Grant will most likely take him to the hole for a time-out.

The hole is where we put people who need a little time to think about their actions. It isn't meant for long-term use like the solitary confinement cells and isn't as friendly as the temporary hold cells at booking. The hole is in a short hallway, separated from the other housing units. It feels darker and colder there. The "bed" is a concrete block, and the "toilet" is a hole in the floor. This room was designed to make someone uncomfortable. Time spent here is meant to remind you that even in jail, you have things to lose. Normally, it doesn't take long for someone in the hole to apologize and start begging to return to their bunk. I have a feeling; no amount of pleading will get this guy back in here before breakfast.

An uncomfortable energy hangs heavy in the air even after they're gone. It's dead quiet, but the previous tension lingers around me as I make my way through the bunks, and I remember why I hate being here alone. Thankfully, I finish my count without further trouble and return to my desk no worse for the wear.

"Um, excuse me. Officer Belk, I'm sorry to bother you. But I think my blood sugar is crashing, and I don't feel very good. Do you mind if we check it?" An inmate walks over as my ass makes contact with the chair. What else could go wrong tonight?

I recognize the man from previous interactions and offer him a seat in the extra chair. Even though it's dark, I can see that he looks pale, and beads of sweat are speckling his forehead. He knows what to do with the testing kit, so I sit back and wait for the results. He's right; his blood sugar level is low. I record this in the book and make a call to the kitchen.

"Stay seated right here until you eat. Then we'll retest before you go back to bed." He knows the drill, but I say it anyways. A moment later, there's a knock at the little door we use for tray pass. I walk over and open it. One of the guys from across the hall in the kitchen has brought a peanut butter sandwich, a small carton of orange juice, and a bucket of ice.

"I wasn't sure if you needed ice, so I brought some with me. Can I get you anything else from the kitchen, ma'am?" Apparently, my ice addiction has also not gone unnoticed by the kitchen workers. It must be even worse than I thought. And did he call me ma'am?

"This should take care of it, thank you. I appreciate it." My gratitude is genuine. The men and women here may have done some illegal things, but that doesn't necessarily make them bad people. Every human being craves acknowledgment and praise, something that's in short supply when you are incarcerated. I don't know. This is my only experience working as a corrections officer. Maybe I'm totally off base.

I return to the desk and set the sandwich and juice on the corner. As for the ice, I slide the new bucket into the empty one next to the computer, and instantly, my mouth begins to water. I fill my cup and start crunching, unable to wait the fifteen minutes it's going to take to finish with this current inmate situation. All I want right now is some time alone with my thoughts and a break from the disorder.

"Quite the commotion tonight. Does that mean no coffee in the morning?" My desk companion asks between bites of his sandwich.

I have to think for a moment before answering, but I settle on giving them the hot water pots and mail during the normal times. I hate the thought of punishing everyone for the actions of one or two people. Plus, the flooded bathroom happened before I walked in here.

"Everything will be given at the scheduled time. So long as the rest of the night is quiet."

It's time for him to retest, so he does. I record the number in the book and send him back to bed without further discussion. Then I make sure to note the previous conflict and resulting action and adjust my inmate total to reflect one less. I hope that jerk is freezing his ass off in the hole.

Finally, some peace. I sit and consider every moment leading to this one. I think about the conversation Kelly and I had as we went through all the empty sections of the building during our perimeter check. I catch myself smiling as I recall a particularly corny joke he told me. The way he struggled to get through the punchline without doubling over from laughter was funnier than the actual joke.

Then I replay our trip through the blocks and the letter that made a mess of my night. I think about the inmate that handed it to me and my choice to turn it over. Maybe I could ask Kelly to throw Jason Hillard in the hole for ten minutes. He could sort things out for me with those who might wish me harm. Of course, I'm not really going to let an inmate fight in my place and defend my honor, but the thought does cross my mind. Regrettably, real life doesn't play out like in the movies.

My decision to report this stupid letter has weighed on me since it happened, and not because the inmate involved was relatively good-looking. The punishment seems unfair. One guy receives 30 days in solitary for writing me a note, while another gets a few hours of being cold and a slap on the wrist after making an obvious threat.

Jason Hillard is the type of guy I would have noticed outside of here. He's tall, muscular, and covered in tattoos. Even in the dim light, I noticed his blue eyes and handsome facial features. He's someone I would have talked to had we met in a tattoo shop or at a concert. After a few drinks, I would've tried to take him home and climb him like a tree. But we didn't meet in a bar, online, or walking along the street. We crossed paths here, in a jail. So, any thought I might have of Jason Hillard being the type of guy I would spend an evening with should begin and end right here and now. Those nighttime daydreams can remain unspoken in the long overdue stillness of what has already been an exceedingly draining shift.

Don't get me wrong, I hate being single, and I'm horny to the point of near insanity. During our nightly meeting, I found myself staring at Kelly, practically undressing him with my eyes. When he caught me looking, he smiled. Then winked at me when we were assigned to the blocks together. Every woman in this place is obsessed with him, but I'm sure he found it hilarious to find my name scrawled across the bottom of his fan club sign-in sheet.

I haven't been with anyone since Kevin left town and desperately crave physical touch. I want to talk to someone about my day. I need to feel connected and seen. I miss being in a relationship, even if they all turn to shit after a few months.

There are days when it takes a concerted effort not to fantasize about the handful of attractive inmates housed within these walls. But that's a slippery slope I refuse to step foot on. You won't catch me tumbling down that hill or falling flat on my face. I don't care how long it's been since I've felt a man's touch. If we met inside this building, you're off limits. Any contact beyond what is required for the job, inside or outside this building, is strictly forbidden.

It's true that my past is littered with horrible choices and despicable men, but even they weren't criminals. Any previous thoughts of Jason Hillard's potential physical prowess are hereby stricken from my consciousness, leaving only the mistakes of my past.

Despite my best efforts, the highlight reel starts to roll inside my head, and it's clear that I'll spend the next hour thinking about each person who took a turn, stabbing me in the back and scarring my heart. Being a hopeless romantic is starting to look a lot less romantic and entirely hopeless.

Six

AT LONG LAST, the sun begins to rise. Usually, my nights here are peaceful, but this shift has been one thing after the next. I complete my final head count before removing the hot water pots from the supply closet. After filling the two large silver and black chafers with water, I flip the switches into the on position and scan the room as the men stir in their bunks. Imagine having so little that being given heated water was enough to keep you content.

Next, I prepare the dining area seating for the breakfast rush. The tables have wheels, so I begin moving them into place, even though the guys here usually take care of that. It feels good to stretch after sitting for so long, and the lights will be coming on soon. This is the final push before I head home and make the acquaintance of sleep.

The last thing I do, while I'm alone, is to replay the night and write out any last-minute notes I have in the log book. In the middle of my shift, Kelly arrived to relieve me for my dinner break. He brought a bucket of ice from the kitchen and a hooded sweatshirt from his locker. Both were greatly appreciated. Sadly, he was called to the sergeant's office before we could talk, and Smith came in to take his place. Once the appeal of staying inside disappeared through the airlock, I quickly followed suit. I wandered through familiar corridors, taking the long way out to the parking lot. As I passed the booking desk and exited through the bay doors, I had hoped someone might strike up a conversation, but nobody did. Of course, none of this is relevant, so I simply write *4:15 am Lunch Break. Smith.*

"Finish strong!" I tell myself.

Like clockwork, the inmates awake and begin shuffling around the bunks and into the bathrooms. No annoying alarm clocks here, and yet, as if on cue, everyone inside the building is a buzz of activity. Grant comes through the door, signaling that breakfast trays will be coming from the kitchen any minute, and I'm happy to see his face again. Tray pass would be a *lot* more stressful on my own. Plus, I didn't get a chance to thank him for having my back.

"Morning, beautiful. How'd you sleep?" He gives me a wink, so I know he's joking. Grant is an attractive man, but he's not my type. "I'm guessing there were no further issues since we didn't hear from you. Here's the mail." He sets a stack of open envelopes on the desk.

"Oh, thanks," I smile back at him. Secretly, I crave these moments of human interaction. They're even better when it's with a guy around my age who isn't incarcerated. "Everyone was *very* concerned about their letters. They'll be happy to see those made it here on time."

Most people would be intimidated by a guy Grant's size, but I know that people are more than what they present on the exterior. So, it's always a good idea to look a little deeper. Plus, I find tall men with broad shoulders and thick arms incredibly appealing. Which is why I tend to notice them. Maybe because I was overweight in high school and physically quite strong. I need a man who makes me feel tiny when I'm in his arms. I want to feel protected and consumed by an embrace.

So, long story short, that smirk on Grant's face and the twinkle in his eyes are enough to convince me that outside of this place, he's probably a big softy.

"My night was alright. I had a guy with low blood sugar, but nothing a sandwich couldn't fix. Was my pen-pal upset about the 30 days in solitary?" I keep the tone playful as I fish for information.

"Nah, he was cool about it. Pretty sure he knew the cost of playing the game. But I told him I witnessed the entire interaction on the cameras and made you turn it over. That way, it seemed like you didn't have a choice. I didn't want him or any of his buddies to hold a grudge. Otherwise, you'd be stuck in here, and I know you prefer being in the blocks. I'm sure he'll be out of solitary before the 30 days."

"Yeah, that makes sense. Thanks for smoothing things over and for having my back. I guess I owe you a batch of cookies or something." Baked goods have always been my favorite way to show my gratitude.

"You don't owe me anything. Looking out for one another is part of the job. That said, I won't be mad if you bake some chocolate chip and leave them at the booking desk."

"Got it!" I say with a grin, making sure my back is turned to the bunk area. "I have the next few days off. So, Tuesday when I get back. I'll make a bunch. Don't want anyone to think I'm playing favorites." The thought of homemade cookie dough makes my mouth water. I don't care what anyone says about salmonella or e coli. Eating raw cookie dough is one of life's greatest pleasures. Some things are worth the risk.

Tray pass goes smoothly. No one even attempts to steal an extra breakfast. Is this progress, or do they not care for the oatmeal? Either way, I'm glad I don't have to make any calls to the kitchen.

Grant takes the cart of empty trays with him when he leaves, and I pass out razors and mail. All the mail is opened and skimmed through overnight at the booking desk, so all I have to do is hand it out. As for razors, not all the guys bother to shave, but the ones who do each have a bag with their name on it. Razors have to be checked out and returned during this 20-minute window. As I'm checking in the last razor, I hear the next shift coming in behind me. I lock the box in the bottom left desk drawer and collect my things.

Quickly, I give the two officers on 1st shift a rundown of the night's events and walk over to the door. When I hear the lock click, euphoria spreads through my veins. The next door unlocks, and I'm so close to freedom that I can almost taste it. I head to the kitchen to return my small stack of plastic ice buckets and wave good morning to the chef.

"The extra food from breakfast is still hot if you want anything." An inmate from the cooking staff informs me as I pass through.

At this hour, the kitchen feels like a different place. All the overhead lights are on, and the air is warm. It smells like toast and sausage links. Normally, I would make a plate for myself, but I'm ready to get out of here this morning.

"Thanks," I say. It would be rude not to respond. But instead of getting food, I turn towards the door.

I still need to swing by the office to drop my walkie off before I can clock out, and that requires getting past Hubble and whoever he's shooting the shit with. My fingers are crossed, praying that no one is in there, but as I get closer to the open door, I hear the guys talking.

"Hey, Belk, heard you're baking cookies. Can I request some peanut butter and chocolate?" Word certainly travels fast around here. Looks like I'm going to need a grocery run after I get out of bed.

"Absolutely, Sir." It seems like a bad move to say no to the boss. Anyways, I enjoy being in the kitchen. By the time I return on Tuesday, I will have baked 3 or 4 different types and sugary confections in an attempt to sweeten the disposition of my co-workers. I wonder what kind of cookies Kelly likes. I still need to return his sweatshirt, so if our paths cross in the parking lot, I may ask him for a list of his favorite flavors.

"Have a nice rest of your day." I slide my walkie into the charging cradle and offer a quick wave before scooting out the door.

One last short hallway leading to the front is all that stands between me and the time clock. I'm so focused on my destination that I never stop to consider my path until I see his fat ugly face glaring through the small window at the center of the door. The hallway I'm walking along is where the two cells we refer to as The Hole are located. I do my best not to react or respond as I pass by, though I strain my ears in an attempt to sort through his vulgarities.

The threat maker is saying something, but the words are distorted as they bounce off the thick steel door. No doubt he's hurling insults of some kind. As much as I try not to be an asshole, an undeniable satisfaction comes as the door ahead of me clicks to unlock. I smile, knowing that I get to walk out of this place, and all that jerk behind me can do is watch as I leave.

Of course, that kind of cockiness can paint a target on your forehead, so I don't turn around. When the inmates decide they don't like you, they find creative ways to let you know about it. I'm sure, like with Officer Smith, there will be a flooded bathroom somewhere in my future.

When I take my first step out into the morning sun and fill my lungs with clean air, a transformation happens. Instantly, the weight of last night is lifted from my shoulders, and I get a bounce in my step. Letting everything go and leaving it at work is one of the best things about this job.

I feel like in the past, though all of my jobs were vastly different, the stress of each seemed to linger and build. Oddly enough, I could describe my relationships the same way. Now, couple that with my unchecked bipolar depression, and it becomes an endless cycle of Hope-Delusion-Doubt-Rejection-Denial. And the stronger it gets, the more I feel like I'm disappearing.

But each new day is an opportunity for a fresh start. A chance to do things differently. Right? What will today hold? It's anyone's guess. I could meet the love of my life at the grocery store later. Anything can happen if you remain open to it.

Kelly is parked next to me this morning, but he's already getting into his car and too far away for me to catch him. Even though the odds are stacked against me, I begin moving faster, and as luck would have it, he sees me. My speed walking across the parking lot must look out of character because he stops, pulls back into the spot, and steps out of his car.

"So? Come on, don't leave me in suspense here. Did he ask you to the prom or what?" His question throws me off momentarily, and the confusion must be painted all over my face. "What was in the letter? I'm dying to know. I was told to adjust the headcount, but Grant wouldn't let slip the reason for the move. Was it bad?"

"No," I laugh, "Alas, I'm still dateless for the prom. He was placing his order for a birthday cake with a key baked inside."

"Ha!... I know you're joking, but that shit would be hilarious. Not you actually baking it, just him asking. Speaking of baking, I heard you're making cookies. Are you being friendly, or do you have a secret crush on someone I don't know about?"

I can't help but laugh, scrunch my face, and shake my head to reset my thoughts. The idea of me having a crush on someone I work with is ridiculous. Isn't it? And anyways, If I did have a crush on someone, I wouldn't be telegraphing my intentions with baked goods. My idea of flirting looks more like shots at the bar and a blow job in the parking lot.

"So you guys were talking about me, huh?" I hand Kelly the sweatshirt that still smells like him and study his expression. "Thanks for letting me borrow that. It's always freezing in there."

Now I'm starting to wonder what else the guys say about me when I'm not around. What is there to say? The people here hardly know me. We've never gone out for drinks after work or met up on a day off. There are nights here that pass without so much as a single word being exchanged. Kelly probably knows me the best out of anyone, and even that's not saying much.

"No worries. I promise you, only good things were being said." A smile stretches across his face, and his big brown eyes ignite as they catch the morning sun. "So, you *aren't* making cookies for Grant?"

"I'm making cookies for everyone. Want to add your favorite to the list?" There was something in that last question, the way he said Grant's name. Is Kelly trying to ask me if I have a crush on Grant? Of all the people here, why him? Have I done or said something to give off that impression? I do a quick scan of my mental files, searching through conversations and interactions over the last couple of months, anything involving Grant. Nothing jumps out at me, so maybe I'm misreading the current back and forth.

Kelly resumes the conversation right where it left off, clearly not noticing my internal multi-tasking. "If I had to choose a favorite, it would have to be sugar cookies. You know, to sweeten me up a bit."

"Ha! Right, because you're such a sourpuss." My response isn't even that funny, but we both begin laughing for some reason. I cover my face with my hands, an unconscious reaction, and wipe a tear from my eye. I guess my body needed a release of emotion. We're both probably a little punch-drunk from lack of sleep.

"You can make whatever. I'm sure they'll be delicious. I'm nobody special. So, don't feel like you have to go to any extra trouble for me." With these words, I can sense that the end of our conversation is near.

"Respectfully, I disagree. You're worth the trouble and then some. Don't ever let anyone convince you otherwise." My joking tone from a moment ago seems to have disappeared with my laughter, and I realize our playful conversation has turned into something more serious. A wave of awkward nervousness washes over me, and I'm suddenly afraid to meet his gaze.

When I finally lift my chin, it's worse than I feared. Kelly has taken a step forward, and the expression on his face is difficult for me to discern. Normally, reading people is my superpower, but he has me stumped. Did my last comment strike a nerve? I hope he knows that wasn't my intention. I feel like I should apol-ogize, but I'm frozen in place, and my throat is suddenly bone dry. All I can do is search his eyes for clues and hope he breaks the silence between us.

The tension holds until he says, "Text me when you wake up. Maybe we can go to lunch or something. You still have my number, right?"

"Um yeah. Totally." As soon as the words cross my lips, I hear how stupid they sound. What the fuck? Hey Heather, the 90s called; they want their surfer lingo catchphrase back. And this, folks, is why I'm single. If I detect the slightest hint of interest from a guy, my brain turns to pudding. This is probably why, in the past, I've missed so many obvious red flags.

Kelly takes a final lingering look into my eyes and turns to get back into his car. Before I reach my driver's side door, I hear him say, "Sleep well." Then he waves and backs out of his spot. I smile back and get into my car, which is all I'm capable of doing at the moment. My brain requires distance from this conversation in order to process what happened.

Did Kelly ask me on a date, or is this a standard run-of-the-mill meal between co-workers? After two months of working together and talking in ten-hour increments, I suppose I'd call us friends. We did exchange phone numbers, but neither of us has ever reached out. At the time, I assumed he did it to be nice. In case one of us needed something at work and didn't want to ask over the radio. I had almost forgotten that his number was even in my phone. Typically, I avoid the K section altogether when digging through my contact list.

Most likely, I'm making something out of nothing, and he's being friendly like always. Maybe he feels bad for me after last night. Or maybe this is some kind of co-worker sympathy because I've been here for a while and have exactly zero friends. I'm sure that's all it is. A guy who looks like that doesn't notice a girl like me.

Seven

I AWAKEN to the unmistakable stench of cigarette smoke seeping through the floor, and it takes my brain a moment to place where I am. For some reason, I can't seem to get used to this apartment, probably because I hate it so much. Whoever lives downstairs is clearly uninterested in getting back their security deposit. If they even paid one. For all I know, it's the landlord's kid or something. That would certainly explain a lot. Funny, I've lived here for months and have never seen who lives there. Then again, I do keep a rather nontraditional sleep schedule. I should stop being nice, call to complain about the smoking, and be done with it. Maybe tomorrow.

My 28-year-old spine feels 82 after nearly five hundred hours on an air mattress. I should look for a bed frame and memory foam mattress when I go out later, but I won't. Furniture would make my stay here feel permanent, and I'm not quite ready for that yet. Living like a squatter in a place I pay for seems ridiculous, but I find comfort in its temporary nature. A tiny part of me still has hope for a better life, and I'm not ready to watch that dream whither on the vine.

I should probably stop being dramatic and get up, but my watch and phone are charging on the other side of the room. So, if I want to see what time it is, I'll have to crawl over there or stand and walk. A vision of myself rolling naked across the room flashes in my head, making me laugh out loud. Maybe if the carpet weren't so gross, I would do it to be silly.

As a kid, I loved making people laugh when they were crying. I would go to great lengths, sacrificing my comfort to ease their suffering. Had I ever bothered to believe in myself, I might have had a bright future as a comedian. Now I'm the unfunny clown renting an apartment in my own personal hell, and there's no one coming to save me.

I get to my feet and search for comfortable clothing. The room is dark, but my night vision is top-notch, so I don't have any trouble finding what I'm looking for. Gym shorts and a t-shirt will do for now. I don't so much as want to look at a uniform on my day off.

When I open the curtains, I leave the mini blinds closed. The afternoon sun filters in at half-strength, which is all I can handle. The time on my watch reads 4:38 pm as I fasten it around my wrist. Since I know my alarm is set for 5:00, I grab my phone and turn the alarm off to avoid the noise. That's when I see the notification.

You have 3 missed text messages.

> Kells: Work called and asked me to come in early. Between us, I wanted to tell them to fuck off, but they sounded desperate. Now I'm stuck working 6 pm - 9 am. Kill me?!? Please.

> Kells: Rain check for lunch? I was looking forward to it, and I hope you were too. I promise I'll make it up to you.

> Kells: Text me when you have a free minute. I need to ask you something, and I've hit my unread message limit. If I send any more, it'll look like I'm obsessed.

I read each message a few times before crafting my response.

44

I don't want to say the wrong thing, and I'm still unsure of where exactly things stand between us. I need to play it cool and see where his head is at.

> : Good Morning. Although, maybe not for you. Sucks to hear about the 14-hour shift. That's going to be a long one. What did you want to ask me?

I take my phone off silent and set it on the window air conditioner before retreating to the bathroom to begin my normal routine. I'm halfway through brushing my teeth when I hear my phone ding. At the sound, my heart jumps, and I nearly swallow a mouthful of minty foam. "Play it cool," I tell myself as I walk back into the bedroom.

> Kells: I am sorry I had to cancel. I feel like an asshole.

> : No way. Don't even worry about it. I would've been their next phone call if you had said no. So, I should probably thank you. :) You spared me from having to go to work on my night off.

> Kells: In that case, you're welcome. It is my honor and privilege to suffer in your place. Since we didn't get to go out, and you don't seem mad at me, I was wondering if we could do something else tonight.

> : What'd you have in mind? I'm not getting arrested so we can have breakfast together in the morning.

I'm not sure what Kelly's plan is, but my anxiety is multiplying by the second as I await his response. I'm too much of a rule follower to willingly get myself into trouble, but I suppose I am cleared to enter the building without a police escort. Maybe he wants to have dinner together in the parking lot. That could be fun.

> Kells: And here I figured you were game for anything. I've been looking forward to seeing you, and you did say I was worth the trouble. Didn't you? Only kidding

> : Fine. Maybe a six-hour hold. LoL. What would be a good crime for that?

I know he's joking, but I'd consider doing almost anything to see him right now. And he's right. I did say he was worth the trouble. Whatever this is, I'll take it. Friends without benefits. Sex without strings. Pity from a co-worker. That all sounds fucking terrible, but I don't care. I'm lonely. I can't spend another night feeling invisible in this ghost town.

> Kells: Public Intox?

> : Hold my beer, Officer. I'm going for a walk. LoL.

> Kells: That sounds kind of fun. Maybe we should get drinks together the next time we both have a night off. But I had something else in mind for tonight. I was wondering if you would text me while I'm at work and help me to stay awake. Unless you have other plans? I don't want to intrude on your evening.

So much for my night in the holding cell and breakfast in the morning. No parking lot picnic for this girl. Kelly wants me to text him so he doesn't fall asleep and get murdered. Good times. I suppose it's the least I could do for the one person who's always first to have my back.

: You are more than welcome to intrude anytime. I don't have plans for the night. I considered going to that $5 movie theater later, but that's about it. I can talk to you if you want. Let me know where you end up, and I'll be your entertainment.

Kells: It's a date.

That didn't end where I expected, but I think it went well. My face hurts from smiling, so that's probably a good sign. I need to be smart about this. Do I want to get into something with a guy I work with? I moved here to work with a guy I was sort of dating and look how that turned out. Would a serious relationship make things awkward? What if it didn't work out? Am I allowed to date a co-worker? I don't remember hearing anything about that one way or another. Am I even interested in Kelly that way? Sure, the guy's incredibly attractive. I'll give him that. But he's three years younger than I am. If only he had blue eyes.

"Stop being ridiculous! He isn't slightly attractive. The guy is fucking gorgeous and clearly flirting with you. You're an idiot if you don't go for it. What's wrong with you? Do you want to be single forever?" I attempt to talk some sense into myself.

Seriously? Can I afford to be so picky and have stupid deal-breakers regarding eye color? Aren't there more important things to consider? I'm 28 years old. If I don't find someone soon, I'm going to have to start applying to those TV shows where they make you marry a stranger. And then, who knows what I'll have to settle for?

It's time to come back and rejoin reality. There are no less than half a dozen things I could be doing right now. Instead, I'm exhausting my brainpower on fantasies about a guy I work with who happens to look good in a uniform. No, the word *good* doesn't even begin to describe it. Kelly is sweet enough to be February on the company calendar and hot enough to pose for June. Less than a dozen text messages in, and he has me thankful enough to picture him as November and grateful enough to gift him December.

I'm not only thirsty. I'm dehydrated.

I should attempt to knock out a few things from my list before heading out to the movies. My days off tend to be spent doing chores since the other days are work, sleep, eat, and repeat. I gather the dirty clothes that have yet to reach the basket in an effort to feel productive. There's a place in town that will clean and fold your laundry for $25, which is a steal if you ask me. I can drop my clothes off in the morning before grocery shopping, and two hours later, they're clean.

Walking into the kitchen, I take stock of my meager supplies. I still have some meals in the fridge from the last time I cooked. So, tomorrow can be a baking day. It's no wonder I'm light-headed all the time. Apparently, I haven't been eating. My ice cravings are most likely to blame since I'm obsessed with fast food and gas station ice when I'm not at work. Perhaps I need to stop ordering french fries and calling it a meal.

As I notice the time on the oven clock, I hear my phone ding in the bedroom. It's 6:26 pm. Let the texting continue.

> Kells: It's weird being here for second shift. I don't like it. Everyone's wide awake and moving around. They have me doing intake for both shifts. So, you can text me whenever you'd like and as much as you want. Did you decide on a movie?

> : I don't know what movies are out right now. Normally, I pick something when I get there. I'm not even sure I feel like going out.

> Kells: Quiet night at home? I'm jealous. That sounds amazing right now. What's your place like? All I know is that you live near work.

Oh, dear lord! Kelly can NEVER come here. If he sees this place, I'm done for. He won't even want to be friends. I should lie. I should say everything's fine and leave it at that. I should change the subject back to movies or throw my phone out the window and die of embarrassment. No. If we're meant to be friends, I should be honest and allow him to make an informed decision.

> : My place is a total shithole. It's old and disgusting and the smell gives me a migraine. I hate it so much that I wish someone would murder me in my sleep. That's why I go to the movies all the time. Normally, I watch a few films back-to-back to avoid being here as much as possible. I keep thinking about getting a hotel room for the night. Does that sound financially irresponsible or utterly ridiculous? I can't decide.

> Kells: It can't be that bad. Can it?

> : No bed. No shower. No couch. Honestly, I would probably be better off sleeping in my car. Or under a bridge in a cardboard box with a pet raccoon named Templeton. Maybe there's a nice local cave I could dwell in. Do you think I could still get wifi if I lived under a rock?

> Kells: I know you're joking, but are you also being serious? Do you not have a shower, a bed, or a couch?

Why did I do that? I shouldn't have said anything about my place. That was stupid. I'm going to have to change the subject. Otherwise, this will be the shortest "date" in history. If he even bothers to message me again.

: It's fine. I'm not planning to sleep in my car or under a rock. That part was a joke. But I am considering getting a hotel room for two nights. The one over by the school looks nice, and I think they have a pool. Maybe I can dig around online and find a deal.

Kells: BRB Cops are bringing someone in.

This conversation is a disaster. Even if Kelly does text me back, it's going to be a while, depending on who the cops are dropping off. I need to find a way to distract myself so I don't obsess over my flirting faux pas.

I kill time by taking my laundry basket out to the car. This stairway is an accident waiting to happen, so I take my time, feeling each step with the heel of my foot before shifting my weight. It's warm out tonight. Too nice to stay inside. I need to figure out where I want to go, and then I need to get in my car and start driving. As I turn to go back in, I notice the lights are on downstairs. Unfortunately, the blinds are all closed, so I'm unable to sneak a peek at my mystery neighbor. I wonder how long I'll have to live here before I find out who my chain-smoking housemate is.

The grocery store is open 24 hours a day, seven days a week, so I could do my shopping tonight and get it over with. Or maybe I'll drive without a destination, get some gas station ice, and listen to music. I wish I had a lounge chair. Then I could find a quiet spot and enjoy the night sky. I need a place to settle my bones and appease the voices. Everything sounds better than being here, but nothing sounds appealing enough to convince me to commit. My mind is all over the place, and I can't focus. What I wouldn't give for a hot shower and a real bed. I wonder how much a hotel room would cost. It can't be that much.

Different ideas swirl around my brain as I walk back to my room. I can already see that my mania will be calling the shots from here on out until I can sleep again. There are two new messages on my phone when I return to my room, but I'm afraid to read them. I pace the hallway between the kitchen and living room, trying to swell my courage.

> Kells: Okay, I'm back. That was a quick one. Six-hour hold. All I had to do was a pat down and fingerprints. Hope the rest of the night goes like this.

> Kells: When you have a minute, can you visit me at Oak Falls? The sooner, the better.

> : Is everything alright? Did you need me to bring you something?

> Kells: A soda would be amazing, but you don't have to go out of your way. I have something I want to give you before you get too busy. And I'm afraid if I don't do it now, I'll lose my nerve, and it'll be too late.

> : Okay, I can drive there now if you want. What do you like to drink? I'll swing by the gas station on my way. They have a decent selection.

> Kells: Diet Coke. Same as you.

I try not to smile, but it's cute that he knows my beverage of choice. Usually, I'm the one who notes those kinds of intimate details about a person. Come to think of it. I can't say I've ever seen Kelly eat or drink anything at work.

> : Well, that's easy enough to remember. I'll text you when I get there. Give me 10 minutes.

> Kells: You're the best!

Everything about the last 24 hours has been weird. I need a change of scenery to collect my thoughts and clear my head. It doesn't take me long to shove a few things into my backpack and grab my keys. I'll stop at the hotel after I leave the jail. At this point, I don't care what it costs. I want a hot shower and won't rest until I get one. The last thing I grab is the pillow from my bed and two 20 oz sodas from the fridge.

Once I'm in the car, it only takes me a few minutes to drive to Oak Falls. That's barely enough time to think about what Kelly could have for me. I hope it's not leftovers from tonight's dinner. If he walks out the side door carrying a white Styrofoam container, I swear, I'll die laughing.

> : I'm in the parking lot by the intake doors. No rush. I'll be out here enjoying this perfect weather and my personal freedom. Try not to be jealous.

The door next to the loading bay opens, and Kelly walks out. I'm not sure how it's possible, but he looks even more striking than usual. My heart begins to race as he gets closer. And when he smiles, I'm nearly undone.

"Fancy meeting you here," he says with a wink. "Thanks for coming to see me. I appreciate it."

"Yeah, of course. Anytime. I'm glad you asked. I needed a reason to leave the house and couldn't decide on a destination. Oddly enough, I hadn't even considered the parking lot at work." I hope my nervous ramblings come across as charming. "Anyways, here's your soda. I don't want to keep you too long."

"I wish you did." There's something about his tone. Kelly's voice sounds drenched in longing.

"What?" I feel like I missed something. Kelly and I seem to be having two different conversations, and I desperately want to know what he's thinking.

"Never mind. The real reason I asked you to come here is that I have something for you." He takes my arm and drops a set of keys into my hand. "I knew you hated your place before I asked you about it. You mentioned it once while we were doing a perimeter check. And I've overheard people saying stuff."

"What kind of things are people saying, exactly?" This conversation is making me feel sick. I'm not someone who likes attention, especially the bad sort. Only one person from work has seen my place, and that was two months ago when I moved in.

"That came out wrong. I didn't mean for it to sound like people are talking shit about you. Not at all. Everyone we work with likes you. I was thinking back to the couch situation when we first met. And Collins said something once about you being the only girl who uses the locker room shower. Then, last week, you mentioned that your back hurt from the air mattress. And then your text confirmed everything I already sort of knew. Lately, you look worn out, and I miss seeing you smile."

"I feel like I should be offended, but I'm willing to hear you out." I lift the keys and give them a jingle. "What are these for?"

"Okay, so I've wanted to make this offer a few times, but I didn't know how you would react, and I didn't want to piss you off. You seem like you need a place to recharge, and I want to be the one to give you that. So, the keys are to my apartment. The key fob is for the main door and the elevator. The silver key is for the deadbolt, and the small white key is for the patio. Go hang out there tonight. Watch some Netflix. Take a shower. There are tons of snacks and a queen size bed. There's even a pool. I swear my place is nicer than any of the hotels in town, and all it's going to cost you is a diet coke."

"Are you being serious right now? Why would you trust me to be in your place alone? We've never hung out or spoken outside of work. You hardly know me." I'm so caught off guard. I can't process my feeling when he's standing in front of me, looking at me like I'm the last dog at the pound.

"You think I don't know you after all the shit we've been through together? All of the conversations and stolen glances. I've been paying attention, Belk. Probably more than you realize. But let's set my feelings for you aside for one second. I trust you with my life every time we work together. You think I'm worried about my gym shorts and body wash?" Kelly reaches across the short distance between us and puts his hands on my shoulders. The second he touches me, my hesitation evaporates, my defenses crumble, and I'm on the verge of tears.

"Are there any strings attached to this offer that I should know about in advance?" I need to know what it's going to cost me, and I want to hear him say it. With men, there is always a quid pro quo.

"I'm giving you free rein to do whatever you want at my place, so long as you promise to text me while I'm stuck here."

"Okay. I'm fairly certain I can agree to those terms." I sound less defeated than I feel. His offer, as generous as it is, feels a lot like pity, and I hate that.

"I promise you'll love it. It's that new apartment building behind the gym on 4th Street, next to the wash-and-fold laundry place. Mine is 602. Take the elevator to the 6th floor and turn right. You can't miss it. Text me when you get there so I know you made it in all right. Otherwise, I'll be sitting here worrying about you all night."

"Alright." I don't know what else to say. Either I've gone crazy, or Kelly has. What kind of guy lets a random girl go to his place while he isn't there? That sounds like some stupid shit I would offer someone if my place weren't a total embarrassment. He can't possibly be this nice. There have to be loads of strings I'm not seeing yet. Even if he's trying to get laid, this is overkill.

"Shit! A cop pulled in. Duty calls." He closes the gap between us and kisses my forehead. Then turns and jogs back over to the side door before I have the chance to say anything.

This has to be a dream. My alarm will go off at any minute, and I'll be alone in my shithole apartment with my dirty laundry still scattered across the floor.

Am I doing this? An evening in a real apartment is exactly what I need, but that makes me even more suspicious. No one ever offers to help me. It's always me bending over backward for everyone else. Is this what it feels like when I go out of my way for people? No wonder I always feel unappreciated. Turns out, being too thoughtful can really make a person feel awkward.

What are the worst-case scenarios if I go? Kelly has hidden cameras in the shower and posts videos of me naked online. Or I fall asleep, and Kelly turns out to be a rapist. Those both seem highly unlikely. Also, I know he's stuck at work until 9:00 am. I can set my alarm and leave before he gets home.

I've been feeling drained since moving to Oak Falls. Laying on a couch and watching a movie might be exactly what I need to feel like myself again. If I get a weird vibe, I can always leave.

Who am I trying to fool? I'm going. I've gone to scarier places for less.

Eight

THERE'S an open parking spot near the front of the building, close to the entrance. I don't see any signs about parking, and the spaces are unmarked, so I pull in with my fingers crossed, hoping my car doesn't get towed. It surprises me that Kelly and I have never run into one another outside of work. He lives in the building next to where I take my laundry and the gym I belong to. I've only seen this apartment building from across the street, but it's even nicer up close. If I lived in a place like this, I could stay in this town forever. I wonder what the rent is for a one-bedroom apartment here.

The elevator is already on the first floor with the door open. It feels a little strange being here, like I'm trespassing. So, I hurry inside, scan the key fob, and press the button for six before anyone takes notice of me. This building doesn't seem to fit with the rest of the town. I sometimes forget there's a college nearby.

I step out and turn to the right when the elevator opens on six. The door for 602 is exactly where Kelly said it would be. So far, so good. Using the silver key to unlock the deadbolt, I take half a step in and run my hand along the wall. The light switch is next to the door, where you'd expect it to be. When the lights come on, I'm surprised to see how clean the place is. Forget about bad vibes. It's the total opposite. This place is amazing, and I'm jealous.

> : I'm sorry I was being weird. I don't want you to think I'm ungrateful. You surprised me, and I wasn't sure what to say. Your apartment is awesome! I'm jelly. You did something nice for me, and I should have been more appreciative. Sorry again, and Thank You. If we ever get to have that lunch date, it's my treat.

> Kells: I'm glad you like it. You don't have anything to apologize for, and you don't owe me anything. I shouldn't have sprung all that on you the way I did. After you left, I was afraid you'd change your mind and go to a hotel. I want to talk to you more than anything, but I have some shit I need to finish here before 3rd shift starts. Why don't you shower and find some comfy clothes in my closet? Nothing is off-limits. Everything I have is yours for the taking, so make yourself at home. The WIFI password is written on the notebook next to the couch, and the remote has a button for Netflix. I'll message you after the meeting.

I want to look at everything, but I also like the idea of getting out of my jeans. When I walk into the bedroom, I recognize the smell immediately. If I didn't know better, I would swear Kelly was standing here with me. I close my eyes and breathe him in. Standing in the room where he sleeps, I can almost feel the weight of his hands on my shoulders, the warmth of his body an inch from mine, and the soft kiss he left behind. He knows how to make a girl melt, that's for sure.

There's a clean pair of sweatpants in his dresser, and I saw a hoodie on the couch. I have clothes in my backpack, but it's impossible to resist wearing something of his. I hang out in the shower until my fingers begin to prune. Then I dry off, comb my fingers through my hair, and dress in his clothes. Kelly must have worn this hoodie earlier today because it's soaked in the memory of him. I pull the hood over my head and let the smell wrap around me like a blanket. Before settling on the couch, I grab my pillow and phone. This apartment is a hell of a lot nicer than any hotel room I could have afforded.

Kells: Looks like I'm working with your boyfriend until sunrise.

: Oh yeah? That's exciting. Are they letting the patients run the asylum tonight?

For some reason, my mind jumps to Jason Hillard and the stupid letter that landed us both in solitary.

Kells: Hahaha... I meant your other boyfriend, Grant.

: Grant could never be my boyfriend. He doesn't have any tattoos.

Kells: Well, that explains the one in solitary. He's inked from head to toe.

: Is he? I've only seen his neck and arms.

I can feel my pulse quicken and my cheeks flush. He needs to stop talking about this before I end up in a puddle on the couch, dreaming of tattooed hands around my throat. I might not be allowed to act out my fantasies at work, but in the privacy of Kelly's apartment, no one will know.

Kells: I was working intake the night he came in. Head to Toe.

: Hahaha... Okay, Stop! I believe you. How was 2nd shift? Are you worn out already?

Kells: I will NOT be volunteering to work 2nd again unless I know for a fact that it saves you from having to be here. This entire shift feels like torture. Time is going soooooo slowly. Except for the part when you were here. That went by too fast. Grant asked me who I was texting. Think he'll be jealous if I let slip that I'm talking to you?

: I don't know why you think there's something between him and I. Grant and I have spoken all of three times since I started working there.

For the first month and a half, I made a point to steer clear of Grant for personal reasons. I thought it was in my best interest to keep my distance, and it was a task easily accomplished. After a while, I got the impression that he was avoiding me as well. Normally, he's at the booking desk on nights when I'm sequestered to minimum or in the tower. And he can be found hanging out in Hubble's office when I'm in a position that offers me free range.

Kells: And what about before that?

: I don't know what you mean.

I might have a pretty good idea about what Kelly is hinting at, but I don't want to offer information he doesn't have. Why Grant would be running his mouth about shit that happened months ago is beyond me, but he can kiss those chocolate chip cookies goodbye if he makes trouble for me.

Kells: We can talk about it another time. When I'm less annoyed. What are you getting into right now? Distract me. Tell me about your night.

> : If you have something to say, please say it. I'm not a fan of guessing games. Nothing is going on between Grant and me. I'm not interested in him. Is this about the cookies? If he said something about me, I'd like to know.

And this is why I don't get involved with co-workers. Lord knows what information Kevin divulged to his friends on his way out the door. We didn't date for long, but knowing me, I was stupid enough to share secrets I wouldn't want to be repeated.

> Kells: He started telling a story about before you worked here, and it pissed me off. I can tell you what he said later, but I'd rather not get into the details while I'm stuck working next to him. Please tell me about your night before I knock him out and get fired.

> : Whatever he said, it's not worth losing your job over. It's probably bullshit anyways. Let it go... Right now, I am talking to you and watching movie trailers. Not sure what I'm in the mood for yet.

> Kells: I know what I'm in the mood for.

> : Oh really? So much for no strings attached. LoL

If talking about sex gets Kelly in a better head space, I'm all for it. I don't need him distracted while he's in that place. The jail is only safe in theory. There are a lot more inmates than there are guards, and I'm not there tonight to watch his back.

Kells: Hahaha. That's not what I meant, though I wouldn't be opposed to it. I'm in the mood to get out of here and go home. BRB. I need to finish up with this inmate that is getting booked in.

: Why is it so busy there? It's a Sunday night. Is there some big party around here that I don't know about?

I select a movie I've seen a few times so I don't have to pay attention. It's been nearly an hour since my last message, and I wonder what's happening at the jail. Hope it isn't someone high on meth because that's the worst. You can't send them to the blocks while they're high as a kite, so they stay near booking, shouting and running into the walls all night. I don't have any personal experience with drugs like that and don't want to. In high school, my friends were content to smoke weed and listen to Pink Floyd every weekend.

It makes me sad to see how many women and young girls filter through the jail because of meth, heroin, and crack. I wish the lawmakers in this country would realize that people need treatment, not incarceration. I can't imagine anyone intends for their life to turn out that way.

Kells: I see another letter in your future.

: Oh lord, what now?

I realize I shouldn't want to hear details about the incoming hotties, but I can't help myself, and Kelly seems to enjoy toying with me. I think he's trying to figure out what I like and what I'm looking for through examples he knows I can't pursue. Inmates are safe because they're off-limits. Kelly doesn't have to waste his time being jealous of someone who can't touch me.

Kells: This huge Viking was here a minute ago. Arms, chest, back, and neck are all covered in the best ink I've ever seen. I escorted him to minimum. I'm certain he's going to love you.

: Does he have a beard?

Kells: Of course. I know what you like.

: Oh shit, look out! Hahaha. Kidding... I think you might be surprised to find out that most men don't even notice me. I peeked in college, and it's been all downhill since then.

Kells: I know for a fact that isn't true.

: You're one to talk. Women fall all over themselves trying to get your attention. When you walk through the women's blocks, I practically have to hand out buckets for the drool. LoL.

I tack on a snide comment about Collins but delete that part of the message before hitting send. I'm not sure what their relationship is, and I'm not trying to make waves. I have enough enemies at work without adding my co-workers to the list.

Kells: You know how thirsty the females in this place are. Their heads snap when Smith walks through the door.

: OMG stop. You're ridiculous.

Kells: Hey, Belk. Thanks for making my night better. I'm glad you accepted my offer, and I hope you're enjoying yourself. It feels good to talk to you outside of work.

: I'm happy to help. Does it count as talking outside of work if you're technically still in the building? What time do you want me to get out of here? I'll make sure I set my alarm. Don't want to overstay my welcome.

Kells: For tonight, why don't you forget the alarm and focus on sleeping peacefully? I want to see you relaxed and happy, just once... And if I'm being honest, I'd be disappointed if you weren't there when I came home.

What am I supposed to say to that? Of all the possible strings, *this* is the one most frequently attached. If I stay, he's going to have certain expectations. Do I want that? I mean, I don't *not* want that. Is it worth the complications? He's been laying it on thick all night, and I'm at his place, in his clothes. Of course, sex was going to be the price of admission. As much as I want to get laid, finally having a friend would have been nice.

: Okay

Nine

IT FEELS like I've barely fallen asleep when a sound wakes me. The time on my watch reads 6:07 am, which means I've been passed out for a few hours. It's too early for Kelly to be here, but when I look past my wrist, I see him standing in the doorway of the bedroom.

"I like coming home and finding you in my bed." When he wants it to, the sex appeal drips off his every word. "Can I lay with you?"

"You scared me. I wasn't expecting to see you." My voice comes out barely above a whisper. It sounds like I'm trying to be cute, but I'm still half asleep.

He pulls a lighter from the bedside table drawer and lights a candle I hadn't noticed before. The flame catches and holds in his eyes.

"You didn't answer my question." There's an intensity folded into the layers of his voice. Normally, when we're both in uniform, I feel like we're on an equal footing. But as I lie here in comfort, I deem myself willingly under his control.

"Of course, it's your bed." His question seemed rhetorical, but I can see now that he was waiting for my invitation.

My breath catches in my throat as he removes his uniform,

pulls back the comforter, and gets into bed wearing only his boxers. I'm still in the hoodie and sweats I put on earlier, though I doubt he'll let me hide beneath their cotton fibers for much longer.

"I like the way you look in my clothes." He pushes a section of my hair behind my ear. Then follows my jaw with his finger-tips and stops when his thumb is against my bottom lip. "I could get used to this." Kelly knows exactly what he's doing. I can already tell that he's about to get anything he desires from me.

"Tell me what you want, and it's yours." He's trying to convince me that I'm in control of what happens next, but it's an illusion. Of course, I have a say, but my consent was implied when I crawled into his bed and stayed until he returned home.

I know what he wants me to say. The words sit on the tip of my tongue, begging to be spoken. But I'm not ready to submit. I need to find a way to slow this down. So, I make him start at the beginning.

"I want you to kiss me." My whispered plea draws him near, but I want him closer still.

His hand moves to the back of my head, and his fingers braid into my hair. I have only enough time to pull in a breath before his lips are on mine. His kiss is pure lustful passion, and I am living for it. I could stop time and burn in this moment forever.

When his kiss stops, and the distance between us increases, I seize the opportunity to get out of his clothes. I can't breathe, and the room is spinning. My body attempts to cool itself with sweat, but the heat radiates off him in waves, evaporating my efforts. I can see that his eyes interpret my actions as a request for more. So, he presses his body to mine, tucking his face into the side of my neck. His exhaled breath is a scalding mist. I inhale, filling my lungs with his scent before I melt.

There is no sense in denying it. Kelly is fire, and I'm engulfed by him.

Ten

BEFORE I EVEN OPEN MY eyes, my mind begins to take stock of the sensations my body is already fully aware of. I can feel Kelly's warm breath as it passes through my hair. The heat of his skin, everywhere it touches mine, feels like we're welded together. One of his arms is under my pillow with my hand in his, our fingers laced together. My other hand on his thigh as his fingers grip my hip bone like a handle. Even our legs are twisted together, my ankle locked between his. We fit together like mirror opposites. Where I give, he takes, and vice versa. I won't be able to escape until he's willing to release me.

Taking a deep breath, I fill my lungs with the air that tastes like him. As he senses the change in my body, Kelly shifts position and wraps both forearms across my chest. His muscles tighten, and I'm pulled even deeper into his embrace.

"How'd you sleep?" He asks, still using his bedroom voice.

"The best I've slept in months. I don't even remember falling asleep." My voice is coated in playful sweetness, and a little moan unintentionally slips past my lips as I adjust my head and neck over his flexed bicep.

"Do you remember what happened before drifting apart?"

"You mean after you came home early and scared me half to

death?" Of course, I know what he's fishing for, but I can't bite on the first cast.

"Joke all you want. I'm willing to remind you if need be. It seems I didn't leave a lasting impression the first time." His voice is deeper now, and I can feel the fire growing in his chest.

Repositioning his body, Kelly starts by kissing my shoulder before biting into me. My back arches away from him in response, but he's prepared for my reaction. He keeps one arm locked tight across my chest. While his other hand returns to gripping my hip. Now my body moves only where he tells it to. And I can already feel how much he wants to remind me.

Every button he presses multiplies my desire until I'm prepared to beg for my release. But no amount of pleading will free me. What Kelly seeks is my surrender. An admission that he will remain forever branded into my memories. As if I could forget.

Eleven

I HAVE a small list of things I'd like to complete today. Laundry, grocery shopping, and a phone call to my landlord. But accomplishing those tasks would require getting dressed in my own clothes and leaving. And therein lies the problem. As I brush my teeth, I consider various ways to broach the topic with Kelly. I'm trying to create the right combination of words to tell him I need to go, but it's proving difficult. When I get nervous, I tend to say the wrong thing, and I'd like to avoid Kelly thinking that I don't want to be here. Maybe my list could wait until tomorrow.

His reflection fills the mirror as he steps behind me and wraps his arms around my waist. Kelly's presence is larger than mine, but he's not quite big enough to rest his chin on the top of my head, so he centers himself over my left shoulder. As I tilt my head to the right, he kisses my neck and brushes a hand down the front of my body.

"Should we shower and get food delivered? I'll let you pick the restaurant." Again, the illusion of choice. My options have been preselected, and the expectation is clear. I wonder what would happen if I offered an alternative plan. I've learned the hard way that most men don't enjoy being challenged, so it's best to tread lightly.

"Sure, lunch sounds good. I have my laundry in the car. Maybe I could drop it off at the place next door while you shower. I'm out of clean clothes for work." My eyes hold onto the reflection of his face, waiting to gauge his reaction.

"I figured you'd join me. It's not nearly as much fun by myself." His smile morphs into a playful grin as he winks at me. "But if you'd rather do laundry…"

"I'm pretty sure I need to eat something before going another round with you." I try to match the playfulness of my tone to his. "You're insatiable."

"What if I promise to behave?" He says before kissing my shoulder. "Then will you come in and keep me company?"

I turn my face to look at him directly. The path is clear, and I can fight it or enjoy it. My body moves to align with my gaze, and I bring my arms up to rest atop his muscular shoulders. As my eyes scan his face, seeking approval, my lips part.

"What am I going to do with you?" I ask, not realizing how much I need to hear his answer.

"Anything and Everything you want." He stares so deeply into my eyes that, for a moment, I'm afraid he's located the place where I hide my secrets. When he kisses me, all of my fear and self-doubt melt away. He's right. There's no place else I need to be and no one else to spend my time with. For today, I remain his.

Every time Kelly's lips are on my body, I want him to know me, to see me, to claim me. I want him to hold on and never let go. I want him to choose me and only me. I want to belong to him and know that he belongs to me. Those are the thoughts running through my head as we shower together.

When he pins me against the wall, with his hand against my throat, I nearly blurt out the request I'm craving. Thankfully, his kiss keeps me quiet. I'll need to be more careful if I want us to remain friends when this is over.

After we shower, get dressed, and order food, we retire to the couch in the living room. Kelly searches the channels for something to put on, but our taste in movies vastly differs.

Hesitantly, I test the waters, dipping in the tip of one toe. "Let me know when you want me to go. I'm sure you'll need to take a nap before work."

"Why would I want you to go? The food we ordered hasn't even arrived yet. And I don't have work tonight. I switched shifts so we could hang out." His tone is matter-of-fact, as if I already know the information he's presenting.

"You did? I wasn't aware of that." With new information in play, my mind starts to wander. Did he switch shifts to spend time with me? Maybe he punched Grant and was fired. That would explain why he was home three hours early. What was that with Grant anyways? What kind of story could he tell to get Kelly that pissed off? It feels like all that happened weeks ago, but it was last night. I'd forgotten about the undefined interaction with Grant until now.

"I thought I told you when we were in bed together. Sorry. Guess I was so preoccupied with your beauty that I forgot to say the rest aloud." His words are intentional, meant to guide my thoughts elsewhere. Meant to distract me. He's going to charm me into oblivion if he keeps moving at this rate.

"I find myself easily preoccupied with you, as well." I don't want to spoil the mood by asking about Grant. So, I let it go. When I'm around Kelly, I feel like I'm high. My head is full of smoke, and the only path I can see is the one he's standing on. The feeling is a mix of hyper-focus, distraction, confusion, and sexual desire. The buzz is enjoyable, but I worry the hangout may be severe.

My heart jumps when there's a knock at the door. Somehow, I forgot that the meals we ordered would be delivered. All morning my thoughts have been foggy, as if I'm on the verge of forgetting my own name. A chill from the air conditioning passes through me like a ghost the second Kelly leaves my side. It makes the muscles in my back tighten as a shiver ascends my spine. I'm pretty sure the hoodie I had on last night is next to the bed. If I'm quick, I can retrieve it and be back before he's finished talking to the delivery guy.

I didn't realize how hungry I was until the smell of the food hit me, and the saliva began to pool in my mouth. The last time I ate a real meal was months ago, before I moved to Oak Falls. Since then, I've been surviving on snacks, ice, and leftovers from the jail's kitchen. Even when I cook at the apartment, it's something basic, like a side dish.

Kelly selects our first round of entertainment, and we eat without conversation. The movie has subtitles, and I've never seen it, so I'll have to pay attention to figure out what's happening. Sadly, I'm not sure I have the mental capacity for reading comprehension with Kelly seated within kissing distance, and I catch myself zoning out.

"Would you like to choose the next one?" he asks, placing the remote in my hand. I set it on the coffee table without making my selection.

"Will you tell me what was said last night at work that pissed you off?" I avoid mentioning Grant's name for fear of fueling his fire.

"I'd rather not. The entire situation was stupid, and I never should have concerned you while you were trying to enjoy your evening. I had a momentary lapse of better judgment, and I'm sorry." Kelly is acting like nothing happened, even though the interaction with Grant was enough to piss him off last night.

"I appreciate that, but I'd like to know if people are talking about me. You'd want me to tell you if I heard something. Wouldn't you?" I wish he'd spill whatever it is and be done with it. I hate being left in the dark without a nightlight. Any story I fabricate in my head will be ten times worse than what was actually said, and it's exhausting chasing after the truth.

"Come here and lay with me." He stretches across the couch and opens his arms, indicating his subtle unwillingness to engage in my chosen topic of conversation. I could press the issue, but what's the point? Turning to face him, I stretch out and settle against his chest, letting go of my need for more. His heart beats like a lullaby against my ear, and if I'm allowed to get too comfortable, I might fall someplace other than sleep.

Eventually, the TV turns off, and we remain still in the quiet darkness. Kelly alternates between rubbing my back, playing with my hair, and holding me. Lying in his arms, I think about the day we first met and the laughs we've shared along the way. Every time he sheltered me from harm brought us one step closer to this moment. I replay the night of the letter and our conversation the next morning. The restrained flirting I registered as friendly banter plays differently in today's light. Thinking back to his original offer to let me hang out here, it was cute to see him nervous. Ultimately, I'm glad there were a few strings attached. I enjoy being tied to him. But I wasn't prepared for his slightly controlling nature, and I'm starting to feel like a marionette.

Only now that I'm with him, how can I complain? I've been so lonely since moving to Oak Falls, and I couldn't take being in my apartment for one more minute. Sure, Kelly is intense. We both are. But he's also passionate, warm, and trusting. I didn't realize how much I would come to need his touch until I had it.

I wish I could have checked off the boxes on my to-do list while I had the day off, but who would choose running errands over spending the day in bed with a gorgeous man? It's not like I want to be a one-night stand. Everything comes at a price. We all know that. And women get used to paying in flesh. I wanted him. I still want him. Don't I?

This new dynamic between us will turn into something, or it won't. Guys like this, the one's made of fire, tend to destroy everything in my life before they leave. I have to decide if these moments are worth the risk. Is he worth the trouble?

"Did you fall asleep?" His quiet voice beckons me back to the here and now.

"No, I'm awake." Filling my lungs with his warmth, I hold him in my chest. Kelly always smells good, though I can't place the scent. I might have to read the label on his body wash the next time I'm in the shower. He's intoxicating, though I doubt it has much to do with his choice of soap.

"Should we order a pizza and find something to watch?" This time when he asks, it sounds more like a genuine question.

"I should probably get back to my place at some point. I have things I need to do, and I don't want to overstay my welcome." I've tip-toed about the issue all day. Even now, with the words hanging in the space between us, I wish to suck them back in.

I can feel the muscles in his chest and arms tighten as the fire inside him spreads. It isn't difficult to guess what's coming. I should have kept quiet and left well enough alone, but now it's too late.

His voice is calm, but his body gives him away. I can feel how hard he's working to hold back. "If you're not interested in me holding on, I'll let you go. But I rearranged my schedule so we could be together because I thought you would enjoy spending time with me."

"I do. I am enjoying it. But I don't want you to get sick of looking at me." There's hurt in my voice, but he isn't the one who put it there. The pain I'm feeling now is much older. It's the kind of damage that takes years to cultivate. Each time someone told me they loved me and then fucked someone else. Every manipulation. Every lie. Every promise they never intended to keep. Each time they burned my world to the ground after stealing the best parts of me, they fed the darkness.

"You honestly think I could get sick of looking at you? You're all I've thought about for the last two months. Do you know how often I've fallen asleep imagining what it would be like to have you next to me? It was torture being at work last night, knowing you were here. All I wanted to do was come home to you." The intensity of his delivery reads a lot like longing.

I wish I could ask him to repeat what he said. Beg him to go slower so that I might absorb each syllable as it's spoken. Were his questions rhetorical, or was he expecting me to answer? What did he even ask me? I don't know how I'm supposed to respond to any of that.

"If you want to leave," he starts to say, but I stop him.

"I don't want to leave. I want to be here with you." I don't like that I've hurt him. I don't ever want to be the reason he feels pain. Whatever the cost, he is worth the price. If I'm meant to burn, let me burn to ash right here in his arms.

Twelve

WHEN I OPEN MY EYES, it takes me a moment to adjust. The open blinds in the bedroom are letting in more sunshine than I'm accustomed to, and the excessive amount of daylight stings like needles. I roll over to playfully scold my companion for his oversight, but the spot next to me in bed is empty. My hand glides across the cold sheet. It's 10:05 am, according to my watch, which is the time I'm usually drifting off to Dreamland. I can't remember when Kelly and I went to bed, but I know he was next to me when I fell asleep.

As I'm getting dressed, I hear the front door open. The interruption makes me pause and listen, unsure if that was Kelly coming in or leaving. I hope he isn't still upset with me. The night ended on a high note, or so I thought. The way his fingers brushed across my skin as if the answers to all his questions were written there in braille, felt a lot like absolution. I don't imagine Kelly's the type to hold a grudge, but I could be wrong. He has a way of disarming me with his touch, and I find myself begging for things I never knew I needed. But something within him, bubbling beneath the surface, frequently renders me silent.

It surprises me when he walks into the bedroom carrying two

laundry baskets, one stacked on top of the other. Both are filled with freshly cleaned and folded clothing that fill the room with the scent of ocean breeze. I recognize the top basket as mine, which I put in my car before coming here. It seems so long ago now that I was last at my place. Time passes differently when I'm with him, like my battery is running low on its charge, and I'm frozen in place.

"You did my laundry?" I'm not entirely sure how I feel about this yet.

"Technically, Linda from Spin Cycle did our laundry. I took it over there this morning when I woke up. You mentioned yesterday that you needed to stop by there, and I was too busy being selfish to let you go. I felt bad all evening and wanted to make amends. Can you forgive me?" He sets the baskets on the bed and walks over to me. Taking my face in his hands, he tilts my gaze upwards to align with his. "I should've given you a little space to breathe. I never meant for you to feel trapped."

"Thank you." My quiet voice does nothing to convey gratitude.

"For what?" His eyes search mine as though some undeniable truth lies far beyond the reach of my words.

"For doing my laundry. And for being amazing." Kelly is more than I deserve. Women dream of having a man like this and rarely find it. He's like something out of a movie, only a thousand times better because he's right in front of me. I can't believe I almost pushed him away.

"I know you said you needed to do a few things today before work, but I'd love to spend as much time with you as possible. That being said, I understand if you have to leave." His tone has a hint of both sadness and sweetness. It makes me want to spend the rest of my day in his arms.

"I need to make a phone call, but it's nothing urgent." I hope my phone isn't dead. I forgot to plug it into the charger last night. "I can wait and do it another time."

"If you want me to leave, I can. That way, you can have some privacy." This overly accommodating mood of his is certainly a 180 from yesterday. I wish I could get him to settle into a place halfway between the two. I'm cautiously optimistic, though slightly doubtful.

"I'd never ask you to leave your apartment. Anyways, it's not that kind of phone call. I've been meaning to talk to my landlord about something, but maybe it's stupid. A little second-hand cigarette smoke from the downstairs neighbor isn't going to kill me. I might not even bother since I haven't been there." Problems that felt so infuriating a few days ago seem irrelevant now.

"No. I think you should. Speak your peace and throw the ball back in their court. You hate that place. And maybe they have no idea about the smoking. You could probably sue them if they advertised the property as non-smoking." His words are all the encouragement I need.

"Well, I don't want to take anyone to court over it. But it would be nice if she could ask them to smoke outside. You're right. She probably isn't aware of the situation. Otherwise, she would've dealt with it. Maybe she'll appreciate me bringing it to her attention. Do you mind if I go on the balcony to make my call? I get nervous when I have an audience." I hate complaining or disagreeing or making waves of any kind. As a kid, I remember thinking how much better life would be once I was an adult. Now I have anxiety over the idea of making a phone call.

"Okay. I'll be in the shower if you need backup. Your keys are on the counter."

When I get to the kitchen, I find the spare set of apartment keys attached to the silver loop that holds my car key. Interesting. Kelly must have hooked them together this morning while I was sleeping. He would've needed my keys to get the laundry basket out of the car. It's not a big deal. I'm probably reading too much into it.

The balcony is even nicer than I expected. Kelly has a blue and white striped outdoor rug covering most of the concrete floor and a round gray and white coffee table flanked by two oversized patio chairs. Each chair has a thick blue cushion and a white pillow, and there's a small potted plant on the table. This would be an amazing spot to have coffee in the morning.

I'm still taking it all in when Kelly opens the sliding glass door and pops his head out long enough to say, "Don't forget to use your work voice when you call your landlord. Let them know you mean business. And if that doesn't work, subtly remind them that we know a *lot* of cops."

I can't help but laugh. Of course, we all have different voices inside of us. The professional one we wear like a suit during an interview. The weak one we hide under when we want to go home sick. The sweet one we dip ourselves in when we want something. And the sexy one we strip down to when we want someone. I have dozens of voices that I carry around in my arsenal should the need arise. The voice Kelly is referring to, the one I use at work, is specially tailored to our job. My work voice is confident, bold, self-assured, and direct, with a hint of sarcasm.

It's unbelievably attractive that he notices those differences. In that way, he reminds me of myself. Usually, I'm the one saying stuff like that.

My call goes straight to voicemail, so I leave a message. "Hello, this is Heather Belk. I rent the second floor of 472 Douglas. You listed this as non-smoking property. But the downstairs renter smokes inside on a daily basis, and it filters into my apartment. If you could speak with them about it, I would greatly appreciate it. Thank you."

I feel lighter after I leave the message and disconnect from the call, mostly because I'm glad she didn't answer. My landlord is on the surly side, and I doubt she'll be thrilled to receive my complaint. Even still, I'm glad Kelly encouraged me to call. I waste so much time being miserable and keeping quiet when I should speak louder.

Too often, strong, outspoken women are painted as a problem. This is society's way of telling the rest of us to keep our mouths shut and to smile more. I would love to see women rise up and take back their power. See them unshackled from the home and watch them break through the glass ceiling. Hear them say, in one voice, "We Are No Longer The Property Of Men." Unfortunately, I'm going to need everyone else to go first. I'm not the one to lead the charge. After all, I required a man's permission to make a phone call.

However, I would say to all the women who are braver than me, "You have my full support. Keep fighting, even though it's hard. Someday, the rest of us will join you."

I stay outside on the patio, letting my mind wander. It's a sun-drenched summer day, but for some reason, I'm cold. Still, it's warmer out here than it is at the jail. I might as well be sitting on an iceberg when I'm in there. If I had a diet coke, a bucket of ice, a hoodie, and my book, I could live out here. As the thought crosses my mind to return inside long enough to tell Kelly I've finished my call, the door opens, and he emerges.

A smile plays at the corner of his lips as he sits across from me. I can't help but wonder what has him so amused. Knowing Kelly, it's probably something that involves us being naked. "Anything else on your to-do list for the day? My name, perhaps? I want to make sure we've checked all the necessary boxes."

"Do you feel like baking cookies with me? I promised the guys at work." I smile at the thought of him in the kitchen. I would love to see Kelly with flour in his hair and sugar on his lips. Getting his hands sticky might be just the thing to loosen the knots he ties himself in.

"You're joking, Right?" The playful smile and overly accommodating attitude turn on a dime, revealing an irritability he's working to keep in check.

"I'm sorry. You don't have to help me." The sun dips behind the clouds, and the temperature drops ten degrees on my side of the patio, even though I can see the fire inside him blazing.

"Babe, I would happily join you in the kitchen, and you can give me as many cooking lessons as you want. I'll be your personal sous chef. But there's no fucking way I'm spending even one second of this day watching you do something for the other guys at work." He finishes speaking and begins drumming his fingers on the arm of his chair, waiting for my response. The repetitive sound causes the muscle in my neck to tighten and pulls my head to one side.

"That's fair. I never thought about it that way." Looking at his face when he's upset makes my chest tighten, so I drop my eyes toward the plant on the table. The Kelly I know doesn't scare me, but he does intimidate me.

I watch his legs as he walks over to stand in front of me. He leans forward and places a hand on each armrest of my chair, making me feel small as he looms over me. Shrinking into the chair and collapsing in on myself, I do everything I can to disappear.

"Please look at me." Our eyes meet, and he kisses me. "I apologize for raising my voice. I shouldn't have spoken to you that way. It was rude, and I'm sorry if I startled you. Is it so bad that I want you all to myself for a little longer?"

"And then what? Planning on getting rid of me?" I try to lighten my voice, but it comes out like the saddest joke ever told.

"Of course not. I intend to keep you for as long as possible. But I won't get to see if they stick you in minimum for the next few weeks. And I'm going to miss you. Now, come on, let's go inside. We can check the kitchen. See what's in there. I'm sure we can find something to cook together." He straightens himself, steps to the side, and offers me his hand. When I take it, he lifts me from the chair and pulls me into his arms. "Sometimes, I think you like making me jealous."

The only thing in the kitchen that resembles a meal is a frozen pizza. I suppose that will have to do. Kelly seems to have it under control, so I seize my opportunity to get a shower. I wouldn't say this shower is the best part of my day, but it certainly ranks pretty high. The hot water feels nice against my frozen skin but quickly makes me lightheaded. I get out and wrap myself in an oversized towel before my vision begins to blur.

I'm only two steps into the bedroom when I collapse on the

edge of the bed. The room spins like a tilt-a-whirl making me want to puke. I feel hot and clammy and the light stings even through my closed eyelids. I need everything to pause long enough to get dressed, but there is no end in sight. Taking off my wet towel, I cover myself with the comforter and pull my hands over my face. Surrounded by darkness, I focus on my breathing.

"Are you alright?" Kelly asks as he sits next to me on the bed. "Do you need me to get you anything? A bottle of water, maybe. Or some crackers." He sounds genuinely concerned. "Maybe we should take it easy for the rest of the day and leave your list for another time."

"I'm okay. I think my shower was a little too hot." My body is starting to cool, and as it does, the room begins to slow its rotation. "I'll get dressed and be out in a minute."

This has been happening more frequently lately, even though Kelly has been pushing meals on me like a Polish Grandmother. My body requires more than diet coke and ice, but my cravings are stronger than my need to survive. I'm not usually hungry. But I am painfully thirsty all of the time.

I get dressed and walk out to find the most handsome man I've ever seen waiting on the couch for me. You know how sometimes, you take a moment to look at someone from a different perspective? Well, I'm doing that now, and it's blowing my mind. Kelly hasn't shaved the last couple of days, and his beard has gone from a 5 o'clock shadow to the real deal. I can't help but bite my lip and smile when I look at him. How did I get so lucky? This has to be a dream.

"Why are you looking at me like that?" He grins at me, and I'm overwhelmed by the urge to be near him. Sitting on his lap so we're face to face, I tuck my knees on either side of his legs, grip the top of the couch with my hands, and bury my face in his neck.

"Well damn, had I known you were in this kind of mood, I would've crawled into bed with you." Kelly's voice is playful.

I laugh and sit back so I can see him. "I simply needed to be close to you for a minute. Don't make it weird." I move to get off his lap, but his arms stop me, locking me in place.

"How about a couple more minutes? I like seeing you in this position." He moves his hands to my hips and pulls me closer. I should have known he would turn my attempt at a cute embrace into something sexual. "You're so beautiful."

My reaction is involuntary.

"Why'd you roll your eyes when I said that? You know, I think you're amazing." I can feel the temperature of his body start to rise as he speaks. "You're everything I have ever wanted. Do you need me to prove it to you? Because I will. I'll do anything to make you mine. What do I have to do to show you this is real?"

It's an interesting question. The problem is, if I have to tell someone what I need, it doesn't mean anything when they give it to me. The kind of proof I require takes time. Pretty words and empty promises are easy. Sex is even easier. What I want is someone to build a life with. I want to know that I'll always have my best friend beside me, no matter what comes. It's great that Kelly knows how to make me melt, but in my experience, Lust and Love don't even run in the same circles.

"Say something, please." He keeps looking for answers I don't have.

"I can't think straight when you look at me like that. And your beard is kind of turning me on." I don't know what to say. So, I go for the easy out. "I think I see cold pizza in our future."

"You're ridiculous." He laughs, and I get a smile.

"True, but isn't that one of the many things you love about me?" Of course, I'm joking. Kelly could never love someone like me. Not when he deserves so much better.

"It is indeed." He wraps me in his arms, and I lay my head on his shoulder.

"Can we take a nap later, before work? We woke up way too early today." If I don't get a few more hours of sleep, I'll never make it through the night to see the morning.

"Yep. Whatever you need." His reply is sweet and to the

point. But something in his tone leads me to think we have two different definitions of the word *nap* in mind.

"Are you going to let me sleep?" I ask though I can already guess what his answer will be. He doesn't seem to require the same amount of rest as I do.

"Not a chance." He says, giving me a squeeze.

I have a feeling I'm in for a long night.

Thirteen

THE ALARM we set for 9:00 rings on the other side of the bed, and if I were alone, I'd be tempted to hit the snooze. For those of us working overnight, it's time to prepare for the day ahead. But when I open my eyes and see Kelly beside me, I find it nearly impossible to get out from under the covers. I want to cross my fingers and toes and pray to the gods that we wind up in the blocks together, but no amount of superstitious gesturing will grant that request. Thankfully, our shift doesn't start until 11:00 pm. So I'm in no hurry to get dressed.

"Can't we have one more night together?" I ask because I know he'll like hearing it and because I wish, more than anything, we could stay home in bed. Being at his apartment was meant to recharge my battery, but I feel more drained than ever.

"I would give anything for that. But people like us have the morning to look forward to. You'll be asleep in my arms again before you know it." He sounds confident that I'm coming back.

"You're welcome to visit me in purgatory whenever you'd like." I try to make it sound like a joke so he doesn't feel obligated, but it would be nice to have something to look forward to.

It tends to be painfully boring in the minimum-security block when I'm alone. I doubt tonight will be any different.

"When Hubble passes out assignments, I'm going to volunteer to go in your place. And if that doesn't work, I'll make every excuse I can think of to be in there with you. I hate when you're in that area alone. It makes me nervous. And I don't like being that far away from you." His voice confirms the fact that he worries about me. It's sweet, even if it is unnecessary.

"The only thing I worry about is falling asleep. Or being bored to death. Other than that, I don't mind being there. It's quiet." If I'm being honest, minimum is my least favorite position and the only place I ever worry about something bad happening. But right now, Kelly doesn't need to hear that. He doesn't need my manic, worst-case overthinking adding to his concern. For both our sake, I decided to keep my worries to myself. I don't want him to spend the entire night thinking about me. He needs to be focused and watch out for himself. "I'll be fine. Text if you think of it and you aren't too busy."

"If I'm in the tower, I can talk to you all night. We can entertain each other, and I can keep an eye on you." He gives me one of those playful smiles that pretty much melts me on the spot.

Regardless of his cuteness, I'm not sure how I feel about him watching my every move for ten hours straight. Having him there might make me feel safer initially, but it wouldn't take long for me to get self-conscious. Then again, if it were me behind the monitors this week, I'd probably keep a closer eye on him as well. So, maybe it's not that strange.

"Be sure to watch out for everyone when you're there. Not only me. I'll be fine." I'm starting to wonder if this is a good idea. Are we a liability to our team if we're together outside of work? Do our feeling for one another become too much of a distraction? I would run into fire for Kelly, no matter what. But that's been true since day one. Like Grant said, protecting each other is part of the job.

I'm probably worried over nothing. By morning, I'll be back

at my place, and everything will have returned to the way it was. I doubt Kelly intends to tell anyone that I was even here.

My mind wanders back to a moment in the past I wish I could let go of.

When I was 16, I went to junior prom with a guy I thought I had a friendship with. He spent the entire dance avoiding me but came to the party at my house after and stayed until late afternoon the next day. When I was 26, I ran into him and his wife out at a bar. He was friendly and bought me a drink. I'm guessing he must have been pretty drunk because he looked me straight in the face and told me, "The reason I didn't dance with you at the prom was because I was embarrassed to be seen with you." Then he kissed me. I was disgusted and mortified and really fucking hurt.

He said something out loud that I had already kind of known. And now that it was spoken, I could no longer deny it. I'm the kind of girl that you have fun with in secret but don't claim out in public. Looking back, I think nearly every person I've slept with has treated me that way.

So, do I think Kelly, the male model, will walk into work holding my hand? Hell No! I wouldn't be surprised if he went in a different door and forgot to look in my direction. However, here in the solitude of his apartment, he is very much looking at me.

"I'm allowed to worry about you, Belk. Even if you don't want me to." He reaches his hand across the six inches of space between us, touching me for the first time since we woke up. With a gentle hand, he brushes a section of hair behind my ear and runs the backside of his fingers along my jaw. "You're important to me."

It's not that I don't believe him. The problem is that I *can't* believe him. Why does he keep saying all these things to me? Why can't we enjoy our last hour and a half together before we say goodbye? We've already slept together. There is nothing else. Stop pretending like you care, Kelly. Cut the shit and call it what it is. This was a one-night stand that lasted for two incredible days. It was exciting and intense and exactly what I needed, but it's over now. For some reason, he seems hell-bent on destroying me. He wants me to fall in love with him so he can rip my heart out and laugh about it.

"Where are you right now?" His question snaps me back.

"What?" I don't know what else to say. "I'm right here with you." I'm not sure what he's thinking or why he's convinced I'm something special. I haven't been able to sort out my own feelings since walking through the door a couple of days ago. I keep trying to remind myself that we're friends, but the way he touches me feels like so much more. I want to be here, but I'm afraid to stay. I want to keep him, but I know I can't. I'm the only place I want to be but disappearing by the second.

"No, you aren't. Or at least you haven't been. I wish you'd talk to me when something's bothering you. Tell me what I did wrong so I can fix it." His tone is commanding but also pleading.

I reach over and put my hand on his. I want him to feel my presence in the moment. "I'm with you."

He pulls me into his arms and kisses me. I wish I could freeze this moment and live in it forever. This will only last a minute, so I have to catalog every detail. I want to replay this interaction in my mind later when I'm missing him. The feel of his lips against mine. The fire burning in his chest. The combination of scents that I've come to know as distinctly him. The way the muscles in his arms tighten, locking me into place. And the little sounds he makes when he forgets to hold back.

The tears begin to puddle and spill from my eyes. Everything about this moment overwhelms me, and any hope of holding it in is lost. The last thing I want is for him to see me cry, but I'm not sure I can hide my face before he notices.

"Babe, please tell me what's wrong. What did I do?" He asks, wearing a look of genuine concern on his face. "Why are you so upset with me?"

"Oh my god, stop! You didn't do anything wrong. I'm not upset with you! It's literally the complete opposite." I'm three seconds from spilling my guts if I'm not careful.

He stares into my eyes, waiting patiently for me to continue. When I don't say anything else, he asks, "I don't understand what you mean. Explain it to me. What feeling is the complete opposite of being upset with me?"

I meant to imply that I was upset with myself, but he interpreted what I said to suggest something else entirely. What feeling is the opposite of upset? What answer is he looking for? I wish I knew more random words. Maybe I should have read more books when I was younger. Or participated in family game nights when they were playing Scrabble.

"Enthralled?" I say hesitantly. It's the first word that pops into my head that isn't *love*.

"You're too much." He takes my arm and presses the button on the side of my watch, illuminating the time. "Come on. We have to get ready for work. And I want to stop for food on our way in. Don't take this the wrong way, but you look terrible. Your face is drained of color, and even your eyes look pale. It looks like I've been holding you hostage and starving you."

Instead of looking in the mirror, I jump out of bed and straight into my feelings, franticly searching for my clothes. This is the second time he has insulted the way I look. I wasn't emotionally prepared for his critique, and it hurt a lot more than it should. All I can do is stare at the floor and start getting dressed.

"I don't have my belt or my handcuffs. They're back at my place. So, I'll get all my shit out of here, and maybe I'll see you later." I try to focus on my breathing as I turn away from him. My chest tightens, and my eyes sting. The interesting thing about pain is that it improves once you let it out, but I don't want to cry in front of him again.

"You're being ridiculous. Maybe you'll see me later? What the fuck does that mean?" He takes off his belt and hands it to me. "Take mine. I have another one in my locker."

I can't tell if he's annoyed, hurt, or mad, so I don't make eye contact.

"Listen to me, Belk. I want you to hear what I'm saying.

We're riding into work together. We're getting dinner. And we *will* see each other as many fucking times as I can get away with. I don't know what kind of emotional hole you've stepped into, but I'm standing here offering you my hand. And if you aren't ready to accept my help, that's fine. But I'm not going anywhere unless it's with you."

We stand silently for a few seconds before he closes the gap between us and gently pushes me against the wall. "Babe, I don't want you to leave."

It's hard to explain. Physically my body is there, but I'm not in control. I'm aware of everything, floating a few feet away, watching helplessly. My silent screams do nothing to stop the pain my shell inflicts. I'm a mere spectator. I'm not the one destroying everything, but they wear my face. I'll be the one who is blamed and the one who has to apologize and accept the consequences. Depression isn't anything like being sad. Depression is shutting down and feeling nothing. Then feeling everything all at once after it's too late.

"Okay." This one word comes like muscle memory.

"What am I going to do with you?" Kelly holds my face in his hands and searches the depths of my unfocused eyes, looking for acknowledgment. "We have to get going if we want to be there on time. I need you in the right head-space by the time we get there. You can't walk into the jail like this. You know that. Those guys will eat you alive."

I follow his words back. "Yeah, I know. I'm fine. I'll pull it together before we get there. I promise."

He holds my hand as we walk through the apartment, across the parking lot, and all the way to the car. Then, in perfect gentlemanly fashion, he opens the passenger door for me and closes it after I'm in. I hadn't noticed, but he must have grabbed my phone at some point because he hands it to me after getting into the driver's seat.

I'm not hungry, but when we stop at the drive-thru, he buys me food anyways. It's 10:37 when we pull into the parking lot at work, leaving us plenty of time to eat. I hate when people take care of me. It makes me feel weak and worthless. However, being ungrateful is a bad look, and I'm not trying to add insult to injury.

"Thank you for getting me food and remembering to ask for lots of ice. I appreciate everything you've said to me and everything you've done. Letting me borrow your belt. Offering to let me stay at your place and wear your clothes. Changing your schedule so we could spend time together. Allowing me to feel human again... I'm not sure how you knew, but I needed all that... I'm sorry I was distant. My mind is all over the place, but not because of anything you did." It feels good to say that while he's in front of me. Gratitude and apologies aren't as meaningful over text.

"Even when you're struggling, you manage to be a good person." He says, taking my hand.

"Another item to add to the list of things you love about me." Jokes are my way of trying to lighten the mood. I'm not great at accepting compliments of any kind.

"Trust me, it's written near the top in permanent ink." He squeezes my hand and smiles. "Unless you want to go back to the apartment and spend the night looking for new jobs, we'd better get in there. Let's get this over with so we can go home."

Kelly holds the door and lets me walk in first. I punch my employee number into the time clock, 37497, and hit enter. As I stand there waiting, I watch him type in 37498. It makes sense that our numbers would be similar since we started the same day, but knowing we're only one digit apart makes me smile. Stepping in front of the door that separates the administrative section from the jail portion, I wait to hear that familiar click.

"I have to get a couple of things out of my locker. I'll see you in there." I'm not surprised when he says it, even though I forgot about him needing another belt. I knew he wasn't going to walk in with me. Guys who look like that don't claim girls who look like me. I was stupid to think this would be any different. One of these days, I'm going to meet a man who isn't embarrassed to be seen with me.

I'm already in Sergeant Hubble's office for the shift meeting when Kelly comes in. He pretends to squeeze in behind me and hooks his fingers under my belt. As expected, I'm banished to minimum again. Kelly attempts to volunteer as tribute, but the sergeant assigns him to the blocks with Collins. Of course.

I've secretly hated Collins for months, mostly because she's annoying. But also because she has a massive crush on Kelly and goes out of her way to flirt with him. The fact that she's over there smiling from ear to ear, trying to get his attention, makes me want to shank her.

He must sense my discomfort because he takes half a step forward and presses his body into mine. Or maybe it was meant as a message to someone else because his action certainly didn't go unnoticed across the room. I try to keep a straight face and pretend to listen to the rest of the meeting. When we're dismissed, he releases my belt, leaving me free to go. But I linger momentarily, filling my lungs with one last breath of him. Hopefully, that will be enough to get me through this shift.

We all exit into the main hallways. That's where I turn left, and everyone else goes right. I'm not sure why I look over my shoulder, but when I do, I find Kelly watching me walk away. Collins is trying desperately to get his attention, but his eyes hold on my location. Pulling out his phone, he points to the screen, clearly conveying his wishes. I mirror his action and remove the phone from my pocket before pressing the home button.

You have 1 missed text message

Kells: I miss you already.

Well, shit! That's super cute. Seeing his message has me grinning like a girl with a crush, and I have to walk away before the rumor mill catches wind of the new gossip. Maybe tonight won't be so bad after all.

Fourteen

THERE ARE 114 guys currently being housed in minimum security. That's a lot of bodies for me to keep track of. The officers on 2nd shift were finishing a head count as I arrived, so I am all set until midnight. They don't have anything too exciting to report, so I'm planning on things being quiet. Most of the inmates are in their bunks for the night. I see a group playing cards, a couple of guys writing letters, and one person reading. Makes me wish I had brought a book with me. I'm in the middle of a decent novel, but it's back at my place. I'd ask Kelly to stop there after work, but I didn't think to bring my keys. Thankfully, I have a few puzzle games on my phone to keep me occupied. After all, I need something to do besides flip through mug shots.

I quickly scan the bunks and notice the idiot from the other night has returned. The mouthy one who bragged about beating his wife. I hate guys like that. Hopefully, Grant pitching him in the hole was enough to straighten him out, but I sort of doubt it. I'm sure I can expect another comment when I finally get around to walking through.

The two officers from the previous shift are headed out, so I'm on my own. I wonder if Kelly and Collins are done with the perimeter check. I'm dying to know if she said anything about me. I want to message him, but I don't want to be obvious about anything. He did send me that text during the meeting, but does that count? Is he waiting for me to respond?

> : Do you have a new girlfriend?

Kells: Fuck, I hope so. You tell me. Do I?

> : I was talking about the president of your fan club over there. The way she bats her eyelashes at you, I assumed she's using echolocation to see.

Kells: In that case, NO. I'm pretty happy with the one I have… BTW Everyone's looking at me like I'm on drugs. Your text made me laugh loud as hell in a very quiet room. Thanks for that.

I'm glad it's dark because I can feel myself blushing. Obviously, we're both joking around, but I'm not mad at the idea. Being with Kelly is a nice excuse to avoid going home.

> : Sorry, not sorry. How's everything going out there? It's quiet here.

I play a word game on my phone to kill minutes between messages and notice it's almost time for the midnight head count. Technically, I can do it any time during the hour, but I usually like to get it over with. At 11:59 pm, as I'm about to stand, I hear the door click behind me, and Kelly walks in carrying a cup of ice.

"My saraph, come to visit me in hell. What are you doing here in the badlands? It's almost time for your rounds." I'm surprised to see him so soon. I knew he would find a reason to sneak away, but I figured he'd save the ice excuse for later in the night.

"I know, I'm wonderful. You're a lucky girl. Thought I'd

help you count. Plus, I brought you a gift." He sets the cup on the desk next to the soda I brought and extends his hand to me.

"You didn't think I could count to 114?" I smile and laugh a little louder than intended. His proximity is giving me butterflies. Not to mention the scandalous way he's touching my hand as he helps me from my chair.

"I told you I would find every excuse to see you. So, here I am. Apologies, I never meant to offend your brilliant mind. Do you want help with the count, or would you rather do it yourself?" He presses his lips to the back of my hand, but I pull it away quickly.

The smile on his face is enough to make my heart race, but his touch pushes the pedal to the floor. I don't need us to get caught doing anything we shouldn't be, and I'm still not sure what the rules are.

"Come on. Let's get it done." I don't know what reason he gave, but I don't want him getting into trouble for helping me. Kelly counts the left side, and I take the right. As I'm walking past the last set of bunks, I hear something along the lines of, "What's the matter, little girl? You scared?" I don't even have to look to know who said it.

"What's the opposite of yes?" I shoot back loud enough for him to hear me before meeting Kelly at the desk to check the count.

"Everything okay? You want me to take anyone with me when I leave?" His question hints at concern, even though I don't think he heard the exchange.

"Yes, please. Take me with you!" We both laugh, and I find myself locked in his gaze. I don't want him to worry about me. It's important that I send him off on a lighter note so he can focus on the night ahead.

"You have no idea how badly I want to." His comment would be better suited for the bedroom. Something I'm sure I'll be thinking about after he walks out the door.

He still has to do the headcount in the blocks with Collins. I understand he has no say in who he's paired with, but that doesn't mean I like it. I want to hold on to him and not let go.

"Text me if you need *anything*. I'll stop whatever I'm doing." He leans closer to whisper in my ear, "If I could kiss you right now, I would." Then he turns and leaves.

I spend the remainder of the midnight hour daydreaming about things unsuitable for work. By the time I've exhausted myself thinking about every known position I've attempted and a few I'd still like to try, nearly everyone is asleep. I look over the ledge of my desk and scan the room for movement. One inmate remains sitting on his bunk, quietly reading. It must be a good book. If he's still awake when I walk through again, I'll note the title and add it to my reading list.

> Kells: Do you want me to come back for the 1:00 count?

> : You don't have to. I'll be fine. Save whatever excuse you have and use it at 2:00.

> Kells: It's a date.

I wish the other officers would walk in here once an hour as standard procedure. The day shifts have two officers posted in this position, but 3rd only ever has one. The social interaction would boost morale. Plus, the constant visits would be a good way to show that we're never truly alone. I wonder if I could suggest something like that to the sergeant without sounding like a scared little baby.

> : By any chance, do you have a hoodie in your locker? I'm freezing.

I place my phone on the desk and stretch my back before beginning my walk-through. There hasn't been any movement in the block, so I don't have to worry about losing count. At this point, I'm taking a stroll around the bunks to make it look good for the cameras. I don't need whoever is watching in the tower to rat on me for not doing my job. For some reason, I can't remember who was stationed there tonight. I must have been distracted by something.

As if a glutton for punishment, I start on the right side. Yet again, I hear another comment, but I don't bother responding this time. My stomach feels weird, and I want to get through this count as quickly as possible. But if that asshole makes so much as a peep at 2:00 am, I'm asking Kelly to drag him out.

Halfway through the left side of the bunks, I begin to sweat. It feels like there's a fire in my chest. My hands get sticky, and my vision blurs. When the room starts to spin faster, I feel like I'm looking down a long tunnel, and my desk is three miles away. I try to grab the edge of a nearby bunk, but everything goes black, and I disappear.

It all happens too quickly. But when a sinkhole opens beneath your feet, how do you keep from falling in?

Fifteen

"HEATHER, I need you to wake up."

Only his voice fills the space, finding me there in the darkness. Everything is black. I can't get a full breath, and I feel like I'm being crushed under a two-hundred-pound weighted blanket. There is no sound except for his. And no light. If he reaches out again, maybe I'll be able to find my way out. I'm not scared of this empty place, I've been here before, but I know this time is different. This time, I need to fight.

One by one, sensations begin to register. Something hot is dripping on my skin. There's a body pressed heavily against me, moving slightly. I can feel someone's breath against my cheek as the cold from the floor absorbs into my fingertips. And there's some kind of electrical current. The blackness begins to spark as little white orbs light pop and disappear.

Then, there is his face, no more than two inches from mine. I don't know this person, and I'm fairly certain I've never met him, but he feels familiar. My ears start ringing, and I feel sick. A metallic taste in my mouth makes me gag, but I can't sort out what's happening. The waves of electricity tingle as they pass through my chest and into my limbs.

Suddenly, the room ignites like a flashbang, and I hear something I recognize. It sounds like boots against a hard floor and men shouting. I've heard this before, two months ago when that fight broke out in the blocks. I take one last look at the face in front of me and realize where I am.

Whatever part of his weight he had been supporting comes bearing down on me. I feel like I'm trapped between a corpse and a hard place. Whoever this man is on top of me, he's not moving.

There's panic in the raised voices as they spread throughout the room. "Where is she? Does anyone see her? Where did you see her last?" They seem to be looking for someone. "Find Belk." And they keep saying my name.

I recognize Grant's voice, "I found her. Call an ambulance." Seconds later, the body concealing my whereabouts is pushed aside, and I can finally breathe. Kelly appears, kneeling next to me, talking on the phone. His touch burns as he presses two fingers to my neck.

"I'm fine," I say, hoping to comfort him, but my ears are still ringing like a fire alarm. The pain is shooting back and forth, from one side of my head to the other, directly behind my eyes.

"Lie still. The ambulance is on its way... This is all my fault. I should have been here." He ends the call and pushes his phone back into his pocket.

"I need to get up. I feel sick." The room is still spinning, but I'll crawl if I have to. I can feel the eyes of no less than 118 people on me, and I don't like it. "Kelly! Let me get up, please!"

"Babe, I can't. I don't know where you're hurt." Kelly sounds shaken, and that won't do. Not here. I need him to be strong so that he can stay safe.

I press my hands into the concrete floor and attempt to find my feet, but my effort is useless. I can't make my body cooperate. The guy on the floor beside me isn't moving, but I recognize him from my dream. Who is he?

"Stop! Is he alright?" I shudder as Grant fastens the handcuffs around the man's wrists. "He didn't do anything!"

Grant doesn't take orders from nobodies like me, so I'm

surprised when he nods his head and unlocks the cuffs. I hear Kelly audibly disagree with this decision, but the action remains unchanged. There's an unspoken argument between them. I can feel it as the tension passes through me. But Grant doesn't take orders from nobodies like Kelly either.

"What happened?" I can't see who asked the question because I'm still on all fours, but it sounded like Sergeant Hubble's voice.

"I don't know. But I want to get off the floor." I can hear the anger rising in my voice.

"Grant, get her to the booking desk. The ambulance will be pulling into the loading bay any minute. Carry her if you have to. Then come back so we can start getting the rest of these guys out of here. Kelly, you're in here with me for the rest of the night. We have to get this under control. Collins, get everyone in their bunk and counted."

What did Hubbard mean by the rest of them? I'm a quarter of the way between kneeling and standing when Grant lifts me off the floor and starts to carry me out.

"I can walk. Help that other guy!" He doesn't deviate from his course. "Kelly is going to be pissed if you carry me." I don't realize what I'm revealing until it's out. Shit, I shouldn't have said that.

"Kelly can get the fuck over it! Right now, you need to shut up and let me help you. It's a fucking blood bath down there, Heather. I don't know how you're alive right now." Grant's tone is harsh, but I'm not sure his anger is meant for me. "Kevin is going to lose his shit when he hears about this."

"What?" I'm having a hard time understanding Grant's statement. None of it makes sense. What does Kevin have to do with anything, and why would he care about what happens to me?

"Keep her ass in that chair until the ambulance gets here. Do not, under any circumstances, allow her to walk around. I have four more people we need to get out of there. Two urgent. Two secondaries. She goes first." Grant relays the information to the officer at the booking desk before returning to the action.

Four more people? The guy from my dream is one. I saw him on the ground, and he wasn't moving. But who are the other three? I wish someone would tell me what's going on. I can hear Grant coming as the first ambulance arrives. He's shouting orders while pushing a sizeable man in a wheelchair.

"She goes NOW!"

"No, I'm fine. Take him first."

"She goes. Then him. Sedate her if you have to."

"Don't you fucking dare! Stop wasting time and take him to the goddamn hospital."

"We can take them both, but we only have one stretcher."

"My officer is the priority."

"Put him on the fucking stretcher, and let's go."

"Get them out of here."

The stretcher looks like a toddler bed with this oversized man on it. He is easily one of the biggest guys I've ever seen. If I had to guess, I would put him at 6'6, 260 lbs. His arms, shoulders, and neck are massive and covered in tattoos. I can't make out the images, but consider my interest peeked. I wonder if this is the "Viking" Kelly mentioned the other night. With his sandy blonde hair, steel frame, and thick beard, he does look like the sort of guy who might have a dragon for a pet.

The EMTs get him loaded into the ambulance and return to grab me. I swear one of them has a needle in his hand, and I'm about to lose my shit. Then I remember that old saying, *"You get more flies with honey,"* and I will myself to relax.

Taking a deep breath, I hold one hand in front of me, and try to speak as calmly as possible. "That's not going to be necessary. I'm dizzy and slightly confused, but other than that, I'm fine." Everything feels like it's taking too long, and I wish people would stop looking at me.

The ambulance ride to the hospital seems to take forever. The EMT sitting beside me in the back keeps asking me questions I can't answer. "What's the inmate's name? What's he in for? What happened? Where are you hurt?"

I would text someone to ask, but I've lost my phone. Thankfully, my companion regains consciousness before we get to the hospital downtown. Turns out his name is Croy Jepsen, and he was in for a DUI. I suppose he could be lying, but I have no reason to think that. Other than the fact that he's dressed like a criminal. I'm sure the hospital will call and get confirmation from the jail.

I reach out and rest one hand gently on top of his leg. I'm not sure why, but I want him to know I'm here. When his hand settles over mine, the circuit is complete. Again, I feel the current of electricity as the floating orbs begin to snap. Everything goes black as my body slumps forward onto his.

There's a stretcher with my name on it at the hospital, and two staff members waiting to strap me down. I attempt to remain calm. Knowing Grant, he called ahead and told them to knock me out. I don't understand why people keep fussing over me. This other guy, Croy, needs the attention more than I do.

They wheel me into a room as someone begins asking the usual questions. "Can you tell me your name? What's your birthday? Do you know what day it is? Is there any chance you could be pregnant? What hurts? What happened?" On and on it goes until it's all a blur.

Someone new comes in and says they need to take blood. Then they leave, and someone else comes in to hook me to a machine. No one believes me when I say I'm fine. And for some reason, everyone keeps threatening to cut off my clothes. Finally, I agree to change into a hospital gown and robe before they can strap me to the bed and pull out the scissors. A lady comes in and informs me that she'll have me all cleaned up in no time.

"Is that necessary?" I'm confused. What does that even mean? Why would I need to be cleaned up? There's nothing wrong with me. I feel like I'm losing my mind. I shouldn't even be here.

She looks at me like I'm crazy, and I think maybe I could be. "Would you like me to get you something to help you relax?"

"No, I would not!" Why does everyone keep threatening to drug me? I'm behaving myself. What more do they want? I finally agree to the stupid sponge bath and lay back with my eyes closed. "Do you know if that guy I came in with is okay?" I ask the nurse, but she refuses to tell me anything. I can't help but wonder if he's also getting cleaned up. Or is this special embarrassment reserved for me?

After I'm sufficiently scrubbed clean, I get to answer more questions, give more blood, and get a bunch of x-rays. I keep thinking about Croy. I wish I knew where he was. Then maybe I could sneak past and check on him. I'd like to talk to him if I could. Maybe he'd tell me what happened. Or who the other three people were that they had to take out. If I had my phone, I could text Kelly, and he could tell me why I'm here.

The nurse puts me into a room and dims the lights. Am I supposed to sleep until they figure out nothing is wrong with me? I have no phone, no clothes, and no one to call when it comes time to leave. I can't even take an uber because I have no wallet and no keys. I'm starting to think that maybe I died on the jail floor and have yet to accept my fate.

I have to get out of here and find someone who will talk to me. Starting with the monitors, I take off everything one at a time, making sure it isn't going to call the attention of the nurse. Then, I take off the oxygen but leave in the IV. If by chance I'm not dead, I don't want them to have to stick me again.

As luck would have it, a certain Mr. Jepsen is in the room three from mine. I overheard a pair of nurses whispering about him in rather unprofessional terms. No matter, they let slip a room number, and that was all I needed. With my IV stand in tow, I'm able to sneak into his room before anyone sees me. This guy must be part giant. I feel tiny sitting in the chair next to him.

"Croy, are you awake?" He doesn't move. "I need to talk to you." When I touch his arm, a shock of static pricks my finger. It must be all the stupid wires coming off him. I rest my hand gently on his arm again. "Croy, can you hear me?" He must be able to hear or feel something because his pulse increases on the monitor. Before I can say more, I hear someone behind me.

"Ms. Belk, what are you doing out of bed? You can't be in here." The voice comes from the doorway behind me. This is a different nurse. One I haven't seen yet. She looks much younger. Maybe I can explain to her what I'm doing.

"I'm sorry. I needed to see if he was okay. We came in together from the jail. I'm a correctional officer there. He was awake in the ambulance. I heard him. He has to be okay. Can I talk to him for one minute?" I can see she's listening, but nothing I say makes a difference. I'm not going to get any of the answers I seek.

"Ms. Belk, I'm fully aware of the situation. Where you came from, and the condition you arrived in has been well documented. But it's 4:00 am, and you need to sleep. There will be plenty of time for conversation after the sun rises. Now, let's get you back to your room and get you settled." Her voice is controlled and assertive. I appreciate her ability to control the room, so I do what I'm told.

She leads me out of Croy's room and back into my own. After reattaching the monitors, she tucks me under the blankets. I notice her retrieve a syringe from the cart and watch as she connects it to my IV. "This will help you sleep."

There's nothing I can do or say. It's already too late. She pushes the clear liquid into the tube attached to my arm, and consciousness begins to fade. "I don't want to sleep."

It doesn't take long for the darkness to find me. Yet again, I am lost.

Sixteen

THERE ARE people in my room talking as I open my eyes. Maybe I should pretend to be asleep so I can finally get a few answers from one of these nurses. As it turns out, Warden Lawson is the other person in the conversation, so it's probably good that I opened my eyes.

"Belk, how are you feeling?" He asks as soon as my eyes flutter open as if he's been watching me sleep, waiting for me to join the conversation in my own time.

"Sir, I keep telling everyone here that I'm fine." I hope Lawson is here to negotiate my release. This place makes me uncomfortable. If anyone can get me out of here, it's him. He has a commanding presence. Even outside the jail, where his title carries less weight, Lawson is an authority figure.

"Well, it turns out you're *not* fine, so I'm going to need you to stay in bed and follow the rules." I assume he was told about last night's visit down the hall. "I brought something to show you, but I need your statement first."

For the first time, I notice his laptop is on the tray beside my bed. This has to be a video from last night, right? Unless he brought the computer to type out my statement. If I answer whatever questions he has for me, maybe I can finally find out what happened.

It's quicker than I thought it would be to get through his Q&A. I suppose it helps that I can't remember anything. Or maybe help isn't the right word. Lawson looks increasingly concerned whenever I say, "I don't know" or "I can't recall," as if he thinks I'm lying to him.

"I have the video files from 1:00 am, and I'm willing to review them, but only if that's something you're prepared to watch. We can wait until after you're released if you would rather."

The warden isn't one to make jokes, but he has to be kidding. Of course, I want to see it. "Sir, I'd like to watch the video as soon as possible. Please. I need to know what happened."

He opens the laptop and clicks on the first of four files. I'm guessing they're all from the same time frame but recorded from different cameras. I see myself walking from the right side of the block, across the open dining area, and through the bunks on the left. My labored steps come to a pause next to the guy reading in his bed. My body sways, and I reach my hand toward the empty top bunk before I drop. The man on the bottom bed catches me with one arm and lays me on the floor. Then he stands and steps over me like I'm not even there. I can tell from his massive size that it's Croy in the video. He was the one reading. Croy is the person who caught me before I smashed into the ground.

All the nights I spent playing out worst-case scenarios in my head, I never imagined this. Sure, I figured someone would try to take me out eventually. But it never crossed my mind that I would be the one to do it to myself. Lawson pauses the video and looks at me.

"Do you know Croy Jepsen, Miss Belk?"

"NO, Sir."

"Have you ever met him before last night?"

"NO, Sir."

"Did you exchange words with him before you passed out?"

"NO. I don't believe so. Chunks of my memory are missing, but I'm certain I would remember him had we spoken. I was never even over there. Second shift already had the headcount done when I came in, and Kelly did that side at midnight."

"Why would Officer Kelly come to help you with the 12:00 headcount? Did you ask him for his assistance? Were you concerned about being in the blocks alone?"

"Kelly brought a cup of ice from the kitchen and offered to help while he was there. That's it. I accepted his offer because an inmate had been making comments, and I thought it could be beneficial to have backup."

"What kind of comments?"

"The usual kind, Sir. Rude comments meant to intimidate. The inmate had made a thinly veiled threat a few days prior, and Officer Grant removed him for the rest of my shift."

"So, Officer Kelly was aware of these threats?"

"I'm not sure if I mentioned it to him or not. Officer Grant could have said something to the other people working that night, but I wouldn't have that information. To my knowledge, Kelly was unaware of the issue. Otherwise, I believe he would have addressed it."

"I'm certain you are correct. What is the nature of your relationship with Officer Grant and Officer Kelly?"

"We're co-workers. Perhaps friends, depending on the day.

Officer Grant and I met before I started working at the jail. Kelly and I were hired at the same time and worked a lot of the same days. I'm not sure why you're asking me about them. What do they have to do with what happened last night?"

"I'm trying to get the facts to paint a clearer picture."

"Okay. I don't see the relevance since neither was present when the incident occurred. Unless one of them was hurt after I left? What aren't you telling me? Did something happen? Did somebody else get hurt after I was removed from the block?"

"No. You and four inmates were brought to the hospital after sustaining injuries. The other three were taken to Solitary. Perhaps we should continue the video unless it's upsetting you."

I nod in response, and the video continues where it left off. I'm on the ground, and Croy is standing in front of me. He's a grizzly bear in a howling forest, and the wolves have begun to circle. The window of opportunity is so small, and I'm defenseless on the floor. How long until they notice in the tower and send the call out over the radios? Apparently, pretty fucking long.

I recognize the fat piece of trash that had been running his mouth. Of course, he'd be leading the pack. No surprise there. As soon as he lunges, Croy swings. The punch connects, and mouthy boy is knocked out cold. The next guy has come armed with a shank. He stabs Croy in the arm and falls back a step. Not the best move. Croy kicks him in the chest, sending the man flying into the metal bunks at his back. One more kick to the ribs for good measure before it's on to the next. The third guy swings at the same time Croy does, and their fists collide in mid-air. I'll assume from the reaction that the little guy's hand is shattered.

What happens next doesn't make sense right away. Three more guys come to take their shot. Coyotes looking to pounce on the weakest prey. I'm ripe for the picking, still motionless on the floor, but they never touch me. The three men move in tandem, having witnessed the results of prior solo attacks. There's a man to the left, another to the right, and a third coming through the bunk I'm lying next to. I don't see Croy get hit, but he falls to the ground. Or rather, he throws himself on top of me. The lesser predators swing and kick wildly, landing blow after blow, as Croy safeguards a body devoid of a soul.

The call must finally go out over the radio because the lights turn on, and officers file into the block one after the next. They don't go straight to the fight. The officers seem to be looking for something, or rather someone. Kelly is there. I can see the panic in his movements. But it's Grant who comes over and rolls Croy off me. Then Kelly is kneeling beside me, yelling something into his phone. He takes my hand and leans toward me. Eventually, I steady myself on my hands and knees before trying to stand. Grant lifts me off the ground like a sack of potatoes and carries me out of the room. Kelly looks like he wants to murder everyone. But his ire seems directed at Croy most of all.

"So, your bodyguard, whom you don't know and you've never met, delivered a broken jaw, five cracked ribs, and a shattered hand. During which he was stabbed for his trouble. He then proceeds to offer himself up as a human punching bag to shield you from harm. Am I forgetting anything?"

"Yeah. You forgot the part where he caught me before I would've cracked my head open on the floor."

"You honestly expect me to believe that you and Croy Jepsen have never met? Never spoken? Never associated in any way? But he would protect you at the cost of his own well-being? A guy who was set to be released 12 hours later."

"I don't have an answer for you. You'd have to ask him why he did it."

"So, you're going to sit there and lie to me, Miss Belk? Let's try this again with the sound on."

It's harder to watch when you can hear everything breaking. This could have ended before it began had the other guys stayed in their bunks after Croy caught me. However, fat boy and his buddies had other ideas. "Let's fucking kill her." That's what he said when he walked over.

"That's not going to happen." Croy's response was not what they were expecting, and the fuse was lit.

Having the audio doesn't change much about the story until I hear, "Heather, I need you to wake up." I remember that voice calling out to me in the darkness. It was Croy who said my name. He was the one who found me and ushered me back.

But it's Kelly's words that make me look like the biggest liar. "This is all my fault. I should have been here... Babe, I can't. I don't know where you're hurt." We've all seen our co-worker Kelly remain calm in the face of immense pressure. But this Kelly, the one who sounds like my boyfriend, is on the verge of collapse.

The last video is from the hallway. It's footage of Grant scolding me as he carries me like a child. "Kelly can get the fuck over it! Right now, you need to shut up and let me help you. It's a fucking blood bath down there, Heather. I don't know how you're alive right now. Kevin is going to lose his shit when he hears about this."

"Would you like to start telling the truth now that we're all on the same page?"

"I don't know Croy Jepsen. And nothing you show me is going to change that. Officer Grant and I met through Kevin Norton, which is common knowledge. As for Kelly, we're co-workers and friends. But if you must know, yeah, we've slept together. I'm not a liar. Forgive me if I don't see where my having a one-night stand is any of your business."

"You know what I think? I think you're sleeping with all of them."

"Well, Sir. You would be wrong."

Lawson slams the laptop shut and storms out of the room without another word. I'm so pissed off I want to scream the building down. He accused me of causing this whole thing and called me a whore. Maybe he thinks I slept with all six of those inmates as well. Is this guy for real? Hooking up with Kelly may have been a mistake, but Lawson is making it seem like I sit on every dick I happen across.

I'm done trying. People only see the worst, no matter how much good there is.

Seventeen

THANKFULLY, when Kelly arrives in the doorway, holding my backpack, Warden Lawson is already gone. It's 9:54 am, and he has to be exhausted. A normal night of work has me dragging myself to bed. I'm not sure how he's standing upright after everything Kelly was left to deal with last night. I motion for him to come in, but he holds his position. My perfect boy looks like he's been destroyed and taped back together.

"Did you come all this way to stare at me?" My question is meant to lighten the mood, but even from here, I can see his eyes filling with tears. I want to wrap him in my arms and repair what's broken, but I can't do that from ten feet away.

Finally, after what feels like ages, he reduces the distance between us but remains intentionally out of my reach. I can feel my heart sinking. I've been on the receiving end of this silence before. Not from Kelly, but plenty of others.

"I'm a little surprised to see you. I know you have to be tired." I'm not sure what else to say. It's clear he doesn't want to talk to me. "Did you, by chance, find my phone at work?"

He reaches into his left pocket and pulls out two phones, mine and his. Instead of handing it to me, he places the phone face down on the table next to my bed. The way he sets it there, I can only assume that it's shattered. It must have broken when I fell. He sets my backpack on the wooden chair, propped against the arm furthest from me and again, I think I might be dead. The look on Kelly's face and how he positions everything beyond my reach makes me feel like a corpse who no longer needs material possessions.

And then I remember the accusations Lawson hurled at me when he was here. The way he used sections of the video to imply Kelly and Grant were somehow involved in what happened. Did something in that video get Kelly fired? Is that why he won't talk to me? I meant to look in the rule book to see if there was anything about dating a co-worker, but I forgot to follow through.

"Thanks for bringing me my stuff and stopping by to see me. I appreciate that you went out of your way for me." I have no idea what's left in that bag. I packed it days ago, and I've been taking things out as needed. I'm hoping for some clothes, my wallet, and keys. But it could be a pair of socks and a dirty t-shirt, for all I know.

Kelly takes one last look at me before stepping back towards the door. If this is meant to be the end, I wish he would speak and leave me with something. If he was closer, I could fill my lungs with his scent or feel his heat against my skin. I'll miss his fire and all the ways it consumes me.

"I guess this is Goodbye." It feels fitting to wish him well as he exits my life. Kelly was the closest thing to a friend I've had in a long time. Two days hidden away in his apartment might not have been enough to make me fall in love, but at the time, it was everything I needed. And two months of working side by side might not have been a lifetime, but it was long enough to change me into who I needed to be. My well-intentioned farewell is enough to stop Kelly dead in his tracks. And all I can do is watch as he crumbles.

"I thought you were dead." He moves the backpack to the floor and sits in the chair next to me. If I can stretch my arm, I might be able to touch him. "I knew I had to be there, even though you told me to wait. There was a sinking feeling in my gut that I couldn't shake. And I tried to get you out of there. I begged Hubble to put me in your place, but he didn't want two *girls* walking through the blocks together. I planned to finish the 1:00 headcount in my area before making my way back to you. That way, I wouldn't have to be in a hurry to leave, and we could sit together until 2:00." He pauses to wipe his eyes before continuing.

"You and I were doing our counts at the same time. Smith was in the tower. He was so focused on unlocking doors for Collins and me that he wasn't watching the other monitors. He never saw you disappear. It wasn't until we made it to the women's blocks that he finally noticed the fight. That's when our radios went off. 'FIGHT IN MINIMUM SECURITY BLOCK.' The doors weren't unlocking fast enough, and I was trapped. I couldn't get to you." Kelly pauses again. I can see how much all of this is hurting him.

"I heard Grant over the radio, 'WHERE'S BELK? WHERE DID YOU SEE HER LAST?' I made it into the hallway and then the airlock, but it took forever. Smith said, 'I DON'T SEE HER. I DON'T KNOW WHERE SHE IS.' When the door finally opened, I was frantic to find you, but it was chaos. There were pools of blood and bodies. When I saw you..." With the force of his voice depleted, Kelly trails off, and his head droops lower.

"I'm sorry you had to see that, but I'm right here. I'm fine." I wish I could make him understand that the only part of me that hurts right now is my heart because he is breaking it. I stretch my arm out and reach my hand toward his.

"I'm afraid to touch you. I don't know where you're hurt. And for some reason, you keep lying to me." He doesn't take my hand, so I allow it to fall away and hang off the side of the bed.

"I'm not lying to you. I'm fine." Why won't anyone listen to me? Why am I even here?

"You can't be fine. You lost so much blood." Kelly sounds mentally and physically exhausted. He needs to sleep.

"No, I didn't. There's nothing wrong with me. If there was

blood, it wasn't mine. I'm telling you the truth. I'm fine." Kelly must have been in a panic when he saw me, and his eyes were playing tricks on him. I wish I knew what to say to make him believe me. More than anything, I need him to be okay.

"If there was blood? What do you mean *if* there was blood? You were floating in a goddamn pool of it when we found you. I spent the entire night with the cleaning crew, mopping it off the fucking floor and wiping it off the bunks. Why are you acting like nothing happened?" The room is getting warmer, and I can feel his anger. "You don't end up in the hospital getting a blood transfusion if everything is fucking fine, so stop saying that!"

I look at the tape on my hand and follow the IV with my eyes. Instead of the tube being clear, it's red. A nearly empty bag hangs from the pole behind me, and the remaining liquid looks like dark tomato juice. The room spins on its axis as my vision dims at the edges. I feel sick. I mean to say his name, but there is no time. I lose my grip and fall back into the darkness.

I really hate blood.

As I open my eyes, I see Kelly talking to the nurse. I can hear that he's using his charming voice, the one he displays when he wants something. He sounds like a memory, and I wish he were talking to me like that. I start to consider that those days may be behind us, which makes me miss them all the more. All I'm getting from him now is the silent treatment or yelled at.

They both begin moving in my direction, but Kelly redirects his charm toward me before the nurse can say anything. "I'm sorry, my love. I have to get going. I need to take care of something, but I'll be back as soon as possible. I love you, more than everything." He leans over me and kisses the top of my head. "Call me if you need anything, and I'll make sure you have it."

Kelly turns and walks out of the room, leaving me confused. I'm having a difficult time following the various scenarios and linking them together. Everyone keeps saying things to me that don't make sense.

"Your fiancé is such a sweetheart. And if you don't mind my saying, very handsome. You're a lucky lady." The nurse is smiling from ear to ear. I think Kelly might have charmed her a little too well.

"Yeah. I'm quite fond of him." Fiancé? I'm not sure why she thinks Kelly and I are engaged. We've never even discussed being a couple. But I won't burst her bubble yet, not when I still hope to gather information.

I try asking about Croy and his condition, but all she'll say is that he's in surgery. There has to be some way for me to find out more. Maybe I could call the hospital later when I'm alone and pretend to be his wife. There's no way a guy who looks like that is spending his nights alone.

Since I'm unable to get any real information on Croy, I change the subject to blood transfusions. She starts to explain, but then the doctor walks in. I don't care who tells me. I want to know what's going on and when I get to leave.

The doctor goes into detail about symptoms, numbers, and treatment options. When I arrived here, they ran a bunch of different blood tests. They had to go looking for the answers I couldn't give them. Turns out I have iron deficiency anemia, and it's become pretty severe. They are certain that's what caused my body to shut down.

According to Dr. Guess, "The symptoms include extreme fatigue, problems concentrating, confusion, memory loss, weakness, pale skin, chest pain, headache, dizziness, lightheadedness, chills, irritability, poor appetite, and craving things like ice." In addition, I also went into shock, most likely caused by the violent incident at the jail.

"Well, that all makes sense when you say it like that." My mind is a jumble of thoughts and images. I've become so accustomed to feeling this way that I never considered something might be wrong. It's been so long that I can't even remember how I used to feel before my ice addiction. I thought it was Kelly making my heart race and my thoughts blurry, but these people are giving it a different name. "I think I need to close my eyes for a bit."

The nurse lifts my backpack from the floor and sets it back on the chair. "Your fiancé said he brought you some clothes. May I help you get changed before I go? It'll make you feel better to get out of that hospital gown and into your own things."

"I'm sure I can manage." My voice sounds distant, like it's coming from another room.

"It'll be a lot easier if I unhook your IV. Let me help. Then I can get out of your way so you can sleep."

"Okay." I find giving in and going along with it easier than fighting another losing battle. What's the point of struggling to convince everyone I'm fine when they already know I'm not?

She opens the bag and pulls out a pair of black sweatpants and a gray hoodie. I recognize both immediately. This is the outfit I put on the night Kelly gave me the keys to his place and told me I had free rein. The backpack contains little else. No shirt. No bra. No underwear. My iPad, earbuds, and fuzzy slipper socks are the only other things Kelly thought to include. "Well, you'll certainly be comfortable."

I put the pants on under my gown and slip the socks onto my feet. Then, worse case, this lady only has to see me topless. She helps me out of the gown and into my hoodie. Kelly must have worn it on the drive here because it's coated in his scent. The nurse reconnects my IV to a new bag of clear liquid. When she asks if I need anything else, I shake my head no.

Finally, I'm alone. I curl into a ball and pull the hood over my head, covering part of my face. Then, I take the deepest breath I can, wrap my arms around myself, and cry.

Eighteen

WHEN I OPEN MY EYES, there's a tray of food, a bouquet of flowers, and a card on my bedside table. The tray table has wheels, so I pull it toward me. I'm not hungry, but even if I were, I wouldn't eat the food here. My tray of food looks like it was prepared and delivered by the kitchen staff at the jail. The sight of it makes my throat tighten and my eyes sting. Looking past the food, I'm more interested to see who the other items are from. A tiny note stuck into the mix of yellow carnations and white daisies reads: *Get Better Soon. We Miss You. 3rd Shift.* My eyes begin to water.

It was nice of them to send flowers, even though the blame for this ordeal rests squarely on my shoulders. It might not be due to the reasons the warden claims, but I still feel bad that a quiet night turned into chaos, and I left everyone else to clean up my mess. I don't care what Kelly says. My co-workers deserve all the cookies I can bake and then some.

The envelope is metallic gold, and someone's drawn a heart where the stamp would be. I wonder which officer ran to the store and picked this one out. From the envelope's quality, I can already tell this will be one of those fancy $8.99 cards. The sort of elegant sentiment that catches your eyes and makes the other cards feel cheap by comparison. You convince yourself this is the one until you see the price on the back. You return it to the display, thinking, *I don't love you that much.*

I slide the card out of its envelope and look at the front. It's blue and teal with gold and silver embossed stars scattered across. In the middle, it reads: In a sea of stars, you shine the brightest.

This isn't the kind of Get-Well card I expected from my co-workers. Inside there's a handwritten message:

My world feels empty without you in it.
No matter where I go, the absence of you is everywhere.
I'm sorry I wasn't there to protect you.
I love you, more than everything.
-Kells

I keep reading his message, wondering if these words are meant for me. Or is he simply trying to bolster the fiancé ruse? Every time I get to the signature, it makes me laugh. *Kells* is the nickname I use for him in my phone, which was meant to be a playful secret. I've never actually addressed him that way out loud.

During our first perimeter check together, he gave me his number. We were outside alone, and there was something deeply personal about the way he kept looking at me. He pulled out his phone before we reached the door and asked if we could exchange numbers. "You need someone local you can call in case you ever get arrested."

At the time, I thought he was being funny because we work at a jail. But maybe there was more to it than that. When I'm in trouble, is Kelly my one phone call?

My thoughts snap back to reality when the nurse walks into my room. "Let's get you out of bed, shall we."

I set the card next to my flowers and push the table back to where it was.

"Oh my, you still haven't eaten anything? Are you feeling any nausea or dizziness?" She presses the back of her hand to my forehead as though I'm a little kid asking to stay home from school.

"No, I'm fine." I'm going to keep repeating myself until someone hears me. Or until I lose my voice.

My response causes her mouth to turn down at the ends. I forgot. People don't want to hear me say that everything is *fine*. I'll have to make an effort to remember that.

"Go ahead and use the restroom. Then we can take a walk in the hallway together. Alright?"

She unscrews the tube from my IV like she did when I was dressing. I'm glad I don't have to take it with me. Wish she would remove the other part from my hand. It hurts. I swing my legs over the side of the bed, preparing to stand. But she's right there, with her arm bent in front of her, like a little hand-railing. I use the bed to steady myself and brush past her. It makes me uncomfortable when people offer to help me. I don't like being perceived as weak or incapable. Plus, I know how to walk. Thankfully, she doesn't offer to help me pee.

Once we reach the doorway, I turn to the right and step in the direction I long to go. I intend to shuffle past Croy's room to sneak a peek, and the nurse doesn't seem to care which path we walk down. One. Two. Third door from mine. As we pass, I casually turn my head and look inside.

"Is he going to be alright?" I can see he's there, so the surgery must have gone well. I wonder what it was for.

"Why do you want to know about him so badly? You keep requesting information even though we refuse to tell you anything." Her tone sounds annoyed, almost suspicious even. It reminds me of Warden Lawson.

"Because it's my fault that he's in here. He saved my life, and I don't understand why." Images from the surveillance video flash through my mind as my legs carry me forward. My body moves on autopilot, but my thoughts remain 20 feet behind me.

Her expression changes, and her tone softens. "How about we make a deal? You promise to eat your dinner when it comes, and on the way back, I'll let you stop in for a moment. Then you can see for yourself how he's doing."

"I think those terms sound fair, so long as you give me a few minutes." I'd like to talk to him before I get discharged, and this may be my only opportunity.

We get to the end of the hallway and turn around. What am I going to say? Was he even awake? I didn't get a good enough look. Why are we walking so damn slowly?

As we get closer to his doorway, I can see that the curtains are drawn, and only the light behind the bed is on. The dim lighting reminds me of being in the blocks at night.

"I have to check on my other patients. Can you make it back to the room on your own? I'll be around to reattach your IV."

"I'll be fine... I can make it back to my room. Thanks." I try to control my emotions by burying them like I do at work. My slippers carry me silently across the linoleum floor like a spirit adrift in a world that no longer remembers their name.

Croy's room looks identical to mine, except no one thought to send him flowers. There's even an untouched tray of food on the table next to the bed. I move the chair closer. Sitting here next to him, he's even bigger than I remember. His upper arms are the size of my thighs, and his feet nearly hang off the end of the bed. I rest my hands on his forearm. I feel a small shock when we touch, like when you run across the carpet and grab a metal doorknob.

I don't have much time. Soon, the nurse is going to come looking for me. If I have something to say, it's now or never.

"I don't know if you can hear me, but I'd like to talk to you. I need to know that you're okay. I'm not sure why you did what you did. You could have sat back and let it play out. You don't even know me. Why would you put yourself between me and fate? I know it might not mean much, but I am sorry. This whole thing is my fault. You saved my life, and now there's a debt between us that I don't know how to repay." My apology is sincere, but my delivery is choppy as I push through the pain of my regret. "I wish you would have let them kill me."

The tears stream down my cheeks, and I'm helpless to stop them. Overwhelmed by the depth of this emotion, my head falls forward and comes to rest between my hands. How much is one life worth? Every ounce of sadness I've held back for 28 years is coming out and dripping between my fingers. This outpouring of vulnerability is the part of me he gets to keep. I can't imagine this is enough to make us square, but it's all I have left. Hopefully, some part of him will know I was here. Otherwise, he's going to wake up and wonder why the side of his bed is soaking wet.

"You are worth saving." His voice is deep and melodic. It suits him.

I sit back in the chair and wipe my face. I said all those things because I thought he was asleep. Now they're out there, and I can't unsay them. Maybe I should apologize again and go. "I'm sorry. I didn't mean to bother you."

"You're good... None of this is your fault." Croy's voice is soothing. How can he be so calm? I feel like I'm one giant knotted-up ball of tension, and he's prepared to be the scissors that have come to cut me some slack.

"Yeah, right! You don't have to do that. You don't have to be nice. I don't want you to make me feel better." A man doling out niceties feels like such bullshit. In my experience, the only time men are genuine is when they're screaming about how much they fucking hate you.

"Fair enough." He lets out a deep, steady breath as though I've somehow disappointed him. "But I didn't stand between you and your fate. You could've blacked out anywhere, in front of anyone. I could've hired a damn lawyer and paid a fine. Either one of us could have changed something, and we would've never met. Yet here we are... I might regret not kicking the shit out of those next three guys, but I could never regret protecting you. Why would I?" His tone is straightforward and honest but not angry. I want to stay and ask him a million questions, but I don't want to push my luck.

"I don't know... I should probably go. I'm supposed to be in my room. But maybe we could do this again sometime."

"I'm here all week." He delivers the line like a comedian at the end of a show, making me smile. I'm surprised by how easily he can soften my mood. I wasn't expecting that.

I walk out feeling lighter than I did when I went in. You don't realize how heavy guilt is until someone lifts it off of you. Returning to my room, I see a familiar face at the nurse's station.

"Where is she?" His tone is firm and direct.

"Hey, are you looking for me?" My voice, more cheerful than I intended, falls silent with realization. When Kelly turns to look at me, I can see he's angry.

Bubble, meet pin.

"Where the hell have you been? You haven't responded to any of my messages. Then I get here, and you aren't in your room." His eyes are black, and his hand burns into my skin when he grabs my arm. I wait until we enter my room to respond. If all he plans to do is yell at me when he's here, I'm not sure why he bothers to come.

"I'm sorry. After you left, I fell asleep. Then the nurse came in and told me I needed to walk around. I didn't get a chance to look at my phone, and I didn't hear it go off." I sit on the bed with my legs dangling over the side. Kelly stands in front of me and wraps his arms around my shoulders. When he pulls me into his chest, I can feel his heart pounding. "I'm sorry."

"No. It's not your fault. I'm the one who needs to be sorry. I drove here expecting the worst and acted like an asshole. All four inmates from last night are still in the hospital, and when I couldn't reach you, I was afraid something had happened. I can't forgive myself for not being there to protect you."

"Will you please lay with me?" I push the button that makes the bed flat and scooch to one side. I need to do for Kelly what

Croy did for me. I need to shoulder his guilt before it crushes him. "Can you come on this side and be careful of my hand."

"I don't know if this is a good idea. I don't want to hurt you." He keeps looking at me like I'm weak, and I hate it. I miss the way he used to look at me when he wanted to be the one to break me.

"Kelly, you can either lay here with me, or you can go! But if you go, please don't come back. I'm not in the mood to beg for your attention." My eyes blur with tears at the thought of never seeing him again, but I need him to start taking me seriously. He sits on the edge of the bed, testing my limits with sympathetic movements, until he's lying flat beside me. Resting my hand on his chest, I throw my leg over his. "I miss *my* Kells."

"Is that not who I am to you anymore?"

"Not when you're so angry with me." I wish I knew all the right things to say. Kelly sounds discouraged and tired, and I need him to be strong. "I don't need a fake fiancé. I want you."

"It doesn't have to be fake." He turns his face to me with a smile. "So, about this Kells things?"

"Do you not like it? In all fairness, you weren't ever supposed to know." I don't care that he looked in my phone. I'm sure he had his reasons. If scrolling through my life and seeing that I had nothing to hide made him feel better, I'm glad he did it.

"No, I like it. You're adorable." He brushes his hand against my cheek, and I melt into his touch. "I miss having you at the apartment. Do you know when you're getting discharged? I'd like to take you home."

He turns onto his side, and repositions himself so that we're face to face. I could stay in this moment forever. I only wish we were at his place instead of here, so I could fall asleep beside him.

"I'm pretty sure I get to leave sometime tomorrow morning. They have to run another blood test, and then I'm free to go." The thought of leaving is exciting until I consider returning to my shithole apartment. Not to mention, I don't even know if I have a job to go back to.

"I'll plan to come straight here after work." He slides his hand over my hip and pulls me a little closer. "I want to ask you something, and I need you to be honest with me."

"I'm always honest with you." We were doing so well. I wonder where he's going with this. I can feel all the things he doesn't say. He's holding back and keeping secrets while asking me to be honest. There's so much he isn't telling me, but I don't know what questions to ask, and I fear I may be unprepared to accept the answers.

"Are you in any pain?" His question is soaked in hesitation.

"No. Not really. My hand is sore from this stupid IV, but other than that, I'm good. Seriously, I'm alright. No one hurt me." Hopefully, this will be the last time I have to answer this question.

He lets out a sigh of relief as his eyes catch fire. "Good, because I need to be close to you." It isn't difficult to read his subtext.

"You're close to me right now." I smile and lean in to kiss him. This is the Kelly I'm used to, the one who makes me feel warm and fuzzy inside. The handsome man with a clever grin who wants to have sex all the time.

"Not nearly close enough." His touch renders me speechless as the hand on my hip migrates to my lower back, making my body turn to liquid.

We talk and kiss until I fall asleep in his arms. Being close to Kelly clouds my judgment, and I forget I'm angry. It's not what the doctor ordered, but he should have.

Nineteen

WHENEVER A NURSE COMES in to check on me, I stir and open my eyes. This time she's grinning from ear to ear as she takes in the affectionate scene. "Aren't you two just the most adorable couple?" Her eyes move from Kelly to me and back again. "Your dinner will be here in 20 minutes. I expect you to eat it."

Kelly kisses my forehead before moving to the chair. He slips his feet back into his shoes, and I have the feeling he isn't putting them on so that we can hang out. I'm so used to knowing him as the handsome guy in black boots and a uniform. It's still jarring to see him in casual attire.

"Are you leaving?" This visit was much nicer than the first, and I'm not ready for it to end. It's hard to let Kelly go when my favorite version of him sits right in front of me, within arm's reach.

"I am. But not because I want to. I still need to get a few hours of sleep in before work. And then I have to shower and find something to eat. You know how it goes." He selects my phone from the table of items, and I watch as he deletes my unread messages and clicks my ringer off silent. "I'll text you before I go in later. If you care about me at all, you'll respond."

"Don't say that. You know I care." I wonder if I'm saying enough. Do I feel more or less? Everything is so confusing. If I had a time machine, I could turn everything back 20 hours and convince him to spend another night in bed with me. In the parking lot outside of work, he joked about quitting our jobs. I didn't know back then that I should've accepted the offer. Right now, we don't even feel like the same people. How could so much change so quickly?

"I wasn't sure when you were getting out, so I brought you a change of clothes and that book you've been reading. In case you need something to distract you from missing me." Kelly wraps me in his arms and kisses me one last time. "I'll see you in the morning, okay? I love you."

He doesn't wait for my response, which is good because I'm not sure I have one. The nurse isn't here this time, so I can only assume these words were for me. I get that we've each been through our own version of the same traumatic event, but is that the kind of thing that induces a complex feeling like love? Rolling the table closer, I run my fingertips over the front of his card. I've read his message several times, and when I close my eyes, I see it written there. I allow myself a moment to miss him, and then I have to move on. Holding the flowers to my nose, I breathe in their fragrance. They smell like a warm breeze drenched in the summer sun. I'll have to make sure I thank everyone when I get back.

The book Kelly brought is sitting on top of my backpack. Seeing it reminds me of last night and the guy who was up reading at 1:00 am. I walk to the nurse's station and ask to borrow a pen. On the dedication page, I jot down a song lyric that comes to mind and a heartfelt addition.

"Thanks for the Memories,
Even though they weren't so Great."
Irregardless, I will cherish them always.
-Heather Belk

It's kind of a dumb message, but hopefully, he understands what I'm trying to say. When I get to Croy's room, his eyes are closed. I might be able to leave the book and sneak out without him noticing.

"Hey, if it isn't everyone's favorite Officer. Making sure I didn't escape? Or did you come to bust me out?" He winks, and I can't help but laugh.

I'm used to guys at the jail flirting with me. When you're one of the only women they get to see, you start to look good to everyone. But this feels different. I imagine his time has elapsed, and he's been processed out. Otherwise, he'd be handcuffed to the bed with a uniformed police officer sitting outside the door.

"The escape plan is hidden in the pages of this book. Memorize it. We go at midnight." I set his gift on the table and turn to leave.

"Can we make it 1:00 am?"

There's a lot to that question, isn't there, even though the conversation leading to it was playful banter. I stop before the doorway and turn around. "I've been wondering about something."

"That doesn't surprise me. You seem like the type of girl who's always wondering about something. What's on your mind?"

Should I be offended that he referred to me as a *girl*? I'm 28 years old. Surely, that's old enough to be considered a woman. Of course, I do the same thing. Anyone younger than me is a boy or girl, regardless of age. How old is Croy? I guess I can let it slide. "Anyways... I was curious about how you knew my name."

"It's on your uniform." He's trying to throw me off with his confidence and playful smile, but it isn't going to work.

"No, my last name is on my uniform, and you called me by my first name, which is interesting because no one in Oak Falls calls me that. So, how did you know?" I would have remembered meeting a guy like this. Not only is he enormous, but he's also sexy as fuck. Under normal circumstances, seeing him would have made my mouth drop open. So, I know that I wasn't the one to let that information slip. Not to mention, I wasn't even at work the night he came in.

"It's kind of a long story." He says as I walk over to the chair and sit, hoping to convey that I'm not going anywhere until he tells me. "Okay. So, when I was getting booked in, the two officers at the desk were talking about you. Well, not talking so much as bragging. The one guy was telling a story about how he met you before you landed a job there, and had you not been dating his friend; he would've tried to take you home. He kept calling you Heather, and the other guy looked like he was about to commit murder. The dark-haired one rattled on nonstop while I was fingerprinted and changed out. The way he spoke about you… Well, Anyways. As soon as I saw you, I knew you were the girl all the fuss was about. And then that same guy, your boyfriend, came in for headcount. That's how I knew for certain that you were her. Heather, the temptress of Oak Falls. So, yeah. Guess it wasn't that long of a story." Croy always seems to have a smile on his face, like he's the only one in on the joke. It's cute. I'll give him that. However, at this moment, it's also making me want to choke the life out of him.

"What the fuck are you talking about? Are you being serious right now? What the hell is wrong with them? This is the type of stupid-ass shit they talk about when I'm not there?" I'm not sure why I'm so angry, but I am. This whole story feels like such a betrayal. At work, we don't use first names or talk about our personal lives. Why would they be so careless, especially if they claim to like me?

"Don't be mad. I was the only one around to hear them, and I didn't repeat any of it. You have my word. If I'm being honest, I was dying to get a look at you. Helen of Troy."

"Yeah, well. Sorry to disappoint." My tone is as sharp as a well-crafted prison shank.

"Quite the opposite. Neither of them did you justice." He sits forward, swinging his legs over the side of the bed. My feet always dangle when I'm seated in that position, but his are planted squarely on the floor. We're face to face, yet again, though quite a bit further apart this time. I can't help but notice how blue his eyes are. The color reminds me of the warm ocean water around the Bahamas. I wish I could get lost there and never be found.

"Would you like to have dinner with me?"

Yet again, I'm caught off guard and swimming in confusion. "You mean like a date?"

The food runner walks into the room carrying a tray. He picks up the uneaten lunch from the table and replaces it with dinner.

"Would you mind bringing the tray from her room? Thanks." It's worded like a question, but he means it to be a command, albeit a friendly one. I get the feeling that Croy doesn't hear the word *no* with any frequency.

"Ma'am, the room number?" This kid wants to get out of here as quickly as possible. I wonder if that's due to a strict schedule or the whispered stories floating around the sterile, air-conditioned corridors. What are people saying about the helpless corrections officer and the would-be killer inmates?

"307, but I can grab it." I don't like to delay people when they're in the middle of something.

"No need. I still have it on my cart. I was headed that way." He retrieves the tray and sets it on the table. "You both have a nice night." And with that, he's off.

"Alright then. Mmmmm. Look at all of this delicious hospital food." My statement is dripping with sarcasm.

"Makes me miss jail." Croy looks at me, and we both laugh.

He's funny in an effortless way. Or maybe I'm desperate for a laugh. Whatever it is, I find it easy to talk to him. I don't feel so weighed down by reality when we're going back and forth about dumb shit.

"Oh, by the way, I'm jealous of your ensemble." He points his fork at me and waves it in a sort of figure-eight pattern.

"Yeah, I know. I'm killin' it over here." Sarcasm is my go-to way of deflecting anything resembling a compliment.

"Comfort is key." It's then that I notice he's still in the hospital gown. No flowers, no clothes, no personal items, and no visitors that I've seen. Does anyone even know that he's here?

"Hey, I'll be right back. I need to grab my phone out of my room. Feel free to eat *all* of my food while I'm gone." I shoot him a smile and speed walk back to my room. It so happens that I am a huge fan of oversized sweatpants and hoodies. Kelly knows this about me, so I'm willing to bet that's what he brought me to change into. Sure enough, a pair of XL men's sweats and a matching hoodie are folded and stuffed in my backpack.

> : Thank you for knowing me so well. You're the best.

> Kells: I'm glad you still think so.

No one attempts to stop me on my return trip. It seems word has spread quickly that Croy is the hero of my story and not the villain. I wonder how many facts they know and how much they've created in their heads.

Walking into his room, I hold the stacked clothes out in front of me and bow as if I'm presenting offerings to the king. "I come bearing gifts."

"If those are your skinny-ass boyfriend's clothes, they aren't going to fit." He makes no attempt to hide his smirk. I can tell he's been waiting to get that dig in.

"One. He's not my boyfriend. Two. They're my clothes. And three. Shut up and put them on. They'll fit." I've stolen enough clothing from ex-boyfriends to know what will fit who.

When Croy stands, it's the first time I fully experience our immense size difference. I suddenly feel tiny, though not insignificant. I wonder if I should look away, but I watch as he gets dressed the same way I did in front of the nurse. The notable departure being, after he gets the sweatpants on, he pulls the gown off and stands there half-naked in front of me. Holy Shit! This guy is the physical embodiment of everything fantasy I had during my hormonal teenage years. "See, I told you they would fit." My 14-year-old self is about to have a heart attack.

Croy sits back on the bed, and I return to the chair. My legs always hurt, for some reason, when I have to sit normally, so I pull them up and sit cris-cross applesauce. I heard a lady use that term while wrangling a group of kids at the library. I thought it was awesome, so I stole it and have used the term ever since.

"You can put your legs on the side of the bed if you want." Croy pats the mattress with his hand.

So, he's funny, intelligent, sexy, observant... and still half-naked. I'm going to need to be careful. This kind of guy could carry me away, and I wouldn't even scream for help. My heart is running in time with my racing thoughts, and I can only hope that my cheeks aren't as red as they feel.

The nurse comes around every hour to check on us, and it reminds me of being at work. I didn't realize how annoying it was until I was on the receiving end of things. When she came in the first time, I asked her to unhook Croy's IV so he could get the hoodie on. I should have kept my mouth shut. Don't get me wrong, he still looks good, but I miss looking at his tattoos.

Finally, I break down and pull the chair close enough to put my feet on the edge of the bed. We discuss all the usual stuff, music, movies, food, and books. We've even seen a lot of the same bands in concert. I'm not surprised by how much we have in common. We'll be the same age on my birthday next week, so it makes sense that we would have grown up seeing the same movies and listening to the same music. Plus, we're both covered in tattoos, and that's kind of a niche group.

Turns out he went to college not far from my hometown. When he mentions that he played football in high school and college, I'm flooded with all my old schoolgirl fantasies. I always wanted to date a football player in high school, but I wasn't skinny enough to be seen with in public.

It's already 10:00 pm when my phone goes off. How did it get so late?

Kells: Do you need anything before I go to work? I have a little extra time.

: I should be okay, but I appreciate the offer. I'd rather not have too much stuff here since I'm getting released in the morning. Did you get some sleep?

Kells: I would have slept better with you next to me. You have no idea how hard it was for me to leave you. I can't wait to have you back.

: Yeah. It'll be nice to get out of here. I have to make sure to take a shower before I leave.

Kells: Why?

: Because I don't have a shower at my place, remember?

"Is that the GQ model or Mr. Guns and Ammo?" Croy thinks he's clever. I can see it written all over his face. He also seems to be fishing for information about my dating life without directly asking.

"GQ," I say, with a laugh tacked on at the end. "Why do you ask?"

"Well, I wasn't going to say anything, but I heard him earlier in the hallway. Why do you let him talk to you like that?" Croy's usual joking tone has disappeared and been replaced with something else. Concern, maybe? I'm not sure.

"He's not himself at the moment, after everything that happened. I don't know. He's different, somehow. Kelly isn't normally an asshole. I'm giving him a pass for the day because he's stressed. Plus, he's my ride out of here. If I want to get home, I can't get too mad at him." I should add that I stood my ground eventually. Croy didn't hear that part because I don't like to engage in public displays.

"So, some horrible shit happens *to you,* and your boyfriend gets to be angrier about it than you are? Explain that to me."

The *boyfriend* thing is beginning to rub me the wrong way. I don't like repeating myself, but I'll say it again for the people in the back. "Kelly is *not* my boyfriend. And he's allowed to feel however he wants. We each experienced last night differently. I'm not upset because I was somewhere else for most of it. You were busy kicking the shit out of people. And Kelly was trapped in a different part of the jail. It's our job to protect each other, and he feels like he failed me. He believes the situation could have been prevented had he followed his gut instincts instead of listening to me." My throat feels tight, and my eyes are beginning to sting. "What am I supposed to do? I don't want anyone to feel guilty. Especially when everything is my fault." I can feel the weight of my guilt returning like bricks being dropped into a canvas bag.

"It wasn't exactly a party for me. I was stabbed." He touches the place where his arm is bandaged.

"Exactly. How do you not hate me?" Cast a few more stones into my bag of guilt. Why not? Croy was stabbed and used as a human punching bag while protecting me from ruffians. Like I'm some goddamn sleeping beauty. And I'm sitting here defending Kelly's hurt feelings. When did I become a complete asshole?

"Because it wasn't your fault." He holds out his arms toward me and motions with his hands. "Come Here."

Croy grabs me by the arms and pulls me toward him the second I get on my feet. I don't have time to react. My legs are numb from being elevated for so long, and I nearly drop to the floor. He scoops my body into his arms and sets me on his lap. One arm cradles my legs, and the other is around my back. I bury my face between his neck and shoulder, fighting back the tears.

"I could never hate you, Heather. Getting stabbed and taking a few hits was a small price to pay. If I had the choice, I would spend the rest of my life protecting you." Everything about Croy makes me feel safe. As I relax into him, he wraps both arms around my body and holds me. My 15-year-old self is falling to pieces.

I feel small, like a little kid with a skinned knee crying in a parent's arms.

"You mentioned that during the fight, you were someplace else. Where do you think you were?" It's late, and the hospital is quiet. I'm still sitting on his lap, held securely in his arms, so when he speaks, the words are barely above a whisper. "Did they ever figure out why you passed out? I kept asking the nurses if you were okay, but they wouldn't tell me anything."

"My iron level dropped so low that my body shut down." I probably shouldn't admit my weakness, but Croy already sees me for exactly who I am. "The nurses wouldn't tell me anything about you either, no matter how many times I asked. As for where I went, I'm not sure. I wasn't in my body. I was someplace dark and empty. It was the complete lack of all things until you said my name. Then your voice bounced from one wall to another. It was like I could see your words. I tried to follow the path they had traveled. And eventually, I was able to locate my individual senses and turn them back on. When I could finally see, you were there. I felt like I knew you before I met you. But not in real life. It was like I knew you from a dream... Anyways, I'm sure that sounds pretty stupid." I can't believe I said all of that. My 16-year-old self is dying of embarrassment. "Do you want me to go?"

"What part of this moment gave you the impression that I wanted you to go?" His mouth is so close to my ear that I can feel his words as they brush past. "If you want to go, I'll walk you back to your room. If you want to stay, you should stay. The choice is always yours to make."

"Well, it isn't appropriate for me to be sitting on your lap." I don't want to move, but I also don't need to get caught like this by a nurse.

"Inappropriate because of where we are or because of who we were when we met?" His tone reflects genuine concern. I wonder if he's worried about the same thing I am. Do we remain forever branded with the titles officer and inmate? If so, we can't know each other.

"I don't know. Either. Neither. Both." This is something I have to think about. I feel bonded to this man. He did save my life, after all. But there are other factors to consider. How would this relationship make me look at work? What's going on with me and Kelly? Would he be okay with me having this person in my life? To what extent do I want Croy in my life? Friends? More than friends? A stranger that I met once in passing? That last one doesn't feel right at all.

Croy moves me slowly off his lap. Once I get my feet planted under me, he lets go. I'm only a foot away, but it feels like a mile. "I'm sorry that we met where we did. I swear to you. I'm not a bad person." The entire mood in the room has shifted. "And I'm sorry that I grabbed you like that. I shouldn't have put my hands on you."

"I know what kind of person you are, so stop apologizing." I take his hands and put them on my hips, wanting to feel connected. Slowly, his grip tightens as he inches me forward. "I told you. I knew you before I met you." I step forward, wedging myself between his thighs, and suck in a breath. I'm so tired of being the girl who follows the rules. I lean forward to align our lips, close my eyes, and kiss him.

My 17-year-old self finally fell in love.

Twenty

I'M BACK in my room, lying in bed, but my thoughts are 30 feet down the hall. What the hell am I doing? Why did I kiss him? I grab the earbuds from my bag and connect them to my phone. I want to disappear. What kind of blood did they give me? This time of night, there's only one distraction available if I'm looking to escape.

> : Take my mind off of everything and force me to forget.

Kells: What's going on, babe? Is everything alright? I'm surprised you're still awake. Not that I'm complaining. I love hearing from you.

> : You know how it is. Vampire sleep schedule. Plus, I took that nap earlier when you were here.

Kells: I remember. I've been thinking about it since I left. You felt so good in my arms. I didn't want to let go. I should've stayed with you. I'm working intake tonight, but I don't want to be here.

: Who's the booking officer?

Kells: Grant. That asshole. He's playing cards on the computer and being as worthless as ever.

Oh, wonderful. Here we go again with these two. I can only imagine what kind of tales they're spinning about me tonight. Or maybe I'm old news, and they've run out of things to say. It's no secret that Kelly and I have been sleeping together. Perhaps that will be enough for him to lock his lips and leave the key at home on the nightstand.

: He's still your favorite person, I see. That should make for a fun night. Try not to spend the entire shift talking about me.

Kells: As if I could sit in this place and think of anyone else. You're all anyone's talking about. Do you not want people to know about us?

: That cat's already out of the bag and living in the next town over. Anyways, that's not what I meant. I was talking about the last time you guys worked together. When you shared stories.

Kells: Well, he did ask about you. Everyone did. I don't think you'll have to worry about getting put in minimum ever again. There are two people posted there now. Think that might be a permanent thing.

Kelly is either playing coy and skirting the issue to avoid a fight, or he doesn't know to read between the lines. I suppose it doesn't matter at this point. Everyone at the jail thinks the worst of me, including the inmates. Imagine the letters I'd get if

Lawson let slip his theory about me being the town whore. Someone would need to order extra envelopes in preparation for all my fan mail.

> : Not sure why they ever thought it was a good idea to cut it down to one person at night. Out of curiosity, do you know if Croy Jepsen booked out? I don't want personal info on him, just a yes or no.

Kells: Why are you asking about the inmate that put four people in the hospital last night?

> : It was only three people.

Kells: Three inmates that he nearly killed and my girlfriend. Grant said he booked out this morning. You don't owe that guy anything. You can't trust him. Babe, you need to stay away from him. Now is not the time to be naïve.

> : Yeah, I know. I was just asking a question.

There's a tapping at the doorway of my room, and Croy is standing there, looking adorable in my spare set of clothes. "Can I come in?"

"Of course." My heart races in my chest as he moves closer, and my body begins to tingle. I find myself staring at his lips, unable to think. Why the hell did I kiss him? And what is he doing here in my room?

"You still want to run away together?" He sounds serious.

What is he talking about? Whatever the question, my body is screaming *yes* at the top of its lungs. I look at the time and remember the book. "I could be persuaded."

"Would you like to extend our date and watch a movie? I'm not ready to let you go." His touch against my leg sends an electrical current running back and forth between us. And I'm starting to wonder if he isn't some kind of fancy robot. That would explain why he lacks a general concern for his own safety. There's nothing to be afraid of when you're indestructible.

"I don't want to be too loud." It might be rude to put on the TV at this hour. I have a bunch of movies on my computer, so that could be an option.

"I could be quiet." Croy winks and squeezes my leg in case I missed the subtext.

"I'm not sure I could be." I bite my lip as my mind slips straight into the gutter. Every time I close my eyes, he's all I see.

"Fuck. You're making it difficult for me to be a gentleman. Please suggest something PG before I lock the door and tear your clothes off." His hand moves slowly up my thigh.

"Umm…" I can't think when he's touching me and talking about locked doors and torn clothes. I want to beg him to give in, not encourage him to stop.

"Do you wanna listen to my gym playlist? I'll let you critique my taste in music." It's the first thing I can think of that isn't sex. We look at each other and laugh. That was a close one.

Croy takes the phone from my hand and starts typing. "You should password protect your devices."

"Nah. I don't like secrets. The second a guy puts a password on his phone, I know he's cheating on me." I'm not sure why any guy thinks he's getting away with something. They're always so obvious about it. If you go from being a normal person to sitting on your phone like it's an egg, you're a cheater.

"A guy would have to be an idiot to have you and look elsewhere." He returns the phone but doesn't let go when I take it. "I put my number in there. If you text me, I'll respond. But if I don't hear from you, I'll know you don't see a place for me in your life, and I won't bother you. The choice is yours." He releases the phone but continues to hold me in his gaze. "Our collective fate is officially in your hands."

I scroll through my contact list and find his name.

: Tag. You're it!

"Do you know how long you'll be stuck in here? I'm sure you're eager to get back to your life." I can't imagine anyone enjoying being in the hospital. It's a lot like jail, except you get your own room.

"I think I'm getting released in the morning." I get the sense that he has more on his mind than he says.

"Is someone coming to pick you up? Does anyone even know that you're here?" I'm curious who Croy's one phone call is. The name and number would be listed in his file at work from the night he booked in. If I'm ever feeling nosey, I could invade his privacy and look it up. Or I suppose I could simply ask him.

"No, I didn't tell anyone where I was headed. I'll figure something out. My car is parked at the jail, and I have to get my wallet and clothes and keys... Which reminds me, if it's okay, I need to buy these clothes from you. I'm pretty sure they might have burned what we came in wearing. So, you could pretty much name your price."

I can't believe they would have done that. The hospital wouldn't throw our clothes away, would they? I'm sure everything is in a bio-hazard bag, labeled with our room number or name, and hung on a rack in a locked storage closet. We have a room like that at the jail, where personal belonging are kept until your release papers are signed. I imagine the hospital might have a room like that. I don't care about the jail scrubs Croy was wearing. That shit was trash when he put it on. But what about my uniform? And Kelly's belt?

"I was wearing my watch at some point, but they must have taken it off." I rub my hand over my wrist. "As for the clothes, they're yours. And if you need a ride, I'm headed back that way. I only live a mile from the jail." I know everyone keeps trying to convince me that I don't owe Croy my loyalty, but that can't possibly be true. The trinkets I'm offering pale in comparison to what he's given me. My life has to be worth more than sweatpants and a half-read book.

"There's no way you'll convince your boy to drive me

140

anywhere besides off a cliff. But I appreciate the offer. It's sweet of you to care. It's only 10 miles from here to the jail. I can walk."

This conversation is stupid. I won't leave him to walk 10 miles in the middle of summer wearing sweatpants, a hoodie, and hospital socks. I can't live with the idea of that.

: Will you do me a huge favor?

Kells: I would do anything for you.

: Okay, don't get mad. Can we give Croy a ride back to the jail if he gets released when I do?

Kells: Have you lost your fucking mind? You're not seriously asking me to do this! You know how that would make us look. If anyone here found out... We can't be seen talking to him. You know that.

I barely have enough time to be nervous before Kelly's response appears on my screen. How quickly we went from "I would do anything for you" to "Have you lost your fucking mind?" I suppose that's to be expected. Maybe I have lost my mind. I thought I could count on Kelly as a friend, but he's behaving more like a jealous boyfriend. No wonder I have to keep repeating myself.

: You're right. Forget I asked. I wasn't thinking about the implications. You don't owe me any favors. I can drive back in my car.

Kells: That's not happening. It's not your job to save him. Why is this so important to you? He can have the hospital call here, and they can send someone with the van.

Absolutely not! I'm not having Croy escorted out of here like some common criminal when he should be hailed a hero. Kelly might not owe me anything, but I owe Croy my life. You'd think the guy who claims to love me would want to shake the hand of the man who kept me alive, not kick him into the ditch.

> : He doesn't need a goddamn police escort. He needs a ride. Forget it. I have my phone. I'll order a ride to the jail and walk home from there.

Kells: No! I'm picking you up. And this conversation is over.

> : I would rather you not. I'm tired of fighting with you. The constant push and pull are more than I can handle. Whatever this was, it's not working. I'm sorry.

Kells: What the fuck is going on? Is this guilt?

"You're right. He hates you." I shake my head and fake a smile. There's nothing else to do or say. I'm on my own.

"Don't do that, Heather. Please don't blow up your life to make a place for me. I never want to be the reason you lose something." Croy attempts to sit on the bed beside me, but there isn't enough room. Without warning, he grips my hips and lifts my ass off the mattress high enough to reposition me between his legs. "Enough stalling. Let's hear this playlist."

We each take an earbud, and I hit shuffle as I lean back against his chest. The first song to come on is Hostage by Billie Eilish. As we listen together, I sink further into his embrace. From now until the end, no matter what happens next, this song will remain tethered to this moment in time.

As crazy as it sounds, I don't know how I'm going to exist apart from him. When our paths intersected, everything changed. For twenty-eight years, I've been living as half a person. Only I didn't know what was missing until I became whole. We've merged in such a way that losing Croy would mean splitting my soul in half again. And I don't know anyone who could survive that.

Twenty~One

I DON'T REMEMBER FALLING asleep, but the room is blanketed in sunshine when I wake up. My phone is back on the table, and someone has tucked me neatly into bed. A tray of breakfast has been dropped off, but I have no intention of eating. Every new day is a great opportunity for a fresh start, and the best way to start any day is with a hot shower. I'd better get one while I can. Worst case, there's always the shower at the gym if desperate times should call for desperate measures.

I have no choice but to get back into Kelly's hoodie and sweats after I finish my morning routine. Wearing them now, after everything that's been said, feels uncomfortable, but I can't exactly walk out of here naked. Kelly and I always stood on solid ground with each other until I ruined everything by having sex with him. I know I feel something when I'm around him. There's a bond between us that grew over time. I care about him deeply, but I wouldn't say I'm in love.

Leaving the hospital is bittersweet. I look forward to being alone and choosing what I eat and when. I'm excited about no more IV or hourly nurse checks. I want to get back to my life, even if I'm not sure what parts are left for me to return to. But I will miss hanging out with Croy. I've enjoyed our conversations and the times we've spent in silence. The more I talk to him, the more I learn about myself.

The nurse walks into my room as I'm exiting the bathroom. "I need to do a quick blood draw, and then you can be on your way. Let's get that IV out of your hand and get you bandaged up."

You'd think a girl half covered in tattoos wouldn't mind a couple of needles, but you'd be wrong. Tattoo needles thrill and excite me. Hospital needles, on the other hand, make me squirm and ache. I have to close my eyes and look away so I don't pass out.

Without the clothes I came in wearing, there aren't many personal items in my room. I'm able to stuff everything into my backpack and carry the flowers. For a second, I consider throwing away my card, but I can't bring myself to do it. I'm upset with Kelly, but I don't hate him, and I'm certainly not excited about the prospect of losing him. What I want is for him to stop being so angry with me. Hopefully, we can still be cordial at work.

I'm nearly certain the nurse has everything she needs from me, so I approach Croy's room, eager to see him. Sadly, my excitement is short-lived when I get to the doorway and see Kelly standing inside. As I walk in, he moves beside me and snakes an arm around my waist.

"Good morning, love. Here, let me take your bag. I wanted to help you pack, but I thought I should stop in here first. I know you're ready to get home so we can relax." He's pretending to talk to me, but clearly, his words are meant for the other person in the room. Kelly's tone isn't charming, it's cocky, and I'm not impressed.

"My girl mentioned that you might need a ride back to jail. We would be happy to drop you off. If you're ready to go?" Kelly presses the side of his body to mine, staking his claim while addressing the competition.

I feel myself on the cusp of blowing a gasket. What the fuck is he doing? No, I take that back. I know exactly what he's doing. He's being an asshole, masquerading as a nice guy.

"Sure thing. It was nice of her to offer. Heather really is the best. Not sure I could walk out of here without her. You know, because I'd still be naked." Croy winks at me, and Kelly is on the verge of combustion.

I rest my hand against his leg, hoping physical contact will help calm him. We don't need to make a scene. This has already gone far enough. All three of us have a lot to lose if a fight breaks out and the cops get called.

"If you two are done measuring dicks and talking about me like I'm not here, perhaps we could go." My annoyance seems sufficient to shove them back into their separate corners long enough to get us moving toward the exit.

Kelly grabs my hand in the hallway and doesn't let go until we're in the car. I feel suffocated by the tension between them. This drive feels like the longest 20 minutes of my life. When we pull into the jail parking lot, Kelly stops near the door.

"Thanks for the ride. I appreciate it." Croy's tone has returned to its usual level of friendliness. When he opens his door to get out, I mirror his action.

Kelly grabs my arm. "What are you doing? We're going home."

"Please don't make this a fight. If you let go of my arm, I'll go home with you. But I'd like to say goodbye." My voice is pleading and reassuring. I need Kelly to tone it down before he starts something he won't be alive to finish.

When I stand, Croy wraps me in his arms and pulls me into his chest. Even in the jail parking lot, he isn't afraid of my skinny-ass, GQ model, fake boyfriend waiting in the car. With his chin resting on my head, I feel calm and safe. He keeps his voice low and says, "Are you going to be okay if you leave with him? You can come with me. I promise I'll never let anything bad happen to you. And you wouldn't owe me a thing. I give you my word." There's nothing empty about his promise, but that doesn't mean I can go with him.

"This doesn't have to be goodbye forever, but I need you to let me go." I'm afraid if Kelly hears any of this, I'm going to be in even more trouble.

"Heather, I'll always be here for you. No matter what you choose to do next. No matter how much time passes. If you call me, I will show up."

Every word he speaks cuts deeper. And I wish I had time to explain. I desperately need Croy to understand I'm not walking away from him. Not the way he thinks I am. I can't jump from one guy to the next and expect him to solve my problems. At some point, I need to be the one calling the shots in my own life. I love that he wants to protect me, but I need him to trust that I can protect myself.

"I have to go... But if you ever have the time or the inclination, come find me." I unwrap my arms from around his back and push against his waist. He's solid muscle layered over a steel frame but releases me at the slightest sign of my resistance.

"I found you in my dreams and inside of a jail. I'm confident I can track you down in Oak Falls." He kisses the top of my head and turns towards the building.

I have to choke back my tears before getting in the car. This moment is only the first hard thing I have to do today.

The ride to Kelly's apartment is quiet. He reaches over and puts his hand on my thigh, stroking his thumb back and forth. I'm emotionally drained, so I'm thankful for this moment of peace between us. When we exit the car, he reaches for my hand, and I let him take it. His fingers remain interlocked with mine until we get into the bedroom.

"Can we please take a nap? I'm exhausted, and all I want is to sleep with you in my arms again." His request means continued peace, so I can't say no.

"Okay." I feel shattered and empty. I feel weak. So much for all that strength I thought I'd found. I guess it's easy to feel strong when 260 lbs. of muscle is wrapped around you.

"Do you want to change out of those clothes? I'm sure you're tired of being in them." Is he asking me because I've been wearing them for a day and a half or because they're his clothes? Either way.

"I'm fine." I don't give a damn about my clothes right now.

"Babe, please take them off and lay with me. I need to feel you next to me." Kelly drops his own clothes in a pile on the floor and gets under the comforter. Then he pats the empty side of the bed where I'm expected to join him. My body goes through the motions like a marionette. Kelly is still very much in control.

"Did you and that guy have sex?" His voice is calm and measured. I doubt it will stay that way for long if I answer his questions incorrectly.

"No. Of course not. The guy is a stranger, and we were in a hospital." Nothing like that came close to happening, even though the desire might have been present. It wasn't exactly a great location. "I had a hard enough time getting a nurse to let me talk to him."

"Did you read the card I left for you?

"Yes. I read it half a dozen times, if not more. Your message was sweet. I liked it." I loved the card and the message he wrote inside. It was the way he spoke to me the rest of the time that was the problem.

"I missed you so much. Tell me you're still my girl, and everything can go back to the way it was." He presses his hand against my chest, directly over my heart. I can feel the fire inside of him growing. If I let him, he will consume me. "Tell me you want me as much as I want you."

"I do." I close my eyes and go to a different place.

Kelly's passion feels laced with rage as he devours what fragments of me remain. I suppose I could stop him, but I don't care, and he doesn't bother to notice. In the end, this is easier than fighting and quicker. I don't think he's a bad person. He just isn't *my* person. If I had said No or asked him to stop, he would have stopped.

Kelly falls asleep in a sweaty heap, with his arm thrown over me. I wait until he's out cold, then slide out of bed and get dressed. Collecting my phone and earbuds off the counter, I unlock the patio door with his keys. All I'm looking for right now is a moment of solitude. It's nice out here, and the summer sun feels energizing. I can almost feel my internal battery recharging.

> : Did you make it home in one piece? I wasn't sure how long your drive would be, and I didn't want to bother you. If you're still in the car, you can text me later.

Croy: Hearing from you is a highlight, not a bother. I'm at home, safe and sound. It was a short drive. I take it you're safe?

> : Yeah, I'm fine.

Is it weird that I miss being in the hospital? At first, I was desperate to get out, but now I miss knowing Croy is nearby. I miss his face and his laugh, and his overwhelming presence. I wish I could tell him I'm thinking about him, but I can't.

Croy: Be straight with me. Are you two together or not? I'll be here for you either way. But I need to know the truth.

> : I swear to you, Kelly and I are NOT together. I don't even know his first name. We work together. He was nice enough to let me come to his place a few days ago to relax because my apartment is a nightmare. But since then, a lot's happened. He's changed. I thought we were friends, but I guess not. Everything is fine. I can find my keys when he goes to work. Then I'll be able to leave.

Croy: What the fuck! Heather, are you being serious right now? I knew something wasn't right. Why did I let you get in a car with him? Tell me where you are, and I'll come get you.

Shit! I didn't word that right. I made it sound like Kelly abducted me from the hospital, and now Croy thinks I have Stockholm syndrome. If I stick my foot any further into my mouth, I'll end up kicking myself in the ass.

> : No. That's not what I meant. I don't want you to think that I'm kidnapped or something. I wasn't trying to make a big thing of it. I probably didn't explain it very well. Everything is fine. I'm out on the balcony getting some air.

> Croy: Please, Heather. I'm begging you. Let me sort this out for you. He isn't going to do anything if I'm there. Guys like that are only tough when they know they can win.

As much as I would love to see Croy's version of "sort this out," I can't have him directing any of that masculine aggression toward Kelly. We might not be cops, but we are law enforcement adjacent. If Croy shows up looking for me, it will make every false claim Warden Lawson made about me shine like truth. And then I'll be the one in jail asking for envelopes and toilet paper.

> : This isn't anything new to me. I put myself in this situation, so I need to be the one to get myself out. I'm sorry. I shouldn't have said anything. Forget that I messaged you.

> Croy: Wait! If you think you can handle it, then I'll stay out of your business with him. We can talk about something else. Anything. I'm not ready to let you go.

Croy and I text back and forth for the next few hours. He doesn't mention Kelly again. But we do spend a solid hour talking about football and Cleveland sports. I ask for his gym playlist because I know he has one, and I listen to each song online. We take turns asking each other questions ranging from favorite color to bucket list dreams. The conversation flows as effortlessly as it did in the hospital, and I can almost picture him sitting across from me on the patio as we text.

Don't get me wrong, part of me would love to have Croy ride in on a white horse and save me, but the other 72% has no interest in being the damsel in distress. I don't want him to think of me as helpless and weak. Plus, I owe him enough already as it is.

Kelly is the current version of the same guys I've been with since I was seventeen. I'm nearly certain that I can handle it gracefully. Sneaking out while he's asleep will only cause more issues. Once he's awake, we can have a conversation and part ways as friends. If Kelly knew me, he wouldn't be interested in being with me.

I go inside to use the restroom and get something to drink. It's hot on the patio, and my mouth is dry from laughing. Kelly must hear me go back outside because he follows me.

"I love it out here" He sits in the chair across from me and appears to be in a good mood. "Have you been awake this whole time? You could've woken me up. I would've rather spent the time with you."

"I couldn't sleep. And I didn't want to disturb you. So I came out here to listen to music on my phone... Do you know where my keys are? I'd like to drive to my place and check on my stuff. I know I don't have much, but I haven't been there in a few days, and there's something shady about the downstairs neighbor."

"I wanted to talk to you about that. Remember when you called and left that voicemail for your landlord?"

"Yeah. Why?" Where is he going with this?

"Well. You left your phone on the desk in minimum, and when I sent a text to check on you, it started glowing. That's why I had it when I came to see you at the hospital. Anyways, your landlord called before I left work, and I answered it. She said that if you hated your place so much, she would let you out of your lease. But she was only willing to give you one day to get out. So I had to make a snap decision. That's where I went after I told you I had to take care of something."

"I don't understand. What are you saying?"

"When I went to your place, I thought you and I were still together. I thought I was helping you get out of a lease you hated. You had so much on your plate, and I didn't want to add anything else to it. Please believe me when I tell you that I only had the best intentions."

"Okay. So?"

"So, I cleaned out your place and turned over your keys. You're no longer stuck in your lease. Anything I thought you might need is in the apartment, and the rest is in your car. I'm sorry. I feel like a complete asshole right now and a total idiot. I thought you'd be happy to get rid of that place, but I never considered that you'd be unhappy here with me."

"So, I'm homeless?"

"Babe, please don't be upset. I feel terrible. You're welcome to stay here as long as it takes while you look for a new place. We can go back to the original deal. No strings. I don't want you to feel like a prisoner here. I'm sorry that I was being so pushy. I should have listened to what you weren't saying and given you time. It was selfish of me to think that sex was still on the table."

"This is a lot for me to process. You canceled my lease without discussing it with me. Then moved me into your place. Not once have we talked about what this relationship even is. And now you're worried about sex and consent. It's all too much. But let me set your mind at ease, Kelly. You didn't make me do anything I didn't want to do. I'm not mad at you. And I don't feel taken advantage of. I was upset about our interactions at the hospital, and I wanted to have a conversation. But what's done is done."

"I'm glad you're not mad at me, but I still owe you an apology. I'm sorry. You weren't in the mood this morning, and I should've respected that. I missed you, and I wanted to feel close to you again. But I wasn't listening to what you wanted, and I should have been." Kelly is doing damage control while my life falls apart. He's afraid he crossed the line, and he's accusing himself of something I can't even be bothered to care about.

"So, I have nowhere to go?" My eyes fill with tears, and I feel the dam about to break. Kelly stands and moves beside me. When he embraces me, his touch is an unwelcome gesture. I don't even want to look at him right now.

"I'm sorry I fucked up." His apology sounds sincere, and I can follow his logic. He seems desperate for my forgiveness, but it's hard for me to trust his motives.

I wish he would have spoken to me before making decisions about my life, but I understand a lot was happening at once. I wasn't exactly clear-headed enough to exercise my better judgment. Honestly, he made the best of a now-or-never offer, but that doesn't change the fact that it's a lot to take in. Where do I go? Should I move back home and start over? What am I even still doing here? I love my job and my co-workers. But how do I go back there after what happened?

"I'm gonna give you some space to think. But I'll be inside if you want to talk. Would you like me to order some food, or are you going out?"

"I'm not going anywhere. If it's okay, I need to make a phone call. I should get ahold of my mom and tell her about the hospital and whatnot."

"Yeah. Of course. Take your time." Kelly kisses the top of my head and goes inside.

All I want to do is scream and jump over the railing of the balcony. If this had happened two days ago, I might have been excited about it. To lose my place right now feels like a trap. I spent the day convincing myself that Kelly was the wrong guy for me, and now I have to live with him. What reason do I have to stay? Why would I bother to look for another place? The men in this town make no sense. He gets rid of my apartment without asking and then doesn't even intend on being with me. What was the point? I'm so sick of boys and their head games.

I can't stay here again for a guy. Figures. Leave it to me to find the man of my dreams right before deciding to move away. Where the hell has he been for the last few months? Why did I have to meet him now? Why did I have to meet him like this?

Why did Kelly have to spend the last few days fucking with my head? And why did I let him? Goddammit! I'm pissed off, devastated, and confused as fuck. I have to stop making decisions based on my desire for true love. That shit might not even exist. I need to focus on myself for once.

After I take some time to silently vent, I call my mom and tell her what's been going on. I keep it all surface-level so she won't freak out. But, as I expected, she told me to move back home. What other choice do I have? I'll make time tomorrow to email resumes and fill out online applications. Getting a new job is always easier when you're currently working. So, if I fill out things now, I can still use the jail as my employer.

I wish I had a group of friends like other people do. Having someone in my life who could help me shuffle through these thoughts would be useful.

> : I'm not sure what your work schedule looks like for the rest of this week, but do you think we might be able to get together to talk? I could use an ear, and I noticed that you have two.

> Croy: Absolutely! Tell me when and where, and I'll get my shoes on. I took vacation all week since I had that stint in the slammer. So, I can make myself available for you day or night.

> : How far do you live from the jail? Maybe I could come to you. I need to clear my head.

> Croy: I'm in the same town. Are you okay to drive? You're welcome to come to my house if you need someplace quiet to hide out.

I'm willing to put my trust in Croy and believe he is who he claims to be. On the surface, going to his house without telling anyone where I'm headed is a horrible idea, but I can't risk having someone see us out together. The rumor mill in this town

154

may not grind out information as quickly as the guys at the jail, but that doesn't mean the people here are oblivious. It is a small town, after all.

> : That works. But I want to say in advance that I'm not coming over for sex. I need a friendly face and someone to listen. Is that okay?

> Croy: Whatever you need, that's what I'm here for. I'm more than happy to sit and listen. The address is 8704 Briarfalls. Come over whenever. I'm finishing a workout, and I need to shower. But I'll leave the front door unlocked so you can get it.

> : Okay. Thanks. I'll message you if I can't get there.

> Croy: Heather, if he doesn't let you leave that apartment, I'm coming to get you.

Kelly is on the couch watching a movie, making a point to act casual. He gives me a half smile and waits for me to speak first. When I sit next to him, he pauses whatever it is he's watching and turns to face me.

"Do you have my keys? I need to go out for a little bit."

"I left them on the counter next to your wallet. They were still in my pocket from yesterday. Are you coming back at some point?" He sounds like he is tiptoeing through the conversation.

"Yeah. If that's okay? I have a few stops I need to make. But I shouldn't be too long. Do you need anything while I'm out?" I want to keep things friendly between us. I do like Kelly. He's an amazing guy. I haven't forgotten all the reasons why he was my favorite person to work with, and I haven't written him off.

He shakes his head no and takes my hands. "I genuinely do want you here. Not just in the apartment. I want you in my life. You're important to me, and I'm sorry I didn't tell you sooner. I should have."

"I'm not mad that you turned over my keys and moved me out of my apartment. I hated that place! The fact that you were able to void my lease is amazing. But I wish that you would have spoken to me about it first… I might need a day to figure out where I'm headed, but I'll keep you in the loop." If we could have more moments like this, I'd be in no rush to leave. It's the fighting that I can't abide. It gives me anxiety.

Kelly wraps me in his arms and pulls me close. "I hope I get to see you before work, but if not, please know that I'll be thinking about you. I still believe in us. I know that we can fix this and be happy together. I'll do anything."

"Be your usual charming self. I love being around that guy." As I look up and lean in, our lips meet. I can't help myself. Kelly is exceptionally kissable when he's like this. Maybe we could see whatever this is through to the end if he could slow down.

I change my clothes and grab my keys and wallet off the counter. I'm not in a hurry to get back, but I'm also not avoiding seeing Kelly before he leaves. Croy is going to lose his mind when I tell him about the apartment. I'm nervous about mentioning it to him, but I also want his advice.

Twenty-Two

8704 BRIARFALLS TURNS out to be so much more than I imagined. I'm not sure what I expected, but it wasn't a brand-new home in an upscale development. I wouldn't call it a gated community, but it's definitely Members Only. Driving around, I'm blown away by the grandeur of it all. There isn't an untrimmed lawn or an overgrown hedge in sight, and every landscaping bed is freshly mulched. I can only assume there's a lawn service that comes in every week, generously paid for by the residents via an exorbitant HOA fee.

I never asked Croy what he does for work, but clearly, he has his shit together. That fact alone puts him out of my reach as far as dating, not that dating was ever an option. There are so many factors to consider, but as it stands right now, I'd accept anything he's offering. It's not that I'm desperate or even lonely. Croy is an anchor I'd like to tie myself to, for the moment, if he'd allow me.

Croy is waiting at the door when I pull into the driveway, and it's the first time I've seen him dressed in his own clothes. He looks like he belongs everywhere and nowhere. He's the kind of guy I would expect to see competing in the strongman competition at the Arnold Classic. Or holding his own in the mosh pit at a metal show. His intricate body art could win him first prize at any tattoo convention. Or garner him smiles and stares in every Vegas nightclub. I could picture him throwing darts in a bar, tossing a frisbee on the beach, and playing football in college, but I never would've thought to look for him here. Maybe he's in a high-priced witness protection program. Or he's an undercover FBI agent making connections on the inside until I came along and blew his cover by exposing him for the upstanding citizen he is.

"Well, don't you look nice? I'm glad you're here." Croy offers me his hand at the base of the steps, and I accept. "Would you like a tour of the house, or are we on a time crunch?"

"I would love to see the inside of your home. This place is amazing from the outside." It's always a good idea to know where your exits are when stepping into some place new, but besides that, I'm obsessed with looking at houses! For fun, I like to scroll through the For Sale listings once a week and dream about someday being an adult.

In hindsight, I should have focused on college and my career after high school. But I was skinny for the first time, and guys were finally looking at me. My quest for love and partnership had officially begun, and all other priorities took a backseat. Despite my dwindling interest, I did well in school. But I wasn't thinking enough about *my* future. Imagine how much further ahead I would be if I knew back then what I know today. I'm going to need Elon Musk to stop focusing on Mars and seriously get to work on time travel.

The tour Croy's giving me is respectfully professional until we get to the master bedroom. Now, I know that I'm the one who said, "I'm not coming over for sex." But standing in his bedroom, the tension between us seems to be physically pulling my body towards his. Croy must feel it too. He slides his hands below my ass and lifts me off my feet in one smooth motion as if we'd rehearsed it a thousand times. My arms come over his shoulders, and my legs wrap around his waist.

For a girl who has always been self-conscious about her weight, this is probably the single greatest moment of my life, and we haven't even kissed yet. Croy has this way of making me feel tiny, like I'm cute and sexy and perfect.

I'm used to guys making me feel small, but their version meant inferior, invisible, and insignificant. After a while, you start to believe that love is sacrifice and pain and something that must be endured. Now I'm beginning to realize that if love feels like work, you're definitely with the wrong person.

Staring into Croy's eyes, I rub my hand over the back of his head. "I want *all* of this with you and then some. But for the time being, I think we should get out of this room and finish seeing the house." I can't believe *these* words are coming out of *my* mouth.

What am I even saying? I've never been more turned on in my life, and I'm asking him to stop. Seriously? I've hooked up with people in the past that I didn't even like because they wanted to. And now that I've found the one guy who checks every box, I'm asking for a tour of his basement instead of getting naked and diving into his bed. I think I might have sustained a brain injury during that fight at the jail.

Croy closes his eyes, exhales, and gently returns me to my feet. He's still wearing his usual smile, so I know he isn't mad. "All right then. Whatever you want, dear. Let the tour continue."

He takes my hand and leads me into the next room. It's a three-bedroom house, with all the bedrooms on the second floor. He only has beds in two rooms and an office in the third. There's a built-in bookshelf behind his desk that covers the entire wall. I let my eyes wander over his impressive collection of books, secretly looking for the one I gave to him.

"What is it that you do for work? I know you told me that you studied computer programming in college."

"I do production planning for an aerospace company near Columbus. My job is to create and manage work orders for all the parts fabricated inside the building." I feel like he's talking to my dad right now instead of me. This must be his work voice. "When I bought this house, I worked from home a lot more, so I needed an office."

"That makes sense. How's your arm feeling, by the way? I've been meaning to ask, but I've also been avoiding the topic because… Well, you know." I can't help but notice the small bandage. I'm surprised it isn't worse since it required surgery. He seems to be using it without any difficulty, but I still feel guilty that he was hurt.

"It wasn't your fault, Heather. And it's fine. There was a piece of plastic they had to go in and remove. No big deal. I could probably take this off. It doesn't even have stitches or anything. Pretty sure they used some crazy glue and called it a day." He makes the whole situation sound like it was no big deal, as if he wasn't stabbed a couple of days ago during a fight over my life.

We finish the tour downstairs. The basement has a gym nicer than the one I paid to join, a gorgeous TV room, and a full bathroom. I want to hide here for the next few days, playing video games and trying out various exercise equipment.

He keeps finding little ways to touch me without being too much. Every time we come into contact, I can feel my skin tingle and my muscles tighten.

This is all wonderful and amazing and heart-breakingly tragic. Croy has everything going for him. He has a beautiful home, a career, a whole life… I have nothing to offer a guy like this. I'm currently waist-deep in the lowest point of my life. I'm homeless, jobless, and without a plan or sense of direction. I can't help but take stock and notice how worthless my life is. Maybe a half-finished book and a pair of sweats are enough to repay such a meager debt. Why did I have to meet him now?

"Should we sit here or go in the living room? I'm dying to hear whatever it is you wanted to talk about." I can hear the eager excitement in his tone. This guy wants to know me and puts forth every effort.

I'm not good enough for him, and I know it. I can feel myself disappearing like I'm shrinking into the carpet. And the only person making me feel this way is myself. Croy is perfect, and I'm nothing. I'm nobody. My throat tightens, and I know the tears aren't far behind. I need to get out of here before I fall apart.

"Actually, I should probably get going. I appreciate you letting me stop by, but I don't belong here." I turn on my heels and head straight for the stairs. I have to make it to the front door before he says my name. I have to get into my car before he asks me to stay. I have to go back to Kelly's and accept that I don't deserve this level of happiness.

"Heather, wait." He catches me a foot from the stairs. I don't turn around. I can't. So he stands behind me and wraps me in his arms. "I'm not going to stop you if you want to leave. But please know that I want you here. I understand you have a lot going on, and I'm not trying to make your life more difficult. If I crossed a line or said something to upset you, I'm sorry. You are welcome in this home any time, day or night. I'm not going anywhere."

"Thanks... You know, for saving my life and all. I'm sorry I can't repay that debt." My body trembles as I battle old demons that never seem to die. I need to get out of here before Croy feels obligated to fight by my side. I know he wants to fix me, but I've been broken so long that I don't even know where the pieces are.

"Please don't do this. You can talk to me." Croy's voice is stable. I can hear our whole future played out in his tone. He is my forever if I stay. If I let myself believe I'm enough, he'll hold on and never let go. If I had done things differently in the past, maybe I could have deserved him in the future.

"Goodbye." I pull myself out of his arms, take the stairs two at a time, and leave through the front door. I don't know where I'm going, but I can't be here.

Without thinking, I drive back to Kelly's building and take the elevator to the 6th floor. Standing in front of 602, I knock. When the door opens, everything I've been holding inside spills out. Kelly doesn't say anything. He slowly pulls me inside and embraces me. We stay like this for as long as it takes for my body to run out of tears. I'm so tired I'm barely alive. "Is it okay if I lay in your bed for a while?"

"You don't even have to ask. What's mine is yours."

I kick my shoes off and walk into the bedroom. There isn't enough energy left inside me to get undressed or lift the blanket, so I lay on top and curl myself into a ball. Kelly walks in with a soft blanket from the couch and covers me from toe to chin. "Do you want to be alone?"

His question bounces around in my head. Do I want to be alone? Isn't that what I deserve? To be miserable and empty. To disappear. I wish the darkness would come back and lock me away for good.

"No. You can stay."

Twenty-Three

"BABE, I ordered food. Do you feel like eating anything?" Kelly's voice is soft. It's a nice way to wake up. I wish I could record it and use it as my new alarm tone. "Also, the hospital called. You have an appointment tomorrow morning."

"Alright, I'll be right there... Hey Kelly, thanks for taking care of me." My voice sounds as weak as I feel.

"It's my pleasure." His pleasant mood is almost too much.

I wish our sexual relationship would have started this way and progressed over time. Whenever someone is too much too soon, I feel overwhelmed. Plus, their words sound disingenuous. Especially looking back after they leave me for someone else. I'm sure as hell not trying to do to Kelly what so many others have done to me. While I stand behind my statement that he is not my boyfriend, it's obvious that we're in some sort of situationship. I can't pretend to be a good person if I'm lying. It's time to be honest and let things fall where they may.

"Can I talk to you?" I sit on the couch beside Kelly, ready to spill my guts.

"I would love that, but first, let me tell you what the doctor said so I don't forget anything." This level-headed, compassionate version of Kelly is the one I could see myself with if he weren't so much like me. Two people who lose control of their emotions can be a dangerous combination. When the mania kicks in, and the highs feel extra high, it can be addicting. Intense passion often leads to incredible pleasure. But there is a corresponding low for every high, and we'd push each other deeper into those emotional pitfalls.

I don't hold Kelly's recent erratic behavior against him because, honestly, I'm guilty are far worse. His emotions are an asset, as much as they are a drawback. Seeing Kelly this way, he feels like a real person instead of a lonely girl's fantasy.

"The blood work results came back, and the transfusion didn't work. Your body rejected the blood for one reason or another. So, they want you to come in tomorrow morning for an iron IV treatment and again on Sunday. Then they'll do blood work again in a few days and review ongoing treatment options, if necessary." He takes my hands in his and looks into the depth of my eyes. "I'm sorry you have to go through all of this. That's probably why you still feel so terrible. Your body doesn't have what it needs, and you want to shut down again. The doctor said if you black out or feel sick, I should take you to the ER immediately."

"Okay. What time do I have to be back there tomorrow?"

"They made the appointment first thing in the morning, at 8 am. Maybe I can leave work early and go with you. It's not a good idea for you to be driving, and I don't want you to be alone."

"You don't have to take off work. And anyways there won't be anyone to cover you. I'll be fine." As I sit here trying to have this conversation, I feel myself sinking. Kelly's words feel slow and heavy, like they're coated in paste. I feel tired in a way that a nap doesn't solve.

"While I was on with the hospital, he sent you a text, and I read the conversation you've been having. I don't care that you went to his house. I assumed that's who you were going to see when you left. I don't like it, but I understand you have reasons for needing to talk to him. Your loyalty and kindness have always been two of your most attractive assets, though I do prefer when I'm the one on the receiving end."

"I don't mean to be disloyal or unkind to you. I wanted to tell you that I went to see him. I wanted to be honest with you. That was my plan when I came in here, but I suppose honesty after getting caught lying isn't quite as meaningful."

"Babe, I'm only asking this because you came back upset… Did something happen while you were there?"

"No. Nothing happened. We didn't even talk. He was giving me a tour of his house, and I started to feel sick. So, I came back. I planned to go to the store afterward, but my thoughts felt slushy, and my vision was blurry." I've always hated secrets. It feels better to be truthful, even if parts are omitted for his benefit.

Kelly and I stay on the couch for the rest of the evening. We eat and watch a movie, and I snuggle into him like he's the only place I want to be. His warmth cloaks around me like a heated blanket. There's a lot of comfort to be found in these arms if I allow myself to accept it. It's going to be hard to leave him when the time comes.

I have no home here, and I've been put on an indefinite leave of absence from work, per the voicemail I received while driving. If I stay, it would be for a guy, and I can't keep doing that. I'm getting way too old to have nothing. It's bad enough that I wasted my 20s chasing after all the wrong things, and science has failed me when it comes to changing the past. All I have left is my ability to take control of the present as I attempt to salvage my future.

I have a few days to tie together loose ends. Then it's back to square one, page one, a fresh start, and a last chance. If I fail again, I'm done for.

Eventually, it gets late, and Kelly has to catch a power nap before work. I'm jealous. I miss being there. It's like walking through a ghost town full of ghosts that want to jump out and scare you to death. It's exciting and tense, and I'll miss feeling important. Endings are always tough.

I look over the back of the couch to see my bouquet from the hospital. The jail is full of so many wonderful people, and even though I was only there for a couple of months, I will treasure those memories. I can't imagine finding another job that feels so much like home and family.

I stay on the couch, reflecting, while Kelly sleeps, showers, and gets dressed. Where I look boxy and butch and silly in the uniform, Kelly looks like he was made to wear it. Somehow, the stiff material complements his sleek waistline and muscular arms. I don't have to guess why my eyes were always drawn to him. I can see all the reasons right here in front of me. I've admired him since day one, but my understanding of his complexity has grown substantially over the last week. Kelly is so much more than I gave him credit for, and I'm thankful we've become friends.

"I don't want to leave you. Tell me to call off and stay home, and I will." He lifts my legs and sits with them draped across his lap.

I sit forward, wanting to be closer to him. "You can't do that. They need you there. It's bad enough that people have to cover for me." We both lean in. Our foreheads touch, but not our lips. "I wish I could keep you."

"Babe, you can. Say the word, and I'll call into work and tell them you're still sick. I'll say that I might need to take you back to the ER. Or I'll tell them that I have PTSD and I need a mental health day. It's not like I'd be lying. I hate being there without you." He pulls the phone out of his pocket. "I'm calling off."

"Please, don't. Our friends are counting on you to have their backs. The overnight crew is already too small as it is. I'm not sure how long I'll be gone in the morning, but hopefully, I'll be back when you get home. You can text me all night if you get stuck someplace alone, and I'll keep you entertained."

"Okay, but I don't think you should drive. Is there any chance your new *friend* could take you to the hospital tomorrow? Then you two could have a chance to talk." He takes my face in his hands and kisses me. "I still don't like him. But if he drives, I won't have to worry about you blacking out behind the wheel. And since you won't let me take care of you, maybe he'll have better luck."

"I can ask him. Okay? Be safe tonight. Make sure you come home in one piece." If he doesn't leave now, he's going to be late. I kiss him goodbye and follow him with my eyes as he walks out. Once he's out the door, I send a text that I hope will make him smile.

> : I miss you already.

Kells: I miss you more than a drowning man misses air.

> : LoL. You're too much in some of the best possible ways.

I plan to spend the night online looking for jobs back home, but maybe I should shower first. I need to get my head in the right space, and a shower is the ultimate reset button. Plus, I need to shave my legs. The hairs feel like cactus needles.

Croy: Can we talk?

> : I'm sorry about earlier. I shouldn't have run out like that. I wasn't feeling well and didn't want you to see me like that. I was about to text you.

Croy: How are you feeling now? Are you at your place or with Kelly?

> : Oh lord, I never had the chance to tell you. I don't have a place anymore. Kelly canceled my lease and moved me out yesterday without telling me. LoL. When I tried to go home, he finally mentioned it to me. That was one of the things I wanted to talk about when I came over.

Croy: WOW! Now that's a fucking move. That
guy has guts. I'll give him that. I'm guessing
you're okay with this situation for some
unknown reason. Or were you looking for a safe
place to crash?

"Hey, you don't know me, but since you were kind enough to save my life and all, I was wondering if I could move into your huge house for a few days?" If only I could be so bold. The idea of me saying something so forward makes me laugh aloud. I'm glad Kelly isn't home to overhear me. I sound like a lunatic. Did Croy honestly think I would swing by his house looking for a place to stay? Either he thinks I'm someone who takes advantage of the kindness of strangers, or he has a serious savior complex.

: I pretty much have to be okay with it. I don't
have much choice. I was PISSED when he told
me, but after I took a minute to process the
information, I was less upset. It temporarily
puts me in an awkward position, but I'll figure it
out. I also found out that I can't go back to
work. So, I'll probably be moving home in a few
days. I have to go to the hospital in the
morning. After that, I should know more.

Croy: Home? Meaning three hours away? Is
Kelly taking you to the hospital?

Does it matter to him where I live? I want Croy in my life, but we could be friends over the phone like we are now. He sure as hell doesn't need me as much as I need him. Going into a relationship with that sort of power imbalance is a trap that's difficult to escape from. I've gathered this information from previous experience, and I'd like to think I'm smart enough to learn from some of my mistakes. Although, if I'm being honest, I don't feel overly intelligent at the moment.

: No. He'll still be at work. I told him I would order a ride, but I'll probably drive myself if I'm feeling well enough. You might not know this about me, but I'm a penny-pinching miser. That's why I'm here instead of a hotel. LoL.

Croy: What time is the appointment? I'll come pick you up.

: It's at 8 am, but you don't have to do that. I don't know how long I'll be stuck there, and I'm sure you have better things to do.

No one wants to sit at a hospital with nothing to do. Even I don't want to go. Croy must be auditioning for sainthood. It's sweet of him to offer, but I'm not great at accepting help. He should consider pouring all of that altruism into a worthier cause.

Croy: You already know that I want to take you. And I already know that you want me to take you. So, let's call it a done deal and move on. I want to prove to you that you can count on me. So please send me your address, and allow me to do this one thing for you.

: One thing in a long list of many. I'm already so far in debt with you that I'll have to hand over my firstborn. Might as well dig my hole a little deeper... It's the new apartment building behind Sterling Gym. I'm not sure what the address is. Give me a second, and I can find it.

Croy: No need, I know where it is. My buddy Eric lives there. Those apartments are nice. Maybe I didn't give Kelly enough credit. What floor are you on?

Too often, I forget how small this town is. Having remained relatively inconspicuous until recently, I've avoided participating in the town gossip. Once or twice, when I forgot to charge my headphone, I overheard conversations at the gym. People on treadmills are willing to discuss anything to pass the time. Even after my music faded, I would leave my earbuds in to avoid conversing with such strangers.

> : I can meet you in the parking lot. That way, you don't have to deal with building security at the front desk.

Croy: Okay. If that's what you want. I was gonna ask Eric if he knows your boy.

> : What floor is your friend on?

Croy: Top floor. He's in 607. I go over, and we drink beers and play Xbox once a month.

It's a Small World begins playing in my head, and I suddenly feel like I'm sitting in a little boat, moving through my life on a track I had no part in laying. Coincidence is starting to feel a lot like destiny. Unless I have it all wrong, and Croy is a stalker. "Mom. Dad. Meet the man of my dreams. He's a serial killer, and we're in love." I laugh again at my unfiltered commentary before returning to the conversation at hand. I don't actually think Croy's the bad guy. He's way too nice for it to all be an act.

> : Of course, you do Because why wouldn't you? Well, it's definitely, most certainly, absolutely NOT that floor!

Croy: Hahaha. Your boyfriend's first name is Matt. In case you were curious. Eric said they've hung out a few times.

Well, god damn. That was fast. I think Croy might have missed his calling as a private investigator. Or maybe he is a stalker. There's always the possibility that he could be lying or

170

merely joking around. Matt Kelly, huh? He doesn't look like a "Matt" to me, but I suppose parents don't truly know what their kids will grow up to be. Otherwise, Kelly's folks would have named him Ares or something equally fitting.

> : Oh, for the love. If I wanted to know his name, I could've asked him. LoL. And he's still not my boyfriend. Why are you texting people at 11 pm on a work night?

> Croy: I was already talking to him. He was asking me about some parts for a project at work. I told you I'm off all week. Let's hang out now. I'll drive over to get you. I want to listen to random songs, watch movie trailers, and talk, even if it's only for a little bit.

> : We're going to see each other in the morning.

> Croy: I know, but if you're gonna leave in a few days, I want to see you. Unless you're tired and need to sleep, then I'll wait.

Well shit! I should've taken a shower earlier while I was busy doing nothing. I still have the essence of Kelly all over me, and it's going to be difficult to live up to my new reputation with prickly little cactus legs. I reach under the leg of my sweatpants and run the palm of my hand over the length of my shin. I suppose they aren't that bad. But they could be better.

> : Okay. You've convinced me. Can you give me ten minutes?

> Croy: I'll be there. Do you need me to have Eric carry you to the parking lot?

> : Don't push it. LoL. I'll see you in ten.

I've never showered and shaved so fast in my life. I'm

surprised my legs have any skin left on them. Getting dressed, I throw on the first thing I can think of. I want to be casual but not too casual. So, I put on jeans, a t-shirt, and my black and white chucks. Then I remember to brush my teeth before grabbing my keys and racing out the door. Everything feels like a blur.

When the door opens, I nearly scream when I see Croy standing next to the elevator. "Jesus Christ! You scared the shit out of me! What are you doing here? How did you even get up here?" I have to clutch the frame of the door to steady myself while my heart knocks wildly under my ribs.

"You're adorable. It was worth the drive just to see your face."

Croy is standing there with a giant smile on his face looking tasty as fuck, and I probably look like I'm on the verge of a heart attack. Why do these boys have to be so damn attractive? I can't handle it. They both make it impossible for me to think.

"I thought you were meeting me in the parking lot. I wasn't expecting you to be standing right there." As I walk toward him, I trying to get my heart to slow down, but it beats harder the closer I get.

"Well, you don't know what I drive, and I thought I'd be a gentleman and walk you out." He holds out his hand to me and bows slightly. "Shall we go?"

I swear, his smile is omnipresent and infectious. I take his hand and walk into the elevator. Once the doors close, he kisses me, and I very much kiss him back. I needed this, but I was too afraid to want it. The feel of his lips on mine as his hands grip my body. I've waited my whole life for a kiss to feel like this, and now that I've had a taste, my appetite is voracious. We manage to stop before the doors open on the ground floor, but he keeps my fingers folded into his.

As I walk beside him, my body aches with need. The buzzing in my nerve endings persists until I'm numb to everything except him. In the parking lot, Croy leads me toward a big black SUV. It reminds me of reality TV shows, where the people get whisked away to random locations. It seems like the days of limos are past. Now, everyone arrives in a freshly detailed Suburban.

He opens the door and holds my hand until I'm seated. Then fastens my seatbelt and leans in. "If you need me to be on my best behavior, I can be, but you have to spell out the rules for me in concise terms."

"I'm sick of playing by the rules." Kissing him might have cost me everything back when I had something to lose, but everything that gave my life purpose has already been lost. Or maybe my priorities have shifted now that my focus lies elsewhere. I'm a shell of my former self, yet I feel more alive than ever when I'm with him.

As we pull into the driveway, I'm shocked to see that Croy's house is even more impressive in the dark. There are lights in the landscaping that illuminate the entire front, and it's rich and warm and gorgeous. This is way too much house for a single guy. He must be recently divorced. Or maybe he's still married, and she's out of town with the kids. Wouldn't that be my luck?

"How long have you lived here?" This entire development seems fairly new. It reminds me of Kelly's apartment building. Not in cost or caliber, but in the way it stands out against the rural background surrounding it.

"I bought it two and a half years ago when it was first built. There's a clubhouse with a pool we could go to tomorrow after the hospital if you feel well enough. Then again, Matt's building has a pool, doesn't it?" Even in the dim light, I can see his smirk.

"Oh my god, do not start calling him that. It's too weird. Plus, I don't even know if that's his real name. You could be making that shit up to screw with me."

"How are you living with a guy, and you don't even know his name? I'm practically running background checks on girls who friend request me online."

"When you have nothing left, there isn't much a person can take from you." I can't even imagine how many girls try to talk to him. I'm not sure I want to know. The idea of Croy's flooded inbox makes me want to run away crying for a second time.

"I'm curious what you mean by that?" We're still standing outside the front door. Maybe my answer determines whether I get to enter or if I'm walking home. Croy's hand is on the knob, and the door is open a crack, but this feels more like a test than a tease.

"Anything I had to offer worth a damn has been lost, stolen, or broken beyond repair. I have nothing left. Therefore, I risk very little by putting myself out there. You have *all* of this." I motion with my hands as I run through the list. "Good looks. An expensive car. A gorgeous home. A decent personality. And a career that affords you this lifestyle. You have everything a person could want. It makes sense that you'd have to be selective about who you let in." It seems straightforward.

"Trust me, I would trade all of this for the one thing I can't buy." He shakes his head and pushes the door open. "Should we go downstairs for a bit?"

"Sure, sounds good." If I had to guess, the basement TV room is his favorite spot to hang out with people. The bedroom would be too suggestive, and the living room on the first floor feels a little formal. Then again, I suppose the location would depend on the reason for the visit. I'm sure plenty of girls have seen the bedroom and nothing else.

"First, we need to make a quick stop in the kitchen." He takes my hand and leads the way. From the kitchen, he goes into what appears to be the laundry room and pulls some clothes out of the dryer. "You have a choice to make. Do you want to wear the hoodie and sweats you gave me, or do you want to wear mine?"

"Which would you be more comfortable in? Or am I the only one changing?" I guess he thinks I'm overdressed for midnight music and movie trailers.

"We're both changing. I'm wearing whatever you don't choose." He holds a piece from each set, presenting me with the choice that will determine the outcome of my life.

"Yours." Of course, I'm going to choose his. I can't decline an opportunity to wear a guy's clothes. And I'm pretty sure he might already know this about me.

He hands me my set and closes the door between us. I change right there in the kitchen and put my stack of folded clothes on a chair. When he comes out of the laundry room, he looks like he did this morning. I understand now what he's going for. This is starting to feel like last night when he came to my room at 1:00 am.

We spend out time in the basement, talking and listening to music. Croy makes life's simple pleasures even more enjoyable, and I'm glad I came over. When the 1:00 am hour comes, he puts on Hostage, the first song that played last night, and I fold into him like origami. Little things like this have always gone unnoticed by the men in my past. Usually, I'm the only one who cares enough to construct memory markers. I'm surprised when he says, "I think this is my new favorite song. I hear it, and I think of you. Or maybe I'm already thinking of you, and I listen to it. Either way, this song is forever tied to you."

It's 2:14 am when I suggest that we call it a night. I'm getting tired. If we stay awake any later, I'm worried I might sleep through my appointment.

"Do you want to stay? Then we can leave from here in the morning. Or would you rather I take you home?" Croy looks as tired as I feel. I should leave, but I don't like the idea of him driving when he appears half asleep. I guess I didn't think this through enough. I know he'll never agree to let me walk home, and I doubt I have enough energy to make it. If I still had my place, I wouldn't be pseudo-single, and this decision would be a no-brainer. "You can sleep in the spare bedroom if you don't trust me."

I laugh at the suggestion. "I wouldn't be here in the middle of the night if I didn't trust you." This isn't even something I have to invest thought into before answering. Of course, I trust him. I would trust him with my life. I trust him more than I trust myself. It feels like, no matter where life leads us or who we end up with, at 1:00 am, we'll always belong to each other.

As I get into bed, I think of everything I would say and do if I were more confident. I shouldn't overthink it. I should live in the moment, especially since I'll be gone in a few days. How can I let pass any opportunity at this point? I won't see this beautiful man again, so I might as well go for it. What do I have to lose? We're both laying on our backs, looking at the ceiling as slivers of light come through the side of each set of window blinds. It's scarcely enough to keep it from being dark.

"Can I ask you something?" Croy's voice is soothing and melodic in the dark, like falling asleep to classical music. "How do you feel about being here with me?"

"I feel a lot of ways about it if I'm being honest." And why shouldn't I be honest? Remember, this is the time to go for it. This is *nothing to lose* time. "Mostly, I'm excited because I enjoy being around you. But I also feel overwhelmed, confused, disappointed, and sad, not because of anything you did but because we met at the worst possible time. I feel like I'm in the middle of watching my life fall apart around me, and it's uncomfortable and embarrassing.... I don't want you to think I'm the type of girl who runs around entertaining other men while in a relationship. I'm *not* in a relationship, but I'll acknowledge that it appears that way from the outside. I'm not trying to hurt anyone or get myself hurt in the process. I want to be happy. I want to make the most of my time with you even though I have nothing substantial to offer. And I don't want to think about leaving."

It felt good to say all that, even if it makes him regret asking me the question. I'm sure this was supposed to be a quick hookup, and I'm laying here unburdening my soul. Leave it to me to ruin a perfectly good moment by talking too much.

"You're worried about me thinking badly of you? That's funny. You're honest, giving, beautiful, kind, thoughtful, forgiving, and self-aware. I have seen you take it on the chin, time and time again, with a smile on your face because you didn't want to hurt anyone's feelings. What the hell would you have to be embarrassed about? I was the one incarcerated when we met. You could have looked the other way without giving me the time of day. Instead, you offered me your only spare set of clothes and a book you didn't even get to finish reading. Not to mention what you wrote in it, which I fucking loved, by the way. You're the one person who should be selfish right now, but you won't let yourself. Kelly was selfish when he made decisions without talking to you and canceled your lease. I was selfish when I asked you to come over tonight because I needed to be close to you. Your boss was out of line, and I know what he said hurt you. But you refuse to get mad at any of us... I can't even think about you leaving."

"How am I supposed to fall asleep after you say all that? Could you stop being so amazing? Please. You can't be this perfect." I truly believe he's either a robot. Or I died and somehow landed in heaven.

Croy rolls onto his side, facing me, and lays his arm across my waist. His hand drapes over my side, and I can feel his fingers against the edge of my back. The feel of his skin against mine starts the race in my heart. "I'm not perfect, Heather. I was recently in jail. And I have it on good authority that my personality is 'decent' at best. Don't take this wrong, but you seem to have a blind spot for red flags. It's no wonder you've dated so many jerks."

"It was a joke. Your personality is spectacular. Five stars. Would recommend... And it's not that I don't see the negatives. I do. But I choose to focus more on a person's potential. Our lowest moments shouldn't be our defining ones."

"I wish you could see yourself the way you see others. Hell, I wish you could see yourself the way I see you. You have so much value. You're worth more, not worthless." Croy leans in closer but waits for me to meet him the rest of the way.

I close the distance between our lips, and the fuse is lit. Wherever Croy intends to take me, I am going there willingly.

Twenty-Four

I'M NOT ready to wake up when the alarm goes off, not after only a few hours of sleep. I tell myself, "Five more minutes," and drift off.

"Good morning, beautiful. I made you coffee." I open my eyes and find Croy sitting on the edge of the bed with a mug in each hand. "I wasn't sure how you take it or if you even drink coffee, so I fixed it the same way I take mine. If you don't like it, I can make you a new one."

"So long as it's not plain black, I should be fine. Normally, I do some flavored creamer and call it good." I'm still so tired, but coffee and the pleasure of his company are enough to persuade me.

"You're in luck. It's vanilla creamer. I'm pretty basic when it comes to my morning beverages. Also, I brought your clothes from the kitchen and put them in the bathroom. We should probably leave here in 20 minutes." Croy sounds like he's been awake for hours. Did he sleep at all?

"How are you wide awake right now?" I have weighted eyelids, and he looks ready to face the day. Maybe he has a cocaine habit I don't know about.

"Well, I'm used to waking up early for work. And I don't

178

have a depleted iron level." He sets a handled cup on the night-stand and heads for the door. "I have a few emails I need to answer for work, but I'll be ready to go whenever you are."

"I'll find you." I swing my legs over the side of the bed and take the mug from the side table. I can't remember the last time I had a cup of coffee at home. I never bought a machine for my apartment, and I didn't notice one at Kelly's place. As a teenager, I loved going for mochas with my girlfriends. We weren't old enough to get into the bars, so coffee shops were the next best thing. Those friendships may have faded, but the memories remain.

I take a quick shower before getting dressed. Hopefully, Croy won't mind that I used the towel hanging on the hook. You never know with people. I've always displayed the towels I use, but I've encountered people who hang the *nice towels* and dry off with the dingy ones hidden under the sink. I wonder if anyone has ever done a physiological study comparing and contrasting those two groups of people. It makes me think of social media and how people flaunt the good moments and bury the real ones.

When I'm dressed and ready to go, I join Croy in his office. He's sitting behind his desk, wearing glasses, and typing skillfully. This look is quite the contrast from the man I saw in a prison fight. This image of him validates my theory that people are so much more than their worst moments.

My phone alerts me to a new message, and I know who it isn't from because I'm looking right at him. That only leaves one possibility.

> Kells: Were you able to find a ride to the hospital?

> : Yeah, I'm good. I'll let you know how it goes. How was your night?

> Kells: Long. I'm ready to get home and go to bed.

Croy looks away from his computer, his gaze fixed on my presence in the doorway. "And how is Kelly doing this morning?"

"He was making sure I found a ride." I don't feel the need to lie. This entire situation is beyond me at this point.

"I hope you assured him you're being well taken care of." A smug grin is playing at the corner of his lips. "Shall we go?" I wonder what will happen to these two after I'm gone. Will they cross paths somewhere and glare at each other, or will they laugh about the silly competition they created centering around a worthless girl? I suppose only time will tell. Regrettably, I won't be around to see it happen.

The ride to the hospital is quiet. It's not that I don't want to talk. I do. I have a lot on my mind, but I'm not sure what this doctor plans to tell me when we arrive. Croy put his hand on my leg after we backed out of the driveway and kept it there until we parked at the hospital. I'm not sure if I'm aware of his touch more when it's present or absent. Both feel equally significant.

We're stuck at the infusion center for hours, so I take the time to fill out job applications on my phone. Croy is able to find a vending machine, so we share an assortment of snacks and split a soda. I'm glad he's with me. The conversation gets my mind off things and makes the time go faster. It's nearly 10:30 am when we finally get to leave. I have another appointment in two days. Then I'm free to move away. Back to square one.

"Are you feeling okay? You look a little out of it." There's a hint of concern in Croy's voice.

"I'm alright. Nothing a nap can't fix." I feel horrible, but I don't want to tell him that.

We're almost to the point in the drive where I have to make a decision. Then again, he hasn't said anything, so maybe he's planning on dropping me off. Perhaps last night, and all that stuff he said, didn't mean what I thought it did. This certainly wouldn't be the first time a guy has turned on the charm and lied through his teeth just to get laid.

I wish I were feeling better. I thought that was the whole

point of getting the iron. Instead, my entire body feels bloated and itchy. I can't imagine this is a good look. I lay my head against his arm and allow myself to drift off.

When the car stops, and I open my eyes. We're back in Croy's driveway. "Do you want me to carry you inside, or are you good to walk?"

"As exciting as that sounds. I think I'll walk. Thanks for the offer, though." I can picture his neighbors peering out their windows, watching him carry a passed-out girl into the house, never to be seen or heard from again. The HOA would have to call a special meeting to discuss options for handling the big scary tattooed guy.

Croy makes me a bed with a pillow and blanket downstairs on the couch. It's the perfect location for a nap. I fall asleep ten minutes into a movie with him rubbing my feet. If heaven is a moment you want to relive for an eternity, this is mine. Don't get me wrong, every second with him is amazing, but nothing beats a shared moment of peace.

The guys from my past always had to be doing something. Concerts, movies, bars, bedrooms, so on and so forth. The second they realized they were bored, they were on to the next worst thing. But I'm looking for my best friend. I'm trying to find the rest of my life. I need someone who can be with me when things stop being fun. Sure, I'd love to find passion and romance, maybe even a dash of adventure, but the older I get, the more I value stillness.

Kells: You aren't still at the hospital, are you?

: Hey Kelly, this is Croy. Heather is okay. She wasn't feeling well after the iron IV and didn't want to wake you. So I brought her to my place, and she fell asleep on the couch. Can she give you a call when she wakes up?

Kells: Looks like she made her choice. Congratulations.

: I don't think that's the case, but you can have that conversation with her, not me. I wasn't trying to start anything. I didn't want you to worry about where she was. I can drive her back that way when she's ready.

Kells: Try not to get drunk before you drive my girlfriend home.

: You need to relax.

Kells: Some piece of shit loser inmate is trying to steal my girl, and I should relax? You have her so fucked up in the head that she feels like she owes you some huge debt. As if you're some kind of hero. You aren't good enough to speak to her, let alone know her. Eventually, she'll see you for what you are.

: I know what you're trying to do, and it isn't going to work.

Kells: She's only there out of guilt. She'll never love you.

"Is that my phone?" The room spins slowly as I open my eyes. Croy is still in the corner of the L-shaped couch with my feet in his lap. His face, cast in soft TV light, wears the unmistakable mask of anger. "What happened?"

"Nothing yet. Your boyfriend struck a nerve, that's all." He takes a deep breath while handing me my phone. "I shouldn't have said anything."

I take a second to read through the text exchange. My chest feels tight, and my heart hurts. I fucking hate boys. "Would you mind giving me a ride, please? I need to get my stuff out of his apartment before he throws it all in a dumpster." Apparently, I'm moving sooner than I thought.

"Yeah, that's probably a good idea." Croy seems less upset as we drive. I feel like he is working hard to control his emotion. "Do you want me to come with you? I'll stay in the hallway and carry stuff out. I'm not sure you should be doing this much right now."

"No, thanks. I'll take care of it. If he sees you, it'll only make things harder. You can drop me off and head home." I don't need this to turn into a pissing match. I want to get my stuff and go.

"I wish you'd let me help, but I understand. I'll wait for you here."

"I'll be fine. Kelly's a good person at his core. He's angry, but he's not going to hurt me." I can't make eye contact. I wasn't ready for this to be goodbye. I knew it had to end, but I never wanted it to be like this. I hope Croy meets someone who can be everything he wants and needs. He deserves that.

"Thank you for everything," I whisper against his chest as he holds me one final time. Getting out of the car, I walk away with my heart broken into bits, taking all our unspoken conversations with me. It's time to focus on what I must do next.

I stand in the hallway outside of 602 and knock. When Kelly opens the door, he looks like he's expecting someone bigger. But it's only me. My head is already spinning, and I haven't even carried my laundry basket to the car yet. All I have to do is hold myself together a little longer, and then it will all be over. Finish strong.

"Can I please come in?"

Kelly drops a layer of his defense and lets me into the apartment. The person standing before me is not the man I know. This Kelly is closed off and silent.

"I'm not here to fight with you. I appreciate everything you've done for me over the last few months, especially this last week. You're incredibly important to me. I hoped we could remain friends, but I'm not sure you'd be interested." I can feel my eyes filling with tears. This is not the goodbye I wanted with him either. "I'm here to get my stuff out of your way, and then you won't ever have to see me again. I'm sorry about blacking out at work and making a mess of everything. I'm sorry that we didn't get to spend more time together. I'll miss so many things about working at the jail, but it's you that I'll miss most of all."

"So that's it then? You're leaving, and I never get to see you again? You're going to quit your job and move in with that criminal. Why? Do you think you owe him your life? Are you seriously choosing him over me?"

"No, Kelly, I'm not... I'm not staying with Croy. I'm moving back home. I planned to talk to you this afternoon, but I didn't expect it to be like this. I was going to stay the weekend and leave Monday, but I think it's best if I go now."

"You have another appointment this week. I know because I scheduled it. You can't leave. And I thought he said the iron made you sick. You can't drive three hours."

"None of that is any of your concern, and I can sort out my own appointments. But I don't know what you brought in from my place, so if you want to be nice, you can make a pile, and I can start carrying it out." I hope there isn't much because what little energy I had is fading.

I start throwing as much stuff as I can into my backpack. Then I get my laundry basket from the bedroom and stack my pillow on top. Kelly stands there, looking lost for words. I guess he isn't planning on helping. "The only things I brought in were the food and your toiletries, and one duffel bag of clothes."

"Alright." I'm going to leave the food and anything in the bathroom. I don't have the strength for the extra trips, and I won't need any of it anyways. I go back into the bedroom and find my bag of clothes in the closet. It's heavy, but I can get it all in one trip if I believe in myself just this once. I put on my backpack, sling the strap of my black bag over my shoulder, lift my laundry basket, and try not to fall over. Then I remember the extra set of keys.

I remove Kelly's apartment keys from my ring and set them on the counter. He doesn't speak. He stands there, watching me struggle. Then he reaches into his pocket and pulls out my watch. "Here, Hubble gave me this to give you. It was in a bag with your uniform and my belt."

I take the watch and put it in my pocket. There's dried blood all over the band, so there's no way I'm going to put it on. I wonder if it even still works. I guess I can find out later after I close the book on this unfortunate chapter of my life. "Thanks."

"Can you at least get the door?"

I don't say goodbye. I don't look back. I take one step and then another, willing myself to get into the elevator as quickly as possible. When the door slides closed, the tears begin to fall. I have only the time it takes to descend six floors to miss him and pull it back together. When the elevator doors open on the ground floor, Croy is standing there against the wall, waiting.

"Oh my god, Heather. Why do you insist on doing everything yourself? Please give me that before you fall over. How did you even get this far?" I keep my backpack but hand over the duffel bag and the basket. "Is this everything?"

"Yeah, that's all I'm worried about taking. He can keep the rest." I'm about 63% sure I would have made it to the car alone. Not bad odds, considering.

When we get outside, I unlock my car, and we throw everything in the backseat. The weight of what happened is starting to hit me, and my throat is on fire. I want to sit in my car and cry. I want to call Kelly and have an actual conversation with him. But I think this situation might require some distance first.

"Are you okay to drive to my place? If not, we can take your car now, and I'll come back for mine later." Croy is clearly under the impression that I'm going with him. I'm not sure how to tell him that isn't the plan.

"I don't know what I'm doing at the moment. I appreciate your help, but I need some time. I may take a nap in my car someplace and then try to drive home." Everything around me is spinning like a top, and my forehead is beading with sweat. I need to make it into my seat before I lose my vision. I can see the handle for the driver's door, and then it's gone.

"Thankfully, you blacked out before you started driving." Croy's voice is my current favorite song. He's the track you keep on repeat and never get sick of hearing. I can feel that we're in a car, moving, but I can't open my eyes. "I wish you'd give yourself time to get better. You're pushing yourself too hard, and I don't understand why. Why can't you relax and let me help you?"

"What are you talking about? You've helped me a dozen times, and it's only been a few days." I can't find my sight, but my voice works.

"Yes, but you never *let* me help you. I have to sneak it in every time you're an inch from death. And don't get me wrong. I love saving you. I'll do it as many times as necessary. I just wish you *wanted* me while you were awake."

"Trust me. I want you all the time." My comment lightens the mood with a shared laugh.

When I finally open my eyes, Croy is smiling.

Twenty~Five

FOR THE FIRST time in what feels like forever, I'm alone with my thoughts. No inmates making comments. No nurses doing rounds. No beautiful boy manipulating me like a marionette. I suppose Croy will be back, but for now, even he is absent.

I decide to close my eyes and sort through the files of the last three months, starting with my choice to move here. Self-reflection can be important when your next step is a new starting line.

My original reason for moving here was a guy. He left before I arrived, and forgiving him for that has been difficult. Even though I didn't love him, I felt rejected when he left without a goodbye. No matter what I do, I can't stop men from making meaningless promises, but I can prevent myself from always taking the bait.

Being in such a hurry to get here made me reckless. I opted to live in a place that had me feeling sad and worthless. I felt trapped by my lease. The apartment fed all the worst self-criticisms I hold. My physical surroundings became the lens through which I judged myself, but I can chalk that up to lessons learned. I'll leave here knowing to always see a place in person before signing a lease.

My job at the jail was an unexpected pleasure. I accepted

employment at a place that both frightened and excited me. My position gave me purpose and a sense of pride. I felt like part of a team, and that team quickly became a family. Our strong bond was forged in trust, which has been painfully lacking in all my previous relationships. That job also facilitated my introduction to both Kelly and Croy. Had I never worked there, I probably wouldn't have crossed paths with either of them.

Where do I start with Kelly? I have admired and respected him since the moment we met. Kelly is engaging and handsome, thoughtful and passionate, intense and overbearing. Before we started hanging out, I always felt like his equal. He made me feel seen. And it was flattering when he started showing interest in something more. I stepped into his web and called it home, never caring that it was a trap. I wasn't important enough to myself to see what I was losing.

Sure, I'll miss Kelly and the way he looks in his uniform. That boy made my heart skip several beats. But sexual passion cannot be enough to ignore several fire engine red flags. I've already let go of everything I'm willing to lose, and I'm afraid that might include him.

I spend so much time building the stock of others, but I never make an effort to invest in myself. I keep thinking that if I care enough about someone, they'll care for me in the same way, and we'll grow together. As they say, "High tide raises all ships." I realize that I need to be able to provide for myself because, right now, my ship is underwater. I'm not looking to come into a relationship and be a burden.

My health has been a hot topic of discussion lately, so it seems worth reflecting on. If I'm being honest, I've known something wasn't right for a while. But again, I didn't care enough about myself to investigate what might be wrong. That needs to change. How can I ever be enough for someone else if I can't be bothered to care about myself? It's not as though I enjoy feeling weak. Quite the opposite. I've always prided myself on being physically and mentally strong. I'm not sure when everything started falling off track, but now I know how to make it right. So, another positive takeaway from my time here is that I finally know what is wrong with me. Even as I sit here, I can feel my thoughts coming into focus, as if the clouds are lifting. Maybe the iron is finally kicking in.

And then there's Croy. Something about him feels permanent. Every time he's next to me, I feel whole. It sounds crazy, I know. But his every word rings in my ears like forever. It's as if we've spent 1000 lives knowing each other, and this is our latest chapter. If I let him close to me, I know that he'll walk by my side until the end.

But am I good enough, as I currently am? I desperately want to look in a mirror and like what I see. It's not about needing to be perfect. None of us can achieve that. But it's right back to what I said earlier. I don't want to be anyone's burden. What value do I add to his life if I remain? Does he even want me to be here? Would I stay if he asked me to?

There are so many negative memories attached to this town. It feels tainted. I'm finding it hard to be here, even with an end in sight. What I need is to go home and regroup. Maybe I'll miss Croy and this town enough to return. I want to be with him, without a doubt, but I need to see that he wants to be with me. It can't be only words.

A prison doesn't always come in the form of cinder block walls and metal bars. It can be built with our pain. I've been constructing my cell for over a decade. Every negative word spoken by a lover. Every bottle thrown. Every lie and indiscretion. Every tear. Every kiss. Every moment that remains only with me. These are the bricks and the bars. These are some of the things keeping me locked away.

As much as I want to love Croy, I can't stay here. I would be repeating the same pattern, hoping for a different result. But leaving feels much easier said than done, especially now that he's walking through the door.

Twenty-Six

"I CAN'T BELIEVE you walked there to get your car. I'm surprised you're back so soon." I feel guilty that I couldn't drive myself. That being said, Croy looks good when he's sweaty. Seeing his shirt soaked with exertion makes me smile to myself.

"It's not that far, but it is hot out. I ran there and stopped for food on the way back. Hope you're not still planning on leaving right this minute."

How will I ever be able to leave when he looks at me the way he does? I'm not sure my newly found strength could ever be enough to push away all of this. I should take the weekend to enjoy myself and my time with him. I want to see what it's like without Kelly's strings tripping up my steps. I'll leave Sunday night or Monday morning at the latest.

"I'll depart whenever you ask me to or at the end of the weekend. Whichever comes first." I can't help but smile. I've been with plenty of guys who have given me butterflies, but this feels more like an electrical storm.

"Don't say 'depart.' That makes it sound like you're dying." He shakes his head as if trying to dislodge the thought from his mind. Then comes to sit next to me on the couch in the living room. "If you'd like, we can go to the pool after eating. It's usually two or three ladies in lounge chairs tanning."

Croy is every housewife's secret fantasy, especially if he's half-naked and dripping wet. I nearly choked on my lunch thinking about it. They're going to take one look at us and think, "What the hell is he doing with her?" I might need to boost my confidence a bit before we walk over.

As soon as I'm finished eating, I run out to the car and dig through my bag of clothes. I know there's a bathing suit in there somewhere. I finally find it tucked away in the corner under my interview sweater. I'm glad I thought to pack for any occasion, just in case. I've had this suit for a few years, but it's one of my favorites. It hugs my body and fits my personality perfectly.

When I get upstairs and turn into the bedroom, I see Croy standing by the dresser, ready for an afternoon at the pool. Tattooed skin layered over well-defined muscles makes my mouth water.

"Holy shit, you look good in those shorts. You should prob-ably take them off." The truth tumbles from my lips before my breath catches. I'm shocked I let those words out of my mouth. Without Kelly or my job, nothing is stopping me from doing anything and everything I want, so long as Croy is willing. My pulse quickens in anticipation before he even takes one step toward me. I'm not sure I'm ready for this much freedom. My pseudo-relationship with Kelly gave me a reason to try and behave. Without that, I'm at risk of losing myself entirely to this moment.

"You've seen mine. Now I'd like to see yours. Fair is fair." His voice is playful and teasing. I'm beginning to doubt our desire to make it to the pool. I go into the bathroom and change into my suit. It's a black bikini that ties together. I look in the mirror, fix my hair, check my teeth, find my nerve, and walk back into the bedroom. Croy is sitting on the edge of the bed, waiting.

"Damn, you look perfect." He doesn't take his eyes off me as I walk slowly toward him. I let the tension of the moment build.

I need him to want me. "We can go swimming later. I have a list of things I need to do to you first."

Croy's touch feels like the 4th of July. My logic shuts off, and my brain kicks over to animal instinct. Even in the intensity of the moment, his actions are never selfish. He makes sure to always give more than he takes. I'm not accustomed to this, but I could get used to it.

By the time we've exhausted ourselves, it's nearly 5:00 pm, and my body feels like a ziploc bag full of pudding.

"Should we go swimming now?" Croy runs his fingers over my skin, and a chill runs the length of my spine, pimpling my arms with goosebumps.

"I would probably drown. I'm not sure I can walk, let alone swim." I feel like I'm still waiting for my bones to grow back. There's no question left remaining. This man is a machine.

"We'll take the golf cart. And I promise I'll keep you safe." He sounds excited about going, so I can't say no.

"Okay, you've convinced me. I'm sure I could use some sun in my life." Working at night and sleeping during the day didn't leave much time for sunbathing. I'm going to need to be careful, or I'll come back looking like a lobster.

"Ha. You are quite pale, like an adorable centuries-old vampire. I'm a little scared you might burst into flames when we get outside." Croy is so much like me, with all his light-hearted joking. He's someone I can be myself with. I only wish I could have met him sooner.

I get back into my bikini and add a pair of shorts and a tank top. I'm excited to see this pool area. I've always loved swimming. When I was younger, my parents had an in-ground pool put in at the house, and I pretty much lived in it for a quarter of the year.

I miss that house. My parents sold it after I finished high school, and my brothers were both out of the military. They bought a motorhome and traveled for quite a few years. The house they have now is lovely, but it's not the same as our home in the country. The new place is on the lake in a small boating community west of Cleveland. Half the people move to Florida over the winter, so it's a bit of a ghost town. I think my parents have been itching to get back on the road lately.

Croy takes my hand and leads me to the garage. His damn golf cart is nicer than my car. It's a magnificent cobalt blue, with black vinyl seats. This is unlike any golf cart I've ever seen on the course. I wonder if he's able to drive it anywhere besides the development. I'm picturing gangs of senior citizens rolling down the streets, waving at one another. It's funny that he would buy something like this.

"I already know what you are thinking. I can read it all over your face. I swear, it came with the house." He smiles at me and laughs.

How does he do that? How does he read me so easily? Is it possible that he feels the same connection I do, or is that wishful thinking on my part? What I'm experiencing goes so much deeper than attraction. It feels eternal. Like we've always been and always will be, a matched set. Of course, I won't be saying any of that to him. He would probably think I'm nuts and lose my number.

Riding on the golf cart is fun, like a miniature jeep, only a lot slower. Temperature wise, it's a perfect day. I'm glad he convinced me to leave the house again. When we get over to the pool, I'm stunned into silence. I feel like I'm on vacation. How is this real? I've been here for months and never knew these places existed. Kelly's apartment and Croy's entire neighborhood feel more like California than central Ohio. Who knew this sleepy little town had so many secrets? Maybe I've been too quick to write it off.

"If anyone should ask, how would you like me to introduce you?" Croy poses the question as we park between two golf carts and a convertible. With his hand resting on my leg, he turns to look at me.

"I'm not sure what you mean?" I have a good idea, but I need to stall for time.

"Let me make it easier then. Heather Belk, will you do me the great honor of being my girlfriend?" He smiles with his entire face. Even his eyes seem bluer.

"Um, well... Okay." I'm not sure what else to say. He asked the question instead of assuming, which is better than the last guy did. So, I give him credit for that. Unfortunately, I'm leaving in a few days, and we've danced around the topic but have yet to discuss it in depth. I wouldn't expect a guy like this to wait around while I sort out my thoughts.

"Not the resounding *Yes* I was hoping for, but I'll take it." Croy closes the distance between us and kisses me. "Ready to get wet?"

Is this perfect person actually mine? Does he genuinely want someone like me? I'm a good person with a lot of fantastic qualities, no doubt, but my depression and mania can be a lot to deal with. I don't usually discuss it with people because they aren't around long enough for it to matter, but I wonder if I should issue a disclaimer before Croy gets too attached.

"Me and every other lady here, once you walk in." I smile and give him a wink, loving a good innuendo.

"BaZing! You're cute." He grabs the towels and walks around to take my hand. Does he do this because he likes touching me or because he's afraid I could blackout at any moment? I suppose it doesn't matter. Either way, I get to walk in holding his hand.

Being at his side as we enter the pool area is pretty much as I expected. I'm sure it's hard for people not to notice Croy. He's taller than most normal guys and fit. Plus, tattoos have always been a beacon for attention. I know this from my own experience of being out in public. On top of that, he's unbelievably attractive. It would've surprised me more if the women hadn't looked at him.

There is, however, one woman who seems to be looking more than the others. She hasn't stopped glaring daggers at him since we walked in. I assume this is an ex or maybe a one-night stand. Although, she seems a lot older than what I'd imagine he would go for. Whatever it is, this woman hates him with brutal intensity.

"What's with the lady across the way? The one in the pink and blue bathing suit?" I make sure to talk behind my hand and keep my voice low. "She looks like she wants to rip your heart out of your chest, Temple of Doom style."

Croy laughs so loud that anyone who wasn't looking before is now. "That is the petty Betty that lives next door. I fucking hate her. She likes to do passive-aggressive shit to get under my skin. More than once, I've thought about selling the house and moving to get away from her. But that's what she wants, so..." He lets his sentence trail off. "Anyways, forget about her. Let's take a dip."

Being at the pool and out in the sun is doing wonders for my health. However, seeing Croy swimming toward me makes me wish all these other people weren't here. It's hard to be good when he's close to me, but I'm not one for being inappropriate in public. I draw the line at a kiss, or maybe kisses. Definitely not making out.

We swim around in the deep end for over an hour, talking about random things while hanging onto the edge of the pool and laughing about nothing. He never misses an opportunity to brush against me. A handful of other residents are in the lounge chairs, but no one else is swimming. Thankfully, the bitch faced neighbor left a few minutes after we arrived, so we didn't have to deal with her glaring. I wonder why she hates him so much. It's unfortunate that people feel the need to be like that. Croy seems like such a well-mannered individual. What's to hate?

After a while, I feel drained from the direct sun, and my stomach begins to grumble. I don't know how I could be hungry again when we ate not too long ago, but perhaps I'm getting my appetite back. "Do you mind if we head back to the house? I'd like to avoid burning to a crisp on my first day outside." I might need to locate some ibuprofen and a bottle of water.

"Are you alright with taking the long way back?" Croy hands me a towel, and I wrap it around my waist. Beach towels make the best summer skirts. I'm not in a hurry to get back. All I need is to get out of the sun before I wilt away to nothing. Thankfully the golf cart has a roof.

"If you're next to me, I'm open to taking the longest path possible." I pack as much truth as I can into every flirtatious response. I don't want to leave regretting everything I didn't say.

As we drive around the development, Croy tells me about the house and his mindset when he bought it. "I wanted the whole package, you know. The house, the dog, the wife, the kids. All of it. I thought if I had the material things, the right woman would find me more appealing. But it turns out that only the wrong girls like it ready-made. I never considered that my better half would want to do it herself." He sets his hand on my leg and stops driving. "I want you to stay. I want to be with you. But I understand why you need time."

"For the record, it's not that I want to do it myself... Unless you were talking about someone else when you said that, then never mind." I thought we would have this discussion later, but now works.

"Okay. Then what's the ideal situation here?" We continue to talk as he drives back towards the house.

"Ideally, I'd like to do it together. It'd be nice to build a life with someone, not step into the life they already have. But I guess I'm getting a little old for that, huh? Maybe I missed my window." I hope I'm not saying too much.

"So, if I get rid of everything, we can be together?"

"Don't be silly. That's not what I'm saying... If I stay here, it'll always feel like your place. I'd have that nagging fear in the back of my head, reminding me that you could kick me out at the drop of a hat. I'm tired of walking on eggshells and feeling inferior." This conversation is starting to feel serious.

"Am I making you feel that way? Like you're inferior? Because that couldn't be further from the truth. I think you're incredible." We pull into the driveway and park. Croy's usual smile has dropped, and his demeanor has shifted. He's not angry, just intensely focused as he attempts to read my response before I give it to him.

"No. It's not anything you're doing. I was talking about people prior to you. Believe it or not, I had to kiss a lot of frogs before I found my prince." I pause, giving him my best princess smile and bat my eyelashes. "Listen, I'm not saying I would never live here with you, but I don't think that's the direction I'm headed Monday morning. Lately, it feels like one hit after another, and I need time. I'm not asking you to put your life on hold for me. But I wouldn't be disappointed if you did."

"I want you to take the time you need and focus on yourself. I've been begging you to do that since we met. You don't have to worry about me disappearing or moving on without you. I'm not going anywhere." Croy takes my hand, and we walk inside. I've never been one for holding hands, but lately, I've been reevaluating my opinions. This one simple gesture reinforces the feeling of being connected. As we walk through the door, I hear the text alert on my phone go off.

"That's probably my mom checking on me. I made the mistake of telling her about all the low-iron stuff. Do you mind if I give her a quick call? I'm just going to change first." I need to get out of my bathing suit and into dry clothes before I call, in case it becomes a lengthy discussion. I drop Croy's hand and take off toward the stairs.

"You don't need my permission to call someone." His response trails from the hallway where he's remained. Croy's voice goes from casual to pissed in three seconds flat. "Are You Fucking Kidding Me?"

I'm not sure what he's upset about, but I can feel his anger stomping up the stairs. My body reacts by freezing in place as I consider my options. There's only one exit, and he's currently standing in it. My chest tightens, my heart pounds, my mind races, and my lungs constrict, making it hard to breathe. I've dealt with angry men before, but they've never been this big. I have zero chance of fighting him off or getting away. All I can do is wait.

Croy holds my phone out in front of him but offers no explanation for his mood. I take three steps forward, leaving as much distance as possible between us, and reach for it. The phone is in my hand, but my eyes are on his expression. I've seen this face. It's the same one he wore in the video the warden showed me. Something is very wrong. I want to ask, but I'm too afraid to speak. Afraid of him.

"I'll be in the shower." He steps forwards and kisses the top of my head before retrieving a pair of basketball shorts from the top of the dresser and disappearing into the bathroom. I remain paralyzed until I hear the door shut behind him. Then I look at my phone.

Twenty-Seven

YOU HAVE 11 missed text messages

Kells: I'm sorry about earlier. I didn't handle things the way I should have. I was trying so hard to hold it together. I was afraid that If I opened my mouth, I would fall apart. But you deserve so much more than my silence, and now I regret not telling you how I feel. You're important to me, Belk. I don't know if you're still in town, but I'd like to speak to you. Can you call me? Please. I don't want us to end like this.

Kells: I meant everything I said to you in that card. I love you. You mean the absolute world to me. I'm sorry that I fucked everything up between us. I thought I was making a grand gesture of affection, and all I did was piss you off and push you away. I promise I'll never do anything like that again without discussing the details with you first. I need you in my life.

Kells: I wish you'd talk to me. I don't know. Maybe you're driving or taking a nap. I shouldn't overthink it, but I can't help it. I need to have a real conversation with you as soon as possible. I'll take a few days off and drive north if necessary.

Kells: I don't want to be your fake fiancé. I want to be the real thing. We can get married and plan a future together. You know I love you. I'll do anything to be with you. Tell me what I have to do to prove myself.

Kells: If you slept with him, I don't care. I'm not mad. I know he's in your head about everything, convincing you he's the only one who can protect you. Don't let him get in between us. Please. If you don't call me back soon, I'm going to go to his house to look for you. You and I belong together. You know that as well as I do.

Mom: Hey hun. I wanted to see how you're feeling. Still planning on coming home for a bit? I want to talk to you about that when you have a moment. Nothing bad. Give me a call when you get the chance.

Mom: Also, I want to see a picture of this new guy you told me about. He sounds impressive. Maybe a little too good to be true?

Kells: Your fucking car is at his house. Guess that's why you aren't answering. I can't believe you're doing this. You're throwing everything away to be with him. Is this why you quit your job? So you couldn't hide away with an inmate. Guess that's harder to do if you're still wearing a badge.

Kells: You're being a horrible person right now. This isn't you. I know the real you. I love that girl more than anything, and she wouldn't do this. I would've given you everything. I still can if you'll talk to me. I'm never going to stop fighting for you. I love you too much to let you go. He'll never make you happy. He's going to use you, break you, discard you, and forget you.

Kells: If you don't answer, I'm going to call the police and have them do a well check. His fancy-pants neighbors would get a kick out of that. Pretty sure I spotted the mayor. You don't belong there. I don't know what this guy is into, but it isn't good. Is he blackmailing you? Because nothing else makes sense. That criminal will never love you. This is a joke to him. He's ruining everything, and you're letting it happen.

Kells: Fuck you, Belk! I fucking hate you! I'm embarrassed that everyone knows I was dumb enough to have sex with you. I didn't realize you were such a stupid whore, but I guess that makes sense. After all, didn't you get your job at the jail by fucking a bunch of officers? Guess you can add my name to the list of guys you screwed. You deserve to be alone. I wish I'd never met you. That guy doesn't give a shit about you. Why would he? You're a broken little nobody. I don't know why I tried so hard to help you. I should have left you in the ditch where I found you. Don't call me crying when he beats the shit out of you, and you're back in the hospital with nothing.

I place my phone on the dresser before knocking on the bathroom door. I can hear the water running over the deafening silence between us. "Are you okay?" I ask through the door, but Croy doesn't answer. Maybe he didn't hear me. Or maybe he doesn't want to hear anything I have to say. I open the door and take a step in.

The bathroom is filled with steam, so I leave the door open behind me. "Do you want me to leave?" I don't give two shits about Kelly or any of the ignorant bullshit he said, but I'm pissed that he has done *this* to me. Croy won't even talk to me.

I wait for a response that isn't coming as the final seconds between us chip away at my emaciated existence. Kelly's right. I'm a broke little nobody, and Croy never wanted me. I was a fool to think that this new life belonged to me. I'm nothing more than a ghost.

The shower turns off, and the curtain pulls to one side. Without grabbing a towel, Croy steps out onto the rug in front of me, soaking wet.

My voice is pleading as I claw to hold on to this fading opportunity, "I'm so sorry. I wish I had never gone to Kelly's that first night. Please don't hate me."

Without a word, he cloaks me in his embrace, pressing me tight against his chest. I'm still wearing my bikini, so we are skin-on-skin, from head to toe. "I'm not upset with you, Heather. I'm fucking furious with that asshole for saying what he did."

"You read the messages?" I'm not sure how he could have since I still had the missed text notification.

"Only the one that came through when I grabbed your phone. I saw it on the table and wanted to bring it up so you could call your mom. When I read the message and saw who it was from, I wanted to get my keys, drive to his place, and throw him off the fucking balcony. Then I saw you standing there, scared of me. Seeing you like that broke me."

"I was confused. I didn't know why you were upset. I'm sorry. It caught me off guard." Now I feel bad for thinking he would ever hurt me. I don't want to keep explaining all the ways my past has damaged me. If I tell him about those things, he'll see how broken I am and want nothing to do with me. Or worse, he'll feel compelled to avenge me. Either way, I lose him, which is what I'm trying to avoid.

"I would *never* lay a hand on you in anger. But your friend is living on borrowed time. I'm not sure if you've experienced things in your past or if it's fear left over from what happened at the jail. Either way, you're the one person I will always fight for, not against. I don't want you to be afraid of me. We're on the same team. No matter what." Croy feels less tense the longer he talks. And while I appreciate his desire to protect me, it isn't enough to divert me from the threat he's tacked on. It might be in everyone's best interest to delete the other messages before Croy reads them.

"Kelly's not thinking clearly. I swear, he's not normally like this. He's running his mouth and being stupid because he's jealous of you and pissed at me. If you want, I can text him and tell him to fuck off, or I can ignore him... If it makes you feel any better, not all eleven messages were from him. Two of the text were from my mom, wanting to hear about the fancy new guy I've been spending time with." I try to lighten the mood with a little laugh.

"What makes me feel better is having you in my arms. What am I gonna do after you leave?" He asks me the one question I don't want to know the answer to. I'm afraid he'll move on with someone else and forget I ever existed.

"Come find me." My words are a whisper that melts into his skin.

Deciding it's time for a change in venue, Croy lifts me off my feet and carries me to the bed. Sex is always a good stress reliever, so I'm not surprised he's ready to go. What throws me off is when he positions himself next to me and doesn't make a move. Instead of initiating something sexual, he holds me. This moment isn't about releasing anger. It's about connecting. Everything about Croy contradicts my previous experiences with men.

My life has indeed been turned on its head as of late, but even that feels manageable with him on my team. I'm unsure if leaving is the best idea, though these texts from Kelly are enough to start my packing. What if I throw away my future because I'm scared? I'm so tired of jumping from one relationship to the next. Why would this time be any different? I don't know what to do.

Kelly says that I'm a whore, but I disagree. Serial Monogamist? Sure. Hopeless Romantic? Absolutely. Whore? No way. I'd have to be the worst whore in history because it seems like the only one who pays the price is me. I know he's only repeating the lies he's heard recently, but it still hurts. I thought he knew me better than they did.

After a while, I persuaded Croy to get closer, resulting in the most passionate lovemaking I've ever participated in. With every fiber of my being, I'm convinced we are two halves of one soul, reunited. At this point, it would take a lot to sway my belief.

The rest of the night is quiet. We make dinner together and watch a murder mystery on Hallmark. With no further messages from Kelly, I ignore my anger and disappointment and focus on the man beside me. Croy tells me I have a surprise coming my way tomorrow, but I can't squeeze any clues out of him. Hopefully, it doesn't involve anyone being thrown over a balcony during the night.

Twenty~Eight

I AWAKE to the smell of bacon and a text message.

> Croy: Rise and shine, sleepyhead. Breakfast is
> ready, and you're going to need fuel. =) We're
> going on an adventure!

An adventure? What does that mean? Knowing Croy, it's probably something physical. Although, the last line reminds me of The Hobbit, so that could indicate a lot of walking in my future. I guess there's only one way to find out. I don't typically love surprises. I need to mentally prepare beforehand, so impromptu activities leave me feeling off balance. I get anxious and closed off when I don't know what's coming my way. But I trust that Croy isn't going to throw me into anything I can't handle. But first, I need to settle something with the other man in my life.

: I'm still pissed at you, even after taking the night to cool off. The things you said yesterday were out of line. I understand that you're upset. You have every right to be. You hate me? That's fine. I deserve that. But your hurt feelings don't give you the right to call me every name in the book and make threats. And stop talking about Croy as if you know anything about him. Your fight is with me. And for your sake, you'd better keep it that way.

Kells: Babe, I'm sorry. I never should've said those things. You're right. I was a complete asshole yesterday and said things I shouldn't have. You know that isn't me. I didn't mean anything in that last text. Had I been smart, I would've stopped after the first few messages. I love and adore you. I want to be with you more than anything. You're my best friend. You're beautiful and amazing and a hell of a lot smarter than I am. I'm miserable without you. I miss you every second of the day.

: You can't mean any of this. Please stop saying these things to me. You don't know that part of me.

Kells: Yes, I do! I've spent months falling in love with you. It's not my fault if you didn't notice. Somehow this guy comes out of nowhere, and he knows you better than I do? That's bullshit.

: It's not about him! This is about you and me. I don't want to hate you. I've had you on a pedestal since we met. I still think you're amazing, even when I'm furious. The last thing I want is to leave here, regretting our time together. If you truly love me, then stop trying to pick a fight with me.

Kells: You're right. You're always right. I'm sorry. Can I please see you one more time before you leave town?

: I don't know. I'll think about it. Maybe if you tell me I'm right a few more times, you can return to my good graces. But if you send me one more shit message, my answer to meeting up will be NO. And I will lose your number.

Kells: You're beautiful and kind and right about everything. I'm still not sure how one person can be so amazing, but you pull it off with grace and charm. And did I mention that you're always right? Constantly right about everything. If it were anyone else, it might be annoying, but you, my love, are walking perfection. All other women pale in comparison. Give me a chance to prove I'm still worthy of being on that pedestal beside you. I need you in my life. I can't deal with the thought of losing you. Will you forgive me?

: That was a whole lot of sugarcoated marshmallow fluff, but it did make me smile. So, I guess you're forgiven. I'm going out for the day. We can talk later.

Kells: Okay. I'll be here. I hope I get to see you soon.

I shift my focus and find Croy standing in the doorway. He looks yummy, per usual. "I promise it's going to be fun. Now get that sweet ass out of bed, and let's eat." He's in shorts and a sleeveless shirt, so I'm guessing it's hot today, and our adventure is taking place outdoors.

"I'm going to need a clue. Can you tell me what kind of clothes to wear... Also, I might need a quick kiss to motivate me." If I had the option, I would stay in bed, kissing him all day. I'm going to have to make sure that I plan the next adventure.

My eyes are glued to Croy as he walks over and sits on the edge of the bed. I want to remember every detail of this moment. The smile that reflects in his eyes. The way his hand slides up my back. The kiss that starts on my neck before reaching my lips. "I promise to kiss you every hour, on the hour, if you get dressed. Our food is getting cold."

"Alright, I'm awake. You go eat, and I'll be down in a minute." It doesn't take me long to locate shorts and a tank top in my bag. I get dressed and grab my phone off the bed. When I get to the kitchen, I catch Croy stealing a slice of bacon off my plate. "Caught ya red-handed."

"I'm helping." He smiles as he places the uneaten half back on my plate. "You eat. I need to take care of a few things before we leave."

As I pass by his chair, I run my fingers along Croy's broad shoulders. "Can you sit with me a minute? I'd like to talk to you about something." I sit in the chair near him and place my phone on the table. "I wanted you to know that I talked to Kelly. If you want to see yesterday's conversation and the messages from this morning, it's all right there. I haven't deleted anything."

"I don't need to go through your phone, dear. I trust you." Croy uses one finger to slide the phone back over to me and starts to stand.

"Wait. Please." I want to have this conversation even though it's unwise. I need him to understand where I'm coming from. Maybe I'm stupid for wanting to be this transparent. The messages could be seen as flirtatious on both sides. Certainly, I haven't done as much as I should have to discourage Kelly's advances. But I haven't earned Croy's blind trust, and I want him to like me with his eyes open. "I don't want to make you mad, especially since you've planned a whole day for us, but I'd like you to read the conversation. I'm considering something, and I'd appreciate your thoughts on the matter. Your opinion means a lot to me." I push the phone towards him and hold it there until he gives in.

Croy takes his time reading through the text exchange before speaking. "Okay, my opinion is that Kelly is an asshole. He's obsessed with you and delusional. The promises he makes mean less than nothing because his word is shit. I hate the idea of you meeting with him alone because I don't trust him. And I'm not going to sit here and encourage you to work things out with your ex because I don't think he's the right guy for you. For the life of me, I can't understand why you're always so quick to forgive him. You keep saying this isn't him, but I've yet to see another version... It doesn't matter what I think. What matters is how you feel. So, why is this important to you?"

"You aren't wrong. Kelly does seem a bit unhinged at times and weirdly obsessed. That's why it's important for me to resolve this situation before I leave. I don't want him doing anything stupid or retaliating against you in my absence. It freaks me out that he knows where you live." It's not that I think Kelly will drive past the house and shoot him in the front yard. But I wouldn't put it past him to key Croy's car or stick a screw in the tire.

"It's cute that you're worried about me. But I assure you, I can handle anything he attempts to do to me. Kelly doesn't scare me. Not the way you think he does." Croy might not be worried, but I am.

"You know how you like to take care of me, right? Well, let me take care of this for both of us. You shouldn't have to deal with my mess." I couldn't live with myself if I knew that something from my past was negatively affecting him in my absence.

"How about we take the day to think about it and discuss it after we get back? Same team, remember?" He lifts my hand and presses it to his lips. "Now, finish eating and get your shoes on. Our adventure awaits."

Croy finishes filling the backpack on the counter while I eat. I keep trying to see what he's stuffing in the bag, hoping for clues, but he's being secretive. When he's done in the kitchen, he places two ibuprofen on the table next to me. "Take these. I've noticed you're prone to headaches. I have more in the bag if you need them later."

I've had a headache every day since I was ten years old, but I think Croy is the first person to notice besides my mom. Little actions like this tug at the ol' heartstrings. He makes me feel seen in a way that never comes across as judgmental. Who knew my prince charming would be tall, muscular, covered in tattoos, and ready for a fight? I love it.

We drive for 25 minutes before I see a sign that reads Cedar Falls. I didn't realize, but apparently, we've driven into the heart of the state park. I've never come here, but I've heard people speak of its beauty. At 9:59 am, we pull into a parking spot at our first location. Croy walks around and opens my door, and as I slide out, I hear the alert on his watch go off. His fingers weave into the hair at the back of my head, and he kisses me immediately. "10:00"

We hike a little over a mile at each of the first four locations. Thankfully, the terrain has been mostly flat. Otherwise, my legs would be burning. The splendor of this place blows me away. There are caves and waterfalls, cliffs and gorges, rivers and trees, and even something called The Devil's Bathtub. How have I lived in Ohio nearly all my life and never knew this existed? This would have been the perfect place to come when I needed to escape my apartment.

We stop for a picnic in the woods near one of the waterfalls, and I'm awestruck by our surroundings. The only thing more impressive than the views is Croy's thoughtfulness. I don't have much to compare it to, but this is one of the nicest dates anyone has ever taken me on. The sun is shining, and there's a warm breeze, but it's chilly in the shade of the trees. Lucky for me, Croy planned for everything and packed a long sleeve shirt in his bag. He's attentive in a way I didn't think possible. It's like he's reading my mind or predicting the future.

The final trail is where the real adventure begins. I was lulled into a false sense of security since the other trails had been somewhat compact. So, when we reach Old Man's Cave and pause at the split, I assume both trails will ultimately take us to where we need to be. One path leads to some stairs, the visitor center, and the parking lot where we left the car. The other path goes to Whispering Cave.

"Should we go to the final cave?" Croy is nice and gives me the option, but not nice enough to tell me how far away it is. I don't want to leave anything unseen, so we take the split. When I finally realize what I've agreed to, it's too late to turn back. "We have to go forward, to go back. Best press on." Thanks, Willy Wonka.

At the top of every hour, Croy's watch signals the time. No matter what we're in the middle of, he stops to kiss me. He's too much, in a way that is exactly the right amount. I love that he's always true to his word, even when it's something silly like a kiss every hour.

Finally, at long last, we make it back to the car. My legs have been jello for the last couple of miles. When Croy offered to carry me, I quickly refused, so he held my hand, and I pushed through. Sinking into my seat, I'm that good kind of tired. The sort of exhaustion that follows a job well-done, that can only be cured by kicking off your shoes.

I must fall asleep on the ride home because we're already in the driveway when I open my eyes. Sleeping is probably my body's way of coping with being in the passenger seat. Otherwise, I tend to get carsick if I'm not driving.

I hope the second half of our adventure takes place in the basement on the couch because all I want to do right now is lounge in Croy's arms and close my eyes. This day has been perfect and amazing and I wouldn't change a thing until my phone goes off.

Kells: Can you come over so we can talk?

: I don't think I can right now. I hiked more miles than I can count, and I'm exhausted. I want to see you so we can talk, but it might have to wait. Can we do it later or tomorrow?

Kells: Hiking? That sounds fun. Wish we
could've done something like that together. I'm
happy to hear that you're feeling better. The
iron treatments must be working.

"You're not going over there right now, are you?" I can read the concern all over his face as he asks. "I thought we'd discuss it first."

"We will. I'm not going anywhere. I'm too tired, and I was hoping you, and I could relax together for a bit." The iron has helped, but I'm still not at one hundred percent.

Croy and I shower and change into comfortable clothes before retreating to the cool darkness of the basement TV room. I normally don't care for basements, but this one is finished beautifully. A large egress window behind the couch makes it feel like a first-floor living room. I could picture a teenager wanting this space for their bedroom.

The thought of children and motherhood cris-crosses my mind. It's not on my bucket list, but sometimes I could see my life headed that way. Of course, if my dating history is any indication, I'll be a single mom for sure. Croy did mention wanting the whole package at one point. I wonder if that's still his goal. Is it too early to talk about those things, or is that pertinent information everyone needs before making a decision?

Croy takes his spot in the corner of the sectional couch, and I lay with my head on his chest. Potentially, we could be nearing the end of our time together, and this fact hangs heavy in the air around us. "Are you still planning on leaving Monday morning?" Neither of us will ever be fully ready for this conversation, so I'm surprised when he asks. I suppose now is as good a time as any.

"That's the plan unless you want me to leave sooner?" I know what I'm doing, and I hate myself for it. I'm offering him an out because I know I don't deserve him. But I also know he isn't interested in taking it.

"I don't want you to leave at all. You know that, don't you? I want more time with you, not less." He gives me a squeeze every time he wants to add emphasis to his words. "What did your mom say when you called her? Anything exciting going on there?"

I talked to my mom while Croy was in the shower so that I could gush about him in private. Turns out, my parents bought a new motor home and are planning to take off on a new adventure of their own. They want me to live in the house instead of getting an apartment. Apparently, someone needs to take care of the plants while they're gone, and I've been selected for the position.

Taking care of my mother's plants is a full-time job requiring an advanced degree in horticulture and no less than five years of experience, with a specialty in orchids. This opportunity doesn't get me any closer to feeling like I have something to offer, but it does potentially give me a chance to start saving for a future of my choosing. Plus, I can leave the plants home alone for a few days if I want to come for a visit.

"Turns out they're headed west for a while and asked if I would be interested in staying at the house. It would save me from signing another lease. I have an interview on Tuesday at 10:00 am for a job I applied for."

"Wow. That all sounds great, hun. I'm proud of you for working things out. But can I ask you something? What does your picture-perfect future look like if you didn't have to worry about money or what anyone else wanted? Where would you live? What kind of house? Do you want kids? Or a pet? Do you have a spouse? If so, what are they like? I want to hear the whole package. When you close your eyes and let yourself dream, what do you imagine your life to look like?" Croy starts to play with my hair as he's talking. If he continues, I'm going to fall asleep before I can think of my answer.

"The house would be a 3000 sq ft modern ranch with two master bedrooms on either side. The kitchen and living room would be in the center of the house, and the entire back wall would be floor-to-ceiling windows. There would be a set of french doors in each bedroom that opened out to the back outdoor living space. The stamped concrete patio would have an in-ground pool and a hot tub. There would also be a building in the back. It would be a pool house/gym with a full bathroom. The house would sit on 4.5 acres, and I would have fruit trees and a small vegetable garden. I would have two red boston terriers, one with an all-white face and one with classic markings. As for children, I could imagine having one. I don't have an image of them beyond that. I don't know. I guess I want my kid to have the chance to be their authentic self, not some version of a child I dreamt of. As for the spouse, I want someone I can grow old with. I want a partner and a best friend. I'd like to feel seen and heard, respected and loved, protected and trusted, and all of the other lovely idealistic qualities that probably don't exist in reality. It would be great if my husband were tall and strong, with blue eyes and a ton of tattoos. But I guess I'm willing to take whatever I can get." I thought at first it might be difficult to answer his question, but once I closed my eyes, I realized a clear picture was already there. It reminded me a lot of how I grew up, only more tailored to my personal preferences.

"Wow, that sounds amazing. I'd like to see that. And your husband sounds like my new best friend."

"Yeah. Well, it'll probably have to wait for the next lifetime. I'm pretty sure I've fucked this one up beyond repair." It's sad, watching my dreams grow, simply to have them wither on the vine. "But if you can find me sooner, before my life falls apart, I'll invite you in for coffee and show you around. Maybe you and the husband can work out together."

"As soon as I'm old enough to walk, I'll start searching... So, housing is all sorted out back home, and you have a job interview on Tuesday. That's fantastic. I know whatever the job is, you'll be amazing." He doesn't sound happy, but I can see he's trying.

"What about you? What's your ideal life look like?" I secretly hope that parts of his imaginary life might align with mine. I'm going to miss the gravity of existing in his orbit, and it would be nice to think we might cross paths again somewhere along the line.

"I'm not sure anymore."

The minutes pass, and the silence continues. If he asked me to stay, sincerely asked, I would strongly consider it. After all, my dreams means nothing if he isn't there beside me. But he hasn't asked. He tells me that he doesn't want me to leave. He says that he wants me to stay. But I need a gold engraved invitation, which has yet to come in the mail.

Croy's watch signals the new hour, and he kisses the top of my head. "I need to go out for a bit. Will you be alright here without me?" His voice is somber, as though he's going out to plan a funeral for the death of romance.

"Sure. Maybe I'll get dressed and see about having that conversation. It'd be nice to get it out of the way so I don't have to deal with it tomorrow." I dread the short drive back to Kelly's apartment, but it's better than leaving the situation unresolved.

"Can't you call him instead? I don't like the idea of you being there alone with him. Let me go with you, and I'll hang out at Eric's. Kelly won't even know I'm around. But I'll be close if anything happens." It seems like Croy has given this some thought.

"Nothing is going to happen. I can text him and suggest a phone call instead of meeting in person if that's what you'd prefer. That's probably more than he deserves at this point, after some of the things he said." My feelings about Kelly are mixed. I'm not happy with him at the moment, but I don't hate him either. I miss the guy I knew before, but he's been unrecognizable as of late. "You go out and do whatever it is you have to do. I'll text you if I decide to meet him anywhere, okay? That way, you don't have to worry."

"Please be careful. I know you like to see the good in people. But that makes it easier for them to hide the bad stuff when you're not looking." Croy talks like I have a blind spot for evil. Maybe he sees something in Kelly that I don't, or maybe he doesn't trust me. Perhaps a phone call is going to have to be enough.

> : I'm available to talk if you're still interested. Can I call? I don't want to leave things unresolved between us.

Kells: I'd rather talk in person. A phone call feels too impersonal. If you feel uncomfortable coming to the apartment, we can meet someplace else.

> : I'm not sure if I should be driving. I'm exhausted.

Kells: What if I come there? I can bring all the stuff you left at my place. We can hang out and talk. Or I can pick you up, and we can go someplace else.

I'm going to need to run this past Croy first. I can't exactly invite another guy to the house the second he leaves me alone. That's not a good look. And the last thing I want to do is disrespect a man in his own home.

> : I'm not sure if you left or not yet. Would you be okay with Kelly coming here? I won't let him in the house. I can talk to him out front. He wants to bring me whatever I left at his place, and it would keep me from having to drive.

Croy: I'm in the bedroom changing.

> : I'll be right up.

I should change my clothes as well, that's a good idea. Kelly has seen me in sweats, but being in Croy's clothes might set a bad tone for the conversation. I don't need him pissed at me as

216

soon as he pulls into the driveway. This whole thing is already awkward enough.

"I didn't respond to him one way or the other because I wanted to discuss it with you first. This is your home, and I understand if you don't feel comfortable with him being here." I hope Croy is agreeable to this plan because now he has me thinking that maybe I shouldn't be overly trusting of Kelly's intentions. That being said, maybe letting him come here is worse than me going there, especially if the whole point is to protect Croy and his property. Shit!

"I'd rather the conversation happen here if it has to happen at all. Let him come to the house, invite him in, sit on the back patio, and talk it out. If you want me to stay, I will. I'll sit in my office and give you some space. Or, if you'd rather, I'll run my errands and text you when I'm on my way back. That way, you have your privacy." Croy seems far more relaxed about this plan than the alternative. "But so you're aware, there are two cameras mounted on the back of the house. I put them there to record the petty ass neighbor throwing rocks in my grass."

"And here I thought you trusted me?" I smile and wink because I know our faith in each other remains fully intact.

"I do trust you. You know that... If Kelly coming here gives you the closure you need, then I think you should sit with him and say whatever you need to say. And if he's willing to drop off the rest of your stuff, all the better. I don't want that part of your life following you back home."

: Okay. Do you know where Croy's house is?

Kells: You know I do.

: You could've been lying about that. Honestly, I was kind of hoping you were. I can't believe you looked him up at work. You're lucky you didn't get caught.

> Kells: We look at people's booking info all the
> time. The sergeant encourages us to do it. How
> many hours have you spent scrolling through
> inmate files? Anyways, that's not the point. I
> had to see it for myself to make sure you were
> okay. It's not like I knocked on the door. Is he
> going to be there?

Maybe this is a bad idea. But leaving things the way they are feels worse. It's okay to make a mess. So long as you take the time to clean it up.

> : Croy isn't going to be here. I want us to be
> able to talk. Whatever you need to say to me,
> this is going to be your opportunity to say it. I'm
> leaving, and I'm probably not coming back.

> Kells: I'll be there in 10 minutes. I have to get all
> your stuff loaded into my car. Then I'll be on
> my way.

All of a sudden, I feel sick to my stomach. What the hell am I doing? This is a horrible idea. Why did I think this was better than going to the apartment? "He said he'll be here in ten minutes." I'm trying not to sound freaked out and failing miserably.

"Do you want me to stay or go?" Croy has a twinkle in his eye that concerns me. He's itching for a fight, and I know if he stays, Kelly is getting knocked out.

"Of course, I want you here, but I already told him you'd be gone." I'm stronger with Croy by my side, but that will only provoke the altercation I'm trying to avoid.

"Well then, I better get going. I need to do a little birthday shopping. My phone will alert me when something moves in the back. Talk to him on the patio. Not in the front yard and not in the house. Please, for me. I need to know you're safe." Croy gives me one more quick kiss, and then he's gone.

He's already down the stairs and out the door, leaving me to talk to myself. "This feels like being in the jail again. Why does everything have to be so stressful? It's nothing I can't handle, but a little backup would be nice."

I hurry and change into my jeans. Then put on a light hoodie over my t-shirt. The patio is in the shade, and I'm not sure what the temperature will be. Plus, I don't want Kelly touching me. The more layers I have on, the better.

Twenty-Nine

KELLY SAID TEN MINUTES, but he's at the house in five. I open the front door and step outside before he moves one toe off the driveway. What am I doing? Why am I so worried all of a sudden? This is Kelly. My friend. The guy I've trusted with my life. He isn't going to do anything to me. Maybe Croy has influenced my thinking about this. I can almost hear his voice telling me to be careful.

Shit! I forgot to make a request. As Kelly approaches, I slip the phone from my pocket and send a quick text.

> : Please don't listen to our conversation.

> Croy: No worries. You can say whatever you need to say. I'm not going to get mad. And if you want, I'll turn the volume off on my phone. Please be careful. Don't make me regret leaving.

"Checking in with the man of the house to make sure you have his permission to see me? Wouldn't want to make him mad. We've both seen what he's capable of." Kelly's remark is snide, and I don't appreciate his tone.

"That's not what I was doing... Anyways, thanks for bringing me all of this. You didn't have to do that." I start grabbing bags from Kelly's hand and setting them in the house to the right of the entryway. It's all food and toiletries. Maybe I'll leave some of it here for when I visit. That is if Croy lets me return.

"Am I allowed inside the house, or do we have to talk out here?" Kelly already sounds agitated. Not a great way to start.

"I figured we could sit out back if that's okay. We can go through the house or walk around the side." As I turn to open the door, he grabs my hand and laces our fingers together. I can see he isn't going to make this easy for me. I try making a beeline for the back patio door, but it's like dragging a dead body through quicksand. "Can you please walk? I don't feel comfortable hanging out in Croy's house without him here."

"Isn't this your home now, too? I mean, you are living with him, aren't you?" Again, with the tone. As if he is trying to goad me into a fight.

"No. I'm leaving tomorrow after my iron infusion. I only stuck around to finish my treatments, and I couldn't afford to pay for a hotel." I keep trying to drag his corpse toward the door. He's pulling against me, and I have half a mind to let go of his hand and let him fall on his ass.

"Give me a hug, and I'll go outside with you." From snide to smug. Kelly is here to play games, not get closure. He must imagine Croy hiding upstairs in the closet. What's next? Is he planning to ask me for a blowjob and some break-up sex? Whatever. Let's get it over with.

I turn on my heels and walk into his arms. He smells good, like the man I once admired. When I close my eyes, I imagine we're back at the apartment, killing time before we have to be at work. He reminds me of a dream I had once.

"I miss holding you." His bravado melts away as my proximity stokes the fire in his chest. "I miss us being together."

I take a deep breath, filling my lungs with him, and sink deeper into his embrace. I didn't realize how much I needed this until he thrust it upon me. Croy was right to worry. I've been trying to convince him that Kelly was never my boyfriend, but I'm starting to question those claims. "I miss certain things as well."

Kelly's feet move forward, guiding me backward until my back makes contact with the wall in the kitchen. Then he cups my face in his hands and kisses me. I push my arms out straight into his chest. The wall at my back gives me added strength I wouldn't normally have, and I'm able to create a gap between our bodies.

"Stop! I'm not doing that." I can feel my face getting hot as my anger rises. "Can we go outside and talk? Please!"

Sliding open the door, I step through the opening, dragging Kelly behind me. This is the first time I've been in Croy's back-yard. It's beautiful, even though it could use a few more plants and a fence. Don't need any future dogs or kids running into the street. The glimpse of that future brings a momentary smile to my face as I realize I could be happy here with Croy. Even though the foundation and the first few floors were in place before I arrived, there's still a significant amount of life left to build together. All I have to do is fall and allow him to catch me.

"Babe, did you hear me?" Kelly's taken my hand again, only this time he's the one leading me. While I was daydreaming of unwritten futures, he moved two chairs so that they were facing each other. The distance between them is so slight that I'm not sure both sets of our legs will fit. He sits first and then pulls me towards him. I have to straddle his legs to get into the chair opposite him. Then, he lifts my legs and positions my feet on either side of his waist. He's intentionally making me look like I've draped myself across him. Clearly, this display is meant for the audience not currently in attendance. "So, tell me about some of these things you miss."

I'm getting a headache, and I wish Croy would come home. I should have asked him to stay. Kelly shouldn't even be here right now. No good is going to come from any of this. I'm such an idiot. At the very least, I wish I had grabbed my sunglasses off the counter. Even in the shade, the daylight is hurting my eyes.

"Okay. Well, I miss the way things used to be before the chaos. Not the discomfort and loneliness. That part sucked. But I miss the calm and the certainty. There was a comfort in knowing that I had some level of control over my day. I miss the jail and the people in it. I felt like I was meant to be there, and it gave me a sense of purpose for the first time in my life. The people we work with started to feel like family. Not the kind you live with, but the sort you see begrudgingly on the holidays. I even miss talking to the inmates about stupid shit. I was hoping for a few birthday letters and some toilet paper flowers, but I doubt they even remember me. I miss working out at the gym and going grocery shopping. I miss french fries for dinner and gas station ice. I miss the way Linda from Spin Cycle would fold my t-shirts into perfect little squares. I even miss my horrible apartment because it was the first thing I'd ever gotten on my own. I had this whole other life, and then I woke up, and it was over. I became a ghost and could only watch as everything was ripped away. Now I'm a different person, in a different life, and there's no going back. Do you have any idea how confusing that is? Sometimes I can't figure out which one is real. Before or Now. And then there's you. But you've changed too. No matter what I say or do or how hard I look, I can't find the guy I remember. I lost my best friend, and I didn't even get to say goodbye to him." Kelly rubs his hands over my legs as I talk, and the touch I used to crave feels hollow. This isn't how I want to remember him. I pull my feet back and sit cross-legged. Now, our knees are all that remain touching.

"I'm right here, babe. I never left. You walked away from me, and I kept waiting for you to come back, but that was a mistake. I should've been the one to find you. Been the one fighting for you. I'm sorry that I let you disappear. I should've been there. Should have held on tighter. I should've saved you, not that *criminal*."

That word, criminal, snaps my attention into focus. "Why do you keep doing that? You keep acting like we're better than they are, but I'm not better than anyone. Are you trying to piss me off? It was a fucking DUI, Kelly. Stop with the goddamn *criminal* bullshit. He's a regular guy. The two of you would probably get along if you stopped looking down your nose at him."

"Look at this fucking house. And his car. That guy spent more on tattoos than we make in a year, combined. Wake up, Belk! Your new boyfriend isn't who you think he is, and I sure as hell don't want to be his friend. No one our age makes this kind of money playing it straight. He's doing something illegal." Kelly's getting desperate. He's throwing shit at the walls hoping it will stick.

"You're being ridiculous. He went to college. He has a good job. Someone having their shit together doesn't mean they're doing something illicit. For all you know, he inherited the money from an eccentric uncle. Or maybe he taught himself how to play the stock market. I don't know, and I don't care. If you came over to talk about Croy, then hang out with him. I'll call him, and you two can chitchat about finances and investment strategies." I wonder if Croy is listening to all this and laughing or looking at the visual of us sitting close and getting pissed off.

"Ah! There it is." Kelly's acting like this is a Gotcha moment, but I have no clue why.

"There *what* is? What are you talking about?" I'm not sure if my brain is still in a cloud or if Kelly has always been this hard to follow.

"'He went to college. He has a good job.' I should have known a college girl like yourself would be a snob." Kelly's tone is mocking, and I've had about enough.

"I'm not a snob, Kelly. Everyone goes to college these days. It's not even special anymore. You went to school too." This isn't the first time I've been accused of this during a fight, but I still argue it's false. I don't think I'm better than anyone. In fact, I would venture to say that I think more of most people than I do myself, college-educated or not. "Can we please get this discussion back on track before I abandon the whole idea of a conversation?"

"What is there left to say? You made your choice." He sits

forward in his chair, splitting the distance between us in half. "Unless you want to tell me that you love me and we can be together?"

"What? No. I'm not going to say that." I huff out an exasperated laugh and shake my head. Is he crazy? Or am I?

In one motion, Kelly pushes back his chair and gets to his feet. As I look up, he slaps me hard across the face. The crack makes my ear pop, and I feel the sting as it spreads across my cheek. I've been punched in the face before, but I think this might be worse. My eyes fill with tears as my voice rises to a crescendo. "What the fuck is wrong with you? We're done. Don't ever speak to me again!"

Kelly stands as a blurred imposter. A cheapened memory of the man I once knew. Until two seconds ago, I would've marched into battle by his side and died next to him as a friend. Even now, as the sting of his disrespect pulses in my cheek, I'm concerned with his safety. Croy will kill him in a fight, and I'm not sure I can stop it.

"Fuck. Belk. I'm sorry. That wasn't..." Kelly takes two steps back as the phone in my pocket begins to ring. For the first time, he looks away from me. And that's when he notices the cameras mounted on either side of the house.

"You need to leave!" My resolve is stronger now because I have nothing left to lose. I let my guard down, and it cost me. I've spent my whole doubting my strength and my value, and I have allowed others to benefit from that doubt. But if Kelly stays in this yard much longer, he'll pay for his lapse in judgment in blood.

I get a text alert, and the message confirms my fear.

Croy: He's a dead man.

"Kelly! Leave! You don't want to be here when Croy gets home." I'm not sure what had Kelly glued to his place, but these words have freed him. Opting for the fastest route, he shoots through the sideyard. Before I can get through the house and out the front door, Kelly is backing out of the driveway. My ringtone sounds for a third time, so I answer it.

"What do you want me to do?" Croy's voice is steadfast.

"Come home. Please. I need you here with me." I need him next to me for selfish reasons. I don't want Kelly hurt. And I don't want Croy to become the worst version of himself because of me. I know what he saw and how furious he must be. And I know what he's capable of doing. He was right about Kelly, and I denied him the opportunity to protect me. I can't imagine that's something he's going to let stand.

Thirty

THE STING LINGERS across my cheek, and there's a high pitch ringing in my left ear. The sound makes it difficult to focus. All I want to do is lay on the couch and close my eyes, but I would rather be on my feet when Croy gets home. I'm still shocked by what happened. It wasn't surprising when Kelly wanted to hold hands, hug, or kiss. I had expected him to push for that. Had I been slightly more receptive, I'm sure he would have kept notching up the *romance* until we were naked on the couch.

There's a fire inside Kelly. I saw that early on. But I mistook his intensity for passion. The man I knew him to be died in the jail, right along with me, and neither of us is coming back.

I would need to review the video and listen to the dialogue, but I'm certain Kelly's slap was unprovoked. I don't remember all the words, but the conversation seemed relatively lukewarm. He didn't have to take it to that place. I wanted to love him. Doesn't he know that. I mean, I get it. I fucked everything up and fell for someone else. But Kelly fucked up too. He made everything about himself and made decisions about my life without allowing me to have a say.

Of course, there's *never* a justification for physical aggression toward a lover. Fault and blame have no place here. Let's make that point clear.

The *This is the End of Your Broadcast* tone in my ear is making me nauseous, and I should probably locate some ibuprofen. I'm certain there's some by the sink next to the mug Croy uses when he makes my coffee. I find the bottle of pills where I thought they would be and pour three into my hand. Now all I need to do is find something to take them with. Nearly twenty-nine years old, and I still have to hide my pills in something like I'm feeding them to the family dog.

My hoodie is choking me, so I pull it off and rest my face against the marble counter. The cool stone feels incredible, drawing out the sting and calming the headache demons. I continue replaying what happened. Kelly's choices may have been out of character, but they were by his own hand. And while I acknowledge his instantaneous remorse, I'm not entirely certain I can forgive him.

I hear the front door as it flings open, and the handle makes contact with the wall. With my luck, Croy put a hole in the drywall, and I'm going to have to patch it and paint before I go. Otherwise, I'll feel guilty forever.

"Where are you?" His voice rings throughout the house, bouncing from wall to wall, up the stairs, and down the hallways until it finds me on my feet in the kitchen.

"I'm in here." His quickened steps start towards my voice before I finish announcing my location.

Croy retrieves an unopened bag of frozen blueberries from the freezer drawer and covers them with a towel. Then, he presses it gently to my cheek before wrapping me in his arms. Now that he's home and has seen me standing, I need to lie down. "Can we go on the couch, please? My head hurts."

"Is there anything I can get you? A pillow? Ibuprofen? Kelly's severed head in a box?" Croy sits sideways on the couch so that I can lay against him. This, right here, is all I need. "Tell me you're okay. That's all I care about right now."

"Yeah, I'm fine. Mostly I have a headache, and I'd like to

close my eyes and wake up in the next chapter of my life. Then I won't have to sit here feeling like an idiot. I wasn't expecting that from him. Not even a little bit." The Kelly I knew from work was always cool under pressure, charming, and disarmingly funny. I'm not sure what happened to that guy, but he wasn't here ten minutes ago. "I know you saw that side of him, but I didn't. I'm sorry I didn't listen to you."

The tips of Croy's fingers trace invisible patterns across my skin. He has an uncanny ability to make everything better. "I knew he was going to be an asshole. At worst, I thought he might curse you out. If I had truly thought he was capable of putting his hands on you like that, I would've never left. I'm sorry that I failed to protect you."

"Stop! You don't need to be sorry. I'm the one who failed. I asked you to leave because I was meant to be protecting you, remember?" I suppose that sounds a little silly now. "But hey, silver lining, I don't think you have to worry about me running off with Kelly anytime soon. I'm pretty sure that slap was the final nail in the coffin." In that regard, I do feel a sense of relief and mourning. I know myself, and I'm someone who requires closure. And nothing says, "We're done here," like getting hit in the face.

"Yeah, that's one way to look at it. But he also killed any hope I had of convincing you to move in with me. So, I don't think I'll be mailing him a Thank You card any time soon."

The ringing in my ear slowly disappears and is replaced by the drumming of Croy's beating heart. I love laying against him. His body is in that perfect sweet spot between hard and soft. He's muscular without feeling like a stone statue. So long as he's here, there's always hope I could find my way back. "Wherever you are, is where I'm going to want to be. So, don't lose hope yet. I need a break from this town. But I don't ever want a break from you."

"I know you'd come back for me, but I'm not sure I want you to." His tone is a somber melody.

As the weight of his words sinks into my chest, I feel my light dim. "Oh." I make an attempt to sit forward but his arms snake around me. "I didn't realize..."

"Stop... Please stop. I love to hear you speak. You know that I hang on to your every word. But for a moment, let me finish what I was saying before you take it out of context."

I don't struggle against him. This is not a fight between us. His words are a fight for the future of us, and I want to hear everything he has to say. "I'm sorry. When you paused, I thought you were done. I'm listening."

"We've spent a lot of our time together talking, getting to know one another, which is how it should be. But these are some of the things I know for sure. You moved here for a guy who didn't respect you enough to be honest. Strike one. You felt miserable and trapped in an apartment that lacked basic creature comforts. Strike two. A person that you deeply respected, your boss, accused you of some ridiculous shit and made you feel devalued. He was out of line, and I know you were hurt by what he said. Strike three. The job you loved has been tarnished beyond repair, not because of the violence directed at you but because of the rumors that poisoned your reputation. Rumors fabricated by the people you trusted. Strike four. Then, you were betrayed and assaulted by a friend and lover. That alone is enough to make a person hate a place. Strike five. In addition to *all* of that, a group of people threatened to kill you, which we can call strikes six through ten. After all that, how could I ever ask you to stay here?"

These are all valid points, but each tally mark feels like a personal attack on my judgment. "To be clear, I don't usually have people slapping me or trying to kill me. It's been a bit of an off week."

Croy laughs so strongly that it nearly bucks me off his chest. "Fair enough." He begins tracing patterns on my skin again, and I'm instantly carried back into my calm. "The point I was trying to make is that this town holds too many negative memories and a few very real threats. I want to be with you. But I don't think moving here will ever be an option for you."

"I hear you. I do. Those are all things that have been weighing on me. But let's be real for a moment. You have this amazing life. You're settled in your career. You have this beautiful home. You have your friendships and your routine. I, on the other hand, have nothing. How could I ever ask you to follow me? I can't! I won't let you start over and risk everything for some girl. That's the dumb shit I keep doing, which is why I have nothing to show for my life. So, if moving here isn't an option, neither is being together."

Croy takes a long, thoughtful moment to reflect before answering. "Where do I even start? You, my dear, are not *some girl*. I know you don't want to hear this, but I've gone on plenty of dates and been in my fair share of crap relationships. What you and I have is once in a lifetime. You complete me, completely." He pauses to release a tiny laugh.

I seize my opportunity to chime in. "You're ridiculous and perfect in an incredibly adorable way. It's kind of annoying, really."

"Hun, I don't give two shits about staying in this town. It's almost an hour from work, and the only people I know here are you and Eric. All my family and friends are up north, on the east side of Cleveland. I could have this place sold in a week in this housing market. Once you leave, nothing is keeping me here."

I love everything he's saying, it rings like music to my ears, but I've heard all these lies before. When it's too much too soon and too good to be true, you need to leave that worm on the hook and keep swimming. I can't fall for this again. "So, what happens in six months when we break up? You leave resenting me, and not only do I start over, but I also lose my best friend."

"Heather, I'm not looking to lose my best friend either."

This is progressing to a place where I need to be able to read Croy's words and his face, so I reposition myself. I have been fooled so many times, but if I had been looking closer, I could have saved myself a lot of heartache.

Once I'm turned around, I realize facing him is a bad idea. My heart begins to thunder in my chest as soon as our eyes meet.

He moves forward and wraps my legs around his waist, which is starting to feel like one of those tantric sex positions. It will be impossible to spot the red flags if my mind is in the gutter.

"If you need me to slow down and prove myself, I will. We can take as much time as you want. I'm not trying to push you into anything, and I'm not trying to convince you." Croy's words always sound like he's pulling them straight from my diary. He says exactly what I've wanted to hear time and time again.

I can't help myself. My willpower has been depleted to zero. I lean in and kiss him. The tingling starts in my lips and spreads to my fingers and toes. My heart already knows what my brain refuses to accept. Croy is my forever. "You've already proven yourself, and I don't require further convincing. My heart belongs to you. But... I need some time and a little bit of space. Not distance from you, just quiet, so I can process everything that's happened. It's all been a lot to take on at one time."

"I understand that. You've been upfront and honest with me from the beginning and every step after that. And I've been honest with you every time I've told you I'll wait for as long as it takes. You're my heart and my better half. I'm nothing without that."

Fuck! My mind quickly spins off into a tangent. Why is he so amazing? I don't deserve someone this incredible. How long is he willing to wait, and how long can I stand to be apart? Why am I even leaving? Croy knows why I shouldn't be here. He was kind enough to list all the reasons a few minutes ago. But does any of that matter in comparison to this need I have to be seen by him? I won't have any more or less to offer a month from now, so all I'm doing is delaying the inevitable. And what is that even, us being together or not?

I hate my stupid fucking brain. Shut up! And let me be happy for one goddamn minute.

Thirty-One

THERE'S a comfort level with Croy that doesn't exist elsewhere in my life, but I still hesitate to tell him certain things. Perhaps, over time, I'll introduce him to my demons and be surprised to find out that he has demons of his own. We'll laugh and cry and share more about ourselves than we ever have. Each time, we'll listen and accept what's offered in whatever form it comes. After all, isn't that the goal? To find your best friend. To grow old with the one person who will love you no matter what?

My thoughts continue to parade through my mind during dinner. Instead of focusing on the negative, I allow myself to fantasize about the life that could be. Croy and I are two corresponding puzzle pieces that clicked into place the moment our sides intersected. We are destined to be.

"Okay. So, let's set reality aside and build a hypothetical future. For fun. What might that look like to you?" It's impossible to hide my smile as I ask. Hopefully, all his future plans include me.

"So, time restrictions and all of that aside. There is potentially a job with my company that I've been scouted for. The position would mean more money. But it would also require me to move back up north. As of right now, it's not posted, but I've had more than one person talk to me about it. This is something I was considering before I took the week off. While I've been home, I've been emailing back and forth with HR, trying to get all the details. I wanted to tell you so many times. But I was waiting until I had more concrete information. I didn't want to get our hopes up if it wasn't an option. And you made it clear that you needed time and space, so I didn't want to scare you off." Croy seems to gauge my reaction before continuing.

"Since we're talking hypothetical futures, I thought it would be okay to mention it. If the job is posted and I'm offered the position, the company will cover some of my relocation costs. They would offer me a housing allowance and help me get into a six-month rental. We could use that time to look for a house. Then, from that point forward, everything would be *ours*. You would never have to walk on eggshells or worry about the rug being pulled out from under you. We could build a new life together."

"What would you do with this house? You could fill a semi-trailer with all your worldly belongings." This is fun, picturing this life, even if we are pretending.

"I would have a moving company pack everything we didn't need into some pods and store it until we found a place. If you want to get crazy and go all out, we could buy some land and build your dream house. We could do anything we want."

"I'll be sure to get those blueprints sent over to you." This may seem odd, but I've searched for this particular house in the past. That's how I was able to describe it so easily. I already have a picture of the blueprints saved on my phone. A quickly scroll through my photos, and I find them. A girl has to have dreams. Otherwise, where would she escape to? "Sent."

Croy studies the images for a few minutes. "Oh my god, you have impeccable taste. This house needs to exist. And might I say? I'm not the least bit surprised that you had these readily available. One day, I need to see your entire Bucket List."

We discussed our bucket list plans in passing, but I only offered a few items. In reality, it's a list of about twenty things.

Some are places I want to visit, others are personal goals, and a few were reserved for after I found *my* person.

"I don't need you making all my dreams come true overnight. I want to savor every moment with you, from exciting adventures to quiet nights on the couch." It's pretty safe to say this is the best dinner conversation I've ever had. I love letting my imagination run wild for an evening, but it's even better with a partner. "Plus, I don't want it to only be about me. If this is a team, your dreams matter as much as mine."

Croy gets to his feet and takes my hand. I'm willing to follow him anywhere, which at the moment, means onto the back patio. The lights are on in the landscaping, and the moon is out. Warm summer nights like this always remind me of being on vacation in Myrtle Beach with my family. My parents had a timeshare, where we would spend two weeks every June. As I entered my teen years, I was allowed to be out alone at night. I was a good kid, so they didn't worry about me getting into trouble. Usually, I would walk around and think. For as long as I can remember, I've always been someone who thought deeply about things from every possible angle. That's why I hate surprises.

The patio feels different now, except for the two chairs sitting out of place. Being with Croy, I'd all but forgotten the ear-ringing slap from earlier. He moves the chairs close together, facing one another, the same way Kelly did. And for one brief second, panic tickles the back of my throat. Then he sits and motions for me to join him.

Croy recreates most of the exchange from earlier, not the words, but the actions. He touches me the same places Kelly did, only this time, it's tender and romantic. Then he says, "What is there left to say? You made your choice." He sits forward in his chair, splitting the distance between us in half. "Unless you want to tell me that you love me and we can be together?"

My heart is pounding, and my breathing is heavy. Croy isn't being cruel. He's replacing my bad memory with a good one. No, not merely a good one, but a perfect one. This isn't the time for overthinking. Say what you feel.

"I love you."

Unable to keep the tears at bay, I allow them to fall freely from my eyes and into the hands that are holding my face. Croy is only inches from my lips. I can feel his words against my skin as I breathe him in. "You are my dream. You're my whole life. I could never love anyone more than I love you."

In one synchronized movement, we fall forward an inch so our lips meet in the middle. His arms wrap around my waist, and I'm pulled onto his lap. I need him, and I can feel that he needs me too. Over the next ten minutes, we say *I love you* no less than a dozen times. I'm not typically into such proclamations, but everything about this moment feels right. Plus, whispering *I love you* in his ear is probably better than screaming *Oh my god, harder* at the top of my lungs.

What the hell? Let that bitchy old neighbor watch out her window. Maybe it'll improve her attitude a bit.

Thirty-Two

I'VE BECOME accustomed to waking up in bed alone, but Croy is still there this morning when I open my eyes. He's wide awake, watching me sleep. "Good morning, beautiful. Did you dream of me?" His usual smile adhered perfectly to his handsome face.

"All my life." I'm such a sucker for cute banter and romantic sentiment. I fall into it without thinking. Now we're both smiling, and my mind trails off to memories of last night. After the patio, we went to bed, but neither of us could sleep. We stayed awake talking until 1:00 am. Then Croy put on our song, and I fell asleep in his arms. I wish I could go back in time and find him sooner, but life doesn't work that way. I might not be able to ask him to prom, but I can ask him to dinner. "Would you like to go out with me tonight? On a date."

"You took the words right out of my mouth, birthday girl." Croy reaches over the side of the bed and retrieves a small box wrapped in gold and black paper and a card.

"My birthday isn't until Tuesday." Of course, he already knows this. He's giving me my present today because I won't be here on Tuesday. A reality I have yet to fully acknowledge.

"Well then, Happy Unbirthday, my dear." His words engage

my internal jukebox, and the unbirthday song from Alice in Wonderland begins to play in my head. I always loved that movie as a kid, and I treasure the idea of celebrating someone 364 times instead of only once.

I sit up, facing Croy and his gift. The box is too big to be a ring, so thankfully I don't have to worry about him pulling a Kelly and proposing marriage after less than a week. I decide to open the card first, which seems like proper etiquette. Anyways, I'm more interested to see what he wrote, as opposed to what he bought. The card matches the wrapping paper, with large gold peony flowers against a black background. Bold, yet elegant. Inside there is an iTunes gift card for $100, along with a note that says:

I measure time in memories,
all of them beginning with you.
I love you, more than everything.
-Croy

"I see what you did there." I can't help but laugh. "Got jokes this morning."

"You deserve to hear that every day from someone who means it." Croy puts his hand on my leg and gives it a squeeze. I've noticed he does this whenever he wants to drive a point home. "Anyways, it's a good line, and I'm stealing it."

"Please do. I like it better when you say it, anyways." My fingers trace over the tattoos on the back of his hand, and suddenly I'm reminded of last night on the patio.

"Hurry and open your present so I can give you the next one." Croy's mind seems to have wandered in a similar direction as my own.

"My appointment at the hospital is at 11:00."

"We have time." Croy sounds like he's on the verge of pitching my gifts off the bed and getting straight to the finale. I'd better get this package unwrapped quickly.

I tear off the paper and look at the picture on the outside of the white box. It's a brand new, rose gold Apple watch. "Okay. I can't accept all of this. It's too much."

"All I did was replace the watch you had. The one I probably broke when I bled all over you. I noticed it never turned back on. And the gift card is so you can buy songs, clock faces, and everything that makes an Apple watch worth having." Again, he squeezes my leg, but this time his hand starts to travel. The card, watch, and gift card move to the nightstand, while our clothes fall to the floor.

There's a time for sweet and romantic, and a time for fast and dirty. This is the latter. Afterward, I have exactly 17 minutes to get my watch on the charger, shower, and get dressed, before I need to be downstairs. Croy is always faster than I am. By the time I get to the kitchen, he has the coffee poured and the bagels toasted.

"Have I mentioned yet today how much I adore you?" He says, handing me my coffee.

"You don't have to tell me. You do an excellent job of showing me." I know we have to get out the door, but I can't help myself. Anyways, it's my unbirthday. Surely there's time for a nice long hug and a kiss or two.

In the end, it's a quick kitchen cuddle and no less than three kisses, but we have officially made it out the door with to-go coffees and bagels. Croy does the 20-minute drive to the hospital in 15, so we get to my final appointment with time to spare. I'll be happy when these treatments are finished, though it's been a small price to pay. After all, this low iron dropped me into Croy's arms and held me here after I decided to leave.

After the nurse gets the IV in, all I can do is sit here and wait for it to be over. Thanks to Croy, bagels taste a lot better than vending machine food. As we sit together, passing the time, I ask him, "So, what's on the agenda for today?"

"Depending on how you're feeling after this, we can go on a date, or we can go home and relax. It's your choice. I'm happy so long as I'm with you." Croy moves his visitor's chair beside my vinyl hospital recliner and puts his arm in my lap. Curling in a ball, I wrap my arms around his bicep like it's my favorite teddy bear and rest my head on his shoulder. I don't want to think about leaving. Not yet.

"Ms. Belk, are you feeling alright?" I know this voice but can't place it until I open my eyes. It's the nurse from Wednesday, the one I made a deal with, so I could talk to Croy.

I wipe the tears off my face before saying, "I'm fine. Thank you." I'm a bit surprised to see her. I'd think nurses have an area where they usually work, but maybe not.

"Was your fiancé unavailable to join you today?" Her lips are pursed, and her eyes are accusing.

I decided to fuck with her by going along with Kelly's lie and her little fantasy. My voice takes on a tone even I don't recognize. "He's at home sleeping after a long night at work. Croy was kind enough to offer me a ride and the pleasure of his company. You remember Mr. Jepsen, don't you?" I'm getting so tired of people and their 'gotcha' attitudes.

"Of course. How could I forget?" She looks him over with the same disapproving scowl painted on her face.

"I know, right? He is quite handsome, isn't he." I turn my face towards Croy, and he meets my gaze. "Impossible to forget." We stare at each other until the tension builds past its breaking point. When we kiss, I hear the nurse walk away with a huff.

We both look at each other and laugh. "Never a dull moment."

I coil back into my previous position and rest my head against his shoulder. "Do you think you'll still love me when the dull moments come?" I'm almost scared to hear the answer because I don't think he'll lie.

"Is that what you're worried about? That I'm gonna get bored? Hun, that's the part I'm looking forward to the most. I'm more worried about you getting bored with me. Your life is way more exciting than mine is." Croy and I continue talking until the first nurse returns to remove my IV. Everything about this day tastes bittersweet. We've spoken at length about crazy hypothetical futures but have yet to discuss reality. What is the plan here?

There's a restaurant that Croy wants to try, so we head that way for some lunch. When we get there, it's nicer than I expected, and I'm feeling underdressed. Then again, it's summer, so everyone under the age of 80 is in shorts and a t-shirt. I need to stop being so self-conscious. The waitress practically forgets how to speak after taking one look at Croy. It's funny, but it also feeds one of my biggest insecurities. Is this what I have to look forward to, girls who are younger and prettier than me trying to get his attention? How long until one of them is successful?

The food looks incredible when it comes out. I ordered a California Cobb salad, and Croy went with the steak. His meal smells so good I want to steal it off his plate. I have fully regained my appetite. Just another thing to worry about, gaining weight and getting fat.

My salad is delicious. Everything is crisp and fresh. But Croy's face when that first bite of steak touches his taste buds leaves me a little envious. An emotion that must be written all over my face because he cuts a piece and holds his folk out towards me. "You wanna give it a try?"

"I *really* do." I'm not great at being seductive, so I take the fork out of his hand and pop it in my mouth. This has to be the best steak I've ever tasted. It is seasoned beautifully and cooked to perfection. I am obsessed. "Oh my god, I might love this steak more than I love you." My joke is topped off with a wink, so he knows I'm slightly exaggerating. Don't need Croy getting jealous and punching the cook. The thought makes me laugh out loud.

"What's so funny? Am I about to lose you to a piece of meat?" Croy reaches across the table, grabs my salad bowl, and replaces it with his plate. "Happy Unbirthday, love."

"You don't have to sacrifice your lunch. You chose wisely. And now I'll know better for next time." My words change nothing. To signal that this trade is a done deal, he takes my side of dressing and drizzles the entire cup over the top of the salad. I'm a *dip the tip of the fork in the dressing* kind of person, and he knows this. Clever boy. "Guess that settles that. Anyways, I wanted to talk to you about something."

"What's on your mind, dear?" Croy eats so fast that I'm not even sure if he chews. "This salad is fantastic, by the way." Maybe a conversation will slow him down.

"Do you still want to see each other after I leave?" Well, that came out wrong. What I meant to ask was, what's the plan for seeing each other after I leave? But that isn't what came out of my mouth. My actual question damn near causes Croy to choke on his food.

"Most of the time, I feel like we're on the same page, but then you say something like that, and it's as though you've opened a different book. What do you need from me that I'm not giving you? How can I prove that I'm in this with you?"

This is going to be a long response, so I take a deep breath and center my thoughts. "I'm not looking for you to do anything but be yourself. The only thing that will prove your intentions is the passing of time. I'm not expecting grand gestures and don't need big empty promises. I'm willing to put forth a genuine effort to be with you and to always make you feel important. But my love is not conditional on you loving me back. I'll give you everything I am. Everything I have. No matter what. Because I don't know how to love less than that. The extent to which you choose to reciprocate is entirely up to you. I'll be honest with you, even if I'm afraid it'll make you run because your happiness is more important than my security. I'd prefer you have the information so that you can make the decision that's right for you rather than love someone I can't be."

"See. You say you don't want grand gestures, but then you say shit like that, and all I can think about is how badly I want to marry you so we can start our future together. You're the most real person I've ever met. I have no reason to question your character. You give even when you have nothing. You afford people the benefit of the doubt even after they've shown you the worst version of themselves. You're loyal to a fault. Honest beyond measure. Bloody brilliant. And ridiculously strong. I see you, Heather. I can't *not* see you."

This moment feels too intense. I hold up my index finger on my right hand, look him dead in the eyes, and say "REDRUM" in my best Danny Torrance impression. Croy shakes his head with a smile..

"That, right there, is exactly what I'm talking about. What other woman is going to do *that* in a nice restaurant, sitting across from the best-looking guy in the room while he's professing his undying love and devotion? No one. That moment only exists with you, and I need it every day for the rest of my life."

Croy has both arms stretched across the table. He's holding my hands and looking at me like I am the only person in the place. So, I take the opportunity to rephrase my original question and try the conversation again. "I'd like to circle back if we could because my question didn't quite come out right. I'd like to discuss the plan, if there is one, for seeing one another after tonight."

"Why don't we get the check and discuss all of this back at the house? We can sit on the back patio and have a drink while discussing the details. I've been thinking about it all weekend, and I have some ideas." Croy looks as anxious as I feel.

The ride home is quiet. I can tell that we're both thinking about our options moving forward. Fingers crossed, we're on the same page because I'm not sure I could handle losing him. I've been trying so hard to keep things at arm's length, to maintain a slight detachment. However, I am failing miserably because there is no doubt I am head over heels in love like a goddamn idiot.

Thirty-Three

THE FIRST SIP of my cherry vodka and red bull tastes like heaven. This has been my go-to drink since college, which I mentioned during one of our first conversations at the hospital. I haven't had one in months because I think it's bad form to imbibe alone, so this drink tastes especially delicious. I have no idea when Croy found the time to run to the store, but I'm glad he did. This is the perfect thing to take the edge off right now. I take another sip and close my eyes, letting the warm breeze and summer rays enhance the experience. "Ah! Sweet nectar of the gods."

Croy is having an Angry Orchard, which is a draft cider. That is usually my second choice if a place doesn't have Three Olives cherry. "The best draft cider, in my opinion, is Original Sin on tap, but it's hard to find," My comment is presented with a level of confidence as if I'm secretly hoping he'll be impressed by my cider knowledge.

"I'll be sure to keep an eye out. If you know of a place that has it, we can make it a date." Croy drinks the same way he eats. His bottle is empty after four sips. I'm not sure I want to be responsible for paying the tab if we go out.

"If you don't want to tell me, you don't have to, but how did you get your DUI?" Probably not the best topic to inquire about when we're having drinks and discussing possible dates, but I have been curious.

"I'll tell you if you want to know. But it's not a very exciting story. Mostly stupid and embarrassing. Eric came over one night to play video games, and we ordered a pizza. The place in town didn't have anyone available to make deliveries, so I told them I could get it. Didn't seem like a problem at the time. The night had barely started, and I'd only had two beers. Plus, the pizza place was only a few miles away. I picked up the order and was pulled over two houses from the driveway. The cop didn't believe me when I said that I lived in this neighborhood and claimed there had been calls about a suspicious vehicle that matched mine. He smelled alcohol on my breath, and I was arrested. He wouldn't even let me pull into the driveway. Fucking asshole had my car towed." Croy pauses to gauge my reaction. Maybe the thinks I'll be offended, since I used to wear a fake gold badge. When he sees I'm unaffected, he continues.

"I could've spent the money and hired a lawyer, but I wasn't trying to argue the fact that I'd had two drinks and drove. I was willing to plead guilty, pay my fine, and keep it moving. So, I took a day off work and went to court. I dressed nicely and looked professional, but the judge took one look at my hands and neck, commented about my questionable life choices, and gave me three days in jail and a $2,000 fine. I'm sure you know how that shit goes. Some people see tattoos and automatically assume you must be guilty of something."

I know the type of people he's talking about. "Sadly, your story reminds me of my interview with the jail. The warden told me I needed to wear something to keep my arms covered. It was stupid. I highly doubted the inmates would be offended by my koi fish and flower tattoos. Or maybe offended isn't the right word. Perhaps he was afraid they might view me as an equal. Certainly wouldn't want that, now do we?" Times have changed, but there's still plenty of prejudice out there. No matter what group you're in, someone, somewhere, hates you.

"Well, as a person with insider information, I can say with confidence that 99.9% of the inmates in that place thought you and your tattoos were hot as fuck. The other .1% was that blind guy. But even he said you always smelled nice when you walked through." Croy can't seem to help himself. He has to say something ridiculous to make me smile.

"Let's not forget the six guys who wanted to kill me." I'm only able to joke about the situation because I was unconscious when it happened, but I sometimes forget that Croy remembers it much differently.

"It was only one guy who suggested killing you, and even he was too much of a pussy to come at you head-on. Plus, that doesn't mean he thought you were ugly." Croy is attempting to keep the mood light, but I can see that this particular topic is triggering for him.

"Anyways... Let's talk about something else, shall we? I'd be interested to hear your thoughts on visiting one another." Random topics keep popping up like dandelions, distracting our attention from the real conversation.

"I'm not sure what your work schedule will look like, but mine is pretty typical. I get out by 4:30 during the week and have off every weekend. We could take turns if you want. I could go there one weekend, and you could come here the next. Depending on how much you want to see each other and how your parents feel about me being there."

Gross. The fact that I'm nearly 29 years old and might need my parent's permission to see my boyfriend is making me rethink staying at their house. Their opinions about my dating life are not something I want to deal with. "Having you stay at the house with me shouldn't be an issue since they aren't even going to be there. And if it is a problem, I'll tell them to piss off and get my own place. As for work, the job I'm interviewing for Tuesday would be a similar schedule to yours."

"Well, there you go. That was easy. Now I feel dumb for worrying so much." Croy says exactly what I'm thinking. That was easy. But saying something and doing it are two different things.

"I was worried too, but now I'm not sure why. Since that's settled, there's one more thing I'd like to do before I leave. I'm not sure if you'd be interested in helping me, but I'd like to bake some cookies to drop them off at the jail tonight. It would be my way of saying goodbye to the people I worked with." I catch myself holding my breath, waiting for his reaction.

"That's incredibly thoughtful of you, and I think it's a great idea. It'll give you a chance to set the record straight and say goodbye on your own terms." Croy smiles and gets up from his chair. "Let's check the kitchen and see if we have what you need. I'll be honest. I haven't done much baking since I moved in. We might need to make our first trip to the grocery store together."

Everything about my relationship with Croy contrasts my time with Kelly. This moment is the latest example.

We find eggs, butter, salt, sugar, and baking soda in the kitchen. That leaves vanilla extract, flour, chocolate chips, and brown sugar. All of which I was able to locate in one of the bags Kelly dropped off. And with that, we're ready to bake. Croy is a good cook, but he steps back and lets me take this one. I start throwing things in the bowl without measuring or consulting a recipe, which he seems impressed by. Or he's waiting for it to come out like an episode of Nailed It.

The dough looks perfect and tastes even better, so I know these will be delicious. There was a double batch at one point, but I'm not even going to pretend like it all made it into the oven. I love cookie dough, and I'm not ashamed to say it. Even Croy keeps trying to steal bites. I have to smack his hand away so he doesn't eat it all. In a last-ditch effort to get a bite, he stands behind me and starts kissing my neck. Once he thinks I'm distracted, he tries to be sneaky, but I'm on to him. He forgets that our brains run on the same frequency.

Twenty minutes later, when everything is out of the oven cooling, the whole first floor of the house smells like a bakery. I don't give myself credit for much, but I know how to throw together a good batch of cookies.

Croy went to his office before the first tray came out of the oven, so he had yet to taste the finished product. I take two off the last tray and slide them onto a plate. Fresh-out-the-oven cookies are heaven on Earth. Plus, I need his feedback. I take the stairs carefully, one at a time, so nothing slips off the plate. I would have no issue eating a cookie off the floor, but I won't do that to Croy.

He's in his office, where he said he would be, reading something on the computer. One of these days, I'll have to ask him to wear his glasses to the bedroom. He's fulfilling every nerdy fantasy I've ever had by existing in this moment.

"Why do you always look at me like that when I'm in here? I feel like you're laughing at me for needing reading glasses." He sounds momentarily self-conscious.

"Oh, I'm not laughing at you. Not even close." I walk towards him and set the plate on the desk, taking notice of the other items around his computer. A framed photo of us from yesterday sits on top of the book I gave him at the hospital. "When did you print that out? You never even showed me any of those pictures."

"I had it printed at Target with the rest of my order, including your unbirthday presents." He glides back in his chair and pulls me onto his lap. "I wanted to be able to see you every day."

Looking at the picture, I'm transported back to the moment it was taken. This was the first short hike we went on. There was an amazing path through the woods along the river. Then, out of nowhere, this incredible waterfall. I didn't want to get my shoes wet, so Croy gave me a piggyback ride out to a little gravel island where some kids were playing. A boy, about 12, offered to take a photo for us, and here it is. We had so many fantastic moments yesterday. I almost forgot about this one.

"I love it. That's a great shot. I'm jealous I don't have one to take with me." Here I was taking pictures of trees and rocks and waterfalls during our hike, and he was being cute and thoughtful. I did get a few candid shots of him, but none of the two of us together.

As he opens his middle desk drawer, I see another gift-wrapped box. Croy takes it out and hands it to me. "This one was for you to take with you. I wanted you to open it on Tuesday, but you can have it now."

Damn, me and my big mouth. I ruined the surprise. And it would've been a good one too. My fingers slide gently across the gold and black paper, quelling my anticipation. "I'm going to wait to open it."

"But you already know what it is."

"Doesn't make me any less excited to see it. Anyways, I can look at yours now and save mine for later when I'm missing your smile." Our lips meet, and I'm nearly overcome. This whole weekend feels like I've been sitting on a ledge, and today is the first time I looked at the drop.

Thirty-Four

SINCE IT'S our last night together and we're celebrating, Croy wants to go out to dinner. My stomach is still full from lunch, but I can't say no to him when he looks at me with those eyes and that smile. I'm not sure I can eat again, but I'll give it my best effort. Anything he wants to do, I'm willing to accept the challenge. Unless he wants to go dancing. I'm a pretty terrible dancer.

Croy has been in his office for hours, and if he were *anyone* else, I would assume he was cheating on me. Every time I walk in there, he turns his monitor off and tells me I need to learn to love surprises. Whatever that means. *Surprise, I'm leaving you because I messed around with this other girl behind your back, and she's pregnant!* Gee, thanks. You shouldn't have.

In an effort to distract myself, I've spent the last hour playing with my new watch. To be clear, Croy didn't replace my broken watch. He gave it a major upgrade. I still think he spent too much, but he refuses to take it back. What can I do? My wrist feels fancy, and I'm looking forward to wearing it out tonight. Guess I have to learn to love surprises.

"Is that what you're wearing to dinner?" The sudden presence of his voice from the doorway makes me jump. "Sorry, didn't mean to scare you."

"I was distracted. I didn't hear you in the hall." I start to laugh as he does an over-exaggerated stealth walk toward the bed where I'm sitting. "And no, this is not what I'm wearing to dinner. Are you ready to go?"

He places his hands on either side of me and kisses my neck. "If you keep doing that, I'm not going to be able to get dressed." It wasn't until recently that I discovered a button on the side of my neck that will send my mind straight into the gutter if it's kissed. If Croy does this any longer, I will cease to function on a human level. "Are we doing this right now or saving it for tonight?"

I can feel his lips curve into a smile. "Why can't we do both?" His hands are at my waist, under my shirt. As he glides his fingers upward, my t-shirt follows until it's removed. He eases me into a new position, laying under him. Wherever his fingers trace looping patterns onto my skin, his kiss travels. "I want to give you a good reason to miss me."

I can't form words. His kiss drives me wild, and I love him all the more for it.

"Do you want me to keep going?" There's no way I want him to stop, and he knows it. But he's moving so slowly, it's almost painful, as if he wants me to beg. I reach for the button on my pants, but he moves my hands away. "I can stop if you want."

"No. Please. Don't stop. I want you to keep going." If he had a mind to, we could be done with this in under a minute. But clearly, he intends to drive me into madness with his slow torture. I'm on the verge of exploding against his teasing touch. "Why are you doing this to me? I thought you loved me."

With one final push, and he sends me over the edge. "I do love you. That's why I did it."

Thirty-Five

LUCKILY, I had some nice, unwrinkled clothes in my bag. Otherwise, I'm not sure the hostess would've let me past the entry. This current restaurant is even nicer than the one we were at for lunch. The drive was a good thirty minutes from the house, but that's almost to be expected when you live in the middle of nowhere.

Croy must have made a special reservation because our seats are in a separate room with a fireplace. At the table where we're meant to dine, there is the usual array of cutlery and drinking glasses atop a white linen tablecloth. The other tables in the room are covered in roses and candles.

"I feel like you're about to propose." I'm searching his body for clues, but he's giving nothing away. My heart starts to beat faster, and it's getting exceedingly hot. It would be completely outrageous if he asked, but I could almost see him doing it. Why else are we here? I don't even know what my answer would be. It's only been five days. But they've been the best days of my life. I'll never find another man like this. He is truly one of a kind. And somehow, someway, he feels the same way about me.

"Let's take a minute to look at the menu and order before we dive into anything too serious." Croy takes my left hand from where it was resting on the table and presses my ring finger to his lips. I don't even need a diamond. I would say yes to his kiss.

I scan the menu for something light. There are no prices, so I know even the cheapest item will be $30. They have french onion soup, and I bet it's fantastic. But I can't risk having onion breath, so I move on. Two of the salads sound appealing. I make a mental note of them both and continue. Shrimp scampi is one of my favorites, but again, there is my breath to consider. I'll have to eliminate anything with lingering flavor, so garlic and onion are out. Honestly, I'm not sure I have the capacity for meat or pasta right now, so it's back to the salads. By the time our waiter has returned, I'm ready to make a commitment to my order, if nothing else.

"Could I please get the grilled shrimp salad with the dressing on the side? Thank you." No matter the restaurant, my ordering voice is always the same. Manners Plus. I hate when people are disrespectful to waitstaff.

"All our salads come dressed, but I will ask the kitchen to use a light hand." The waiter turns towards Croy as if his statement were the end of the matter. "And for you, Sir."

"I suggest you ask the kitchen to use a light hand while pouring her dressing into a small cup and placing it on the side." Croy pauses to ensure his message is received, then continues with his order. "I'll have the prime rib, rare."

"Certainly, Sir." The waiter collects our menus before turning on his heels to leave.

A few minutes later, a distinguished-looking older gentleman enters the room. Apparently, this dressing thing has become a situation. "I'm here to ensure your evening goes perfectly, and I you to receive everything you need. Was there a different dressing, perhaps, that you might prefer? We have several options if you'd like to review the menu."

I'm about to open my mouth when Croy speaks in my place. "All she wants is the dressing on the side. What's the problem? She didn't ask you for the world... It's my job to give her that."

"Please forgive my intrusion, sir. I'll make sure the kitchen staff is made aware."

I swear, if the owner comes in next, we're leaving and going to McDonald's. I can't possibly be the first person to order a salad this way. And what was that line about giving me the world? I've watched thousands of movies about falling in love and never heard anything that smooth. How does he come up with this stuff?

"You good?" I can read the emotions written on Croy's face, and I can tell that he's on the verge of anger. Everything, this entire room of flowers and flickering light, all the effort he put into arranging this, is about to be derailed by salad dressing. I should have ordered it the way it was.

"I'm with you, love. I'm great." He's holding my hand over the table like he always does. Physical touch is Croy's love language, whether he admits it or not.

"You're allowed to be mad or frustrated or disappointed. Hell, you can be all three. But don't tell me you're *great* when I can see you're not." It isn't healthy to bottle things up. People shouldn't be expected to bury their negative emotions and only show the good ones. Croy doesn't have to be perfect all the time. I'd prefer he not be.

"I was all three of those things for about 20 seconds. Then I looked at you, and now I'm fine. I hear what you're saying, and I appreciate it. I'll be more open about the good and the bad in the future. However, right now, nothing is more important than *this*." He squeezes my hand, and I understand exactly how he's feeling.

Yet again, when the food comes out, Croy's meal smells amazing. I consider messing with him and asking for a trade, but I'm afraid he'll do it. There is no possible way I could eat more red meat and keep it down. I'm just going to sit quietly, enjoying my dressing-free salad like a little lady.

"When we set down, you said something about a proposal. I'm interested to hear what your thoughts might be on that.

What would you say if I asked you?" Croy sets his silverware on the edge of his plate and waits for my response.

"Are you asking me?" It seems like cheating to know the answer before you pose the question. I think he should have to put himself out there if he wants to know my thoughts on the matter.

"Do you want me to ask you?" His expression is set, but I can't read it. There is no hint that he's joking beyond the back-and-forth questions. "Because you told me you needed time to process and space to breathe, and I want to respect that. You've also told me that grand proclamations early on are a major red flag."

"True, but in all fairness, I said those things four days ago. I thought we'd moved on since then. I thought we were on the same page?" I'm joking. But I'm also not. Sitting here and getting my hopes up about something I said I didn't want was stupid. This right here is one of the worst parts of bipolar depression. The crash. It's irrational, but I'm about to ruin everything. "I'm kidding... No, you're right. That would've been ridiculous. I'm glad you didn't ask, even as a joke. I don't need another Kelly situation."

"Yeah, exactly. Who needs that?" Croy looks like a deflated balloon. I can't handle being near him right now. "You good?"

"Sure, yeah. I think I need to find the restroom or some-thing." I slide out the side of my chair and head for the exit. I don't need a bathroom. I need an escape hatch.

What am I doing? Why am I here? Did I want him to propose, or did I convince myself he would, and now I'm disap-pointed because it didn't? I'm taking his non-proposal as a rejec-tion, even though I'm the one who told him not to ask the question. This has been an incredible night, and I'm leaving in the morning. I only have a few hours left with him. Why am I destroying my chance of having the only thing I've ever wanted?

I pace back and forth on the sidewalk to the left of the door. "Please stop doing this. It's not too late. Go back inside and finish eating." I can't do it. One more bite, and I'm going to vomit. "Fuck!"

"Heather, is everything alright?" Croy exits the restaurant in time to catch me mid-breakdown.

"What are you doing? They're going to think we ran out on the check!" I don't even know what he said because all I can picture is the cops pulling in with flashing lights and arresting both of us.

"It's fine. My wallet is on the table. They aren't going to think we dipped out."

"You left your wallet sitting in there? What are you doing?" I'm starting to get confused, and I wish he would walk away. I don't want him to see me like this.

"I'm out here checking on you. What are you doing? You walked out after telling me I would have to be a complete idiot to want to marry you."

"What? I didn't say that. And you don't want to anyways, so what does it even matter." There's a part of me that is freaking the fuck out right now, begging my mouth to stop moving. I'm going to say something I won't be able to fix. That's the point, after all, isn't it? To sabotage my chance at happiness because I can't allow myself to believe that I deserve what he's offering.

"Is that what you think? That I don't want to marry you?" He cups my shoulders and looks me in the eyes before dropping to one knee. Croy holds onto my hand while retrieving a small box from his pocket. When he looks up at me, I'm not ready, and I'm afraid I might pass out.

"I know what I want, and I'm pretty sure you want the same things. I want to spend the rest of my life laughing with you. I want to build our foundation and grow our life together so that neither of us ever has to question where we belong. I want to put down roots with you. I want to buy a home together, get a dog, and maybe even have a kid. I want to marry my best friend because she's the love of my life. You're my missing half. I know you're my forever, and I will do whatever it takes to prove that to you. I'm not going anywhere unless you ask me to, and even then, I would beg you to come with me. I've been killing time, waiting, and now that I've found you, I can't let you go. You're my whole world. I love you beyond measure. And nothing could ever change that."

There's a diamond ring in the box, and even in this dim light, it shines.

"Heather, will you accompany me on this adventure as my wife? Will you marry me?

The front door swings open, and it's the older gentleman, who I assume is the manager. He takes one look at the scene playing out in front of him and closes the door. I can't help but let out a small laugh.

"Please stand up. My knees hurt looking at you in that position." I try to pull, but he's unyielding.

"I'm not standing until I have an answer, one way or the other."

"Well then, stand up and kiss me because the answer is yes. Of course, it's yes!" Tears are raining down my cheeks, and I'm about to look crazy when we walk back in to pay the check.

Croy slides the ring onto my finger, and I'm surprised by how well it fits. I expected it would need to be resized, but this hugs like it was made for me. When he kisses me, I fear we might drown. Even though I am over the moon, I can't stop crying. There are a few minutes of holding one another and laughing about the absurdity of the situation. People will think we're lost our minds, and for some reason, we can't be bothered to care. Croy wipes my cheeks and gets any makeup from under my eyes. Of course, he's extra careful with the left side, as it's still a bit sore.

Back at the table is a bottle of champagne, two glasses, and a giant slice of chocolate cake. "Did you order this before you came out? What if I had said no?" There is no world in which I could have said no to him, but he doesn't know that.

"I didn't order any of this. But hey! Good news. My wallet and phone are still here." Croy holds them out to me as proof.

"Another bit of good news, you're officially engaged.

Congratulations! Not sure how that happened exactly, but allegedly it did." When I don't know what to say, jokes usually come out. "Also, I'm sorry that I ran out before. I needed some air and a quiet place to think."

Croy stands and moves his chair next to mine. Then he wraps me in his arms, and I melt into him. "I've been sweating bullets all night waiting for the perfect moment. When you left, I was afraid I drove you away because I wasn't listening."

The manager pops in to inform us that it is nearly 10:30 and they will be closing soon, but we should take our time and savor the moment. He also apologizes about the earlier incident with the salad dressing and insists that our bill has been taken care of. The waiter asks for Croy's keys so that he can carry the flowers and our food out for us.

We eat the cake, but the champagne remains unopened. The waiter carries the bottle to the car with the last bouquet of roses, and it's time for us to leave. I can't stop looking at the ring on my finger. This feels more like a fever dream than reality. I wonder how long it will take for the information to sink in.

Thirty-Six

WE'RE NEARLY home when Croy reminds me that there's one more stop left to make. The cookies and the jail have been the furthest thing from my mind. At this moment, I wouldn't be bothered to forget the whole thing. "Run in. Say your goodbyes. And we'll be home in bed before you know it." I'm surprised Croy is so supportive of me walking in there again. I guess he figures I won't be in danger if I stay near the booking desk.

He pulls into the parking lot and stops near the bay door. There's a camera there, so hopefully, they recognize me. I get out of the car and retrieve the container of cookies from the back seat. Before I reach the door, Collins and Smith come around the back of the building. That's an interesting combination I can't imagine either is thrilled about.

"Hey Belk, what are you doing back here at this hour? Miss us?" Collins is friendlier than usual. Maybe Kelly finally gave her the dick she's been after. Then again, she always was phony as a three-dollar bill.

"I wanted to make good on my promise to bake cookies before I left town, and I thought it might be nice to say good-bye." The door lock clicks as the three of us approach, and Smith holds it open for me as I walk through.

Grant is behind the booking desk. No surprise there. And, of course, because why not? Kelly is working intake. He looks exactly like I remember from my life before. "Here you go, boys. Don't say I never did anything for you." I casually address them both to keep it from being weird.

"How the hell have you been? I didn't think I'd be seeing you again out of uniform. And looking beautiful, if you don't mind my saying." Grant, that big softy, had to say something nice. Or maybe he's trying to get under Kelly's skin. Who knows? "Hey Belk, can we talk for one second in private?"

"Sure, Grant. What's on your mind?" I follow him over to the phones about ten feet from the desk. I'm certain anyone interested in listening can still hear everything he says, but the illusion of secrecy has been created.

"Are you alright? I mean, are you safe?" Grant looks at my face with intention as though he's seeing it for the first time. His concern surprises me. I can't imagine what stories are floating around about me, but he's never cared before about my life outside of work. Why start now?

"I'm good. Why do you ask?" I can't wait to hear what's being said behind my back. Knowing Grant, he'll sugar-coat every criticism and make it sound like a compliment. I'd rather people start being honest.

"I know it's not my business, and you can tell me to butt out, but I notice you look like you've been crying tonight, and there's a bruise on your cheek." My hand reflexively goes to my left cheek when he mentions the bruise. It's faint but visible under the fluorescent lighting here in the jail. "And that's a hell of a diamond, so I'm going to shut up now."

Shit, I didn't mean for the people here to see that. Dropping off cookies sounded so simple in theory, but I never took the time to think it through. I was too busy falling in love.

I hear boots and feel someone behind me. There's no need to turn around because I already know who it is. The heat is coming off him like a damn furnace, and he smells as good as ever. "Let's see it then."

"Can we not do this, please." I take a step towards the door, but Kelly catches my arm. His grip is confident yet gentle, like the unyielding caress of a lover seeking absolution. I could pull away if I wanted to, but we both know I won't. It isn't in my nature to make a scene. And I would rather forgive him and leave here unburdened than carry the guilt of our mistakes with me into my new life.

"Is he out there? Maybe I should go out and say congratulations." Now it's Kelly who is headed for the door, a step ahead of me.

"Kelly, don't! If you walk out there after what you did. I won't be able to stop him." This night has been an emotional roller coaster. A fight between Kelly and Croy is the last thing I need. Maybe he thinks poking the bear and getting his throat ripped out will make us square, or maybe he's counting on having backup.

"After what *he* did? That's rich coming from *you*. Aren't you the one who cheated on him with some inmate?" Collins can't help herself. This shit, right here, is why I never liked her. She's so desperate for attention that she involves herself in situations that have nothing to do with her. If she's fucking my ex, so be it.

I never even considered Kelly my ex until three seconds ago. But now that the facts have been laid out in front of me for what seems like the hundredth time, I suppose I can no longer deny reality. Ignorance was bliss while it lasted, but as it turns out, I'm the asshole. Kelly's reactions make a lot more sense when viewed through this lens, but he and I can discuss that later. For now, I'm the one feeling provoked.

"That's not even what we're fucking talking about! So, why don't you run along before I finish what you're trying to start... Go choke on a dick, Collins." I want to argue and claim my innocence, but maybe she's right. I never cheated with an *inmate*, but depending on the perspective, I can see where I might be guilty of cheating. For the life of me, I'm not sure why I wanted to come here. These people are not my friends. They never were. Their loyalty was a perk of the badge, not a bond forged in a shared experience.

"Grant, it was good to see you. Tell Kevin I said hello the next time you talk to him." Again, I step towards the door, and again Kelly stops me. Only this time, he laces his fingers into mine. Maybe I'm not as alone in here as I thought.

Collins storms off. Grant grabs the cookies and returns to his seat. And Kelly and I stand like statues holding hands. This is turning into a real soap opera. "I need to go. I have to be awake early, and it's a long drive. I don't want to be tired, and I don't want to fight with you."

"I don't want to fight with you either. Come on. I'll walk you out. After all, you need me... To get out the door, that is." Kelly's hand burns into mine, and I'm afraid he won't let go. Or maybe I'm afraid he will, and I won't want him to. Funny, Grant is all concerned when he thinks Croy smacked me around, but when the guy who bruised my cheek grabs me twice right in front of him, it's no fucks given. There's a lot of clouded judgment being weathered in this storm, but it's always *us* standing at the center.

"Okay." I don't know why Kelly and I can't let each other go, but whatever happens next, I can't allow him to leave this building. "If you need to say anything, I'm listening."

"There are a lot of things I need to talk about with you, but you no longer owe me those conversations. Not after what I did. I fucked up, and you might never forgive me. But I will love you forever." We walk through the intake area and into the loading bay. I'm almost to the door when Kelly pushes me against the wall and kisses me.

With my forearm across his chest and my back against the wall, I try to push him off me. "Kelly, I didn't come here to see you. Please don't end this with a repeat of last time." My understanding of the dynamics has changed, but I've made my choice, and he's waiting for me in the car.

"I'm not... I'll *never* do that again, to anyone. I feel horrible about what happened. I've started so many text messages to you, but it never feels like enough. I'm sorry. I never should've hit you. I will regret that moment for the rest of my life."

"I need to go." There's a little piece of me that wants to wrap my arms around him and let go of everything bad word that's ever been spoken between us. Not because I want him back but because I want us both to be freed from this baggage. "You'll always matter to me, Kelly. What you did hurt me, but not in the way you think. Take care of yourself, okay? And stay away from Croy."

"I guess this is goodbye for now. But I hope we can find our way back to being friends." Kelly kisses me again, and this time feels like goodbye. We take two steps closer to the door, and I hear the click. "I miss you already."

I open the door one last time and walk through it. "I miss you too." I don't look back for fear that it will encourage him. The night air feels like freedom, and I'm walking in the direction of my future.

As soon as I get into the car, I dry my tears and I throw my arms around Croy's neck. I take a moment to look into his eyes and rub my hand over the short hairs on the back of his head. Touching him like this always makes me feel sparks. "This was a terrible idea. Can we go home?" We share a kiss and then pull out onto the road. "I never want to see this place again."

On the way, I tell him every detail I can remember. I do my best to recite conversations word for word. Of course, Croy isn't happy about Kelly grabbing me, holding my hand, pinning me against the wall, or kissing me. He also isn't surprised since this isn't any different than the shit Kelly pulled yesterday at the house.

It's late, and I'm ready to crawl into bed. Croy unloads the car while I change out of my dress clothes and wash my face. I make sure to slow walk the process until he joins me in the bedroom. One of my favorite times is when we are both in the bathroom brushing our teeth. We take turns pushing each other out of the way, pretending to hog the mirror or the water. It's silly, but I'll yearn for this when I'm gone.

Tonight, when he's done, Croy stands behind me with his arms around my waist, looking at me in the mirror. "Don't feel like you have to leave when I do in the morning. Sleep in, have breakfast, go for a swim, whatever. I'll be home a little after 5:00."

"If I stick around until five tomorrow, I think I might be here to stay." The idea doesn't sound as bad tonight as it did earlier in the week. How could I not stay, now that the situation has evolved?

I could visit my parents for the week, then come back. When I decided to move and applied for the job, it was in reaction to Kelly getting rid of my place and me being suspended from the jail. If Croy is serious about getting married, which I'm assuming he is based on the size of this diamond, then why shouldn't I call this place home? We could build a life here.

"What if we don't move and start over? What if I stay? I'm sure I could find another job." I feel like my thoughts are giving me whiplash. Croy is probably as confused as I am at this point. It can be difficult to keep track when my mania goes one way, and my depression goes the other.

"That's a conversation we can have if you'd like. But you should visit your parents and interview for that job. That way, no matter what direction we decide to go, you still have all your options. Plus, I'll find out tomorrow about that supervisor position."

"I thought when I accepted your proposal, I had made my choice. Didn't realize I needed to keep my options open. Maybe I should text Kelly back!" I make sure to use a joking voice.

Croy playfully smacks my ass. "You're terrible. The Kelly option is emphatically off the table... And you know what I meant. It's nice to have options regarding jobs and what area we want to settle in." He keeps talking as we walk into the bedroom and take our spots under the blanket. "Let's see how this week goes, get as much information as possible, and talk about everything next weekend. I want to visit so you can show me around. And I'd like to meet your parents before they leave town. What do you think they'll say when you tell them we're engaged? Or are you going to keep it a secret?"

"Nah, I don't do secrets. I think keeping skeletons in a cupboard eats away at your soul." In the past, I've not always said and done the right thing, and I carry a lot of guilt for that. There are also things I feel immense guilt about, and I'm certain I did the right thing. So, damned if you do, damned if you don't, I guess.

My eyes insist on closing, but I fight to keep them open. I want this night to go on forever. When I wake up in the morning, Croy won't be here. The thought of that weighs on me, even though I'm nearly 99.9% certain I'll see him again next weekend. Something about that 0.1% nags at me. Eventually, sleep overtakes me, despite my best efforts.

Thirty-Seven

THE SUN IS SHINING HERE. It's bright to the point of nearly blinding, and I don't have my sunglasses. I can feel the sand shifting under my bare feet and take notice of a large body of water in front of me. I'm at the beach. The sea air tickles as it brushes through my hair. But this isn't the ocean. It's a lake. I know this because the water is like glass, reminding me of the freshwater at home. But I can see across to the other side. So, this isn't Lake Erie. It's more like a big pond.

In the distance, I can see a red and white puppy that's too small to be on his own. I start walking faster than usual as discomfort leaches into my pours. Something doesn't seem right. I'm anxious, and my stomach is in knots. Why is this puppy alone on the beach?

I start sprinting. But the faster I dash, the further away he seems. Now, he's on the other side, walking dangerously close to the water's edge. I'm not a good runner. I never have been. But I am a fast swimmer. I used to practice propelling myself, fully clothed, across my parents' pool. I wanted to know that if I fell in with jeans and a hoodie, I wouldn't drown. So, I'm certain I can get across this lake.

I wade into the shimmering liquid to my waist and then dive under. The water is crystal clear, and I can make out tiny details on the bottom. I'm about two-thirds of the way across when I notice the first shark. It's too late to turn back, so I swim harder. The sharks lurking below me aren't the ones consuming my thoughts. It's the one I know is behind me. I'm only 20 feet from shore when I see the puppy tumble from the edge and go under.

I scream, "JoJo," and give it one last push. Finish strong. My hand reaches forward, and I wrap my fingers around the red and white boston terrier, lifting him to the surface. I'm right there. My head is above the water, and I'm only a few feet from the edge. But this isn't a pond. It's a swimming pool.

A black door slides open on the side of the pool, and another shark enters the water. I have to get out. I have to get this puppy safely to the side. Otherwise, everything I did, was for nothing. Kicking my legs as hard as possible, I stretch my hand over the ledge. My red boston with his white face is back safely on the concrete. Now all I have to do is pull myself out. My hands grip the rounded pool edge, but when my feet kick, I make contact with something big.

"NO!"

I hear the word still ringing in the cool air of the bedroom as I spring into a seated position. My skin is wet from sweat, and I feel short of breath. My hand instinctively reaches forward, but JoJo isn't there.

"Ow, babe, what the fuck?" Croy's voice brings me back.

"What's wrong?" My mind is still adjusting to the darkness, even though my eyes are already in focus.

"Nothing, sorry. You kicked the shit out of me. I thought something was happening. I'm sorry. I think I was still half asleep when I yelled. Are you okay?" Croy sounds half asleep still. Like he's trying to sort out dreams from reality. I'm pretty sure that's how I feel most of the time, even when I'm awake. He reaches over and starts rubbing my back.

"I'm sorry I kicked you. It wasn't on purpose. I was dreaming, and I thought you were a shark." We both laugh.

I tell Croy about my dream and snuggle back into his arms. Hopefully, I'm done swimming for the night.

Thirty-Eight

WHEN I WAKE UP AGAIN, the sun is coming through the blinds, and half of the bed is empty. I run my hand over the sheet where I last remember feeling Croy, but it's cold. He's gone, and I'm alone. The time on my watch reads 9:28 am. Guess I better get moving and start packing.

I decided to take an assortment of clothes from my bag and leave them in a drawer of Croy's dresser. Only one pair of pants was housed there, the sweats I gave him at the hospital, so I don't think he'll mind. The toiletries Kelly brought have already made their way into the bathroom so they can stay. I slide the unopened box with the black and gold paper into my backpack and carry it with me as I descend the stairs.

Whatever food Kelly brought of mine, I unpack and sort into the kitchen cupboards. My parents don't need groceries, and I don't feel like hauling all those bags back and forth. Plus, now I have my reusable shopping bags for vases full of flowers. I carefully place two bouquets in each bag and support them at the base. I wedge Kelly's hoodie between glass vases, resisting the urge to smell it before stuffing it into the bag. I forgot I still had it with me until now.

I need a second sweatshirt to support the vases in the other bag, so I grab one from the closet by the door. My eyes are drawn to a hoodie I recognize, the one from the hospital Croy borrowed and never returned, but I leave it. I opt instead to take one of his. Hopefully, it will still smell like him later after I get home.

I check my pocket and realize I've forgotten my phone on the nightstand. Taking the stairs two at a time, I run back to get it. That's when I see my ring laying atop the hibernating screen. For a moment, I almost thought I had dreamt that part of the evening. I slide the ring onto my finger and hold out my left hand. This doesn't feel real. As if on cue, my text alert chimes.

> Croy: Good Morning, love. Hope you slept well and there were no more sharks.

> : The seas remained calm and clear until daybreak. I'm getting everything packed up and out of your way. I'll probably get on the road in ten minutes or so. Thanks for letting me stay here this week.

> Croy: Okay. You don't have to thank me for that... A little part of me was hoping you would stay, even though I'm the one that convinced you to leave. I should've kept my mouth shut.

I wish Croy would stop fancy footing around the issue and come out with it. "Tell me to stay, and I will! You know I want to be here." I make my plea whole-heartedly into the air-conditioned emptiness of the bedroom, then allow my fingers to change the tune.

> : I'll come back any time you ask me to. After all, it's not like I have a job.

Croy: You might after tomorrow. Fingers Crossed. Unless you'd rather not work, which is fine by me. I love the idea of you staying home, but I support your decision as long as you're happy.

I'm grateful for the emotional support, but that isn't going to pay my bills. Having a job is unavoidable when you're an adult. I need to replenish the cash flow into my checking account before a dip in my savings becomes inevitable. Croy is a dear sweet deer who is far more agreeable than he should be, but I won't hold my hand out and ask for an allowance.

: I appreciate that, but I can't stay home and do nothing. Maybe if we had kids, I would consider it.

I enjoy the idea of having kids until I remember that I'll most likely pass on my debilitating depression like a haunted family heirloom. No one should have to feel the way I did growing up. Every day of my life has been a struggle. Even now, as Croy promises to make my every dream come true, I'm crippled by insecurity.

Croy: I'm happy to come home right now and work on that if you'd like.

: Or we could wait a little while.

Croy: How about a little JoJo potato, like from your dream?

: JoJo potato? Hahaha. Did I say that? I only remember saying that his name was JoJo.

If we're talking about getting a dog, Croy has my full attention. I could easily be persuaded to stay home and be a dog mom. Maybe I could set up shop in Croy's office, doing some mundane tasks on the computer.

> Croy: JoJo, the red boston terrier with an all-white head. In my mind, he looks like a little potato. So, there we have it. I love him already, and I haven't even met him yet.

> : He sounds perfect. I'll consider staying home if we find a little guy like that. Then he'll love me the most. LoL.

The way Croy speaks about the future, with unshakeable certainty, makes me think it could be possible. He acts like he's prepared to give me the world at my first request. Maybe finding my soulmate will be enough to fill in all the pieces of me that are missing.

> Croy: Deal. I'm online looking now. Please drive carefully and text me when you get there. I'm sorry. I have to start this meeting, but I'll call you at lunch. I love you, more than everything.

I get everything I'm taking loaded into the car and search for directions on my phone. You'd think I'd know the route by now, but I don't make a point of visiting home. I'm pretty sure I'll be good to go after I make it to Columbus. Then again, having directions at the ready won't hurt anything. I shift into reverse, and I'm about to back out when someone pulls into the driveway next to me.

I recognize the car immediately. It's Kelly's.

Thirty-Nine

I SHIFT BACK into park but leave the engine running, unsure of my next move. Kelly's not in his uniform, so he must have gone home before coming here. Why is he at Croy's house? This feels wrong, but I can't drive away and leave him here alone. I kill the engine and step out.

"What are you doing here?" I'm not even sure anymore if I can leave. I'll feel personally responsible if any of Croy's property gets damaged. Kelly's sudden appearance makes me feel like I might need to stay and stand guard. This is ridiculous at this point. "You know you shouldn't be here."

"Don't be mad... I couldn't stop thinking about you after you left last night. I broke down and told everyone the truth. Well, most of it. There were rumors about you and him dating before the fight, but I said it was bullshit. And Grant's convinced you're being abused, but I said that wasn't the case either. I didn't admit that I was the one who hit you, and maybe I should have, but I was afraid of the consequences. Everyone at work wants to make the two of you into the bad guys because you aren't there to defend yourselves. Whenever someone mentions your name, it kills me. I'm the one who mistreated you, and they're consoling me. It's fucking disgusting. I feel horrible about everything. The things I said and did to you this week aren't me. I keep telling you that I love you, but I'm not doing a great job of showing you." Kelly walks towards me and takes my hands. "I only came by to tell you that I'm sorry. I can see that you've moved on, but I haven't. I'm not sure I know how. But I can't keep hurting you just because I don't know how to accept losing you."

"Thanks for defending me. I'm sure the last thing you want to do is say anything nice about Croy or me. It sucks that you would even have to, but I appreciate it. I realized last night that my co-workers weren't quite the family I gave them credit for." Respect goes out the window pretty quickly when folks are willing to believe outlandish falsehoods over the authentic truth you walked day in and day out. I'm still confused by the tale Warden Lawson was attempting to spin.

"As for you and me, Kelly. I'm struggling with that bit." My intention here is not to lead anyone on. I want to be honest with him and myself. My whole damn life changed overnight, and it's been hard to adjust. "I didn't choose Croy over you. I know that's what it seems like because everything happened at once, but things between us fell apart on their own. I'll admit, I never fully comprehend your feelings, which was my mistake. I should have done things differently. But I'm not always certain which parts I would go back and change."

Kelly has yet to release my hands. His touch has always been like fire. Kelly is a taker. He consumes all. I knew he would burn me to ash if I let him, and for a time, I considered it. He's a difficult man to say *no* to. Had I not absorbed so much of Croy's considerable strength, I think I would still be under Kelly's spell. He would still be pulling the strings, and I'd be thanking him for it.

"I don't want to let you go." His eyes lock on my face as he begins to lean toward me.

"Please don't," I say, as I take a step back. "Another kiss isn't going to make me forget, and it won't make me change my mind."

My phone is still in the car cup holder, but I can hear it ringing. Either my mom is calling to see if I'm on the road, or Croy is on his way home. Until now, I forgot about the doorbell camera on the front door. The camera has a full view of the driveway, and nothing about this situation looks good.

Kelly hears it too. "Do you have to get that?"

"I probably should." Kelly releases my hands, and I grab the phone from my car.

> Croy: Are you good? Did you know he was coming over?

> : I swear, I didn't know. He pulled in as I was leaving.

> Croy: That boy needs to learn a lesson. Why must he always touch you? Is he still in love with you, or does he have a death wish?

> : I'm sorry. Are you mad?

> Croy: No. I'm not mad at you. But your friend is lucky I'm 45 minutes away. I need to get back to this meeting. But I can't until I know you're alright.

> : I'm fine. I promise. Have your meeting and call me at lunch. I'll find a way to get rid of him.

> Croy: If ANYTHING happens, call the police. They can get there faster than I can.

"Does he watch your every move, or what? I thought you hated that?" Kelly would have a point. I always hated the thought of someone watching me all night on the cameras at work.

"It's not me that he's watching. He doesn't trust you to keep your hands to yourself." I wonder how much more of this bull-shit Croy will tolerate before he decides I'm not worth the trouble. Maybe that's Kelly's plan, to be so annoyingly pesky that I end up single. If the shoe were on my foot, and some girl kept chasing Croy, I'd be pissed.

"Is that what *you* want? For me to keep my hands to myself? Kelly tucks his fingers into the front pocket of my jeans and pulls me towards him. "Because that's not what it felt like last night when you kissed me back."

"Okay, well, I'm not a fucking robot. When an attractive guy kisses me, I'm not going to pretend to be repulsed. However, I would prefer you exercise a little restraint. I get that you don't respect me or my relationship, but you're going to make friendship impossible." I haven't stepped back, so I'm still dangerously close to him. I can't imagine what this looks like from the outside, but I'm willing to bet it's not good.

"Good! I don't want to just be your friend." Kelly locks me into place by gripping his free hand around my belt. It reminds me of the night in the office before that version of my life ended.

"Kelly, it's friendship or nothing! Are you ready to say goodbye?" Now that I say the words aloud, am I ready for that? Every time I start to forget, he surfaces. I don't want to be with him, but am I prepared to lose him? Friends are hard to come by these days, and the less you have, the more one's worth. With only one friend to my name, he's damn near priceless.

"That's bullshit." I can feel his grip tighten as he prepares for my retreat. "But if those are my only options... Then we're friends. I can't lose you."

I can't tell if it's the morning sun or Kelly, but I feel like a toasted marshmallow. If I don't get into the air conditioning soon, I'll need a nap before my drive. "Kelly, I need to go. I have plans with my parents for lunch. Can we text later after I get settled in at home?"

"Wait, you're actually moving? I assumed the ring meant you were staying with Mr. Perfect." Kelly's grip is unyielding. He's leaning against my car, and we are pressed together from the waist down.

"I've told you this a dozen times. Do you not believe me

when I speak, or do you not listen?" My tone is getting annoyed. If I don't get the car on soon, I'll have four dozen wilted long-stem roses. Plus, I'm sweating. "Seriously, I need to get on the road. Can you please release me?"

"Can I have a hug first? Then I promise I'll go." He pulls harder still. The sleeves of his t-shirt conform to his flexed muscles. Last week this would have made my mouth water. Everything with Kelly comes at a price, even his absence.

"Fine." I wrap my arms around his neck and press the length of my body against him. He released my belt, but only so that he could snake his arms around my waist like a vice. I get the feeling this hug isn't going to end anytime soon.

Kelly whispers things in my ear that would drive even the good girls wild. I find myself in a death spiral, straight into the gutter. He seems to know exactly what to say to make me want him. My legs feel like they might give way at any moment as I begin to melt.

Goddammit! What the fuck am I doing? Kelly makes me weak. He likes me vulnerable and wholly dependent on him. He wants me broken. This has to stop! I can't. I won't be that person again. This isn't love. It's manipulation. I know that... "Okay. You promised."

"Fuck! I want you so bad right now. Can we go in the house? I know you feel something, too." He's turned on. That's obvious.

"I'm not fucking you in Croy's house. Are you out of your mind? We're not doing this!" The only thing I feel right now is regret and my rising anger. Why do I continue to entertain this? Nothing I do is ever going to be enough for him. He'll keep asking for more until there is nothing left.

"Follow me home. He won't find out. I'll make sure it's our little secret." Kelly is confident. I'll give him that. And sneaky. He also doesn't think much of my moral code, as if I would cheat and lie and not give it a second thought. "Let me do this for you."

"NO! I'm not that kind of person, believe it or not."

"I know. This is me and you we're talking about. I didn't

mean to imply anything else. I'm sorry. If you change your mind, you know where to find me." He kisses my forehead and finally releases me.

I wait for Kelly to get in his car, back out, and drive away. My mind is still racing. I wish I could talk to Croy, but I don't want to bother him. Maybe a quick text, and he can respond if he wants to. When I get in my car and start the ignition, I know it won't help, but I turn the air conditioning on high.

> : Do you think it's okay for me to leave? I don't imagine he's going to come back. But I would feel guilty if he did.

> Croy: I don't care about stuff that can be replaced. That's what I have insurance for. I only care about you. If you leave now, we can meet for lunch.

> : I would love that.

> Croy: 2731 N. Grand Ave Columbus. Call me if you have any trouble finding it.

With the new address in my phone, I start the directions and back out onto the street. There's a lot to think about on my drive. As much as I would love to live on the bright side and focus on the possibilities ahead, I'm leaving this town a failure, and that's a pill that never goes down easily. I failed at living on my own. I failed at my job. I failed as a friend and co-worker. And now I've failed as a girlfriend and a fiancée. Over the last few months, I've done nothing right. When faced with a choice, and 50/50 odds, I have chosen poorly every time.

Forty

ACCORDING to the lady on my phone, the destination is on my left. I haven't spent much time in Columbus, but it feels about the same as driving around Cleveland. Pulling into the parking lot, I look for Croy's black SUV until I'm 90% sure I've found the right one.

> : I made it here in one piece. I'm parked under a tree near you.

> Croy: You are indeed. I can see that part of the lot from my office, and I'm headed your way.

I catch sight of a familiar form in my rear-view mirror and unlock the doors. Following him with my eyes, I watch his torso as it passes from one window to the next. I can't help but smile with giddy excitement as the anticipation builds. His tattooed hand reaches for the door handle, and my nerves threaten to burst my existence at the seams. By the time Croy climbs into the passenger seat and hugs me, I'm overcome with a need to be closer. I didn't know I would get the opportunity to see him today, and now that I'm here, I'm uncertain how to behave, which is silly. I allow his calm presence to quench my illogical nervousness so I can meet him where he is.

"You have no idea how happy I am to see you." He says he's happy but sounds relieved. "Are you hungry? We can split my lunch." Croy pats his lunch box, and I think it's cute that he packs. Although, let's be real, I think everything he does is endearing.

"I'm alright. I might steal a bite, but I'm not overly hungry." I'm curious to see what he's made himself. I half expect it to be a protein shake and some beef jerky. Then again, I've seen his culinary prowess firsthand. Croy seems to have a talent for *something* in every room of the house.

Sitting here next to him, I would love nothing more than to drift off into unfiltered fantasies, but my mind has been racing for forty minutes, and there are other conversations to be had. Guess I should pull off the band-aid and get it over with. "Do you want to talk about the whole *Kelly showing up* thing, or are you tired of having that same discussion?"

"I couldn't hear what was said, but I kept the video on during my meeting. It's not that I was trying to invade your privacy. I needed to know you were safe, that's all." Croy holds out his sandwich before taking the first bite. This one action is indicative of the kind of man he is. "I have a couple of questions, but I'm afraid to ask."

"I didn't think you were afraid of anything." I get the sinking feeling that this conversation isn't going to fall in my favor. And why should it? Croy has offered to move Heaven and Earth to be with me, and I keep stepping back into the arms of the man who gives me Hell. Choosing between them should be simple, yet I insist on overcomplicating everything. And for what? My indecision reads like wavering loyalty, even though that couldn't be further from the truth. It's a wonder Croy's tolerated it as long as he has.

My hand trembles as I slide off my ring and set it on his leg.

"What the fuck? You're leaving me?" His words sound choked. I've never seen him cry, but I think I'm about to.

"No. I thought you were about to break things off with me. I figured giving the ring back would be better than you asking me for it." Maybe I misread the situation.

"Is there a button somewhere that I can press to adjust your programming? Why do you always assume I want to leave you? I just wanted to ask you a few questions." Croy picks up the ring and slides it back onto my finger.

"Well hun, that button you're looking for is hidden in a secure location. And it's buried *pretty* deep. You're gonna have to *really* get in there if you want to press it." Again, with the jokes. It's not that I'm incapable of having a serious conversation. I am. But I hate seeing him with that concerned look on his face.

"If that's the case, you'd better turn around and head back in the direction you came from so I can have you thoroughly reprogrammed by morning. The days of you thinking you could lose me are done." Croy lifts the back of my hand to his lips and presses a kiss against my skin. "Unless I'm the one who's at risk of losing you."

"You're not at risk of losing me. I swear." I shouldn't have taken my ring off. That was a stupid move. It planted a seed of doubt into Croy's heart, and now he thinks I'm willing to abandon ship at any moment.

"All right, then answer me honestly. Is Kelly in love with you?" His question comes slightly out of left field, catching me off guard.

"I don't know. He says the words, but his actions tend to speak louder. I never realized we had the kind of relationship he claimed, so I might be the wrong person to ask about feelings. There was a time when we were close, but that was when we were friends. Who am I to say how someone else feels, especially about love? He might love me, or he might not. Personally, I think Kelly doesn't like to lose."

"That's fair. I can't expect you to read his mind." Croy takes a bite of his sandwich, effectively pausing the conversation, but only for as long as it takes to chew and swallow. "So, the question I should be asking is, do you love him?"

"Why would you even think that?" I guess seeing us together painted quite a different picture without the dialogue.

"Do you want to see the video? You two looked like you were about to have sex in the driveway. I assumed you left and followed him back to his place."

"You did? Seriously? I mean, okay, I'm not gonna lie. He did put the offer on the table. But you actually thought I would do that?" I'm starting to regret coming here.

"I'm not mad at you, and I'm not accusing you of anything. I'm sorry if it came across that way. I don't know how to say this..." Croy seems nervous, which is out of character for him. He's always so cool, calm, and collected, not to mention confident. "Kelly is a good-looking guy. We can all see that. And you two have a recent history. I've seen him be charming and manipulative. And I've seen you be far too kind. The guy was so angry when you rejected him that he hit you in the face. But what's worse is that you forgave him almost instantly and you still want to be friends with him. You knew I would have gone after him that day, and you protected *him*." Croy's words, while true, do sting. "I don't understand why you can't let him go. And it scares me. I'm afraid he'll hurt you again, and you'll never let me protect *you*. I'm afraid there's more between you than you lead me to believe, and there's still a chance you'll choose him over me. But for the life of me, I don't even know why he's an option. Help me to understand. If you want to be with me, why is it so important to you that he remains in your life?"

"Because he's all I have left... I'm sorry that he keeps showing up and that I haven't done more to push him away. Are you asking me to choose? But I have chosen you. Kelly is *not* more important to me than you are." I hate that we're even having this conversation again. Maybe there isn't room in my life for both of these men. "I'm not in love with him, but he is important to me. He's the only person in my life who remembers me. It's like there's a tiny invisible thread made up of our shared experiences that ties me to him and the memory of who I used to be. And if I let him go. If I cut that tie. The person I was a week ago won't exist anymore. The version of me who had confidence and purpose will disappear. And that's scary because I don't know who I am anymore. I'm sorry I don't know how to explain it to you. It doesn't make sense to me either."

"I think you explained it beautifully. I'm sorry I made it seem like you had to choose between us. You don't. You're struggling with things you aren't ready to tell me, and he makes you feel connected in a way that I don't. I understand. I want to be everything for you, but that takes time. So, if talking to Kelly helps sort through what happened, you should do your best to repair that friendship. But if he doesn't stop touching you against your wishes, I'm going to kill him. Even if it breaks your heart." Croy leans over and kisses me.

What starts sweet exchange quickly evolves into passion. "How am I going to make it till Friday without seeing you?" His hand starts at my thigh, but it doesn't stay there. "I need you at home with me. I can't wait to marry you."

"Croy Belk. That has a nice ring to it." I laugh, clearly joking.

"I'd change my last name for you if that's what you wanted. I don't care about the name, so long as we're a family. You, me, and JoJo."

The rest of the hour is spent laughing, talking, and kissing. I don't want to say goodbye to him, not yet. Even though Croy isn't asking me to choose, maybe I should. I don't want Kelly to be a burden on my relationship. I already know I'll spend the next two hours debating with myself as I drive. However, for now, I want to enjoy these last few seconds.

"When you have a minute, can you text me and let me know that you made it to your parent's house? You know I worry." He asks, even though he doesn't have to. I was already planning to text him when I pulled into the driveway.

The image of Croy breaking a guy's jaw in a prison fight never quite aligns with the man I've fallen in love with. Right now, he's wearing a long sleeve button-down shirt, with the sleeves cuffed to his elbows. I run the tips of my fingers over his forearms, hoping that the memory of my touch will linger.

Having a tattooed man in work attire sitting close enough for me to touch is getting me turned on. If he had his glasses on right now, my brain would probably overheat.

"Kelly doesn't have your parents' address, does he?" Croy asks with a raised eyebrow.

"Yeah. Didn't I tell you? It's a race. The first one to find me wins." I'm nearly certain Kelly doesn't know where I'm headed, but now that Croy's mentioned it, the thought will grow in my consciousness like a burning bush. I'll need to make sure I keep an eye out.

"If that's the case, I'll be following behind you and meeting you there." He's joking, of course. Still, I like the idea of him being with me when I arrive. Friday feels painfully far away. "I don't want to leave you, but I should get back to work. I'll give you a call when I get out."

"Okay." I've been dreading this part. The last kiss goodbye. "I hope the rest of your day goes smoothly." There are so many things I want to say, but time has run out on me. I have to hope he feels the same way I do and believe we'll speak again. Considering the lengths he's gone to and the quality of the time we've spent together, you'd think our being together would be a given. However, my past has convinced me otherwise. Nothing is a sure thing, especially if it seems perfect. Then again, Croy isn't anything like my exes. And I've never felt this strongly.

"Please don't be sad." Croy kisses me one more time before he opens the door. "We'll be together again before you know it, I promise."

"I know. Leaving you is a lot harder than I thought it would be." Every ounce of my willpower is being exhausted, damming my tears. I'm not sure how much longer I can hold it together.

"It isn't easy for me either, but we can make this work. The distance is temporary. Any time it gets too hard, we'll make an effort to see each other." Croy takes my hand and kisses the back of it. He has one leg out the door, but he's as tethered to this moment as I am. "I love you. Nothing could ever change that."

"I know. I love you too… Now get out of here, and I'll talk to you later." That is the last thing I say.

Croy exits the car and closes the door behind him, leaving me alone. Not a full second elapses before my eyes begin to water. I have to let it out while I'm still parked. Otherwise, I risk backing into someone. One minute. That's all I allow myself. After sixty seconds of sobbing like a baby, it's time to get it together and return to the road.

Music is normally my go-to distraction, but every song conjures images of his face. And it doesn't help that the car is flooded with the smell of roses. Or how the sun keeps illuminating the diamond on my left ring finger. There's no escaping the unrelenting thoughts of him, not that I would want to. I miss him already, and it sucks.

This sadness feels ridiculous. I'm going to see him again in a few days. All he did was go to work. We can't exactly spend every second together for the rest of our lives. Someone has to be responsible and make some money. Lord knows I'm not exactly helping there. Plus, if I want to be with him, I can go back. No one is forcing me to stay here. I'm not even sure anymore why I made the drive. Maybe I should skip the interview tomorrow, enjoy my birthday, and then go back and surprise him.

Per usual, I start running through worst-case scenarios. "Surprise, I'm here," I announce from the front door. The image of Croy with some random girl on the couch. Or even worse, in bed together. Croy, livid and blaming me for arriving at his house uninvited. My existence shattered in an instant. Broken beyond repair. Would I run back to Kelly and beg him to forgive me? And what if he had moved on as well? After all, I'm the one who left them.

Forty-One

IT'S BEEN months since I was here last, but it feels about the same. My mom must have been watching for me out the window because she was at the door before I even finished parking the car. I have mixed feelings about returning here. Perhaps I should think of this more as a visit and less of a walk of shame. Knowing myself, I'll spend the rest of the week wallowing in self-pity, waiting for all the shoes to drop. I text Croy as soon as the car finishes rolling to a stop.

> : I wanted to let you know I've made it here in one piece. I'm glad that we were able to sit together for lunch. Also, I borrowed your black hoodie from the hall closet. Hope that's okay.

> Croy: I love when you wear my clothes. Send me a picture later if you have it on. That lunch hour went way too fast. I keep thinking you'll be at the house when I get home later, but you won't be... I have to keep telling myself that Friday will be here before we know it.

: Yeah. I'm trying to convince myself of that same lie. Call me when you get home later. My parents are waiting impatiently for me to exit the car. LoL.

"Hey stranger, welcome back." My stepdad has joined my mom at the front door. "Need help carrying in your stuff?"

I open the back door and pull out the two bags of roses. I can deal with the rest later, but for now, these flowers are my top priority. They're the closest thing I have to Croy being here with me.

"Oh my lord, where did those come from? Are you dating a florist?" My mother's voice is full of questions and surprise. One bouquet is a sweet gesture, but four must seem like overkill.

"I'll explain while we eat. Tell me there's lunch. I'm starving." My stomach has been grumbling for hours, and I seem to have lost track of the time. I kept meaning to pull off the freeway for food, but the idea of adding additional time to my drive was enough to keep me set on my path.

"Lunch was three hours ago, but I made you a plate." Her response doesn't at all surprise me. Good mothers never let their children go hungry, even when those children are adults.

I take the two bags to my old room and unpack the four vases. One by one, I space them evenly across the top of my dresser in front of the long mirror. Now I'll be able to enjoy them from every angle. I take Croy's hoodie from the bag and hold it to my nose. The smell of him is faint but present. No question, I will be sleeping with this tonight, so I lay it on the bed next to my pillow. The hoodie in the other bag is Kelly's. I locate his essence, still clinging to the fibers, and allow myself four seconds to miss him. Then I hang it on the back of the door and head to the car for round two.

All my stuff is already in the entryway when I reach the front door. Not surprising since I didn't have a whole lot with me. I carry most of it to my room and pile everything behind the door. My bags can be sorted out later. Right now, I need a meal.

Taking my plate into the sunroom, I eat while we talk. I've never cared much for sitting at the table like a proper adult. My parents ask question after question, and I do my best to give enough information to appease their curiosity without causing undo panic. Regarding Croy and how we met, I leave out everything that happened while I was unconscious. So, the current truth is that we met at the hospital. "From the first moment, everything clicked into place, and we've been inseparable ever since."

"So, how does your new boyfriend feel about you moving? Or has your plan changed?" My mother has gone out of her way to not mention the ring, though we both know she's seen it.

"Well, I'm sure he doesn't feel great about it. Neither do I, for that matter. There are a lot of factors to consider, and we're still weighing our options. If he visits this weekend, I plan to show him around the area." The thought of not seeing Croy until Friday makes my heart hurt. I would give anything to have his arms around me right now.

"So, you're trying to convince him to follow you?" The tone of their questions seems laced with something I can't place. Speculation? Doubt? Distrust? Whatever it is, it's negative.

"No. He's already convinced. But it would make more sense for me to stay there and get a new job. Croy already has a gorgeous home and a good career. He's settled. Why would I ask him to throw that away for me? I have nothing to offer and no reason to stay here." The more I talk about it, the more I'm convinced I need to go back. My heart is with Croy, and so is my future. Why would I want to be here, alone?

"When we spoke a week ago, you wanted to come home and start fresh. Now, you meet this guy, and everything's changed? Don't you think it's a bit sudden? What kind of person proposes after a few days?" Her tone seems annoyed, and her expression is rigid.

"I suppose the same kind of person who would say yes!" I can feel the anger seething below the surface of my skin.

My parents have had front-row tickets to every one of my

relationship shit shows, and they don't want to see me make the same mistakes. I get it. However, I can't sit here watering the plants with my tears for the next year because I walked away from the best thing that ever happened to me. When I called and asked to come back, I felt trapped at Kelly's and had nowhere to go. The situation has changed substantially since then, and I no longer require a hiding place.

"Does this mean you're blowing off the interview you have scheduled for the morning?" Nothing about her tone has changed. It's still shit.

"No. I'm going to the interview. It's not like I have anything else going on tomorrow." I carry my plate to the sink and watch as it sinks below the soapy surface. "I need to lie down. I'm not feeling that great." I retreat to my room and lock the door behind me. My brain needs a break. I think I'll take a nap before I talk to Croy. Maybe he'll be able to help me sort through all of these racing thoughts.

This has already been a long day, and it's only 4:00 pm. I collapse onto the bed and use Croy's hoodie like a blanket. The empty sleeves drape over me, and it's as though he's here in spirit. I can't remember when he gets out of work, so I make sure my ringer is turned on before I close my eyes.

When the phone rings, it jars me awake. And it takes me a moment to get my bearings. I was in the middle of that dream again, with the puppy and the sharks, only it was different this time.

Croy must leave work at 4:30 because it's only a few minutes after. I ask him about the rest of his day, tell him about the house, and repeat select sections of the conversation with my mom. Then I mention the dream, and he laughs. "It's a sign. We're meant to find this puppy and save him." I laugh with him, even though I don't think that's what the dream means.

When I ask for his advice on the interview, he tells me again that pursuing every available option is worthwhile. I get the feeling he doesn't want me living there with him, but he doesn't want to come right out and say it. It's best to be straightforward, so I ask him outright. I'd like to avoid any further confusion. "Would you be mad if I wanted to come back and stay with you?" "Of course not. I would love to come home to you. That's the goal. But I worry about you living in this particular town." There's more, but Croy doesn't say that part out loud.

"Because of Kelly? You think I'll be unfaithful if I lived in Oak Falls." If the roles were reversed, I would be concerned about getting cheated on as well. I'd like to think I'd never do that to someone, but I guess none of us knows for sure until we're in that position.

"I'm not worried about you cheating on me. I worry about him pursuing you relentlessly. I mean, I get it. I wouldn't be able to handle losing you, either. But I would try to respect your decision. Honestly, Kelly isn't my biggest concern. I know we don't talk about it, but those guys I put in the hospital, they have friends on the outside. It doesn't take a genius to find someone's address on the county auditor site. If I'm at work, that means I'm not home to protect you. And if anything ever happened to you..." He trails off and call remains silent for several seconds. "My love, I would hire Kelly to stand guard at the door if it meant keeping you safe."

Some of this conversation we've had before and some of it has remained unspoken until now. He wants to be with me but isn't comfortable with me living at his house. And his points are all valid, even if I don't want to hear them. But where does that leave me? Does he expect me to stay here without him? Does moving here keep me safe, or does it simply keep me away? In my experience, distance doesn't make the heart grow fonder. It makes the mind grow forgetful.

The faint scent of him mixes with the roses, and I'm transported back to last night when he proposed. Everything always feels like a lifetime ago, as if years have passed during our hours together. I want to get back in my car right now and drive home. It isn't about the house or the town or the other people living there. Home is with Croy. Wherever he is, that's where I want to be.

"So, do you think you're ready for your interview? Do you want me to ask you some practice questions?" Croy has a list of questions at the ready as if he conducts job interviews for a living. He inquires about my strengths and asks me to list my weaknesses. I keep my responses professional and sugarcoat the flaws, but I can't help but wonder if this is a future wife interview. He digs into previous employment records. And I list off the job titles I've held. But I draw the line when he asks me to describe my co-worker relationships.

After my mock interview is complete and he's unofficially offered me the position, I turn the tables and begin asking questions of my own. "Speaking of interviews, did you hear anything about the job transfer? Was the position posted? Do you think you'll hear something back this week?"

"The position was posted today, and I already submitted my application. I think they're looking to fill the vacancy quickly. So, I might hear something, one way or another, by the end of the week. The real question is, do you think we should start looking for a house, or would that jinx it?"

I grab my iPad and go to my usual sites. I love a good home search, so this is right up my alley. The rest of his drive is spent listening to me describe places listed for sale. There aren't any houses currently on the market with decent-sized yards, but a few empty 5-acre lots are available for building. When Croy gets home, he heads to his office to join me in the search. We spend the next two hours discussing square footage and taking virtual tours.

Croy makes it fun to dream. He makes me feel like anything is possible. I don't have the heart to tell him that everyone else thinks we're crazy.

There's a diet coke in the fridge next to a plate of food. I take everything back to my room so we can have dinner together on the phone. I feel like I'm a teenager again. Talking to him makes me giddy, and I never want that feeling to end. My twenty-eight-year-old self is head over heels in love, and I wonder what twenty-nine-year-old me will think about my choices.

It's 9:00 pm when we start to say our goodnights. We both need to shower, and Croy has to be awake early for work. It's hard to hang up, so we spend another twenty minutes stalling for time. My interview isn't until 9:30 am, but I want to make sure to give myself plenty of time.

Finally, I say goodbye one last time. "I love you more than I ever thought possible. I know I'll see you soon, but it's not soon enough."

"I'm the man of your dreams, remember? You always know where to find me." This is the part where he would kiss me if I were there. "Sleep tight. I promise you. We'll be together again before you know it. I love you, more than everything... Goodnight"

"Goodnight" With that final word, he's gone, and I'm alone.

Forty-Two

THE BLINDING light stings my eyes, and I know where I am without looking past my feet. I'm on the beach, yet again. I lift my head and scan the water's edge for JoJo, but he isn't there. This dream is different. This time, there's a boat where the sand meets the water. It reminds me of the metal rowboat my parents had at their old house. I would spend hours going back and forth across the pond, to the point where the wooden oars would give me blisters. Why is this here? Am I meant to go somewhere? Why do I keep coming back to this place?

The water remains flat as marble and clear as glass, but I can no longer see the beach on the other side. The sand and water run parallel, as far as my eyes can see. There is nothing to the right or left, only the metal boat and its wooden oars. This is my safe passage across the vast stillness ahead.

Placing my hands against the bow, I push the rowboat off the sand and jump in. It's small and light, making it easy to move. There's a metal bench seat in the middle and another small seat in the front. I position myself between the oars and start rowing. If I were looking to go quickly, I would sit with my back to the bow and use my legs to help power my strokes. But I'm not sure where I'm meant to go yet, so I face forward and keep my pace slow.

There's nothing here. It's empty and quiet. The light reflects off the water, blinding me from above and below. I don't understand what I'm meant to find. And then I hear his voice skipping across the water's surface like a stone. Croy is here, somewhere in this enormous emptiness sprawled out before me.

There's something on the horizon, but I can't quite make it out. It has to be him. Now is the time to see what I'm made of. With my course set, I turn 180 degrees on the seat and pull. This is a motion my body is familiar with. I've spent years on the rowing machine at the gym, both in college and recently. I could get across this lake in my sleep if I had to.

I check over my shoulder every five strokes to ensure I'm still headed in the right direction. Croy is there, arms flailing, shouting my name. I don't see the sharks, but something must be wrong. Otherwise, why is he yelling? I'm only a few feet from him when something knocks against the side of my well-worn vessel.

Croy reaches forward, grabbing the boat's rounded edge, but he's unable to pull himself in. I grip his arm and lean back so we don't capsize. It'll be impossible for me to haul him over the side on my own. My voice is pleading. "You need to help me. I can't do it on my own." He's right there. My hands are on him, but he won't budge. Goddammit! Why did I have to fall in love with someone so heavy? Why won't he move? He must be stuck on something.

"I can't lose you. I need you to do this with me. Please!" My throat is dry. I clench my jaw and pull again with everything I have. Finally, he's in the boat to his waist. "Pull your legs over!"

There's some sort of thick black seaweed wrapped around his ankles. When I try to remove it, the tendrils tighten. This isn't seaweed. It's a goddamn squid tentacle. I lift the wooden oar and smash it against the black arm, avoiding Croy's legs. There's a sound, like a high-pitched scream, and the arms release.

Croy sits with his back against the small seat at the bow.

Seeing him there, safely extracted from harm's way, a wave of relief washes over me. I hook the oar back into place and prepare to get us out of there. But before returning to my seat, I look at him and say, "It's okay. I found you."

Something wraps around my waist the yanks me over the edge. I feel my body smack against the water's surface, expelling the air from my lungs. Croy's face is the last thing I see before I'm plunged into the darkness. There's no getting free of this fate. I've traded my life for his, and now my debt is paid in full.

I wake up drenched in sweat, confused by my surroundings. My hand slides over the sheets next to me, but the only thing there is my phone. It's 1:00 am. Everything is fine. It was another stupid nightmare.

: You were right. I found you in my dreams.

Croy: I hope it was a good one.

: Seeing you is worth any cost.

Croy: So, not a steamy sex dream, I take it? Another nightmare?

I would give anything to have Croy here with me. Being in his arms is all the comfort I need. But I chose to leave for some reason, and I'm still not sure why. Croy is afraid of a faceless threat looming in the shadows. But retaliation has never been one of my concerns, and I typically stress out about everything. If the monsters want to come for us, then let them come. I won't spend the rest of my life being afraid of shadows.

: It doesn't matter. I'm sorry I woke you.

Croy: Don't be sorry. 1:00 am is our time. Also, Happy Birthday, my love.

: Thank you. I'll let you get back to sleep. Goodnight.

There's no way I'll be able to fall asleep right now. If I tried, I would end up back on the beach. What does any of this even mean? First, a puppy and sharks, now Croy and a squid. I swear, the blood they gave me in the hospital must have come from a total nutter because I haven't felt right since.

It's the middle of the night. At this hour, I need a fellow vampire to talk to.

> : Do you mind if I bother you for a moment? I don't want to sleep.

Kells: You're never a bother. What's going on? Something on your mind?

> : Just a stupid nightmare. I need a distraction. And I thought you might be bored.

Kells: You know I'm always here for you. And you were right. I'm in minimum, bored out of my mind. They didn't have a second person available, so it's me and the quiet. I'm glad you thought to message me. I need the distraction as much as you do.

Kelly never shies away from mentioning work, even though it was the stage for a performance that cost us nearly everything. "The Jail giveth, and the jail taketh away," I laugh to myself. Maybe someday I'll stop hiding behind jokes and take the necessary steps to process what happened. But not tonight.

> : Glad I could help. Have things pretty much gone back to normal there now that I'm gone for good?

Kells: The inmates are back to normal. The staff, who knows? After I defended you last night, no one will mention your name in front of me. That's probably what landed me down here alone for the night. When you told Collins to choke on a dick, I nearly died. She was PISSED the rest of the night.

: Yeah. Sorry about that. It seemed like there was something between you two. Did you finally have hook up?

Kells: Hell No! Babe, I only want to be with you. I can't stand Collins, and I know you hate her. Can you imagine how much worse she'd be if I had sex with her? Gross! After everything that's happened, I'm thinking about leaving. Too many memories here. I feel haunted by your ghost every time I'm in here. Like you died, and you're trapped here, and you're pissed at me for letting it happen.

: I don't want you to feel that way. I'm not dead.

Kells: Just lost.

: That's not your fault. I've felt lost all of my life.

"... until Croy found me." I don't say that last bit to Kelly because I'm not looking for a fight. But that's how I feel. I've been locked away my whole adult life, trapped in a prison I helped to create. Somehow, Croy found me in that infinite darkness and freed me. He is the key to my future.

Kells: I've found you a few times. Maybe one of these days, I'll get to keep you.

: Stranger things have happened... Anyways, I should probably get to sleep. I have to wake up early for my interview, but I appreciate you talking to me. I'm glad that I messaged you.

Kells: You know where to find me if you can't sleep. I would love to hear from you any time. I'm always here for you.

: Thanks. You can call me if you ever need someone to bail you out.

"... and I'll send Croy because I'm poor." That last bit makes me laugh out loud. I wish I could say those things to Kelly without him getting mad. It would make being friends a lot easier.

Kells: I'll keep that in mind. Goodnight, babe. Hope you sleep better.

I drop my phone on the bed and close my eyes. Why did I ever think that being here would make things less complicated? I could be home, in bed, sleeping next to my fiancé. Instead, I'm here, texting my ex. Why fight it when giving in is much easier and quicker? I walk across the room and grab the hoodie hanging on the back of the door. Slipping it over my head, the smell of Kelly fills my lungs and floods my senses. I crawl back into bed, close my eyes, and allow sleep to overtake me.

Forty-Three

WHY DID I set my alarm for 7:45 am? I'm still so tired. It would be easy to snooze through the morning, but I don't want to feel rushed before my interview. My plan is to get there early so I have time to meditate in the car with some music before going inside. My depression and mania are in a throuple with my anxiety, so it's not uncommon to see two of them go hand in hand. I tend to overthink everything, and job interviews are notoriously triggering. The rejection feels so personal. I can already sense myself spiraling as my apprehension rises. I need something to calm my nerves, and I know the perfect guy for the job.

: GOOD MORNING!

Croy: Why are you shouting at me?

: Because you let me die last night while I was saving you from a squid.

Croy: I would never let that happen! You know
me better than that. Also, Good Morning and
Happy Birthday! The last year before 30. Or are
you one of those girls who plan on being 29 for
a while?

: I have to make it through the year. Then I'll let
you know.

I take off the hoodie I'm wearing and return it to the hook on
the back of the door. Part of me feels guilty for putting it on last
night but not guilty enough to admit what I did. I told Croy
about the text exchange with Kelly but omitted any mention of
the sweatshirt for obvious reasons. He's far more level-headed
than I've ever been, but even someone as understanding as Croy
has his limits.

My text conversation with him continues as I dress, undress,
and get dressed again. I want to look professional, but I also
need to be comfortable. If I walk in wearing a sweater in the
middle of summer, they'll know I'm hiding something.

It's only a quarter to nine when I'm ready to get out the door.
Even though I know where I'm headed, I put the address into
my phone and double-check the directions. My parents are on
the front deck looking out at the water, planning for the day
ahead, so I say a quick hello and goodbye. Lake Erie is calm this
morning. And seeing the water this flat reminds me of the lake
from my dream.

I take a final moment to debate the pros and cons of eating
before I leave the house. In the end, I decide to skip both coffee
and breakfast. I don't want to have anything in my teeth or on
my breath. Plus, I want to avoid needing the restroom. Easy
enough to wait and eat afterward.

The drive is simple enough, even though it's not an area I
frequent. As a teenager, I used to drive around for fun. Gas was a
lot cheaper then, and it was better than sitting at home. Being in
the car allowed me to be alone with my thoughts or to escape

them. These days, it seems there is no escape. I can't even have a moment of peace while I'm asleep.

> : I'm sitting in the parking lot, trying to remember how to breathe normally. Going to give myself 10 minutes to get centered. Then I'll go in. Wish me luck.

> Croy: Good Luck!!! You're going to be great. I know it.

The list of Croy's attributes continues to grow without end. I make a mental note to add Cheerleader to the positive column and file it away. This is the first time I've had someone invest in me, and it's nice. I hope I'm not a disappointment.

The building is bigger than I expected and full of people waiting to see their caseworkers. I let the front desk know I'm there for an interview, and a woman comes around to open the door and escort me back. This place is the complete opposite of my last job. If the jail is a ghost town, this place is a beehive. Sometimes, organized chaos can be soothing. It can quiet the negative voices by keeping my thoughts focused on the task at hand. But most of the time, chatter feeds the madness within. If too many people are talking at once, my attention is pulled in every direction simultaneously. The more I think about it, this might not be the right environment for someone like me.

The lady interviewing me is older, maybe in her 50s. She has a thin face, faded red hair, and gold wirerimmed glasses perched on the end of her nose. Her style is a dated, as though she came to work thirty years ago and never left. It gives me a whole Shining vibe, reminding me of my lunch date with Croy. I have to resist the urge to answer her questions with my talking finger.

Overall, the interview is pretty straightforward. I appreciate that she doesn't bother with any of the typical gotcha nonsense. Mostly, she seems intrigued by my time spent working at the jail and keeps asking for stories. If we had coffee, this would feel less like an interview and more like two friends conversing.

I walk out with a good feeling. The interview went as well as it could have, and I'm excited to discuss it with Croy. He's the biggest supporter I've ever had, and I appreciate his faith in me even if I struggle to accept it. I'm still not sure I want the job, but I do want them to offer it to me. No one likes to feel excluded.

: I think that went pretty well.

Croy: That's awesome. I have an interview later today for the position I applied for. I'll let you know how it goes.

: Are you going to be in town? I'm in Elyria right now.

Croy: I'm sorry, love. I wish that were the case. My interview is happening over video chat.

: Well, that's still exciting. Good Luck!

So, it appears the hypothetical might become our new reality. If Croy gets this job, I know he'll want to sell his house and move here to be with me. At this point, he's made it abundantly clear that my living down the street from the jail is not going to happen. And if I get this job, or even if I don't, my life is wherever Croy is. It's weird how quickly everything has changed.

What I need is a place to think. After all, isn't that the whole reason I came here? There's a park next to my parent's house that overlooks the water. It even has a little beach, depending on the time of year. That might be the ideal spot to spend some quality time with myself. Water can be a great place for reflection, even if it is distorted by the occasional ripple.

On the way home, I stop for food. Thankfully, places are serving lunch already because I'm not in the mood for powdered eggs. Two months of breakfast at the jail has given me my fill of fake protein for a lifetime.

There's no one here, so I pull into a spot of my choosing,

open all the windows, and kill the engine. It's peaceful sitting at the lake, looking out at nothing. There have been times when my depression has felt overwhelming. More than once, I've considered jumping into the water and swimming toward Canada. I figured, eventually, I'd get so tired that the vast emptiness would swallow me whole. Sometimes, *nothing* can feel like a better option. But today, I have other things on my mind.

I've been working on building a five-year plan. My relationship with Croy feels like a given, so a lot of my goals include him. All I want is to be settled and somewhat happy. But what am I willing to sacrifice? How much am I willing to give? What are my negotiable wishes and my non-negotiable sticking points? I close my eyes, recline my seat, and try to picture the future I long for:

Croy is as handsome as ever, but he's starting to get a couple of gray hairs in his beard. We walk hand in hand through the fruit trees in the backyard, and I still feel sparks when he touches me. A red boston terrier with an all-white face chases after a little girl, trying to get her to play. The girl is laughing. Her light brown hair shimmers like gold in the summer sun. I see the pool and the house and the love that is our foundation.

I think about family and new traditions. I look forward to decorating for the holidays and spending Christmas in our pajamas. The thought of carving pumpkins and passing out candy is especially appealing. I imagine dressing our daughter and the dog in corresponding costumes for Halloween. And Croy having to carry them both home when they're too tired to walk after a full night of trick or treating.

I think about friendships and what they're worth. Will Kelly still be in my life, or is he temporary? Will I meet new people at work or volunteering at the school? Does it matter? I already know I'll grow old with my best friend by my side. Isn't that enough?

I try to picture our wedding day, but that's never been a dream of mine. Fingers crossed, I can get Croy on board with a destination wedding or a quick stop at the courthouse. Maybe the two of us, at the beach next to the lake, committing to a life-time together. I probably should marry him sooner rather than later, or would that make him more desirable to other women?

I think if we did have kids, I'd like to be a stay-at-home mom. I don't know. I never considered it an option, but now that every-thing's on the table, I keep coming back to look at it. I guess that's a conversation for another time. We might never have kids. Is it possible to be a stay-at-home dog mom? Croy did joke about that the other day. I wonder what he would say if I wanted to accept the offer. Then again, I'd most likely get bored and spend the entire day missing him. My mind is such a mess. I can't even make hypothetical decisions.

As the hours pass, variations of my future float in and out of my mind like clouds. It's after 2:00 pm when I finally decide to rejoin reality and move my car over to my parent's driveway. I've never cared much for my birthday. This one, today, feels even more unremarkable than the years prior. Maybe I'll hide in my room and wait for Croy to call after he finishes work.

When I get to my bedroom, I retrieve the present from my duffel bag. Even though I already know what it is, I'm still excited to open his gift and hold it in my hands. My fingers run over the top of the paper. The gold flowers against the black background are as beautiful as I remember. Croy has good taste in wrapping paper. I'll have to make sure my gift-wrapping game is on point come Christmas time.

There's a light knock on my bedroom door, and I hear my mom say, "Are you going to come out and open your gifts?" She may or may not know this is my least favorite day of the year.

"Yeah, I'll be right there." I don't feel like being around anyone, but I can pretend to be happy for twenty minutes. What's the point of visiting if I don't interact? I can't hide in my room until Friday evening, a day that feels painfully far away.

Before leaving my room, I scroll through Facebook. It's the usual messages from people I haven't seen in 10 years and a post from Croy. I get emotional as I read over it again, absorbing every character and punctuation. Attached to the message is another photo of us from Hocking Hills. We were encircled by an incredible rock landscape that seemed too perfect to be real. I remember the man who took this photo for us that day. He was middle-aged and sporting a walking stick and ranger hat. He reminded me of Allen Grant from Jurassic Park.

There's another knock on the door. This one is a bit louder, and the sound makes my heart jump. "Alright, I'm coming," I yell through the door, more aggressively than intended. I don't mean to be an asshole, but my excitement about this visit home is virtually nil. I set my present from Croy on the bed. His gift is special, and it's private. I want to unwrap later when no one's around to see me cry.

Pulling open my bedroom door, I nearly go into shock. Croy is standing on the other side, looking unbelievably perfect. "Found you." He says as he opens his arms for a hug.

I can't contain my emotion and let out a scream of excitement as I throw my arms around his neck. "Oh, My God! What are you doing here?" I have to be on my tiptoes to hug him like this, so he lifts me from the floor and presses my back to the wall. I wrap my legs around his waist and bury my face in his neck. It's taking everything in me not to scream again, but I don't want to deafen him.

"My interview wasn't over Zoom. It was in Elyria. When you asked me earlier, I almost broke down and told you. I hated lying to you, but I wanted it to be a surprise." His kiss is the best gift I've ever received. "Happy Birthday, love."

My poor little heart is pounding in my chest like a drum. This doesn't seem real. My emotions have never swung from one side to the other so quickly, and it's overwhelming in the best possible way. "I can't believe you're here right now. I needed this so badly." To hell with presents. I want to go back into my room and lock the door.

"Alright, geez, you saw me yesterday." He pretends not to be as excited as I am, but his smile gives away his joke. "Come on. You still need to introduce me to your parents."

My eyes are flooded with happy tears, and I can't bring

myself to share him. Not yet. "Didn't you meet them when you came in the house?"

"Your stepdad let me in. He was in the garage when I parked in the driveway. But I haven't met your mom." I loosen my grip, and he eases me to the floor. "Come on, let's see what they think of me."

My parents are friendly but guarded when we go out on the deck. Their smiles seem a little fake, and their questions are a bit too pointed. It's making me angry. Croy drove all this way to see me for my birthday, and they're treating him like an internet stalker.

After thirty minutes of negative attitudes, I've had enough. "Babe, let's take a walk over to the beach. I want to hear all about your day." I'm disappointed by what I witnessed. Croy was respectful, pleasant, engaging, and open. All the things I would have expected from him. My parents, on the other hand, were bordering on rude.

"Lead the way, my love." Croy takes my hand, and we walk out the front gate together.

Forty-Four

ONCE WE GET to the beach, I kick off my shoes to feel the sand under my feet. Croy and I are still wearing our interview clothes, and I wish we had thought to change before leaving the house, but we're here now. He takes a seat in the sand and leans back against a rock. Sitting in front of him, I curl into his chest. When I close my eyes and breathe him in, I'm at peace. The real thing is so much better than a hooded sweatshirt. "So, how do you think the interview went?"

"The interview for the job went great. I'm confident I'll receive the promotion. The interview with your parents, however, was not as reassuring. I'm certain they thought I was a good-for-nothing, semi-obsessed, tattooed bum who would never deserve their daughter. I wouldn't be surprised if they spend the next few days convincing you to file for a restraining order." He sounds defeated.

"Well, the only opinion I care about is yours. But I am sorry they were acting like that." I'm not sure what more I can say. I would rather talk about anything else right now. "Do you think you'd still accept the position and move up this way, or did this visit ruin our plans?"

"Unless you're telling me right now that you've changed

your mind about living here, I have every intention of moving. Forgive my saying so, but to hell with what your parents think. I love you. And if you love me, that's all that matters. I don't care what city we live in, so take your pick, and I'll make it happen. All I ask is for a shorter commute to work than I have now." Croy is as easygoing as ever.

I swear, he rarely seems stressed. I'm completely freaking out about everything all the time, and he's cool as a cucumber. We're exactly alike in so many ways, but we couldn't be more different when it comes to emotional levels. Croy is composed, logical, and even-tempered, whereas I'm erratic and overly emotional. Oddly enough, it works for us. He soothes me and makes me feel safe. I don't know. Maybe it only works in my favor. Loving me has to be quite the adventure. "Never a dull moment," as he likes to say.

"So, we're doing this?" I can't even wrap my head around the enormity of what needs to happen. This is crazy. It all feels like too much. And I'm not confident about what I'm bringing to the table.

"Hun, you're worried about everything, and you don't need to be. I can feel how tense you are." He runs his hands over me, sending a chill along my spine. "Relax and trust me. People relocate for work all the time. That's why there are realtors and moving companies and short-term leases. Once I get the job and have a start date, we can get a six-month rental agreement at a condo or put in an offer on a house. Everything we need can go with us, and the rest can sit in storage. You don't need to worry. We have this under control, okay?"

"It sounds like you have this under control. I'm still not sure what my part is." It's important to me that I'm contributing in some way. Otherwise, I'm riding his coattails and being worthless.

"This is a team effort, but I won't have enough time to see everything. I need you to work with the realtor and sort through the options. And I know how you are about spending money, but I want you to dream big. We can afford it." He gives me a squeeze and a kiss on the top of the head. "There's a lot that might fall on your shoulders, but I promise you're never alone."

"None of these people are going to take me seriously. I'm just the girlfriend." Even I don't take myself seriously. I demoted my own relationship title.

"Fiancée," he says, holding up my hand. "And if you would rather it be wife, we can make that happen anytime you want. I'm leaving that timeline up to you." He looks down at me the same moment I look up, and we kiss. Where's a justice of the peace when you need one? We're on the beach in fancy dress-up clothes. Let's get it done.

"You have so few doubts about us that you would marry me straight away?" I know I would say yes, but would he?

"Sweetheart, I would marry you right this second without hesitation. There is not a doubt in my mind that you and I are meant to be together." Croy is certainly convincing. "Do you think you'll stay up here until the move?"

"Absolutely Not! I want to be home with you. I know you worry about me being there, but I can't stay three hours away from you. I can't. It's fucking torture." I can feel myself on the verge of tears. Last night was harder than I want to admit, and I can't bear the thought of doing it again. "I was planning on talking to you tonight and leaving in the morning unless you tell me I'm not welcome back."

"Please don't do that. Of course, I want you home. You know damn well I hated every second of being apart last night. If I have to make a deal with Kelly, I will. Whatever it takes to keep you safe and happy." Croy always sounds less confident when Kelly gets brought up. As if he thinks there's a chance I could be lured away. Or maybe he's still worried about invisible monsters hiding in the shadows.

"Kelly isn't going to be an issue." I've given this a lot of thought lately, and I can't keep asking Croy to accept something from me that I wouldn't be willing to accept from him. "If you ask me to stop talking to him, I will. There's no way I want to risk our future for anyone."

"As much as I still hate him, I would rather he be in your life. But I want your word. If he touches you again without your permission, you'll let me be the one to handle it." Croy's words land in my lap like stones.

"Okay. I hear you, and I understand. So, you're saying he can touch me as long as I say it's okay first?" It's not the best time to make a joke, but I can't help myself. I don't like when he's upset. I'm like the court jester, and it's my duty to make him happy.

It seems to have worked. Croy laughs and says, "I hope you plan to visit me in jail."

"Wherever you go, I go. I'll get a job there, and then we can see each other every day. Don't forget. I do have experience." I laugh and sink deeper into his chest.

We spend the next hour mostly in silence, and I'm on the edge of sleep when Croy suggests that we walk back to the house. "Let's change into something more comfortable and figure out where we're sleeping tonight. I don't want to wait until 10:00 pm to find out that I need a hotel room."

"We don't have to spend money on a hotel room unless you plan on being loud." I give him my signature wink so he knows I'm attempting to be cute.

Croy and I walk back to the house hand in hand. He grabs a bag from his car, and we head to my room to change. I can't believe I made it this long in these clothes. Once we're in my room, I lock the door and close the curtains. It's my birthday, dammit, and there is only one present I want to open. I do my best impression of a girl being sexy and slowly unbutton his shirt. Croy looks so damn good. I can't believe he's mine. When we kiss, I feel his energy spread through my body in waves. The tips of my fingers tingle as I fumble with his belt. It's been a long time since I last undressed a guy while making out, but I imagine it's a bit like riding a bike.

As everyone learns during their teen years, the bed is too loud. When you have to be quiet, the floor is the best option. We take turns teasing each other and whispering our intentions. I'm finding out that Croy can be quite dirty, and it's incredibly sexy.

When we're done, he holds me in his arms as we attempt to catch our breath. I can't say one way or another if distance makes the heart grow fonder, but it certainly makes the sex more exciting.

As anyone would do in the situation, we get dressed and act like nothing happened. I find leftovers from dinner and make each of us a plate to take outside on the deck. It's quiet here. My parents are nowhere to be seen, so they must have gone for a walk or something. This is probably for the best. I don't need a repeat performance of earlier.

Croy and I sit outside talking until it's time for bed. He has an extra-long drive ahead of him in the morning, and I don't need him asleep behind the wheel. When we get to my room, I sit on the bed and open the present wrapped in gold and black paper. As promised, it's my copy of the framed photo from his desk. I add it to the rose display on my dresser and smile back at the adorable couple.

"If you open up the back, there are a few more photos behind that one, so you can change it up if you want." He picks up the frame and slides the clip on the back, removing the panel that holds the photos in place.

There's a picture of me leaning against a moss-covered rock, Croy standing in the opening of a cave, and a copy of the photo he posted online for my birthday. Each reminds me of a different trail and a day spent falling in love. I like all of them, but the one in front is my favorite. I couldn't imagine ever changing it.

"Do you want me to wake you up before I leave in the morning or let you sleep?" Croy says with a yawn. His voice is sleepy and extra sweet. It's ridiculously cute.

"I want you to wake me up so I can walk you out and say goodbye. Then I'll probably hang out for a bit and leave after breakfast. If you want, I can time it so I'm in Columbus around lunch again." I have every expectation that my parents will be pissed about my leaving so soon, but I'm not going to burden Croy with that information. All I care about is getting home and sleeping next to him again tomorrow night.

"If you stay up here for the week, I'll be back again on Friday." Croy sounds half asleep and fading.

"No. I want to be home with you." I feel strongly about this, and I need him to understand.

"Alright. Whatever makes you happy. I just don't want anyone thinking I came here and forced you to leave. You know I'm fine with anything you choose... I'm sorry dear. I'm really tired... I love you." His eyes close, and he's out almost instantly. Oh, what I wouldn't give to be able to fall asleep like that.

There's nothing that could be said in the morning to change my mind. I'm 29 years old, and I'm going to follow my heart. If things end up not working out, that would be devastating, but those things happen. That's the risk we all take regarding love's uncertainty. But if I go back, I'll know I tried. I won't have to spend my days wondering what might have been had I found my nerve and taken the leap.

Kells: Hey, I heard what today is, and I almost missed it. Let me know next time you're in town, and I'll take you to lunch or something. Happy Birthday!

: Thanks. I had a job interview this morning. Not exactly a party.

Kells: Oh cool, what kind of job? Do you think you'll get the position? I'm surprised to hear you aren't coming back. How does your dude feel about being long-distance?

: Hahahaha... My dude? You can use his name. I know you know what it is... If I get the job, it'll be in an office. Mostly data entry and case review. But things with Croy won't be long-distance.

Kells: He lives down here, and you'll be staying up there. How is that not long distance? Does he own another mansion up north? The drug business must be good.

It's times like these when I wish Kelly would stop talking. Maybe I need to set a few ground rules if we're meant to be friends. Talking about Croy is the quickest way to piss me off, which he should have realized by now.

: Don't be stupid. He doesn't sell drugs. And he doesn't live in a mansion. If you're going to be an asshole, I'm going to bed.

Kells: Whatever. I tell a nurse we're engaged so that I can see you in the hospital, and you freak the fuck out. Then you go and actually get engaged to this stranger a few days later. And I'm the asshole? He makes you quit your job and move away, but I'm the one who was controlling? Give me a goddamn break. All I did was try to help because I care. I never asked you to change for me. I love you the way you are. Or the way you were before he showed up and destroyed everything. He doesn't do a very good job making you happy.

: Do you feel better now? Croy isn't controlling me. I was put on leave, and the warden accused me of being a whore and fucking everyone. Forgive me for getting pissed. You know I was never going to feel safe there after what happened. Were you going to protect me?

: And I came back up north because I'm from here. Croy didn't send me away or whatever you think happened. As for the fake engagement, I wasn't mad at you about that. I didn't care. I was mad you showed up all pissed off and treated me like shit.

: You made the whole thing about you, like I wasn't the one who could've been killed. Oh, boohoo. Kelly's upset because he didn't get to be the hero. FUCK THAT! If you loved me so damn much, you would've been thanking Croy for saving my life.

: I get that you're mad because I started dating him. And I agree that the engagement was fast and probably seems crazy. But I don't care what it seems like to anyone else. If Croy and I are happy together and we want to run off and get married, so be it. We won't be the first couple in history to get married after a week or a month or whatever it ends up being.

My heart is pounding as I hit send on the last message. I know I'm ranting like a lunatic, but I can't keep playing nice and staying quiet. Kelly is important to me, and I owe him my honesty, even if he is pissing me off. Normally I avoid conflict to the best of my ability, but it feels good to let it out right now.

Kells: Is that what you're planning? Are you getting married right away? I thought women only did that kind of shit when they were knocked up. Are you pregnant?

: Be serious? We've been together for a week. It takes a lot longer than that to find out you're pregnant.

Kells: Well, it could be mine. I didn't use protection the last time we had sex.

Is he being honest right now, or is he trying to hurt me because he's upset? I know we had sex a handful of times, but this is the first I'm hearing about condoms or a lack thereof. Either way, I'm angry.

: Are you dumb or stupid? First off, what the fuck are you even talking about? You didn't use protection? When? Where the fuck was I when this happened? And secondly, I'm not pregnant!

Kells: The day you checked out of the hospital. I was so happy to have you home. I wasn't thinking straight. All I knew was that I needed you. I thought you were okay with what happened. You didn't say anything, so I never brought it up.

: I was so out of it I barely remember having sex. But hey, thanks for that. I need to go to bed. I can't talk to you anymore. That slap should have been the final straw, and it wasn't. But this shit right here, I'm done.

Kells: Babe, I'm sorry. Please. I didn't do it on purpose. I was caught up in the moment and didn't think about it until after. Don't do this. I need you.

I'm too angry to respond and too worked up to fall asleep. "Fuck!" I don't mean to say it aloud, but it slips out.

Croy reaches a sleepy arm over and wraps it around me. "What did he do now?"

"Nothing. He just said something and pissed me off. I'm sorry I woke you up." There's no possible good that comes from a continued relationship with the boy I once called my friend. I see that now. Croy doesn't even have to ask. I'm going to shut that door and lock it.

"Can I read it? Helps me know what buttons to avoid in the future. You know, Happy Wife, Happy Life, and all that." Croy sits up and holds out his hand, waiting for the phone. Maybe I shouldn't let him read it, but I've woken him from a dead sleep, and it'll look worse if I say no. I hand him the phone and wait, trying to read his expression as he scrolls.

"Wait, what?" He seems to be searching for the right words. "Okay, so which part is upsetting you? The dig about me doing a shit job of making you happy, the part about not using a condom, or the end where he tells you he can't live without you?" He continues to scroll, reading and rereading the messages.

"The not using protection. I honestly wasn't aware of that, and it makes me mad. Everything he did those last two days felt like a trap, and I feel like he did that shit on purpose. He's so frustrating. And I'm mad that you're always right about him. The two of us cannot be friends, and it pisses me off." Of course, I'm not mad at Croy. I'm mad at myself. Kelly keeps finding new ways to make me look stupid, and I let him.

"Alright. Well, I don't want you mad at me, but we didn't use anything the first time either. So, if you're pregnant, we're looking at 50/50 odds." Croy laughs and hands me back the phone.

"This is not a joking matter. And I'm not pregnant, but what if I was? I not sure if I even want kids. And now I'm going to end up a single mother. Why would you even laugh about that?" I feel like getting up and going for a walk alone. Then jumping in the lake for a swim to Canada.

"Why would you say that? You wouldn't be a single mother. I don't care what color eyes that baby comes out with. You and I are in this together. That would be our kid."

"Right, because you'd stay with me if I were pregnant by another man? And not just anyone, but the guy you hate most in the world. I don't think so." This hypothetical situation is too much for me to process.

"You have every reason to be mad at him. But you said it yourself. It's too early to know. And we both know Kelly likes to say shit to get you going. Maybe he's lying about not using a condom." Croy pulls me into his arms and kisses the top of my head. "No matter what happens, I'm here. And I support any decision you make, so long as you don't decide to leave me for that asshole."

His calm washes over me, and I can feel myself relax. "I never considered that something like this could come along and split us up." I take another breath and sink deeper. "I'm glad you're here. Having you by my side makes everything better. And for the record, you do an incredible job of making me happy."

"Nothing is going to come along and split us up. I promise. I love you too much to let that happen."

I snuggle close and fill my lungs with him, letting myself drift off. The only thing I want to dream about tonight is our happily ever after.

Forty-Five

THE SOUND of an alarm will never please me. It's still dark when Croy wakes up for work, and I'm still tired. While he's in the shower, I make coffee and pour us each a cup with vanilla creamer. I hate these constant goodbyes. Croy always tells me to think of it as a See You Later, but my self-doubt doesn't allow it. I could lose him the same way I found him, unexpectedly and without warning.

I watch him closely as he buttons his shirt between sips of coffee. There's no time for funny business, but I make sure to store the mental images. Here I am, looking comfortable in my sweats and hoodie, and he looks like a goddamn fitness model going to a board meeting.

"Babe, can you put your glasses on for a minute?" I have my phone at the ready and snap a photo. "Oh, dear God! Please come home looking like this later. I'll be waiting in the bedroom."

"Whatever you want, dear. You're being silly, but I'm not mad at it." He comes towards me and leans in for a kiss. "Are you ready to walk me out?"

Standing in the driveway watching him leave is the hardest

318

thing I'm going to have to do today. Best to get it over with, I guess. "I'm ready if I have to be."

We take our time saying goodbye until all the free minutes are exhausted. "If you're staying awake, you can call and keep me company on my drive to Columbus. But only if you want to. Otherwise, text me later and let me know if you're coming for lunch. I'll order food." He pulls me into his chest and wraps me in his arms. I feel tiny, like a little mouse. I want to hide in his pocket and stay with him all day. "I don't want to leave you, but I must get going. Do you still love me?"

"Even more today than yesterday, which I didn't think was possible." I look at him, my eyes asking for one more kiss.

"How am I supposed to leave when you say stuff like that? I need to make you my wife before you run off and find someone better." He seals his statement with a kiss and gets into his SUV, shutting the door behind him.

Better than Croy doesn't exist, not even in the pages of fiction.

I watch as he backs out of the driveway and pulls onto the street. I know there are three stop signs before he gets to the main road, so I send a quick text.

: I love you, more than everything.

Croy: I love you beyond measure.

Once I get back into my room, I lie on the bed and make my phone call. Croy and I talk for nearly two hours, which is how long it takes him to drive to work from my parent's house. I wonder if a day will ever come when we run out of things to say to one another. Somehow, I doubt it.

I have two hours until I need to get on the road if I'm going to meet him for lunch. Figuring that it's best to get my shower out of the way, I get cleaned up before packing. There are shorts, tank tops, and bikinis in my dresser that Croy has yet to see, so I empty my bag and fill it with new clothes. For date nights and lunches, I throw in some nicer items. And, of course, I pack sweats for relaxing. I double-check to make sure I have all my charging cords and devices in my backpack, then zip it shut. I'm pretty sure I have everything I need, including the photo from my dresser. The last thing I pack is the hoodie from the back of my door and the one next to my pillow.

I debate on taking my roses but decide to leave them behind. One at a time, I carry each vase to the living room and arrange them on the various tables. My mom can enjoy them for me. Maybe seeing the roses every day will be a visual reminder that I have a good man in my life and I'm happy. If the next time my parents meet Croy goes anything like yesterday, they shouldn't expect us for Christmas.

There's a second cup of coffee with my name on it this morning, and I'm excited to make its acquaintance. I head out to the front deck for one more moment with the lake. The goodbye with my parents goes about as smoothly as sandpaper. They think I'm making a mistake by moving in with a guy I only recently met and implore me to reconsider the engagement. I'm starting to think their invitation to the wedding might get lost in the mail.

It's not that I disagree with their logic. After all, they only know bits and pieces of the story. They measure our time together in days, whereas for Croy and I, it feels like lifetimes. I wouldn't expect them to understand, so I don't bother explaining it. Croy isn't an option. He's my priority.

There's enough time for a twenty-minute power nap after I load my bags into the car. Before pulling out, I used part of my birthday gift card from Croy to buy some new music and curate the perfect playlist for my drive. If I leave right now, I'll have time to stop for gas and still be there early.

: I'm on my way. Lunch date in the parking lot?

Croy: I'll never turn down an opportunity to spend time with you. Drive carefully, and I'll see you in a couple of hours. I'll order your favorite.

The drive feels faster and significantly more relaxing. Probably because I'm excited about where I'm going and who I get to see. Plus, the new playlist helps. When I get to the parking lot at 2731 N. Grand Ave in Columbus, I'm able to find an open spot next to Croy's SUV. I have about fifteen minutes to relax and close my eyes before he joins me, so I open my windows and recline my seat.

The air is different here in the city. More complex. I try discerning the various layers while I wait. It's an odd sort of game but satisfying in a strange way. Even with my eyes closed, I can smell Croy as he approaches the car. "Are you awake, my love?"

"Resting my eyes while I want." I unlock the doors so he can join me on the passenger side. If given the option, I would make this drive every day simply to have this hour with him.

Even though so much remains in the air, things feel more settled than they did two days ago. We eat and talk, and at no point does my ring come off. Croy points out Eric walking from his car. "He asked if we'd like to come over Friday to celebrate and hang out one last time."

"Celebrate? Did you find out about the job already?" My words come out excited as my thoughts spin. We haven't had any time to prepare.

"Not officially. But Eric heard a few whispers, and he's confident I'll get it." I can hear the pride in Croy's voice. And why shouldn't he be proud? His stock value rises by the day.

"That's awesome! Guess I better get home and find us a new house." I'm not even sure where to start, to be honest. We've looked, but there's nothing that jumps out at me.

"I have an idea, but maybe we could discuss it over dinner tonight. I have to get back to work." Croy kisses me and opens the door to get out. "Do you want my key for the house, or are you okay going through the garage?"

"You don't have to take your key ring apart. I can manage." I remember seeing a keypad on the inside frame of the garage door. My parents used to have one at the old house, so I'm sure I can figure it out.

"Okay, the code is 1981. Type it in, press enter, and you're in. If you have any trouble, call me. Your house key is on the kitchen counter in case you want to go anywhere... I love you. I can't wait to come home to you." Croy smiles and kisses me one more time.

"Okay, go before I take you with me. I'll see you at home." I watch as he gets out and shuts the door. "Love you."

It's interesting how things change when you meet the right person. I used to hate saying *I love you* to people. Family included. It felt like something people would say out of obligation instead of meaning it. But with Croy, my heart feels like it's bursting at the seams with love for him, and I can't say it enough.

The drive home is uneventful since there isn't much traffic at lunchtime on a Wednesday. With three hours to kill, I search for possible house options online. Then, as promised, Croy meets me in the bedroom with his glasses on.

Forty-Six

THE NEXT COUPLE of days are a blur. Croy's housing idea was a six-month lease at an upscale condo, which he has already called about. We sat together and decided on a city, which was easier than expected. I love the town my parents live in, and the schools are good. That's all it took for me to convince Croy that Vermilion was the place to be. He put in an offer on a 5-acre lot and bought the plans for my dream house.

As we discussed our future, I learned more about Croy's financial past. After he made an all-cash offer on the land, it was clear there was something more than a good job funding our endeavors. Apparently, his grandfather started investing money in tech every year for Croy's birthday and holidays. As he prepared for adulthood, he took over the accounts and became proficient at stock trading. His exact words were, "We aren't rich, but we're comfortable." Whatever that means.

By the time lunch on Friday rolls around, Croy has news to share. "Start packing, my love. The job is mine, and our condo deposit has been sent. We leave in a week."

As for my interview results, I didn't get the job. When I broke the news to Croy about my lack of employment, he sounded happy. I remember he said something along the lines of, "You don't have to settle for a job you would have ended up hating. Take advantage of this time and build your dreams. I would much rather you be in charge of everything at the new house since you're the one with the vision. Whatever you say goes, and I'll make sure everyone knows it. Plus, you have to give some thought to what kind of wedding you want. Again, I defer to you. If you decide you want to work, I'll understand your decision. But I'd prefer you wait until after the house is built and we move in. I'm not great at asking for help, but I really need your support while I adjust to my new position at work."

I agree to go to Eric's apartment later to celebrate Croy's promotion. Eric and his girlfriend will both be there, so Croy assures me it wouldn't be boys, video games, and beers all night. I've already showered and picked out my outfit, so now I'm waiting for Croy to get home from work. And I'm pretty sure I just heard him come through the door.

"Honey, I'm home," Croy calls from the door before taking the stairs two at a time and finding me in the bedroom. "Are you excited to start our new life together?"

"I am so proud of you. I've been bragging about you all afternoon. My parents said, 'Congratulations.' They can't wait for us to live closer, and my mom wants to know when she can expect some grandkids." I laugh and motion for him to join me on the bed. "So, throw the condoms away, and let's make some babies."

The excitement of the day has gone to my head and made me loopy. I don't even know what I'm saying right now. My mania is working overtime, and I'm going to end up pregnant before the wedding.

Croy doesn't wait for me to retract my statement or say that I'm joking. He's on me faster than Sonic on a gold ring. I get the feeling he's been waiting for me to give the go-ahead, and now that I have, there's no turning back. I'm not sure what we'll have left if we knock out our entire five-year plan this year. But who cares? It feels amazing.

As we catch our breath, I trace my fingers over the tattoos inked into his skin. I've yet to pick out a favorite. He takes my hand and presses it to his lips before lining my arm with kisses. "Mmmm. My deliciously salty girl. Would you like to shower with me? We're all sweaty."

I had already showered before he came home, but I should probably rinse off. I only go in long enough for Croy to wash my back and kiss me half a dozen times. While he finishes scrubbing the sex off with a loofa and some cedarwood body wash, I dry off and get dressed. Since he has the bathroom mirror all fogged over, I do my makeup in the other room. By 6:45 pm, we're ready to go and walking out the door.

Even though we're still early in our relationship, I was afraid things might change after I accepted Croy's proposal, but if they have changed, it's only been for the better. Most guys back off once they know they have you, but he's remained constant in his chivalry. We walk to the car hand in hand. And when we get there, he opens the door and helps me in. His car is much higher than mine, but I'm certain I could get in on my own. Of course, I would never say that because I think it's cute that he always offers, and I don't want to discourage him from being attentive.

The exact location of our destination doesn't hit me until we arrive in the parking lot. I haven't spoken to Kelly since my birthday when I told him I was done trying to be his friend. He hasn't stopped being important to me, and I've thought about him more than I should admit, but the constant push and pull is exhausting. Hopefully, missing him will become less painful over time.

Eric is already in the parking lot, waiting for his girlfriend. I recognized him straight away when we pulled in. He looks different away from work, in cargo shorts and a black t-shirt, but his face and muscles are the same.

It makes me think of Croy and all the different looks I've seen him in since we met. Gray scrubs and orange crocs, a hospital gown, my extra set of clothes, camouflage shorts and a sleeveless t-shirt, board shorts, and the button-down shirt and tie he had on the night he proposed. He always looks nice when he's dressed for work, and don't even get me started on the pants he wore to his interview. But my personal favorite is when he wears nothing at all. Much like the songs we listen to, some of his clothes have become memory markers. I want to display pertinent items from our story behind glass in a museum dedicated to the existence of love at first sight.

Eric's girlfriend pulls in after us, and the three of us make it to the front door at nearly the same time.

"Damn, you all look amazing. I've clearly underdressed for tonight's festivities." Eric reaches out his hand toward me and offers me a hardy handshake. The strength of which causes my bones to rattle. "Heather, I've heard so many good things about you from multiple sources. It's as though we've become friends by proxy. I'm glad we finally have the chance to meet. This is my girlfriend, Sarah."

Eric's playful dig doesn't go unnoticed, but I decide to let it go and direct my attention to the other girl at the party. Sarah is about two inches taller than I am and stunning. She has long, thick caramel-colored hair that cascades down her back, beautiful green eyes, and a waistline that would make any woman jealous. Eric's a nice-looking guy, but this girl is in a league all her own. "I can't believe you two are leaving next week, and we only get to hang out this once." For a second, I think she's about to shake my hand, but she wraps me in a hug like I'm her long-lost best friend. I don't want to be rude, so I go with it.

Eric opens the door and holds it as we file into the building one after the other. In typical Croy fashion, he takes my hand and doesn't let go. The four of us ride the elevator to the sixth floor in relative silence. I can't help but notice the door marked 602 as we exit the elevator. When we enter Eric's apartment, Sarah offers to make drinks, and he retreats to his bedroom to change. The apartment is a mirror image of Kelly's. They must all come fully furnished because everything is the same. I feel like I've stepped into a dream.

After a couple of drinks, Sarah makes a request that causes my mouth to drop open. "Heather, I am dying to see your ex.

Eric said he's even better looking than Croy, and I said that's impossible. Do you think you can get him to join us for a drink?" I nearly choke on my vodka and red bull. "What?" Croy is sitting in a chair to my left, laughing like he was expecting this. "I don't think it's a good idea. And I doubt he'd drink with us since he's probably working tonight."

"Please, can you go ask him? I have to see this guy." Sarah is almost begging in that playfully annoying way that comes across as taunting. Better looking than Croy? I call bullshit. Kelly is top-tier, as far as looks go, but Croy is the whole package. I can't even begin to guess how Eric could have described "my ex."

Sarah is doubling down, looking at me with puppy dog eyes as though her life depends on seeing for herself if the rumors are true. Maybe she's trying to sort out how someone like me could catch the attention of men who might otherwise swim in her dating pool.

"Okay, I can ask." I pull out my phone and compose the most awkward text in history as a crowd looks on.

"Walk your cute ass over there and knock on his door. He won't say no if you ask him in person." Sarah is giving me the hard sell, and I feel like I'm in college, with someone daring me to run naked through the hallway. And the guys are no help. They've remained quiet to this point, but not detached. Both are egging her on with grins and shared glances.

I fix my eyes on Croy. "Why aren't you saying anything? I can't imagine you're good with this."

"The love of my life has agreed to be my wife, and the pieces of our well-deserved future are falling neatly into place. Kelly coming here for a drink doesn't bother me because you'll still be by my side at the end of the night. Who knows? Maybe we can finally bury the hatchet." Croy chooses an interesting turn of phrase, and I can hear the beers kicking in.

"Look at me and hear my words." I look at Croy like he's the only person in the room. "No matter what he says or does, you have to promise me you won't touch him." My eyes have not left Croy's face.

"What if he swings first?" Croy says, smiling. I can see he's hoping for this chance to even the score. But the likelihood of Kelly taking a swing at him is slim to none. Guys like Kelly are only tough when they know they can win. Croy knows that as well as anyone. After all, he's the one who said it.

"In the unlikely situation that he hits you first, I'll take him down." When it comes to defending myself, I'm a pathetic punching bag. However, if I'm called upon to defend someone else, I can be a tough opponent. Plus, I've learned a few useful techniques during my time at the jail.

"Deal. I would love to see that... Remember, you've made promises to me as well. If he touches you without your permission, he's mine... Now, go get your boy." Croy is way too excited about this. I'm not sure I trust him to stay out of jail tonight.

Finally, Sarah chimes in, "Shit, I didn't know it was like that."

"I don't think he'd try anything with all of us here, do you?" Eric's question is directed at Croy, so I get up and set my drink on the counter.

"Oh, he'll try something. I guarantee it. Kelly has a hard time keeping his hands to himself, right dear?" Croy winks at me and finishes his beer. And all I can do is shake my head and wonder who the blame for tonight is going to fall on. This is not going to end well.

I walk towards the elevator, hoping Kelly is either at the gym or in the shower. I don't care if he's in there having sex with Collins, so long as he doesn't open the door. When I step in front of 602, I take a deep breath and look back in the direction I came. All three of them are peeking out the doorway, making sure I don't chicken out. "Please don't be home." I ball my right hand and knock. "And please don't hate me."

A few seconds later, the door flings open in front of me, and Kelly grabs me. "Oh my god, what are you doing here? I thought I was never going to see you again." We stand there, locked in each other's arms for a solid minute before I remember how to speak. Kelly has a way of sucking the air out of a room and leaving a girl lightheaded.

"We're having drinks with some friends, and I thought I would stop by and see what you're plans were for the night." My arms are still around his waist, absorbing the heat from his core.

"Which friends?" Kelly turns his head and lifts on his toes as if straining his body will grant him temporary x-ray vision.

"Eric, who I guess you know, and his girlfriend, Sarah... They wanted me to ask if you'd be interested in coming over for a drink." I let go of Kelly's waist when he looks like he's about to kiss me. "So, what do you think? Would you like to hang out for a bit?"

"Sure, if it means getting to spend time with you. How the hell do you know Eric? I'm assuming Mr. Wonderful is there as well?" Kelly's already getting his shoes on, so my answers must not matter.

"Yeah, he's there. Please play nice." This whole thing is a powder keg waiting to explode in my face. I can't believe I'm about to put them in a room together. Croy is eagerly awaiting a fight. I could see it etched into every inflated muscle. And Kelly is quick to lose his composure whenever we're within arm's length of each other.

He grabs my hand as we walk toward Eric's apartment. I know this is a bad look, but it might be the only way to get him in there, so I go with it. Anyways, Croy is already expecting this kind of display. I only hope he can stay in his chair.

Kelly and I walk in together, and Sarah's mouth drops open. "Ooooooo... I don't know. I'm sorry, Croy, but this might be too close to call. This man is giving you a run for your money." She gives me a wink.

Croy stands, and my heart drops. I shoot him a look in hopes of reminding him of our deal. *You promised me.* Unphased by my nonverbal cues, he walks over and leans against the counter within swinging distance. "So, what's it gonna be? Beer or booze?"

I hate this stupid dare so much. I want to run downstairs and drown myself in the pool. Before Kelly can answer, I offer him an out. "You probably shouldn't drink if you have work tonight." I try to let go of his hand, but he's not reciprocating.

"It's all good. I have the night off, and I'd love a beer... Plus, I can't refuse an opportunity to spend the evening with my favorite girl. Come on, babe, don't be a buzz kill. We never did get the chance to have drinks together. What do ya say we get drunk and have a threesome." Kelly's joke makes my heart drop into my stomach. Sarah spits her drink across the table, and Eric bursts into laughter. Croy stands there, smiling through his discomfort. This shit is worse than my beach nightmares.

"You're welcome to as many beers as you want, but I'll be taking *my* girl back." Croy grabs a beer from the fridge and holds it out.

Kelly drops my hand and takes the bottle from Croy as I grab my drink from the counter. I remain positioned between them. Tension knotted into my shoulders. If Croy is waiting for me to heel at his side like a dog, it's not going to happen. I don't particularly enjoy being stuck in the middle of this pissing contest, but I won't walk away and let them kill each other.

"Can you guys stop hating each other for one night? For my sake? I would like to have a nice time with both of you." My words seem to break through the tension, and I can see Croy relax. He steps forward and kisses the top of my head. Kelly's beer is gone, so he walks past us to get another from the fridge.

The three of us move to the table, but only two chairs remain available. "Eric, does your place have a patio?"

Once we're all outside, the mood shifts and everyone is laughing and having fun. Sarah asks me to help carry a round of drinks but leaving makes me nervous. I check both my guys to make sure it's safe to turn my back to follow her into the kitchen. "Girl, holy shit! How did you do it? Those two sexy ass men both worship the ground you walk on." Sarah is obviously letting the vodka do her thinking.

"I don't know about all that. Croy, maybe... Okay, probably... But it isn't like that with Kelly. We're friends. He hates Croy because of some things that happened, so he's extra flirty with me to get under his skin." I pause to listen for the conversation outside. Seems okay. "When Kelly said that thing about the threesome, I almost died."

"Girl! I wanted to die so I could possess your body and take your place or hover in the corner as a ghost and watch. You need to make that happen. That would be the hottest threesome in history." Sarah's enthusiasm is over the top, and I can't help but laugh. We grab drinks for everyone and head back outside.

Kelly accepts a beer, and Croy swallows another Angry Orchard. We should probably slow down before someone passes out or pukes from six stories up. Everyone looks a little drunk and far more friendly than I thought possible.

Sarah must be younger than I am because she says, "Let's play Truth or Dare."

"I already did my dare when I brought this one back with me." I point at Kelly, who is sitting across from me. When I gave Croy his drink, he asked me to sit on his lap, so I did.

"Croy, truth or dare?" When Kelly is the one asking, I'm shocked. This game is a horrible idea with this group of people. There are too many strong egos at play and merely the illusion of control. This is a recipe for disaster.

"Truth." He wraps his arm around my waist and kisses my shoulder while awaiting his question. Every time he places another small kiss on my skin, it makes my body tingle. I want to go home right now.

"When did you know you were in love with Heather?" Kelly doesn't ask the question I was expecting. I assumed he would ask when Croy and I had sex for the first time, wanting to hammer out the details in a public forum where I couldn't skirt the issue of my infidelity.

Kissing my shoulder one last time, Croy answers with his truth. "I knew I was in love with Heather the night you and I met. When you couldn't stop talking about her. You went on and on in detail, running through a checklist of qualities. And I already knew the girl you were describing because I'd been dreaming of her all my life."

No one says anything, so Croy's words hang there in the air between us. Is that true? Is Kelly the reason Croy fell in love with me? Is that why he saved me? Because he thought someone else found me worthy.

After a minute, the game continues, but my thoughts remain on the night Croy and I met. Eric chooses truth, and Croy gives him a softball question. "Who is the hottest girl you've ever slept with?" His answer is Sarah though I'm willing to bet that is true. She's annoyingly attractive and not the least bit shy.

Sarah picks dare, and Eric dares her to lick Croy in a place of her choosing. I stand so she can shoot her shot while I look on with a clenched jaw. It seems to be a well-known fact that she has a crush on my date, and her boyfriend is giving her the go-ahead. She lifts Croy's shirt and licks his stomach along the length of his belt. To say I'm annoyed would be an understatement. He's a good sport about the dare but doesn't seem to be entertaining any of her flirtation. I suppose I could take comfort in that.

Kelly chooses dare, and I wish it were anyone but Sarah assigning his task. My heart starts pounding as soon as she says, "I dare you to kiss Heather."

I knew this was coming. This dare is why she suggested the game in the first place. Kelly can't risk telling the truth in front of this audience, not when he knows it'll make me look bad.

Croy grabs the back pocket of my pants and pulls me back into his lap. "Kelly, if you kiss my wife against her wishes, I will make you regret it. She can't protect you forever."

I turn my face momentarily towards Croy and whisper, "This is a game. What you and I have is forever." Then I press my hand into the center of his chest and close the distance between myself and Kelly, kissing him full on the lips. Kelly must figure that if he's about to die, he's gonna make it worth his while. One hand pulls me tight against him at the waist as the knots into my hair. I know this kiss. I remember every one he's ever given me. And Kelly isn't holding back.

Forty-Seven

AFTER A FEW HOURS, I'm ready to go home, but neither Croy nor I am sober enough to drive. For a moment, I considered walking, but with my luck, we'd still get public intox. We can't stay at Eric's because there's no way I want to overhear Sarah in the bedroom calling her boyfriend by my fiancé's name.

As Croy and I head for the elevator, I settle on my suggestion. "Let's sleep in your car for a few hours and then drive home. I'm too tired to go all the way to your house on foot. And the hotel isn't any closer."

Walking in front of us is Kelly, who turns in response. "That's a bad idea, and you know it. Every cop in this town knows who you both are, especially on the overnight shift. You can stay at my place."

"Are you still trying to make that threesome happen, Kelly?" I laugh to myself, but neither of them joins in. Croy refuses to offer an opinion, so it looks like the decision is mine to make.

"It's a genuine offer, Belk. You really don't need to overthink it. I like knowing you're safe, and leaving isn't worth the risk. You know as well as I do that the cops around here get bored and look for any stupid little thing." He's right about that. "Your fiancé will keep me on my best behavior. I'm sure of it."

"Okay. Thanks." As the three of us enter the apartment, I'm struck with the weirdest case of Deja Vu. It feels like this moment has already happened. Maybe it's because Eric's apartment looked the same as Kelly's.

"You two can have the bed, and I'll take the couch." Kelly's offer surprises me even though it shouldn't. He seems to be finding his way back to the man I know him to be. Someone who is thoughtful and giving and loyal. Croy makes himself right at home and locates the bathroom, leaving me alone with the man I once lived here with. It's funny how quickly things can change.

"That hardly seems fair since it's your place. I'm not going to kick you out of your bed." When Croy comes out of the bathroom, I go in. I can't remember the last time I had to pee this badly, and I didn't even have that many drinks. It's anyone's guess how my two guys are still standing, the way they were chugging drinks like it was a competition for my hand.

When I open the door, Kelly is standing there. "He's in the bedroom, two seconds away from passing out. Why don't you join him and get some sleep? Unless you want to stay on the couch with me, for old time's sake."

When I reach the bedroom, Croy is stretched out on my side of the bed, holding his arms out to me. "My only love, come lay with me so I can hold you."

"Don't you think we should let Kelly sleep in here?" I can't help but feel bad. The whole night has been awkward. But this is the cherry on top.

"We can do whatever you want, dear. Just tell him to come in here." Croy's statement confuses me. I'm not sure he understood what I meant.

I hear Kelly come out of the bathroom, so I call his name. When his face appears in the doorway, I pat his spot on the bed. "Come sleep in here with us. There's room."

Croy throws his arm around me, and I put my arm over Kelly. We're like three spoons stacked in a drawer. One side of my body tingles while the other side burns. The three of us fall asleep, lying there together.

When I finally wake up, the sun is shining, and I'm in bed alone. I find Croy and Kelly out on the patio together, talking over a cup of coffee. Leaning against the doorway, watching them go back and forth, one would think they're old friends.

It's Croy who sees me first, "Good Morning, beautiful. You want me to get you some ibuprofen and a mug of the good stuff?" He stands and starts for the door, pausing to kiss me as he passes. "Take my seat. I'll be right back."

I wouldn't say I'm hungover, but I do have a headache. In the future, when I want to get crazy, I think I'll skip the booze and stick to diet coke. I feel every bit my age this morning and then some. It's interesting being out here again with Kelly, alone. Croy's coffee is sitting on the table, so I take a sip and attempt to talk. "How'd you sleep last night?" My voice feels scratchy.

"That was the best I've slept all week. I'm not gonna lie. It felt good having you next to me again." He gives me that look, and this Kelly is every bit the man I once adored.

"Yeah, that was an interesting night. Not at all what I expected when I agreed to leave the house. But I'm glad you and I had the chance to hang out." Part of me wishes they could be friends, so I could be greedy and keep them both. "Thank you for not getting into a fight with Croy. I know being around him isn't easy for you. So, I appreciate you letting us sleep here."

Croy returns with another chair, my coffee, three ibuprofen, and half a breadstick he found in Kelly's fridge. "I ate the other half to make sure it was safe. You're good."

Kelly laughs, "Should be fine. It's only been in there since lunch yesterday. I'm surprised to see you eat carbs, Croy. Or is this a cheat day?"

I feel like I woke up in an episode of the Twilight Zone. These two getting along, while lovely, is a bit unsettling. How long was I sleeping? It seems like I must have missed a lot. Both of them are notorious for waking up hours before I do, so lord only knows how long they've been hanging out this morning without me. I can't take it anymore; I have to know. "What's going on?

Why are you two so chummy all of a sudden? And where did you get coffee?"

Croy answers first. "Your happiness means everything to me, so I'm not going to hurt you by fighting with him. I'm willing to leave everything in the past and move forward from here, because I love you. I know what your heart wants, and I won't ever be the one to deny you." Croy moves his chair closer to mine and puts his hand on my leg, giving it a small squeeze. "The coffee came from Eric's. I have keys to his place. That's how I get in the building."

It all makes so much sense now. I take a sip of my coffee and smile as I recall the night he nearly scared me to death in the hallway. And the kiss we shared in the elevator.

Kelly leans forward in his chair, drawing my attention. "Yeah, well. If I keep being an asshole, I'll lose you for good, and I can't be the reason that happens. I figure he's bound to fuck up eventually, right?" Kelly smiles at me and winks. "Seriously though, I am sorry I disrespected you. I hurt you in ways I never intended. I was stupid and shortsighted. I let my damaged ego cloud my judgment, but I am taking steps to work on that. Do you think you could ever forgive me?"

"You know I can't stay mad at you. Not when a piece of my happiness is tied to yours. So... Now that all is forgiven, does this mean we can have that threesome?" I try to lighten the mood with a joke, but the thought of their hands on me causes me to bite my lips as my heart quickens.

Croy squeezes my leg again before sliding his hand along the inside of my thigh. "Whatever you want, my love. All you ever have to do is ask."

The look on Kelly's face changes to a Cheshire grin. "Oh shit. I'm in."

The three of us laugh, and the rest is a story for another time.

Forty-Eight

CROY and I hide in the basement for what remains of the weekend, watching movies and cuddling on the couch. I love all of our moments together, but the quiet ones are my favorite. It's peaceful, hibernating underground, while the hours pass without notice.

The living room is crowded with empty boxes waiting to be filled with essentials. Everything else the movers are going to sort out. Anything we don't take to the condo is going into the pods and getting dropped off on our empty lot. The thought of moving again makes me anxious, but Croy does a good job of soothing my nerves.

On Sunday night, I have another dream. This time, a little girl is sitting in the sand building a castle.

"Daddy, can you help me make it taller?" I look around to see who she's talking to, but the only person standing there is me. She doesn't seem to notice. It's as though I'm irrelevant to the point of being rendered invisible.

The sun here is always blinding, and it burns behind my eyes. I wish I had an umbrella to shade the little girl from its harsh rays. I want to shield her from harm and protect her from threats I've yet to identify. Looking along the beach again, I see a large figure coming from the left, and there's a dog with him. To the right, I notice a second person headed in our direction, but he seems to be running from further away.

Nausea rises in my throat. Something isn't right. I try to propel myself forward but remain confined to my location. The little girl is the center of everything, and I'm a mere spectator. She pushes more sand into a pile. "Daddy, I need your help." The sweetness of her voice drifts out in all directions, splitting my heart to scraps.

When each figure is positioned about 15 feet away on either side, they come into focus. Croy and Jojo are to the left, and Kelly is on the right. In one synchronized movement, the guys drop to their knees and begin calling the girl toward them.

I hear Croy say, "Come on, sweetie. It's time to go. Mommy is waiting for us at home." As a reflex, I wrap my arms around my stomach and look closer at the girl's face.

"We can build a sandcastle tomorrow, little bug. It's time to go home now." Kelly reaches forward. But the only thing within his grasp is air.

The girl remains planted front and center, with her brown hair shining like gold in the blistering sun. The men seem glued in place as well, unable to move closer. They call out to her using familiar voices, attempting to coax her to their side. Jojo, however, has free rein. He runs over and flops down in the pile of sand, making the little girl laugh. "Are you my silly boy?"

I try to move closer, but I'm buried in the sand to my waist. The light stabs at my eyes as I try to focus, but the pain is too much. My hands come over my face as I squeeze my eyes shut.

I wake up, hands still shielding my face from the light filtering through the blinds. My jaw hurts from being clenched, and I have the making of a migraine. Clearly, the stress is getting to me. I decide to close my eyes and stay in bed until lunch when Croy calls.

When the phone rings, I emerge from where I'm hiding under the blanket. Croy's voice sinks into me, making the tension in my shoulders melt away. He listens as I recount what I can remember from my dream and tries to focus on the positive.

"Hey, this one didn't have sharks or a squid, so that's progress, right?" He tries to ease my mental strain by remaining level-headed. "I think these dreams are your way of processing everything you refuse to discuss. Hopefully, you'll get your period this week, which will be one less thing weighing on your mind."

"I thought you wanted to have kids right away?" This was a conversation we had the other day after throwing a half-empty box of condoms in the trash.

"Trust me, I do. I'd be over the moon if you were pregnant. I thought maybe that text from Kelly was still bothering you. That's all." Regardless of the situation, I can always count on Croy to be supportive. He's beyond amazing. "I feel terrible. I was so absorbed in the excitement of the move that I didn't think about all the pressure I was putting on you. When I get home tonight, you lay on the couch and supervise, and I'll take care of filling the boxes."

I finish talking to Croy and push myself to accomplish something. I'm leaving the office, gym, and TV room to his discretion, but I could probably start in the kitchen. Worst case, we order takeout for the rest of the week. There isn't much left to eat in the fridge and freezer, so I pack the cookware, dishes, cutlery, spices, and other nonperishable items. If we can survive this week without it, it's going into a box this afternoon. The kitchen is 90% empty by the time Croy comes through the front door.

"How did you get all of this done? I told you I would help when I came home." He walks over and puts his arms around me. The reality of the situation is beginning to sink in. We stand together, looking at the pile of packed boxes, both knowing this is only the start.

"Are the movers only doing the pod stuff, or are they bringing all the furniture for the condo?" If we have to move the bed and the couch, that's going to require renting a truck and coming back for whichever vehicle we leave behind. Croy keeps telling me everything is fine, but this is not going to be as pain-less as he claims.

"It's all taken care of. Certain rooms are going into the pods, and other rooms are getting moved to the condo. We can load as many boxes as we want into the cars so that we know that stuff will make it to the right place. Honestly, you don't have to pack anything. I thought you might feel better knowing where things are, but I don't want you to push yourself too hard. For some reason, I wasn't thinking about how much work it is to move. Why don't you pack like we're going on vacation for a week, and I'll take care of the rest." I see what Croy is doing, and I appreciate it, but it's unnecessary.

"I'm not afraid of hard work, and it's important that I do my part. So, I'll keep packing the essentials. And when I'm done with that, I'll start on the rest. After all, I need something to do all day." I wrap my arms around Croy's waist and look into his eyes. "If it gets to be too much, I'll leave it to the professionals. I promise. I have no problem letting them do all the heavy lifting. Little items, I can handle."

Moments like this never fail to prove what kind of man he is. I feel respected, cared for, seen, and understood for the first time. I truly feel loved. I've had grand gestures and empty promises in droves, but genuine conversations have always been hard to come by. These mundane things might feel insignificant, but I assure you, this right here is the best part. From here on out, I need a partner 24/7, 365, until the end, and with Croy, I feel like I have finally found that.

I spend the next few days organizing everything and securing items in boxes while Croy finishes his last week of work here in Columbus. I try to get as much done as possible during the day so that we can relax together after he gets home. We could spend the next 70 years together, and I could never get tired of being wrapped in his arms. He is, without a doubt, my person.

On Thursday evening, Croy wants to go out to dinner, and oddly enough, he invites Kelly to join us. I guess they're trying to be friendly, for my sake. The final move is happening tomorrow at some point, so this will most likely be the last chance to see my only friend and say goodbye. I'm impressed with both of them tonight. Kelly is respectful for once and doesn't insist on pawing at me. And, of course, Croy is his usual self, funny and outgoing. This dinner has been the perfect note to leave things on.

When we get to the parking lot, I walk Kelly to his car. I could use one last hug, and I doubt he'll be disappointed by my request. "I am going to miss seeing you. Maybe you'll consider visiting sometime now that you and Croy can stand to be in the same room with each other." I take half a step closer. "I hope we'll still talk, but if we don't, I want you to know you were worth the trouble. And there will always be a place for you in my life." I can't hold the tears back. I don't even bother to try. He takes half a step forward, and we embrace one last time. "I'm sorry for all the ways I hurt you." I hope my words repair some of the damage I've caused. Knowing I'm leaving things here so broken doesn't sit right with me.

"If I had it to do over again, I would live in those days with you for the rest of my life. I should've told you sooner how I felt. I should've asked you out on day one. I know you don't believe me, but I will love you forever. I miss you every second of every day." Kelly's words bring about more tears. Neither of us is ready to let go.

Despite the distance and our unresolved feelings, I hope we can maintain a friendship. Without him, there is a hole in my heart that can never be filled. I cry myself out of tears and give Kelly one final squeeze. I know it's time to walk into my future with Croy, but I don't know how to let go.

Sensing the end of our embrace growing near, Kelly pulls me in as close as possible and whispers in my ear. "I love you."

I've never said these words to him, but part of me has always known. "I love you too."

A fresh batch of tears makes their way to the surface as I walk back to the SUV and the man waiting for me. Croy opens the passenger door but stops me before I get in. He encases me in his arms and allows me to sob against his chest. Three months' worth of heartbreak, rejection, hope, disappointment, confusion, excitement, joy, and regret come crashing to the surface. If Croy wasn't here holding me above water, I think I would drown in the depths of my sorrow. Without him, this would all be too much to accept.

"Let it out. Let go of everything that's happened since you moved here. I will always catch you when you fall." Croy's words crumble the last of my weakened defenses, and I fall to pieces right there in his arms. I'm not sure how long we remain in that spot, but it's long enough for me to have soaked the front of his shirt. When I'm finished crying, he helps me into the car and wipes the tears from my face. Then he kisses the top of my head and closes the door.

The drive home is quiet. Croy holds my leg while he drives, and I rest my head against his arm. As soon as we're home, I brush my teeth, strip out of my clothes, and get into bed. I feel drained, and all I want to do is close my eyes. All these years, I thought I was strong because I held back and stayed quiet. It wasn't until my soul reunited with its better half that I discovered what true strength is. Croy accepts me for exactly who I am and loves me unconditionally.

The energy in the room changes when he walks in and sits on the edge of the bed. "Are you okay? Would you like me to get you anything?" His touch is comforting as his fingers lace into mine. "I have a few things I need to do in my office, but I can lay with you first if you want?"

"I'm okay. Go ahead and do whatever. But when you come to bed later, will you hold me?" My eyes are heavy, and I can feel myself walking into the darkness. I'm asleep before he gets the chance to respond.

Forty-Nine

I WAKE up in Croy's arms, which is unusual for a weekday. Or any day, for that matter. Normally, he's out of bed long before I open my eyes, but today is Friday. Moving Day. Yesterday, his co-workers had a small party at the office to wish him the best and say farewell. Quite a different sendoff than the one I received at the jail. No matter. The only real goodbye I needed was the one I said last night.

For the time being, the house is quiet. The movers will be here at 11:00 am and the realtor at 1:00 pm. Barring any unforeseen circumstances, this should be our last day in this house. I've packed everything that can fit into a box, and Croy has labeled everything with color-coordinated Post-it notes and duct tape. Pink goes into the pods, and blue goes to the condo. It's starting to feel like we're decorating for a gender reveal party.

I want to stay in his arms for as long as possible, absorbing his tranquility. For now, everything remains peaceful. I take a minute to close my eyes and center my thoughts. His heartbeat thumps against my ear, drumming out his melody. I will never take for granted the feel of his touch and the energy passed between us. It'll always remind me of the night my story ended and our life together began.

"Are you gonna miss it here?" I've only been here for two weeks, and this house already feels like home. I can't imagine how Croy feels after being here for years.

"Not as much as I thought I would. This is a house and nothing more. I'm so excited about the home we're building together that I don't care about anything we're leaving behind. Maybe it'll all hit me next week, and I'll be the one crying in your arms."

"Somehow, I doubt that. You never cry." If I were to think of stable, centered emotion as a 0, Croy is lucky to hit a 2 in either direction. Even in the middle of the prison fight, he remained stoic. I imagine a lot might be buried under the surface, but he's learned to maintain an impressive level of control.

"That's not true. I've cried a few times since meeting you, but I do it when you aren't around to see me." Croy brushes a stray hair behind my ear and kisses me. "When you came into my hospital room and cried on my arm, I wanted to take your pain away. And then you said I should've let them kill you, and it nearly broke me. After you and Kelly dropped me off at the jail, I came home and had a good cry in the shower. Watching you ride away with him and thinking I would never see you again was difficult to accept. Then, the first time you came here, I cried after you ran out. Honestly, I get choked up any time I think about losing you."

"I'm sorry that I walked away when I should have stayed."

"You did what you needed to do, and now we're here together. I don't have any regrets, and neither should you." Croy kisses me, and it feels like time has slowed to a stop. Everything else fades away, and only the pair of us remains.

Once we're out of bed, the real work begins. Croy makes the coffee while I strip the bed and pack everything into one last box. Then I carry out a few personal items and load them into my car before moving it out of the driveway. I didn't bring much, barely enough to fill my trunk and half of the backseat. So, it doesn't take me long to get that squared away.

When the movers arrive, Croy gives them the rundown of

what goes where. He's labeled everything in the house, so all they have to do is carry it out and load it in. I try to peek when no one's looking to double check colors and locations, but they seem to have it under control. Mostly, I feel like I'm in the way, so I retreat to the back and sit on the patio until the real-estate agent arrives.

I get the feeling Croy has been corresponding with her all week because all she has to do is walk through and take photos. The movers have made quick work of the main floor and upstairs, so she starts there. By 2:00 pm, everything is finished, and it's time for us to get on the road.

We take one final walk-through with the realtor before leaving. This place feels even bigger now that it's empty. I can't help but wonder what the new house is going to feel like the first time we see it finished. Croy has been so hush-hush that I don't even know where the new condo is located. No matter how many times I tell him that I hate surprises, he can't help himself. Since it's only for six months, and I know he has good taste, I allow it.

On the drive, I follow behind Croy's car since he refused to give me the address. He calls me a few times to check in, but other than that, I listen to music and daydream about the chapters that lie ahead. The movers worked swiftly and left before us, so they might be unloaded and gone before we even arrive. If I had to guess, around 75% of Croy's house was packed into the pods and dropped off at the property, so there isn't much coming to our temporary home.

As we get closer, I assume he's being funny and driving to my parent's house for a pit stop. But we turn a mile up the road at the sign for Driftwood Shores. I know these condos. I've seen them listed online, and I've walked over here before with my mom. Now I see why he's been so secretive. Of all the places he had to choose from that fell within his 40-minute commute parameter, he moved us into a condo less than a mile from my parent's house. I need to hear his thought process and consider his reasoning before deciding how I feel about it. Despite the neighbors, this place is pretty incredible.

Directly ahead, there's a pair of parking spots labeled 202. Croy pulls into one, so I park next to him in the other. When I exit my car, he walks over and takes my hand. "Surprise!" He scans my face for a reaction, looking slightly concerned. "Did I do good, or did I fuck up?"

I can't help but laugh. "I mean, this place is amazing. I'm wondering why you picked *this* location." I'm not mad or disappointed. How could I be?

"Well, I know your mother was concerned about her plants. And you seemed so peaceful when we sat on the patio looking out at the lake with our coffee. I figured this place had it all. You can walk to your parent's house, we can have coffee on the patio, it's only seven minutes from the new house, and my drive to work has officially been cut in half."

"Alright. Well, in that case, I love it. And I love you for being so thoughtful. How did I get so lucky?" I look at the smile on his face, and I can't help but smile too. He never ceases to amaze me.

"I'm the lucky one. A guy like me could never deserve a girl like you, but I'm hoping it takes you the rest of our lives to figure that out. Now come on, let's go check it out." Croy had the movers leave the door unlocked with the keys on the counter. I guess that's one of the many perks of living in a small town. We take a set of stairs to the second floor and stop in front of 202. Croy opens the door and lifts me into his arms.

"What are you doing? You're supposed to do this after we get married." I'm not even sure what the significance is of carrying a bride over the threshold, but it makes me laugh. I'll have to google it later to make sure it's nothing too misogynistic.

"Shhhh. This is good practice. Let me have my moment." He carefully maneuvers us through the doorway without so much as a banged elbow and sets me down on the other side.

The condo is unbelievable. I don't even want to know what this is costing us a month. These units were built within the last few years, so the fixtures and paint colors are modern and adorable. There's a clubhouse that has a gym and an in-ground pool with a hot tub. Now Croy can work out and swim and make a whole new set of housewives drool.

The movers were nice enough to sort the furniture into the corresponding rooms. They even took the patio chairs out to the back. Whatever Croy paid them, it was worth it. I'm so used to moving on my own, which is such a horribly-stressful, back-breaking ordeal. I understand why he was so calm and kept telling me to relax. How am I twenty-nine years old and only finding this out now? For the moment, unpacking can wait, as well as everything else.

I open the french doors, and we both step onto the patio to check out our new view. I can almost see the beach where we sat on my birthday, dreaming of what-ifs. As I lean against the railing, Croy stands behind me with his arms wrapped around my waist. He places a kiss on the top of my head and holds me against his chest. Since the moment I first laid eyes on him, I knew he would always protect me. As we look out at the lake, I think about how our relationship started. Somehow, against all odds, we landed here, smack dab in the middle of this shared life. The rest of the year is sure to bring its fair share of challenges and surprises, but it's nothing that we can't handle as a team.

After finding each other in the most unlikely place, our paths will be forever entwined. I hope I bring as much joy and comfort to his life as he does to mine. May our conversations be long and our years many. He is my newfound strength, my endless devotion, my best friend, and my greatest love. I will cherish him and our memories, always. Wherever we come to rest at the end, I know we will have traveled there together. Hand in hand.

Fifty/Fifty

MOVING DAY WAS MONTHS AGO, and our six-month plan has remained on track for the most part. The house is coming along, and the builder assured us everything would be finished before Thanksgiving. Fingers crossed. Croy loves his new job, and I love that he's home by 5:00. I wake up early so we can have coffee on the patio together every morning, even though I've had to switch to decaf. And I still meet him once a week for lunch.

My parents traveled across the country, so I'm on plant duty until they return. When they call to check in, they make a point to ask about both of us. I guess that's progress.

We received multiple offers on Croy's house the first week, and 15 days later, it was sold. I think I miss that house more than he does. Part of me wished we could have kept it, but I never said that out loud.

As for Kelly and I, we've remained in contact and are still working on being friends. We usually talk late at night when I can't sleep. I do miss him from time to time. He tells me stories while he's at work, reminding me of the life I left behind. Croy is convinced that my friendship with Kelly is no longer a good idea, but I'm not ready to say goodbye, so he doesn't push the issue.

He still likes to say that with me, there's never a dull moment, and I hope that's a good thing. We were only in the condo for a few weeks when we found out I was pregnant. The highly anticipated addition to our family has Croy excited beyond words. There's still some debate on whether the wedding should be before or after, but it makes little difference.

We've already been through so much as a couple. And yet it feels like our story is only just beginning...

About the Author

Amanda Bryk is a full-time mother and part-time author who had nearly given up on the idea of LOVE... Until she found The One. Now, a decade later, Amanda and her family have dropped anchor in the small boating community of Vermilion, OH, where they share a home with their boston terriers.

Other books by this author:

Drifting Apart
(book two in the locked away series)

Between The Holidays
(a spicy holiday romance)

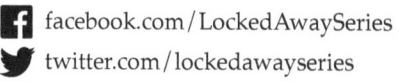

facebook.com/LockedAwaySeries
twitter.com/lockedawayseries
instagram.com/locked_away_series

CPSIA information can be obtained
at www.ICGtesting.com
Printed in the USA
JSHW010843170723
44831JS00004B/9